"To the grave."
-Birde Isles oath

To Free the Waves

Kingsport Chronicles Book 3

C.H. Carter

C.H. CARTER BOOKS

C.H. Carter Books

Paperback ISBN: 979-8-9888820-5-3

eBook ISBN: 979-8-9888820-4-6

Book Cover & Chapter Graphics by Maldo Designs – https://maldodesigns.com

Map Design by Cartographybird – https://www.cartographybird.com

Edited by Rowe Carenen – https://www.thebookconcierge.com/

First edition 2025

For Toni,
None of this would have been possible without you.

Notes & Content Warnings

Notes:

The full cast of characters, including name and birthplace pronunciations, can be found in the Index at the back of the book. (Seriously though, I'm not a stickler for name pronunciation, this is just how they sound in my head!)

The *Kingsport Chronicles* is a high **romantic fantasy** series, meaning it is a fantasy epic first and foremost with romantic subplots that develop over time for various characters. If you are looking for **fantasy romance**, or "romantasy", where the plot centers around the romance between characters set in a fantasy world, I understand this may not be the series for you.

Content Warnings:

The *Kingsport Chronicles* series contains themes that may be distressing to some readers including serious injury, physical violence and bloodshed, character death (on and off page), child abandonment, drowning or near-drowning, mention of aquaphobia (fear of water), panic attacks (on page), parental manipulation, implied assault (off page), mention of coerced sex work (off page), consensual sex work (off page), and consensual sexual relationships (off page).

As much as I hope everyone who picks up this book will be able to read and enjoy the whole story, please be kind to yourselves.

CONTENTS

The Known World   XVIII

The Birde Isles   XXI

Prologue: AITHNE   1

Chapter 1: THE RIDDLES   7

Chapter 2: PASHA   15

Chapter 3: ALLY   21

Chapter 4: MAHER   25

Chapter 5: ALLY   33

Chapter 6: THE RIDDLES   37

Chapter 7: SWAIN   41

Chapter 8: MAHER   43

Chapter 9: PIMM   47

Chapter 10: PIMM   53

Chapter 11: FORAOISE   59

Chapter 12: MAHER   67

Chapter 13: ALLY   75

Chapter 14: MARIELLE   79

Chapter 15: PASHA   83

Chapter 16: ALLY   87

Chapter 17: PASHA   91

Chapter 18: FORAOISE   95

Chapter 19: ALLY   99

Chapter 20: PASHA   103

Chapter 21: ALLY   107

Chapter 22: MAHER   111

Chapter 23: LUTHAIS   117

Chapter 24: MARIELLE   125

Chapter 25: MARIELLE   131

Chapter 26: ALLY   137

Chapter 27: MAHER   143

Chapter 28: MAHER   149

Chapter 29: MARIELLE   155

Chapter 30: PASHA   159

Chapter 31: ALLY   165

Chapter 32: MAHER   169

Chapter 33: SWAIN   175

Chapter 34: PIMM   181

Chapter 35: ALLY   189

Chapter 36: MAHER   195

Chapter 37: MAHER   201

Chapter 38: LUTHAIS								207

Chapter 39: MARIELLE								213

Chapter 40: PASHA								217

Chapter 41: LUTHAIS								225

Chapter 42: ALLY								229

Chapter 43: ALLY								233

Chapter 44: PASHA								239

Chapter 45: ALLY								243

Chapter 46: LUTHAIS								247

Chapter 47: PIMM								255

Chapter 48: LUTHAIS								259

Chapter 49: MARIELLE								263

Chapter 50: LUTHAIS								265

Chapter 51: PIMM								269

Chapter 52: MAHER								273

Chapter 53: PIMM								279

Chapter 54: MAHER								283

Chapter 55: ALLY								287

Chapter 56: LUTHAIS								293

Chapter 57: MAHER								297

Chapter 58: SWAIN								305

Chapter 59: PASHA								311

Chapter 60: ALLY								317

Chapter 61: FORAOISE 321

Chapter 62: SWAIN 325

Chapter 63: FORAOISE 329

Chapter 64: SWAIN 333

Chapter 65: FORAOISE 337

Chapter 66: SWAIN 341

Chapter 67: MAHER 345

Chapter 68: MARIELLE 351

Chapter 69: PIMM 355

Chapter 70: PASHA 361

Chapter 71: LUTHAIS 365

Chapter 72: ALLY 371

Chapter 73: ALLY 377

Chapter 74: MARIELLE 383

Chapter 75: PASHA 387

Chapter 76: ALLY 393

Chapter 77: PASHA 397

Chapter 78: FORAOISE 403

Chapter 79: MAHER 407

Chapter 80: MAHER 413

Chapter 81: ALLY 419

Chapter 82: FORAOISE 427

Chapter 83: MAHER 429

Chapter 84: SWAIN   433

Chapter 85: LUTHAIS   437

Chapter 86: MAHER   441

Chapter 87: PASHA   445

Chapter 88: MAHER   449

Chapter 89: ALLY   455

Chapter 90: MARIELLE   459

Chapter 91: PASHA   461

Chapter 92: ALLY   465

Chapter 93: MARIELLE   469

Chapter 94: LUTHAIS   473

Chapter 95: PIMM   479

Chapter 96: MAHER   483

Chapter 97: PASHA   487

Chapter 98: PIMM   489

Chapter 99: ALLY   493

Chapter 100: MAHER   497

Chapter 101: PASHA   501

Chapter 102: PIMM   505

Chapter 103: FORAOISE   511

Chapter 104: SWAIN   515

Chapter 105: MAHER   519

Chapter 106: MARIELLE   523

Chapter 107: MAHER   527

Chapter 108 : MARIELLE   533

Chapter 109: PASHA   539

Chapter 110: ALLY   543

Chapter 111: PASHA   549

Chapter 112: ALLY   551

Chapter 113: PIMM   555

Chapter 114: LUTHAIS   559

Chapter 115: PASHA   563

Chapter 116: ALLY   567

Chapter 117: PASHA   571

Chapter 118: ALLY   575

Chapter 119: PASHA   577

Chapter 120: ALLY   581

Chapter 121: FORAOISE   585

Chapter 122: SWAIN   589

Chapter 123: ALLY   593

Chapter 124: PIMM   599

Chapter 125: FORAOISE   603

Chapter 126: PASHA   613

Chapter 127: LUTHAIS   615

Chapter 128: MAHER   619

Chapter 129: ALLY   623

Chapter 130: LUTHAIS   627

Chapter 131: MAHER   631

Chapter 132: MARIELLE   635

Chapter 133: PIMM   637

Chapter 134: LUTHAIS   643

Chapter 135: MARIELLE   647

Chapter 136: PIMM   649

Chapter 137: FORAOISE   655

Chapter 138: SWAIN   659

Chapter 139: ALLY   663

Chapter 140: FORAOISE   669

Chapter 141: ALLY   673

Chapter 142: FORAOISE   677

Chapter 143: PASHA   681

Chapter 144: PASHA   685

Chapter 145: LUTHAIS   689

Chapter 146: ALLY   693

Chapter 147: MAHER   699

Chapter 148: MARIELLE   705

Chapter 149: PIMM   709

Chapter 150: MAHER   713

Chapter 151: ALLY   717

Chapter 152: PASHA   721

Acknowledgements 723

Index: Places 725

Index: Cast of Characters 729

About the Author 735

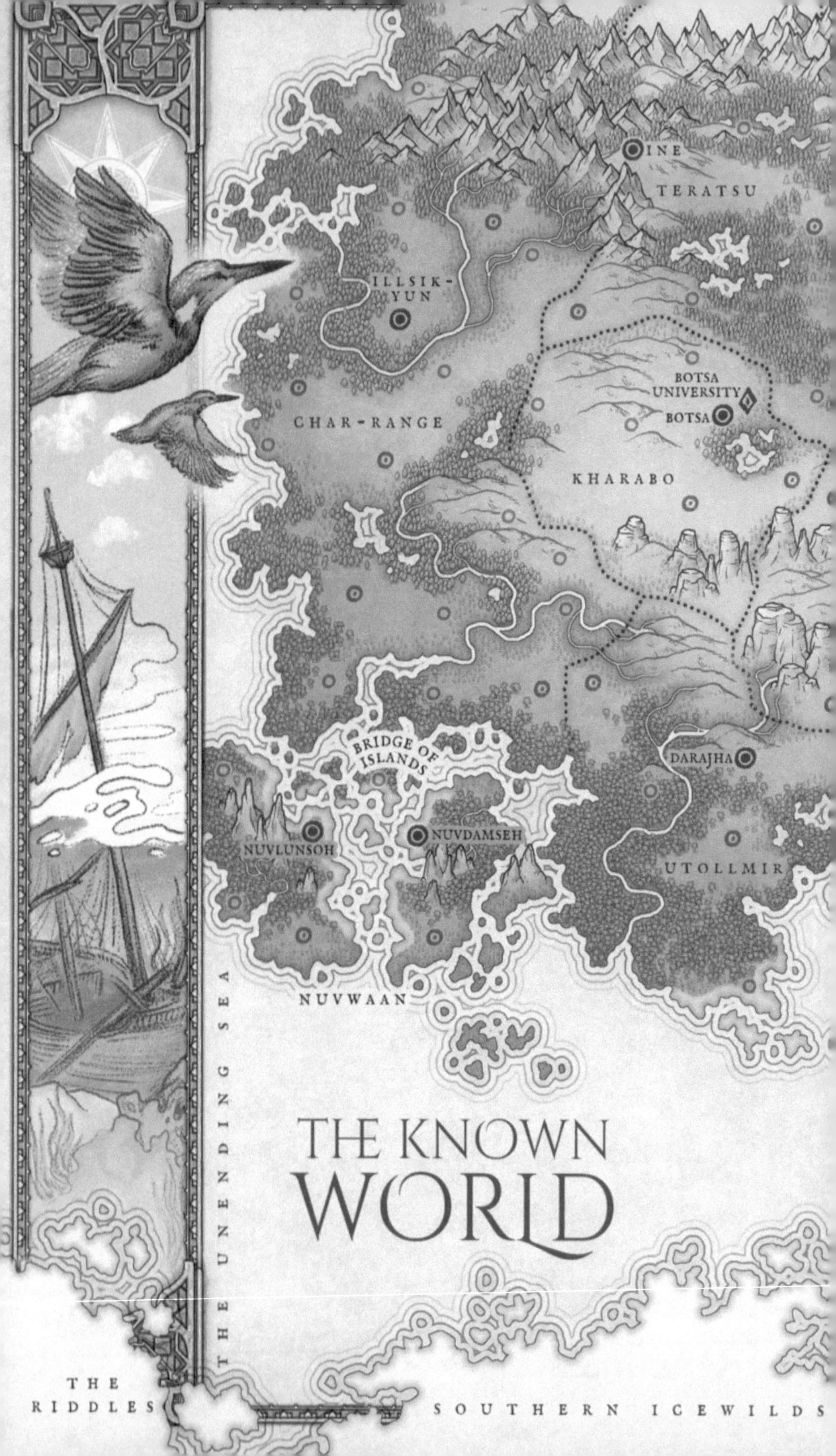
THE UNENDING SEA
INE
TERATSU
ILLSIK-
YUN
BOTSA
UNIVERSITY
BOTSA
CHAR-RANGE
KHARABO
DARAJHA
BRIDGE OF
ISLANDS
NUVDAMSEH
NUVLUNSOH
UTOLLMIR
NUVWAAN
THE KNOWN
WORLD
THE
RIDDLES
SOUTHERN ICEWILDS

FRAOLLKIN FLEET
THE PASTURES
HORN
CAVATLEO
FRAOLLISH TERRITORY
LALESEIR
APREA
VEVAT
AGRIYA
MYRRE
SAN AVETH
FRAOLLAND
LAIVASTHO
THE SPLIT SEA
TJORDUN
MIDTHE
EHLAFI
BALAH
MEREDIA
PRAVIL
EAST TO THE BIRDE ISLES
THE SOUTHERN STRAIT

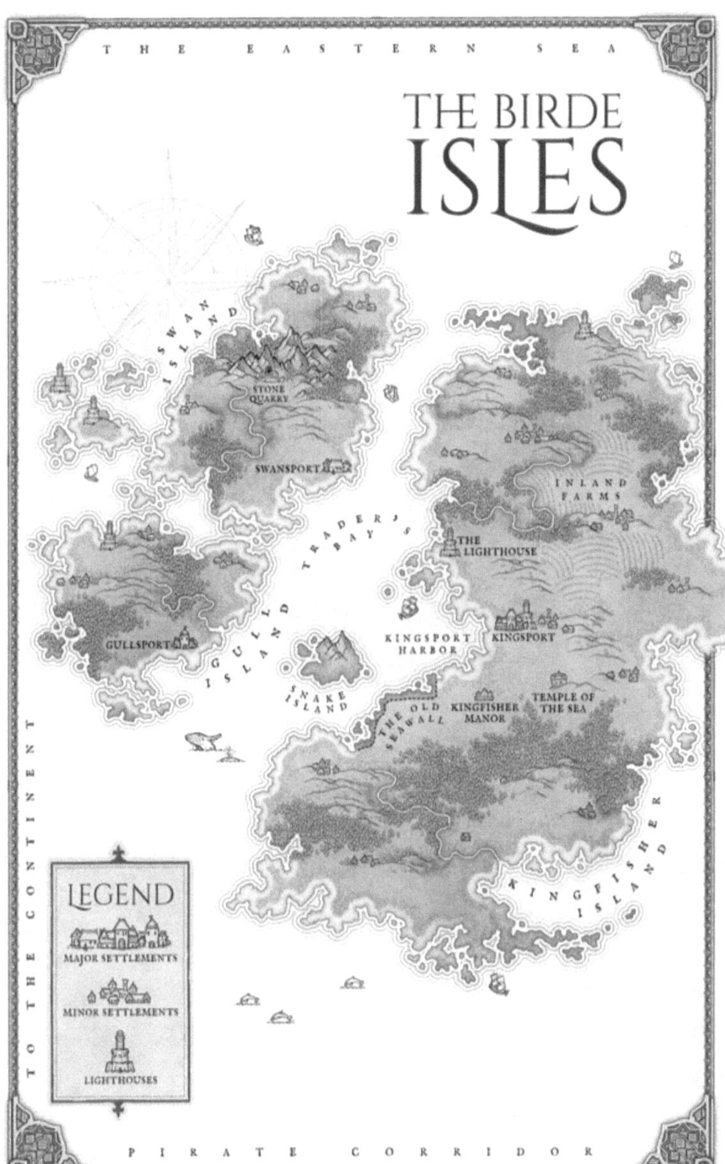

THE EASTERN SEA
THE BIRDE ISLES
SWAN ISLAND
STONE QUARRY
SWANSPORT
INLAND FARMS
THE LIGHTHOUSE
TRADER'S BAY
GULL ISLAND
GULLSPORT
KINGSPORT HARBOR
KINGSPORT
SNAKE ISLAND
THE OLD SEAWALL
KINGFISHER MANOR
TEMPLE OF THE SEA
KINGFISHER ISLAND
TO THE CONTINENT
LEGEND
MAJOR SETTLEMENTS
MINOR SETTLEMENTS
LIGHTHOUSES
PIRATE CORRIDOR

AITHNE

PROLOGUE

The docks were deserted when Priestess Aithne stepped out from the shadows cast by the newly built trade guild headquarters. Its size and detailed construction were a testament to how much the city of Kingsport had grown in recent years. There was no moon out to help guide her and the predawn mist was rolling in off the sea. The lantern in her hand trembled and creaked as she held it up to get a better look at the ships moored into Trader's Bay for the night.

Her other arm was wrapped tightly around a small bundle, tucked beneath her cloak. By the grace of the goddess, no one had seen her as she'd made her way down from the temple of the sea to the wharf. The bundle shifted and Aithne peeked inside. A small face, barely a few hours old, scrunched into a frown before relaxing again into sleep. Aithne's heart ached. This was the first time she'd been sent down to the wharf in the dead of night with a baby girl and, from what she could piece together, this was not the first child brought here since the rebuilding of Kingsport.

Even if they asked this of her a hundred times, it would never get any easier.

When Head Priestess Eschina approached her to take on this task, Aithne thought surely old Lord Kingfisher must have gone mad. Sending away his own daughters and granddaughters in the dead of night? Into the hands of strangers? And the old man only sent away the children who were born daughters, it was only a matter of chance that none of the other children had come to know themselves and become daughters later on. None of it made any sense.

Aithne was the only one, besides Eschina and old Gaius, who knew the truth about the Kingfisher children. The official announcement by the family was always that the child had passed shortly after birth or had been stillborn.

Her first thought had been to refuse Eschina's order but, as a confirmed priestess at the temple of the sea who'd taken her vows and chosen her new name, Aithne felt she had little choice. Now she stood there in the dark, shadows and mist swirling around her, almost clawing at the babe held firmly against her chest. The still air of the wharf judged her with its silence.

Aithne peered around the corner of the building again, still no sign of the captain of the *Agate*. Maybe he wouldn't come. Maybe his conscience had finally caught up to him. If he didn't appear soon, Aithne would hide the baby somewhere until a suitable home could be found, perhaps on Swan Island where her own family lived.

A match was struck in the shadows to her left. Aithne gasped and nearly swung her lantern at the man who stood calmly lighting his pipe. When the light hit his face, she recognized the captain from their brief meeting a few months before. Eschina had arranged everything, in the event the child was a born daughter.

"Captain Bassett." Aithne sagged against the wall behind her. "You startled me."

"Apologies, priestess." Bassett puffed on his pipe, the glow from the match turning his white mustache orange. "It took some time to get our other cargo settled for the voyage tomorrow."

Cargo. Aithne's arm tensed around the sleeping baby. The Balahn captain likely didn't realize what he implied by calling the child cargo, his Trader's Tongue was muddled at best. Or perhaps he didn't care. Either way, old Lord Kingfisher paid him handsomely to take the baby girls far away.

How many? She wanted to ask the man calmly smoking in front of her. *How many children have you taken from their home?*

Captain Bassett looked over his shoulder and Aithne saw his wife approaching through the mist. It wasn't unusual on the Birde Isles for spouses to sail and work together, but Aithne had been surprised to see a Balahn couple do the same.

"Good evening, Priestess Aithne." Mrs. Bassett bobbed her head and held her arms out. Giving the child one last squeeze, Aithne carefully passed her over to the captain's wife. When she started to fuss, Mrs. Bassett hugged the babe to her plump bosom. "I assume the little one doesn't have a name?"

"That's right." Aithne drew her cloak tighter around her shoulders, feeling the loss of the baby's warmth. Of course, the old lord wouldn't risk the child discovering her family name.

"Well, we will make sure she is given one."

Captain Bassett blew out a large puff of smoke. "Yes, yes. The child will be fine. We must return to the ship now." He looked at Aithne expectantly.

"Of course." She set the lantern down and reached to untie the second, much heavier, bundle that had been strapped against her lower back. Holding out the satchel, Aithne watched as the captain quickly glanced inside at the payment for his services. The ends of his mustache tipped up into a smile and Aithne tamped down on the nausea that rolled through her stomach.

"Very good. Please tell his lordship there is nothing to worry about, all will be taken care of." He slung the satchel over his shoulder and tipped his hat before striding across the docks, leaving a trail of pipe smoke behind him.

"He's right, you know. I realize this is your first time, but we do our best for them." Mrs. Bassett turned to follow her husband. "Goodnight, priestess."

"Wait." Aithne reached into a pocket of her robe and passed Mrs. Bassett a small purse. "Please, take this and make sure it stays with the child. It's not much, but she can make the choice of how to use it. Perhaps it could give her a start in life."

Mrs. Bassett nodded, took the purse, and walked away.

Aithne waited until they were out of sight, then retrieved her lantern and started the walk back to the temple. How many more times would she be asked to do this? Neither Eschina nor Lord Gaius Kingfisher I were much longer for this world. Would the family be told to abandon their daughters even after they were gone?

As Aithne passed through the gates to the temple of the sea, she looked up at the guardian mermaids carved into either side. She felt their unblinking eyes follow her, assess her, and find her wanting. Aithne put out the lamp, her feet knew the rest of the way through the temple by heart. A plan began to take shape in the back of her mind. She would continue to do as she was asked and provide what she could for the children they sent away. Then, when Gaius I and Head Priestess Eschina were both gone, she would see how the next Lord Kingfisher acted when the next daughter-born child arrived.

Chapter One

Heinriche trekked through the dense, unfamiliar forest. Roots pushed up from beneath the ground threatened to trip him, while vines hanging from the surrounding trees made him think a nest of snakes would drop onto him at any moment.

This was what he'd been reduced to in the last year. The former Meredian ambassador to the Birde Isles, a position of prominence and respect, now demoted to act as a lowly delegate at a trade meeting on the Riddle Isles. Weeks at sea. Disgusting food. Transferring from the large, elegant Meredian ship to the oddly shaped boats used by the islanders to traverse the place where the seas met. The beauty of their surroundings was not enough to make him feel any relief about the fact that they'd have to cross those same waters to return home.

All this time, Heinriche thought the stories about the currents were an exaggeration, that the people of The Riddles made them up to discourage visitors. He thought they were going to die, more than once. No wonder hardly anyone came from or went to this godsforsaken place.

They'd told him not to wander. Warned him of predators in the trees, so quiet, so cunning, he wouldn't know he was being hunted until they'd already caught him. Ridiculous. He didn't brave that unnatural sea just to sit inside and sweat the entire time. As long as he stayed on the path carved into the forest, Heinriche was sure he could find his way back again. He'd planned to buy his wife and children each a gift that afternoon as well, perhaps some of those odd, decorative earpieces worn by the islanders. If he could find them for a decent price, at least.

"Why is it so blasted hot, even in the shade?" he puffed, mopping his brow and receding hairline with a handkerchief. Pausing to drink from the wineskin strapped across his chest, Heinriche listened to the sounds of life around him. The buzz of insects, the calls of birds that sounded so close yet were completely hidden in the canopy above, the rush of a nearby stream. The thought of cooling his feet in the crystal-clear water that these islands were known for was tempting, perhaps this path would end up at the stream's edge.

What time was it? How long had he been walking? Pulling out his pocket watch, Heinriche frowned at the hands frozen in the same place they were when he'd left that morning. Holding the watch to his ear, he heard the faint ticking of the gears and cogs still moving, but it was no longer keeping time. Of course he was going to be late now, the gods only knew how long it would take to walk back to their accommodations in the Riddles capital city.

Turning on his heel, Heinrich stuffed the watch back into his unbuttoned waistcoat and started back the way he'd come. It took only a few steps for him to notice the sudden shift in the air around him. All the noise that had accompanied him into the forest had completely, and inexplicably, gone silent. No bugs, no birds, nothing. He couldn't help but recall a story his nana had often told, about how the great pine forests of Meredia would go quiet when wolves were on the hunt. But there were no wolves here, and surely the beasts the locals had warned him about couldn't be that large, not on a group of islands as isolated as this...

Heinriche's head snapped sharply to the right. Through the stillness, a faint and familiar sound reached his ears. Someone was singing. Without another thought, he stepped off the path and followed the sound deeper into the forest.

Sweat was pouring down Heinriche's face by the time he came to a break in the trees. His jacket was torn where a branch caught his shoulder and his trousers were splattered with mud, but none of that seemed to matter as he got closer to the source of this beautiful song. All the while, the singing had grown fuller, filled with emotion. The words escaped him, but the melody was comforting in a way he hadn't felt in years.

Stepping into a clearing, Heinriche blinked in the bright stream of sunlight pouring through a hole in the canopy. The ground beneath his feet gently sloped down to a sandy edge that dropped a few feet into a brilliantly blue lagoon. An inlet connecting the lagoon to the sea wound into the trees on the opposite side, then disappeared. To his right, a small rock formation rose above the water, its overhang providing a small spot of shade and giving the impression of a cave tucked into its base. The perfect hideaway.

A breeze swept up from the water and cooled his brow. Sighing, Heinriche looked down into the pool, trying to find the source of the music that had drawn him here.

Floating alone in the lagoon was the loveliest woman Heinriche had ever seen.

She was on her back, eyes closed as she soaked up the sun like a flower. Only her face and bare collarbones were visible above the surface, arms swinging lazily back and forth, just enough to keep herself afloat. He didn't see her clothes lying anywhere on the bank, but it was obvious she was naked beneath the water.

It dawned on him that he was intruding. Heinriche started to back away, but then she began to hum again. It was so delightful, surely he could stay and listen a little while longer. There was a flash of skin, white and delicate as an eggshell, as she lifted her arms overhead. Droplets of water sprinkled over her head like diamonds.

Heinriche almost couldn't believe his luck. She was perfect. He must get closer. He must know her name. He must... Water splashed, the music faded away, and a pair of wide, sparkling blue eyes were staring up at him. He didn't remember leaving the cover of the trees, but found himself standing on the bank, nonetheless.

She was even more exquisite up close. He almost couldn't breathe; afraid any sound might scare her off. He bowed in greeting, but she drifted further away.

"Don't be afraid! Please," Heinriche dropped to one knee, wrenched his hat off.

If this beautiful creature was the reason he'd braved the Riddles' currents, then the gods had surely blessed his journey. She drifted closer, giving him a small smile. A dimple appeared in her left cheek. Long golden hair floated behind her like a flaxen cape. He wanted to shower her with jewels, wrap her in the finest silks and satins, bring her back to Meredia and make her his bride... Wait. He already had a wife. And children. How could he have forgotten that?

Heinriche shook himself. "I apologize, madam, I don't know what's come over me."

The woman sang a few more notes. She skipped her fingers across the water, splashing the front of his shirt. He chuckled. "You are the most stunning creature I've ever seen, but I... I am not a free man." It was harder to say than he'd imagined.

She sighed, her chin dipping into the pool. "I'm so lonely here." Her soft voice set his blood racing, her accent and the language she used were achingly familiar.

"My dear lady, are you from Meredia?"

She only smiled at him again, one delicate bare shoulder lifting out of the water. How did she not burn in this relentless sun?

"What is your name, good sir?"

She really was speaking Meredian. An older dialect, one that hadn't been widely used in ages, but still it filled him with homesickness. Her full, pink lips wrapped deliciously around each word. She was like a princess from one of his nana's stories, waiting to be rescued by her true love from whatever circumstances held her prisoner. He pulled his tongue from the roof of his mouth. "Heinriche. My name is Heinriche."

"Heinriche." She smiled wide now, showing a perfect row of pearly teeth.

The way she *said his name*. Heat raced up his spine and he braced himself against a rock, his hat dropped somewhere behind him.

"Heinriche." She said it again and he groaned.

He couldn't stop his eyes from roaming over every bit of her that was exposed above the surface of the lagoon, but the water was moving too much for him to make out what was concealed beneath.

"If you must leave me, will you at least give me a kiss to remember you by?" She was floating right beneath him now. Her pretty hands rested on the bank, near his feet. "Please? Just one kiss?"

Heinriche licked his suddenly dry lips. It was just one kiss. His wife would never have to know. Maybe he wouldn't go back to Meredia after all, he could stay right here. With her.

His skin was on fire, his clothes stifling. Heinriche didn't even know he was leaning down until her petal-soft palms were cupping his face.

"Just one kiss," she breathed.

"Just one kiss," he echoed, daring to wrap one hand around the back of her neck. He needed his other hand to stay balanced, if not he would fall in...

Her lips molded against his and Heinriche was no longer capable of rational thought. They were as plump and soft as they'd looked. And sweet, so sweet. Almost sickly sweet, like fruit that had been left out too long in the sun. A feeling of complete and utter peace swept over him, starting from the place where their lips met and spreading over his face like a fine mist.

Water sloshed as she lifted out of the pool. Heinriche ached to see her, to behold a body as glorious as he'd imagined. Her palms slipped from his face. One arm snaked around his middle; her other hand trailed down to cup him through his trousers. He'd never wanted a woman so much in his life. And she wanted him. *She* wanted *him*.

Meredia, the trade delegation, the provost, his wife who couldn't even compare to the vision kissing him, they could all rot where they were. He wasn't going anywhere.

Dragging his lips over her cheek, Heinriche opened his eyes and looked down, anticipating the softness of her curves, the pale skin that he would soon see flushed with pleasure. He was rewarded with a view of her perfect breasts; droplets of water ran between them as pink nipples pebbled in the breeze. Then Heinriche saw what waited just below, and his desire deserted him.

Crimson flesh and hanging ribbons of skin wrapped around her ribcage. They pulsed and twitched in the open air, like the gills of a fish trying to breathe on land. Like some great beast had ripped open her sides with a swipe of its claws.

"You... you're hurt?" His voice sounded far away.

"Of course not, lover." She smiled again and a pair of hooked fangs dropped from the roof of her mouth. The creamy skin around her eyes and mouth had gone translucent. Blue veins spiderwebbed over her face. The whites of her eyes were shot through with streaks of red.

Heinriche thought he should be afraid, he really did. But he didn't feel anything. Out of the pool a thick, mottled green tail had slithered up to wrap around his waist. The narrowed tip was hooked around his thigh, pressed between his legs.

So, that's what he'd felt, not her hand at all. It still wasn't enough to make him react in any particular way.

Heinriche thought he might ask her why he wasn't terrified, surely she'd know the answer, but he never got the chance. Pushing off from the bank, she flipped back into the water. The tail locked around Heinriche stretched, tightened, then pulled him beneath the surface of the pool.

The next day a search party was sent out to look for Heinriche, the missing trade delegate from Meredia.

They tracked his winding path through the trees until it ended halfway down the trail cutting through the undergrowth. All they found of Heinriche was his hat, lying discarded at the edge of the trail. The Riddles Islander leading the search picked up the hat and scanned the forest around them, lips pulled into a tight frown against the gold capping several of his teeth. Nothing stood out in their surroundings, but he knew well of the lagoon nearby. There was no helping Heinriche now.

Tucked back into the trees, a man with a long, graying mustache watched the search party through a small spyglass. He waited until they turned back, carrying the hat he'd left for them on the path. With a grunt, he pushed off the fallen trunk that helped conceal him and made his way back towards the lagoon. He may not have been able to stop the fiend from luring that fool in, but he could damn well keep the others from finding their ship hiding in the inlet.

It wouldn't be long now; they'd keep their end of the bargain. As soon as he got what was promised, those wretches could hunt to their heart's content.

PASHA

Chapter Two

Pasha moved slowly through the deep-sea tunnel, her tail barely stirring the water around her. Everything was quiet and still. Darkness enveloped her, the luminescent corals lining the stone walls kept their glow dampened, refusing to acknowledge her presence. The only light came from the corals still lit in the great chamber behind her, but that grew dimmer the further she went.

Her quarry was close by, she could feel it. The subtle shifts in the current rippling out in her direction. The faint trail of energy left behind tickled her nose, she could practically taste it on her tongue. Pasha's own energy pushed against the tight rein she'd looped around it before the hunt began. It wanted to call out, to elicit a response. But that would be cheating.

Pasha kept one hand on the ropes carved into the side of the tunnel, her sharp nails making almost imperceptible clicks against the braids.

Tick, tick, tick.

Where are you? The words echoed in her own mind, causing her energy to fight her hold on it again. *Don't give yourself away.* Pasha rested the tip of her tongue against the sharp points of her teeth and stifled her own energy until she could barely feel it thrumming beneath her skin. She swam a little farther, scenting her prey in the water like the sharks she so resembled. Her nails scraped a little harder against the wall.

Tick, tick, tick.

Something crossed the tunnel near the end, from one cave to another. The resulting ripple was small, but still noticeable.

There!

Pasha shot down the tunnel, arms tight against her sides to create as little wake as possible. She stopped just before the alcove and pressed her back against the wall.

Now she could feel the energy buzzing in the next room, the fear of getting caught making it hum like a smack of jellyfish. She could sense the quick breathing of her target. Had they been on land, she probably would have heard it too.

Taking a long, slow breath herself, Pasha edged her way around the doorway to the cave, taking care not to scrape the scales of her tail against the stone. Homing in on the energy source pulsing in the opposite corner, Pasha lowered herself near the sandy floor and crept closer.

Pasha decided to give one last chance to notice her presence. She closed the distance with one strong flick of her tail. The water swirled, her prey gasped and darted for the tunnel. Pasha drew a tiny charge between her fingers and threw it. There was a high-pitched yelp, followed by a human curse at the gods.

Light bloomed around them as the corals awoke. Pasha grinned at the beautiful mermaid currently scowling at her.

"Hello, sweetheart."

Ally humphed, hazel eyes snapping as she pushed aside the brunette curls swirling around her head. "I was so sure I was going to avoid you this time, with all the corals putting their lights out. What happened?"

"You didn't hide your energy trail,"

"I *tried*," Ally pursed her lips and puffed out her cheeks in a very human expression of frustration. Pasha found it adorable, but now was not the time to mention that. The corals flickered and Ally sighed. She gently stroked the nearest cluster. "I know you were trying to help, thank you."

"You'll get the knack of it, I promise." Pasha swam closer. "If it weren't for that trail, I would've had a much harder time finding you, Ally."

She stuck her tongue out at Pasha and rubbed her side where the charge had landed. "You didn't have to shock me so hard, you know."

"I'm sorry," Pasha caressed the dip in Ally's waist. "Can I – what was that phrase you used? – give a kiss to make it better?"

"That would be a start."

With a smirk, Pasha bent and placed a kiss on Ally's hip, just above the place where the azure scales of her tail ended and her skin began. "How's that?"

"I don't know, it was a pretty bad shock." Ally threaded her fingers into Pasha's dark blue hair. "It's still tender."

"We can't have that," Wrapping an arm around Ally's ample waist, Pasha pulled her closer and mapped a trail of kisses from her side across the soft flesh of her belly and up past her navel. While Pasha had every intention of pausing her journey around the swell of Ally's breasts and the shark tooth-shaped scar that marked her breastbone, a tug on her hair brought them to eye-level.

"You're trying to distract me, aren't you?" Ally's longer fluke curled around hers.

Pasha shivered, "Is it working?"

"For now," Ally kissed the pulse point beneath Pasha's jaw. "But we've got to figure this out. I can't even feel the energy in the sea unless you pull it towards us. Is it because I'm a made mermaid, do you think?"

"I'm not sure, but we will solve this. First, though, let me make up for catching you."

"You love this part," she chuckled.

I love you. Pasha nearly said the words aloud, but they stuck in her throat. Instead, she cupped Ally's face and tried to pour what she couldn't say into a kiss.

Every time Pasha wanted to tell Ally how she felt, one of the lessons Elder Nerys had drummed into her stopped her cold: *Love is a bond. It protects and keeps us from losing ourselves. Never profess your love without first being sure of your partner. There is danger in false love.*

The trouble was, Pasha also couldn't bring herself to ask about Ally's own feelings. They cared for each other, there was no doubt about that, but what if Ally wasn't ready to profess any stronger feelings than that? It would seem like Pasha was pressuring her into something before she was ready.

Ally's arms locked around her, hands smoothing over the skin and scales of Pasha's bare back. A tendril of energy brushed against Pasha's mind and the tight hold she'd kept until then shattered.

CHAPTER THREE

Ally sighed when she felt Pasha's mind give way to her gentle nudge. The corals surrounding them flickered at the shift, then dimmed slightly. Their peculiarly considerate way of giving the mermaids some privacy. She couldn't help but laugh the first time it happened.

Keeping her hold around Pasha's waist, Ally curled her fluke further over Pasha's shorter fins. Her own mind opened, falling easily into the place that allowed them to communicate solely with mermaid language.

Capturing Pasha's lips in another kiss, Ally felt the hum that sparked from every place their bodies touched. Pasha went rigid from the top of her spine to the tip of her tail. Then she melted against Ally, trembling hands finding purchase against her hip and into the hair at the base of her skull. Wave after wave of pleasure swept over them both, until Pasha broke the kiss and buried her face into Ally's neck.

It wasn't lost on her how starved Pasha had been for affection of any kind, spending so many years alone beneath the Birde Isles. But only after learning just how tactile mermaids really were did Ally realize how far this went beyond simple intimacy.

The mermaid way of making love was fascinating. Floating there, locked together yet hardly moving. Letting the energies that lived within the very core of their beings mingle and caress one another. They were wild things, chasing each other across Ally's skin and scales, then to Pasha's. Jumping up to weave through Ally's hair and slide down Pasha's fins.

It could last anywhere from a few moments to a few hours, depending on how fully they'd thrown themselves into that initial brush of power. Sometimes Pasha teased her, sending little pulses of electricity laced with yearning across the caverns until Ally felt she'd go mad with desire. And each time always felt a little different than the last. There was no comparison, no better or worse, it was simply the two of them existing together in that particular moment.

Sinking into the sensation, Ally reached the now familiar experience of floating out of herself. True, she found herself blocked, time and again, from tapping into the energy around them and manipulating it the way Pasha could. But this, this came as easily as breathing. So easily, in fact, that she spent the first few weeks of her new life as a mermaid accidentally sending Pasha – for lack of a better phrase – mating calls. Which resulted in a series of intensive lessons in keeping her emotions to herself.

And quite a lot of love making.

But Ally still felt as if they'd only just begun exploring each other. She knew going into this that it would be one year before she could set foot on land again. What Ally hadn't realized was that she'd spend that first year without feet at all. For some reason, she'd imagined she could change into her more human form underwater.

Apparently not. And because Ally hadn't changed in all that time, neither had Pasha.

There were many things Ally looked forward to as her first year as a mermaid drew to a close. Feeling the dry sand and grass beneath her feet. Taking a deep breath of fresh air. Seeing her family and Maher again, learning everything that she'd missed while living beneath the sea.

And Ally wanted to give Pasha the same gift she'd received. Pasha had shown Ally what it meant to love beneath the sea. Ally wanted to show Pasha what it was like make love on land. As much as they'd been affectionate when Ally was still human, Pasha still had no idea how different this would be in their other forms.

A sudden pulse of pleasure pulled Ally out of her thoughts. They were both breathing hard now, clinging together as they poured unfettered emotion each scale and inch of skin. She was herself and she was Pasha. She tasted the skin of her own neck; smelled the scent of her own hair; felt her own softer, rounder figure molded against Pasha's angular body. And Pasha was experiencing the same. They couldn't read each other's minds in this state, it was more than that, more concentrated.

The sharp points of Pasha's nails pricked her skin and Ally had just enough time to clamp her mouth onto Pasha's shoulder before their combined energies spiraled into a peak.

"Ally!" Pasha groaned into her neck.

A thousand tiny bubbles fizzled in the back of Ally's skull. They traveled down her spine and through her tail to the ends of her fins. For a split second, all her senses sharpened and she had a flash of what it had felt like when Pasha changed her.

When it ended, everything felt muffled at first, her body readjusting to being only herself again. Slowly, very slowly, they both drew back until they were in their own minds. Lifting her head, Ally kissed the faint mark she'd left on Pasha's silvery-gray skin. It would heal quickly, small wounds usually did, though Ally'd not inherited that particular skill either. Despite the frustration of not accomplishing even the tiniest talent, Ally loved being a mermaid. And she loved being with Pasha.

Leaning back until they drifted down to the floor of the cave, Ally kissed Pasha's temple. They stayed wrapped around each other until their heartbeats slowed and their breathing relaxed.

"If this is what happens every time I fail to master a mermaid skill, I'm not sure I will have much motivation to improve."

Pasha chuckled, rolling up onto her elbow and gazing down at her. "Don't fret, I'll find an even better reward for when you succeed."

Chapter Four

The bright summer sun warmed Maher Villaon's shoulders as he made his way through the crowded streets of Kingsport. He was grateful now that he'd chosen a lighter weight suit. This season had barely begun and already it was promising to be hotter than the summer before.

Most people greeted him as he passed, in one way or another. Others avoided eye contact, wary of drawing the attention of the Intelligencer of the Birde Isles.

That was the role he played today. The crest of his station – a slightly altered version of the Kingfisher crest, the bird holding a scroll in its hooked beak instead of a fish – was prominently embroidered on the front of his moss green jacket. Not as fine a job as Ally would have done, but he'd made do with the manor seamstress.

Thinking of Ally made his chest ache. He missed her so dearly. Often, he still caught himself walking towards her room, ready to steal her away for a stroll through the Kingsport market or a picnic in the manor gardens. Then, he would remember, Ally wasn't there. She was in the sea with Pasha, somewhere beneath the island out among the waves. Only the knowledge that he would see her again before the year was out kept Maher from sinking into melancholy.

That, and the fact that he was far too busy.

Beneath Maher's jacket, pinned to his waistcoat, was the tiny enamel magpie Ally'd given him before she left last autumn. The symbol of his other role within the city.

His double life had developed more than he'd imagined, but he wasn't so dimwitted as to not notice the physical toll it was beginning to take. Maher was burning his candle at both ends, perhaps even down the middle some days. The enchanted shark tooth he wore tucked beneath his shirt, another gift from Ally, kept the pain in his left shoulder at bay most days. The spiderwebbed scar, a holdover from the downing of the *Pike* the summer before, was as healed as it was going to be. Already Maher could tell it would give him trouble for the rest of his days.

And if he didn't find some kind of relief soon, that wouldn't be too much longer.

Pimm was right, as they so often were. As winter ended and spring began, Kingsport saw renewed activity from the street crews that had been plaguing the city for over a year. Funded from a seemingly bottomless supply of Saprean coins that were made of very real silver, but came from dubious origins. Maher had finally shown one of the coins to his father, asked if he'd heard of any major thefts within Saprea in the last few years. Not that it was an easy task, he'd had to corner Khafra in the manor after a meeting in Lord Kingfisher's study.

Ambassador Villaon was no help, but his obvious surprise at the coin resting in Maher's palm was the most emotion he'd gotten from his father in months.

Their relationship had been lukewarm at best, their words stilted and relegated to government matters and only spoken in the presence of others. They'd not had a real conversation since Maher had his father followed and caught him in league with one of the vilest criminals in the history of the Birde Isles. Ezmira. She'd gone into hiding through the winter but, like the street crews, Maher suspected she would reappear soon.

Maher couldn't forgive Khafra's scheming, but held out a last kernel of hope he'd change for his own safety if nothing else.

Maher made his usual rounds and reached his last stop, the harbormaster's office, by late afternoon.

"Exactly how long were you expecting me to wait, Mr. Villaon?" The harbormaster scowled when Maher entered the room, gray eyes showing no hint of amusement.

"As long as necessary, Mrs. Heper. We can't predict how much time every meeting will take." He shut the door, the lock turned with a soft click.

"If you think to find me here cooling my heels at midnight, you're quite mistaken."

Bracing his hands on the desk, Maher regarded her for a long moment, until a grin broke across his face. "No late-night assignations then, Agnes?"

Mrs. Heper snorted and shooed him back. "Enough of that talk, Mr. Villaon. Have a seat."

Still chuckling to himself, Maher sank into the offered chair, glad to be off his feet. He liked Agnes Heper. They'd known each other a long time, she was on the shipbuilders' council when Maher and his father first arrived in Kingsport. When the old harbormaster chose to take an early retirement – a decision that was undoubtably related to Lady Rochelle Kingfisher's kidnapping and the subsequent upheaval of the Birde Isles sailing trade – Maher was pleased to see Agnes put forth as a one of the candidates to replace him. She was fair and cared about the sailors' welfare, but tough enough to bring the whole wharf up to scratch after the chaos of the last year.

After exchanging a few pleasantries, Agnes said, "I suspect I know why you're here, and it has nothing to do with how the wharf is operating. I send those reports each week to his lordship."

"You're right on that count. Why do you think I'm here?"

A heavy weight seemed to settle on her shoulders as she unlocked a drawer and pulled out a rolled map. Spreading it out across her desk, Agnes placed a weight on each corner. Maher counted the red inked marks scattered through the Southern Strait that ran beneath the continent situated west of the Isles.

"Two more since we last spoke?"

"Aye," she ran a hand over her close-cropped, steel gray hair. "We saw a lull during the winter, then there was the one found in the spring, and now two more."

"Gods above and below," he shook his head.

Ghost ships. All found in or near the Southern Strait with their crews gone. Not a single soul on board but with all cargo still accounted for. Nothing of value taken, not even the longboats. The sailors had simply disappeared.

When Pimm first brought them to his attention, Maher hoped there was some mistake. But the size and berth of the ships was too varied for it to be a string of mutinies. Pirates would have ransacked the cargo. No sickness reported on land to indicate an epidemic. Before she left, Ally swore none of the sea monsters she and Pasha had called up were responsible. There was just... nothing.

"What do the sailors believe?"

"Most still think it's naught but scuttlebutt." She admitted. "Still, we can't keep this from them much longer."

"I'd feel better giving the warning if we knew of some way they could protect themselves. We don't even know what's happened to the others."

"That may be," Agnes thumped a fist against the map. "But I know this much, the minute any of our own vessels turns up as one of these ghost ships, I'll halt our entire fleet until you find an answer. Trade negotiations be damned."

The sun was already slipping behind the surrounding buildings when Maher left Agnes' office.

Stretching, he scanned the sea of masts scattered throughout the harbor. Luthais' ship was due back more than a fortnight ago, but they were delayed. When Cal, the youngest Kingfisher brother, was declared a danger to himself and others, he'd been sentenced to life imprisonment. Lord Kingfisher couldn't bear to see his on son put to death or exiled, no matter that he'd tried to take control of the Isles for himself. Nearly getting Ally and her mother killed in the process.

Now Gai, the eldest brother, was off on a sabbatical before taking on more of a role with their father. Lord Gaius Kingfisher couldn't be everywhere, so the bulk of the duties surrounding their trade relationships had fallen on Luthais. Lord of Trade though he might be, another thing Khafra had attempted to steal for himself, it was still a tremendous amount of responsibility to lay on one person.

Maher had objected, at least in private, but Luthais had insisted Gai take this time for himself. Apparently, the whole thing was Ally's idea, a parting gift to Gai before he eventually became Lord of the Birde Isles by right of birth. Who was Maher to argue with something both Ally and Luthais wanted? Especially considering the two had hardly spoken for the first twenty-one years of Ally's life and now they were planning a grand tour for their elder brother.

With a heavy sigh, Maher finally walked away from the harbormaster's office. He really ought to return to the manor and grab a few hours of sleep. But something pulled him down into the wharf, his feet crossing from cobblestone to the thick wooden boards of the docks.

As if Luthais is going to magically appear if you stay long enough. Maher snorted to himself.

The brief flirtation they'd begun the year before was practically nonexistent, with how much they were working in their respective positions. Luthais had warned he could be away as long as a year, visiting each of their trade allies to allay their concerns over the diminished fishing catches that the Isles would be producing from now on. A result of the severing of the misguided bargain Pasha once struck with Ally's great-grandfather, Gaius I.

But there was a marked difference between hearing Luthais might be gone this long and experiencing it. Efforts were made on both sides to stay in contact, but they'd barely spoken in the last few months. Letters were brief and infrequent, and Maher wasn't even sure anymore if they'd truly been flirting, or if it was all in his imagination.

It surprised him how much he missed Luthais and his surly disposition.

Go home and go to sleep. Maher turned back, grateful that the day was cooling off at the very least.

He'd not gone five steps when Luthais called his name.

Surely not. Maher shook his head.

Luthais called out again.

I must be hallucinating.

"Godsbedamned, Maher, will you stop?"

Spinning on his heel, Maher found Luthais Kingfisher himself striding up the dock. His skin had acquired a ruddy glow and his already blonde hair was blanched to the color of wheat from the months spent at sea. The sleeves of his shirt were rolled up; Maher noticed fresh nicks and rope burns as he drew closer. Of course, Luthais would pitch in on whatever needed doing on his ship.

"Luthais? By the gods and all their grandmothers, are you really here?" Maher extended a hand.

"Lost in your own head, were you?" Luthais finally reached him. Warm moss green eyes drank him in from head to toe and Maher swore all his blood now resided in his face.

Nearly at a loss for words, Maher said the first thing that came to mind. "You're a bit late, you know."

Bypassing his hand, Luthais scooped Maher up into a tight embrace. Maher might have been more than a head taller, but Luthais nearly lifted him off his feet. Too flummoxed to do anything but hug him back, Maher hooked an arm around Luthais' neck. His other hand was trapped between them, but Maher didn't particularly care. He was too busy attempting to catalogue all the slight changes in Luthais. He was a little thinner, no doubt from months of ship's rations, but still solid as a tree. The thick, blonde beard that had filled in his jaw was tickling Maher's neck.

Luthais' long hair had come loose from its braid and Maher was at just the right height to let his chin rest against the side of the other man's head. He smelled of brine and sweat and wet rope. And he surely had been holding Maher for a long time and...

Someone cleared their throat from behind Maher's back. "Captain, a word?"

Realizing they were on a dock surrounded by people, Luthais sighed and reluctantly released Maher. When he turned around, Maher came face-to-face with a tall woman with deep brown skin and a crown of long onyx braids, each one capped in a colorful enamel cuff.

"Kamharida Anyanwu!" Maher beamed, only a little breathless from this unexpected reunion. "It's good to see you."

"You as well, Maher. A handshake will do just fine for me." One corner of her mouth tipped up at a sly angle as Maher flushed anew and quickly took her offered hand.

"You needed to speak to me, First Mate?" Luthais' face had settled into the stern mask he wore when dealing with official matters.

"Aye, you're needed aboard sir." Kamharida backed up a step, hands locked behind her back, letting them know she wasn't going to walk away without him.

"Right, well," Maher coughed into his fist. "Duty calls, and all that."

Cocking one sun-bleached brow at him, Luthais leaned in and murmured, "Will you be at the house tomorrow night, or do you have other *errands* to attend to?"

Maher didn't need to ask what he meant. "I have one meeting tomorrow evening, but I should be back by midnight. Why?"

Luthais' face was unreadable. "I have a surprise for you."

CHAPTER FIVE

Ally held an arm close to the glow cast by the nearest corals, watched as the scales dotting her skin glistened. A ribbon of different blues wrapped around her wrist, then spread over the top of her hand. Capping each knuckle like a gauntlet. A lone copper scale sat on the inside of her wrist.

The final days of her first year as a mermaid were dwindling quickly. She'd have legs again when reuniting with her family and Maher, but Ally knew from watching Pasha shift between forms that the scales would remain. So would any of the other small alterations that came about during the ritual Pasha performed to change her.

The elongating of her pupils that enabled her to see clearly underwater. The faint sleekness to her skin that mirrored Pasha's, allowing the water to slide over her and protecting her from the copious amount of salt around them.

Ally longed to see her loved ones, but would they still see her? Or would they focus on all the ways she'd changed? Would they be afraid to approach her? To embrace her?

"Ally?" Pasha laid a gentle hand on her shoulder. "Are you alright?"

"Yes, I am." Ally chewed her lower lip for a moment. "I'm so excited to see everyone again. Mama, Father, Gai, Luthais, Maher. But what if this is too much for them?" Her wrist turned and the scales flashed.

Pasha nudged Ally until they faced each other. Sharp nails grazed her jawline before Pasha cupped her face. "They will be *thrilled* to see you. It may take some time for them to adjust, but these changes are all on the surface. You are still yourself, Ally, and anyone who truly cares about you will surely see that."

"Thank you," Ally turned into Pasha's hand, kissing her palm. "I only…"

"Still not convinced?"

"I wish I wasn't so nervous" she admitted. "A year seemed like such a long time, I thought I'd be more prepared."

"I'll be right there with you the whole time." Pasha hesitated. "If that's what you want. I would understand if you'd rather I wait in the waves when you first see them again."

"Of course I want you there, Pasha. Why wouldn't I?"

"You do realize, all differences in appearance aside, that you're stunning, don't you? Whereas I'm fairly certain I would only remind them of a shark. And even though becoming a mermaid saved you from the fate of other Sea Kissed before you, I'm still the one who *changed* you, I'm the reason you're no longer human. They may not feel so forgiving about that."

Ally snorted. An impressive feat, she felt, to perform underwater. "Now who's making assumptions about themselves? You did everything you could to help me, Pasha. You saved my life, and I would be proud to introduce you to the rest of my family." She took Pasha's hands, lacing their fingers together. "Besides, you should know how stunning you are as well."

Pasha tugged her closer, using the leverage to steal a kiss. "Then I wouldn't miss it."

Chapter Six

Water sluiced over the creature's head as she slowly breached the surface of the lagoon. The skin of her face felt tight and parched no matter how much moisture hung in the humid island air. Cloudy blue eyes narrowed and her ears pricked at the sound of human voices wafting out of the trees.

The little balding man had sustained her for a time, but now that sustenance was fading fast. With all the magic they'd taken from the mermaids burning through their energy faster than it could be replenished... It was pure luck that she spoke his language, which made it much easier to trap him. The southeastern portion of the land mass to the west had once been part of her hunting territory.

But they would need more, much more, if they hoped to cross the sea and reclaim all that once belonged to them. A delicious shiver ran from the crown of her head down to the tip of the serpent's tail coiled beneath her.

After centuries of careful planning, they were so close. All that remained was to retrieve the key to their freedom. To undoing the curse placed upon them by the mermaids, regain their wings, and once again rule the land and skies. There will be so many humans ripe for the picking. Stupid creatures that had grown fat and complacent with no predators to hunt them.

Without a steady supply of humans, her kind wouldn't necessarily die. But was the agony of living in a state of perpetual starvation any better?

One of her sisters had a whole herd of humans hidden nearby, but had made some ridiculous pact to keep them safe. For now. It wasn't as if she needed all of them, only the older one, the one who would help them retrieve the weapon they required.

A handful of sisters were strong enough to swim out to sea and hunt entire crews of humans. But then they'd fallen into a pattern of consuming more than they brought back for the rest of them. She'd put a swift end to that.

The voices drifted closer and her hunger rumbled. Swimming towards the bank, she opened her mouth and began to sing.

Across the island, in a secluded inlet, waited a similar creature with bright red hair and a striped tail. She watched as the old man paced back and forth on the sand. A small boat was beached nearby, guarded by a surly woman who often refused to leave his side.

Wavelets lapped around her waist as she rested her chin in her hand. "Swain," she signed his name, grinning wickedly as he slid to a stop. "You will wear a new inlet into the shore at this rate."

He rounded, barely hiding the contempt simmering beneath the surface. "How much longer?"

"These things take time. You knew that when we made our agreement."

"Yes, but it's been months!"

"We are putting her back together, piece by piece," she purred. "You wouldn't want us to rush and miss something, would you? Or we could just make her like my friends waiting beneath the waves, like your new crew. A rotting puppet."

"Don't you *dare*," Swain advanced on her, a hand going for the dagger at his hip.

Faster than either human could follow, she shot up on the powerful coils beneath her. One hand snatched his wrist, while the end of her tail slithered up his chest to wrap loosely around his throat.

"Sir!" the sailor abandoned the boat and drew her sword.

Swain had gone perfectly still. "Stand down."

"But – "

"I said, stand down!"

"Aye, sir." The sailor backed away, sword pointed down into the sand.

She gripped his chin, forcing him to look her in the eye. "Don't forget our agreement, Swain. We give you your ship and you retrieve the machine for us."

"I remember," Swain ground out, muscles flexing against the tail looped around his neck.

"I should hope so, and now that the warm weather has returned, it's time for you to find where the turbine is housed and figure out how you're going to take it." He flinched away when the tip of her tail stroked his cheek. "Don't worry. She will be ready when we say she is, and then it's your task to ensure she fulfills the rest of our bargain."

"The rest?" his eyes narrowed.

"That's right," she hissed. "There's a task to be done, and we will need her to do it."

SWAIN

CHAPTER SEVEN

It took every ounce of Swain's willpower to hold still. The muscles in his neck and shoulders burned as he strained not to touch the slick scales circling his throat.

The creature had never threatened him like this before. In the bright light of day, he could see the strips of white, black, and crimson banded around her tail. He could also see the ragged, heaving gill-like wounds on either side of her ribcage. She wouldn't be able to stay out of the water much longer, but it would be nothing for her to drag him into the sea.

"Do we understand each other?" her rotten fruit breath made him nauseous.

"Aye, we understand each other."

"Good," her tail coiled tighter for a moment, then she released him.

Swain stumbled farther up the beach. The creature blew him a kiss and dove beneath the waves. Rejoining Smith at the longboat, Swain shook his head when she opened her mouth to speak. Together, they pushed the boat into the surf.

"Let's get back to the ship."

MAHER

CHAPTER EIGHT

Maher stumbled up the front steps of Kingfisher manor. Fumbling for the key Gaius and Rochelle had given him, so he wouldn't bother the servants with his comings and goings, he let himself into the darkened house. A single lamp was lit in the front hall. Maher took it from the hook, unsure of where exactly Luthais had wanted to meet.

It was a fairly large house, after all. Was he supposed to start with the cellar and work his way up? Nonsense. Luthais was probably in his room, which meant Maher would have to walk all the way to the family wing. This thought made him more irritable than he wanted to admit.

His burning curiosity about whatever it was Luthais had for him was the only thing that kept Maher from sliding down the wall and sleeping right there. He was exhausted, and distracted. Tonight's disastrous meeting in the Lantern was proof enough of that. A small, irrational part of his mind wanted to blame Luthais. The sudden return and quite literally sweeping Maher off his feet had left him rattled in a way he'd not experienced before. Enough that he'd made a stupid mistake with one of the blue lantern business owners...

How long have I been standing here? Maher shook himself once and finally moved further into the house. *Why we couldn't meet over breakfast, I suppose I'll never know.*

A well-defined arm hooked through Maher's and hauled him into the empty drawing room.

"What the –" Maher lowered his voice when the lamp illuminated Luthais' face. He already looked more put together than when he'd arrived back in town. Maher noticed he'd shaved off the beard. "Luthais, what do you mean hooking me in here like a fish on a line?"

"Quiet," he put a finger to his lips and shut the door.

"Luthais, what..." Maher trailed off when the other man took his elbow and towed him to a sofa on the far end of the room.

If this is a secret assignation, he's chosen a horrible place for it.

Anyone could still see them if they walked into the room, it wasn't exactly private.

Oh dear gods above and below, don't tell me that Luthais Kingfisher is an exhibitionist. Maher snorted out a laugh, even as he gave thanks that the darkness hid the blush that instantly covered his face.

Taking the lamp from him, Luthais adjusted the wick and set it on a low table in front of the sofa. They sat, knees turned towards each other but not quite touching, and Maher found himself unexpectedly feeling quite nervous. Him, of all people. While he couldn't speak for Luthais – not even the Birde Isles sailors would gossip about their beloved Lord of Trade – Maher was by no means inexperienced. Were he a braggart, he might even go so far to say his reputation in town was well deserved. But Luthais? Maher had no idea of his interests or experiences.

Maher shifted in his seat. "Well? What did you want to tell me that couldn't wait for daylight?"

Luthais glanced at the closed door. He leaned closer and Maher's lips parted in anticipation. "I know how the Saprean coins are being made."

"You..." Maher blinked. "You *what?*"

"About seven years ago, a coin press was stolen from the Saprean government. They kept it as quiet as possible, as you can imagine."

"Of course they did, it would be an abject humiliation if word got out. How in all the gods' names did you learn this?"

"When we extended the last leg of our voyage, we docked for supplies in Saprea. I met one of the guards who'd been on duty at the royal treasury the night of the theft. He'd been demoted since then, and now serves as a night sentry for the anchored Saprean trade ships.

The sentries started up a game of chance with some of our crew. When I approached to see why they were gathered, he assumed I was just another sailor."

"Sounds about right," he smirked. "Even so, why would he blab such a secret to a stranger?"

"Apparently, he'd just learned that the royal guard meant to demote him further. Word has finally reached the Saprean government about what's happening here, businesses refusing to take any Saprean currency. He pulled me aside to ask about the Birde Isles, if it might be worth leaving Saprea and finding work here. Once he started talking, he couldn't seem to stop."

Maher smoothed a hand over the waves pomaded into his hair. "Did you learn anything else?"

"Nothing of note. Afterwards he was more interested in inviting us all to drink with them after their watch ended."

"And did you?" The question came out sharper than Maher intended.

"Of course not." Luthais' head tilted, as if the idea had never occurred to him.

"If whoever is behind this has a real press, it would be relatively easy to duplicate the imprints on the plates."

"And they've had plenty of time to print as many coins as possible."

"This is unbelievable." Maher thought for a moment. "We still don't know where they're minting the coins, nor does it explain who has access to that much silver. And why make real coins when counterfeits would be cheaper and still hard to detect if done right?"

"That's the question, isn't it?" Luthais crossed his arms, leaning back against the sofa and looking rather pleased with himself. "Well, Intelligencer, what are you going to do with this information, now that you have it?"

Maher felt as if a cog had sprung loose in his brain. It wasn't as if he'd been expecting a declaration of love, perhaps a declaration of lust at the most. Instead, Luthais just provided the only clue they'd found in a solid year of searching for the origins of the damned coins that had flooded the Birde Isles.

He could only imagine the look on Pimm's face when he told them.

BEAR'S DEN

PIMM

CHAPTER NINE

Pimm struck a match, feeling the familiar spark of heat near their face as they lit a freshly rolled cigarette. The slight twinge in their lungs quickly subsided, leaving behind nothing but the steady stream of blue smoke curling from their nose like a dragon in one of Ms. Orel's old Zavatleon fairytales.

Although now that they knew mermaids and sea monsters really existed, perhaps Pimm shouldn't be so quick to dismiss the fire-breathing creatures that once supposedly inhabited the mountain ranges stretching from Zavatleo, through Teratsu, to Char-range.

The heavy knocker thunked from the other side of the front door. Pimm stood from their chair, checked the membership tokens of the patrons waiting outside, and let them pass through into the lounge. Taking another long drag of smoke, Pimm scanned the crowd gathered that evening at the Bear's Den. A decent number, given the trouble they'd had with street crews harassing patrons. They caught a glimpse of the spry lad weaving between polished oak tables and crimson-cushioned sofas. A head of golden curls standing out like a candle in a coal mine.

Kit Naumenko paused to deliver the last of the drinks on his tray, then nipped back across the room to collect more from the barkeep. Pimm chuckled to themselves, they'd taken Kit under their wing, so to speak, when he'd lost his job at the Whistle and Bells, an orange lantern club that catered to patrons seeking the company of men. They were just finishing the repairs after the establishment was vandalized by another of the street crews.

The lad had grown confident working at the Den, and now alternated between tending bar and assisting Pimm at the door. And Pimm was glad, Kit deserved a bit of luck after a rough start in Kingsport.

Settling back into their chair, Pimm stubbed out the cigarette in a standing brass ashtray shaped like a bear's paw. They pulled a small notebook from their breast pocket and flipped it open. Inside were rough sketches of each district in Kingsport, broken down by neighborhood and then by street. Precise marks ticked off each area that had been searched so far. Finding a pencil in the same pocket, Pimm checked off the final street in the market district.

Months of meticulous searching, and still they'd found no sign of Ezmira. Maher believed she'd most likely left town to hide elsewhere on the Isles, but Pimm wasn't so sure. Something deep in their gut said that she was still lurking nearby. That her soured pride wouldn't allow her to go scuttling off because of a warning from Pimm. Even if they had reminded her of the Madam of the black lantern's edict; Ezmira was banished from Kingsport five years ago for tricking newcomers to the Isles to work in her Lantern establishment against their will. To return was to sign her own death warrant. And yet, Pimm had discovered her in the city last year, holding Kit captive in an empty shop. It still made Pimm's blood boil to think of how she'd harmed the lad, trying to force information from him that he didn't have. There were moments when Pimm went to a dark place, wishing they'd just shot Ezmira then and been done with it. But at the time all Pimm could think about was getting out of there safely with Kit.

Afterwards, when they were both healed from the injuries they'd sustained at one time or another, Pimm offered Kit a room in the building they owned in the northern district. The lad had agreed more readily than expected. Though they both still spent many consecutive days and nights at the Den, it was nice having Kit around to help with the needs of the older tenants. Ms. Orel was especially happy to have someone to converse with in Zavat. He'd also proven gifted at earning the trust of the guests sent by the Madam for temporary stays.

Pimm had grown rather fond of Kit. They'd never had any family to speak of, except the one they'd made for themselves. And Kit fit into that family as if he'd always been there.

Ezmira was the topic of a meeting held by the Lantern business owners just a few nights before. Maher had been uncharacteristically distracted; they weren't sure why. Pimm was there to represent Mama Bear and the Bear's Den. They'd just shared their progress searching the city. Slow though it was, even with the help of a few select employees from the black lantern.

"And what if she is simply moving between locations after you search them?" A well-known proprietor of a blue lantern establishment asked pointedly. A crown of thick, raven's wing hair was piled atop her head and threaded through with a lilac scarf.

"Is that likely?" another asked. "Who in their right mind would shield the likes of her?"

"More folks than you'd think, if there was enough in it for them." Archie, the owner of the Whistle and Bells, spoke for the first time since the meeting began.

Pimm and Maher shared a sympathetic look, then his attention quickly drifted away.

"What do you suggest then, Nitya?" the Madam drew the conversation back to the blue lantern owner.

"My daughter is close to both leaders of the street crews that once worked the wharfs before all the chaos began, they all came of age together. She assures me, they want these interloping crews gone and their old relationships restored. They could help cover more ground faster and reassess the districts Pimm has already searched."

Maher snorted softly. Pimm nudged him with an elbow.

The Madam considered the proposition, while some of the owners shifted uncomfortably. They were wary of any of the street crews getting involved, even the ones that had been active in Kingsport for a century or more. Not that Pimm could blame them. They still had no way of knowing if the crew that attacked them last summer was new, or one of the older groups whose numbers were swelled with out of work sailors.

The Madam leaned back in her chair. "What additional compensation would they want in exchange for this assistance?"

"Nothing. They only want the old order restored."

"I doubt that," Maher grumbled. Pimm kicked him under the table and Maher blinked, realizing he'd just spoken that thought aloud.

"Are you accusing my daughter of lying?" Nitya snapped.

"He's calling your daughter's so-called friends liars," Archie muttered.

"Right!" the owner next to him piped up. "Why should we trust them?"

Chair legs scraped the floor as Nitya stood, along with the two other blue lantern owners at the table. "If you think, because my establishment trades in empathy instead of flesh, that you can disregard my insight, you are sorely mistaken."

"They're not saying that." Maher tried to make peace.

"Why are you even here?" a young green lantern owner scoffed. "The Intelligencer of the Birde Isles has no place at this table. You're probably going to report everything we say to the Kingfishers."

"Shut it!" Archie slapped a palm on the table. "You have no idea what you're talking about."

Others began arguing amongst themselves. Pimm locked eyes with the gunfighter stationed by the door. Marielle shook her head and stayed where she was, hands clasped behind her back.

The growing din came to a halt when a low growl rumbled from beneath the Madam's chair. Those standing quickly found their seats as the massive dog pushed onto her feet. A blocky gray head swung around, eyeing each person until the room was completely silent.

After Ezmira made threats against her, the Madam began taking Sweetpea to all meetings in and outside of the black lantern. The dog was so well behaved, Pimm often didn't realize she was in the room. Everyone was very aware of Sweetpea's presence now.

"That's enough," the Madam patted the dog's back and she thumped onto her haunches. "We cannot afford to bicker like this. We will all consider Nitya's proposal and put our decision to a vote in three days' time. Agreed?" When everyone nodded, she continued. "That does not discount the work Pimm has already done, they have been exacting in their efforts. And Mr. Villaon's involvement in these gatherings will not be questioned again. In this room, he is not the Intelligencer, he is the Magpie. A figure who has been part of the Lantern longer than even some of you." The green lantern owner fidgeted under her gaze. "I think this is a good place to end for now. I trust we have all reached an understanding and will be ready to cast our votes soon."

BEAR'S DEN

PIMM

CHAPTER TEN

Pimm was stirred from their thoughts by another knock at the Den's door. The young woman on the other side smiled wide when she saw them, showing several gold-capped teeth. Light from the green-paned lamp outside made her short black hair shine.

"Marielle," Pimm shook her hand and ushered the gunfighter inside. "What brings you here? The votes aren't to be collected until tomorrow."

"Maybe I was lonesome for your company, Pimm." She winked.

"You're a shameless flirt," they chuckled.

"Makes life far more interesting."

Kit appeared before them, tray in hand. "Evening, Miss Marielle. Care for a drink?"

"I bet most patrons find it hard to say no to those pretty blue eyes," she grinned when Kit blushed. "But sadly, I can't stay long."

"Shameless." Pimm sighed. "It's alright, Kit. I'd love a cup of tea when you get the chance."

"I bet that lad has doubled your spirits sales," Marielle said as Kit blended back into the crowd.

"I decline to comment. What can we do for you, if it's not about the vote?"

"I have a message for Mama Bear from the Madam." Marielle rested her hands on her thick leather gunbelt, a posture Pimm knew well by now. While she might appear relaxed, leaning one wide hip against the wall, Marielle took her work for the Madam seriously.

"She's with a guest right now, but she'll be downstairs soon."

"I'm in no hurry," she replied smoothly.

This must be a very important message. Pimm thought.

They talked a while longer until Mama Bear made her entrance down the main staircase. No matter what else was happening in the nightclub at the time, Mama Bear always became the sole focus of everyone in the room. Her expressive blue eyes skimmed over the lounge, noting the number of patrons even as she smiled and greeted each person vying for her attention. Long, wine red skirts flowed over her ample hips and swirled around her with each step.

When Pimm finally caught her eye, they nodded at Marielle, still leaned against the wall next to them. Mama Bear sauntered over, never breaking the part she played as the Den's proprietor. Sizing Marielle up, Mama Bear tossed her fawn brown hair over her shoulder and the gunfighter snapped to attention. "To what do we owe the pleasure?"

Even Marielle couldn't withstand the full force of Mama Bear's attention. Color tinged her bronze cheeks as she gave a short bow. "I have a message for you from the Madam."

She extended a hand, waiting expectantly. "Well?"

Marielle's voice lowered. "It's for your ears only ma'am... miss... um..." she looked to Pimm for help.

"Have some mercy, ma'am." They smirked, enjoying the sight of a flustered Marielle.

"In that case," Mama Bear purred. "You had better come with me, hadn't you?" Hooking a finger through the top of her gunbelt, Mama Bear led Marielle though the lounge and up the stairs.

Marielle cast one last, marginally panicked look back at Pimm. They gave an almost imperceptible wave and turned their attention back to the notebook.

An uneventful hour passed. Pimm was contemplating another smoke when the latch clicked and Maher strolled through the door.

"Evening, Pimm." Maher gave the same greeting he'd used for all the years they'd known one another. There was something comforting about his consistency.

"Maher," Pimm nodded, noting that their friend must have come straight from his Intelligencer duties. He still wore a jacket emblazoned with the crest of his position. That must have been a treat for some of the tattlers of the Lantern to see. Not that Maher's two roles within Kingsport were a secret. But it drew a great deal of observation. That was to be expected, Pimm supposed, but they were growing concerned about the toll this was taking on Maher.

"You look exhausted, care to sit down?"

"And here I thought I looked fresh as new lamb," he tried to laugh off Pimm's words, but there were dark tell-tale circles beneath Maher's eyes. "Actually, I was hoping we could talk somewhere alone. I have news, my friend."

"Is that so?" Pimm found Kit across the room, catching the lad's eye and waving him over.

"Something you will be very interested to hear."

"Yes, Pimm?" Kit arrived quickly. "Good evening, Mister Villaon."

"How many times must I insist you call me Maher?"

Kit flushed for the second time that night. "Perhaps once more and it will stick."

"Kit?" Pimm cut in before Maher could turn the lad's entire face crimson. "Would you watch the door for a bit? Maher and I need to have a quick chat."

He nodded and signaled to Barkeep that he was taking Pimm's post. "You'll be upstairs?"

"My usual room," Pimm thanked him and led the way to the fourth floor.

"Cheeky lad, that one," Maher remarked as Pimm closed the door behind them and stoked the small pot-bellied stove in the corner. "I wonder if I can set a record for how quickly I can make him blush?"

They ignored the comment. "What did you want to discuss?"

"Spoilsport." Maher lowered himself into a chair by Pimm's worktable, visibly relaxing for the first time since he'd walked into the Den.

"What's this news, then?" Pimm filled a kettle from the pitcher on the bedside table and set it on the stove.

Maher leaned forward, bracing his elbows on his knees. "To the grave?"

They slid a finger along their lower lip. "To the grave."

"I know how the Saprean coins are being made."

Water was boiled, tea was steeped, and their cups were half-empty by the time Maher finished relaying everything he'd learned from Luthais.

Pimm could scarcely believe it. All this time, all the theories they'd tossed back and forth, and the simple truth was that these were *real* Saprean coins. Except they weren't being minted by the Saprean government. As Pimm stared into their teacup, wishing they could divine the final piece of this puzzle in the dregs, Maher's stomach growled.

"When was the last time you ate something?"

"I'm not sure, to be honest. This morning?"

With a sigh, Pimm stood and pulled twice on the cord hanging next to the narrow bed. Down in the kitchen, a bell would signal Olga to send up some food.

Maher's head tilted. "When did you have that put in?"

"After our last run-in with Ezmira. Mama Bear insisted, as long as I was staying here to recuperate." Pimm shrugged. "They're going to put one in each room, eventually, in case any of the employees need something."

"Smart. I hope they'll finally get Olga some help."

"Oh yes, the promise of a second maid was the only reason she agreed to the new arrangement."

"Good," he smoothed a hand over his short, black beard. "How goes the search?"

Pimm took out their notebook and opened it atop the map of the city currently spread across the table. "Let's start from the market district."

FORAOISE

CHAPTER ELEVEN

In the moments when Foraoise Dare thought about death, what the state that comes after living might be, it was never like this.

There were several points throughout her life when she thought she might die. When a horse threw her off onto a stone path at age nine. When red fever swept through the countryside and she spent nearly half of her thirteenth year recovering in bed, being nursed round the clock. When she left home at seventeen to run off with Jon and the fiercest storm she'd ever witnessed struck their ship that very night. In countless battles, as she learned first to defend herself and then how to attack before defense was necessary.

And finally, the day Jon tried to kill her. With the side of her head split wide open, blood running into her eyes and coating her hair, Foraoise really did believe she'd die that day. Before she'd barely gotten to truly live. That made her angrier than anything else, that yet another person was trying to control her fate. If it had been the horse, or the fever, or the storm? She could have accepted that. But another person? A man? Even worse, a man who was no longer the same one to whom she'd given her heart.

But Jon didn't swing his sword hard enough, he didn't think to aim for her neck instead of her skull. He'd already descended into madness by then. His skills simply weren't what they'd once been. Nothing was as it had once been.

Jon Dare was scheduled to die on the day they met. Public hangings weren't as common in Meredia as they once were, but this was to be an exception.

Her friends had dragged her to the square that day, gathering in a flurry of skirts and giggles. They claimed a place next to the antique war machine, a massive, mounted bow that had been put on display earlier that year. The girls all made wagers, not on how long it might take the condemned man to die like some of those gathered were doing. Instead they wagered on how *handsome* they thought he might be. When Foraoise's turn came to speculate, she pretended she hadn't heard them. Even talking to the maid who'd accompanied her was preferable to such twaddle.

It wasn't long before the staccato sound of drums echoed through the square. Murmurs turned to taunts and jeers as the people got their first look at the pirate whose execution they'd all come to witness.

A real *pirate*.

Foraoise had never seen a pirate. She'd only heard stories and songs from the servants about the criminals that plagued the seas. Her governess had refused to discuss such things. The crowd parted as a wheeled iron cage rolled past, pulled by a rather drab horse and an equally drab driver. Though his head was bowed, they could make out the pirate's profile. Dark hair swung forward over his eyes, brushing the high bridge of his nose. His strong jaw was clenched, full lips pressed tightly together and hands clasped in front of him. They'd clapped him in irons, a heavy chain linking between his wrists and secured to the floor of the cage.

"Oh my," one of the girls fluttered her pink-dyed silk fan. "I do believe Hilda has won the wager."

"I *told* you he'd be handsome," she preened as the cart moved out of sight. "Pirates are always mightily good looking in the sonnets."

Rolling her eyes, Foraoise lifted her skirt to step up onto the statue's pedestal for a better look.

"Miss! Please be careful!" her maid fretted.

After the cart reached the scaffolding erected at the edge of the square closest to the sea, the pirate was led out by the chain securing his wrists.

Noise rose around them as they took him up the steps to the gallows. A couple of Foraoise's friends looked as though they'd swoon at any moment. She wondered off-hand if any of the maids trailing them thought to bring smelling salts.

Some magistrate or other kind of ruffle-collared official stepped forward to read the charges against the man. His head was still bowed, but she didn't get the impression it was out of any sense of remorse or despair. He seemed to be concentrating very intently on something.

"What is he doing?" Foraoise muttered to herself, stepping higher onto the statue.

"Please miss!" Now the maid sounded as though *she* might faint.

"Did you bring smelling salts?" Foraoise glanced down at her. "Good, use them for yourself."

The list of charges against the pirate was lengthy indeed, but so far, she hadn't heard anything that heinous. Mostly petty thievery. No murder or massacre. No theft of some nation's crown jewels.

"And finally," the words rang out over the square, "the accused is charged with the theft of the good ship *Prosperity*, property of the lord provost of Meredia, and all goods contained therein."

Ah, that was it. He'd crossed the lord provost.

"Does the accused have any final words before sentence is carried out?"

The pirate finally looked up. Foraoise could have sworn he was laughing.

"Only that I have no intention of dying today." His voice carried over the crowd. "The sea and I have more work ahead of us, yet."

Crouching low on the platform, the pirate threw his arms up, sending the irons flying into the air.

Foraoise watched in awe as the lanky young man escaped his shackles and slipped from the grip of five guards before they noticed anything amiss. The maid panicked, screamed her silly head off, and tried to drag Foraoise away by her skirts when Jon darted past them. But Foraoise wasn't afraid, far from it. She was impressed. The scoundrel actually took the time to pause and wink at them on his way through the crowd. Foraoise scowled, ready to tell him exactly what he could do with that wink, and he grinned at her. One of his canine teeth was capped in silver.

A man destined for the gallows, sentenced for piracy of all things, yet he slid right out from under the officials' noses.

She could only assume he'd gotten away, back to the freedom of the seas.

It would be a whole year before she saw him again. Caught him watching her from the outskirts of a summer festival packed with special goods and food and people dressed in their finest. His hair was a bit longer and he'd grown in a short beard, but it was him. She was sure of it. Foraoise slipped away from her friends, it was as easy a decision as choosing a dress for the day. She made her way around to a stall stuffed with imported fabrics, eyes studying – but not really seeing – the wares before her. One moment she was alone in the crowd, and then he was standing next to her.

"It's impolite, you know, comin' to see a man hanged without proper introduction." His voice was deep, but not harsh. The words rolled over her, a gentle wave for each soft-spoken syllable that burrowed into her ear.

"But you weren't hanged." She picked up a bolt of maroon cloth and held it out for him to admire. "Therefore, I didn't see a hanging and I believe that negates the need for introductions."

He chuckled, a low sound that started somewhere in his chest and traveled up into his throat. "Apologies for denying you the spectacle, but I quite like my neck in its current, unbroken condition."

Color swept over her cheeks, but Foraoise continued to stare at what she now knew to be the ugliest brocade she'd ever seen. "You must have had somewhere better to be."

"Aye, somewhere much better. But I find myself here once again, in the arms of the very city that wished me harm. You weren't pining away for me, were you lass?"

Foraoise dropped the cloth. She braced her hands on her hips and arched a brow at him in a look of disdain that would have made her mother proud. "What sort of insolent presumption—"

"There it is!" He crowed.

"There *what* is?"

"That look you had when I was taking my leave of the gallows. Like you had something important to say. T'was all I could do not to stop for a chat right there." He moved closer, she glanced around but the shopkeeper was busy with another customer across the stall. "Don't see green eyes like that much around here."

"I know." She took half a step back. It was only a matter of time before someone noticed them standing so familiarly. And gossip in New Pravil spread faster than the plague.

"Like looking at sea glass shining in the sun."

Foraoise's eyes had been compared to many things by many ridiculous would-be suitors. Emeralds, spring leaves, even once to fresh celery. All meant to flatter, including the celery surprisingly enough, and all of them were wrong. But sea glass, that one she liked.

"Nope, don't find many eyes like that in this stuffy corner of the world. But I've seen quite a few east of here, as a matter of fact."

"Where?" She grabbed the sleeve of his rough sailor's jacket.

The pirate's dark eyes, like tea that had been left to steep too long in the pot, flitted down to her hand. She quickly let go. "Maybe I'll take you there sometime. Would have to know your name first, though."

Foraoise's heart did a little flip. "It's..." Was she really going to give this stranger, this *pirate*, her name?

"Foraoise!" One of her friends called out.

Gritting her teeth, Foraoise waved at the other girl, hoping she'd take the hint and wait there. Turning back, she found the young pirate had already begun to distance himself. Without thinking or caring about how it might look to passersby, she grabbed his hand. Rough calluses scraped against the pads of her fingers. "It's Foraoise."

"Fora-shuh." A smile passed across his face as he tried her name out. "Jon Dare, at your service." He bowed low and kissed her knuckles, whiskers tickling her skin.

"Dare? Is Dare really your name?"

"You'll have to find out, won't you?"

"Alright," the word left her mouth before she'd had time to think of it.

"It's a deal then. I'll see you soon, my green-eyed girl."

By the time her friends reached her, Jon had disappeared.

Yes, she'd thought many times of what death might be like, about how she'd reach that final state, and she'd been very wrong. This wasn't peaceful or still. There was no world hereafter or quiet void. This was a stifling, crushing weight holding her down for all eternity. Filling her head and choking her just enough to cause a steady stream of twisting pain, but not nearly enough to die.

That was the fate that awaited her. Foraoise Dare, captain of the greatest pirate fleet on the Eastern Sea. The woman who'd cheated death and struck fear into the hearts of every sailor before the mast. Cursed to drown for all eternity.

Or so she'd believed.

Until a strange glow broke through the barrier of her murky prison. Something hard was pressed against Foraoise's chest and the cold sting of the sea was chased away by a fire roaring beneath her skin.

The oppressive weight holding her down began to lift, and when she could finally see again, Foraoise beheld yet another creature that was not meant to exist. Bright, otherworldly green eyes observed her with cool, calculated detachment before a smile stretched across a pale face.

"Hello, Captain."

MAHER

CHAPTER TWELVE

Maher walked down the hall to Lord Kingfisher's private study, mentally preparing himself for another long advisory meeting in a marginally comfortable chair. His left shoulder twinged at the thought.

Suppose I ought not to complain, at least Al's good luck charm has made these things slightly more tolerable. He found the heavy, gilded door sitting ajar and pushed it open with a grunt.

Coming to a stop, Maher took in the long table already prepared with fresh sheets of paper, ink pots, and pens for those attending. Everything looked as it normally did, save one thing: His seat, that had once matched the intricately carved set arranged around the table, had been replaced with an elegant, tufted chair in a vivid shade of spruce. The curved, padded arms and high, wide back would no doubt support his shoulders better than anything he currently owned. But how did it get there?

Circling the room, Maher pulled the chair back from the table and found a small white card tied to one arm. The card read: **Property of Maher Villaon. Do not remove except under instructions from owner.**

Maher had been dreaming of a better seat for this room where he spent much more of his time than he thought necessary, but no one else knew that except...

"He *didn't*!" Maher bent to check for an import stamp on the underside. Sure enough, there was the country-of-origin stamp,

Zavatleo, the Birde Isles diving kingfisher, and the stamped seal of the Lord of Trade. "I'll be damned."

"Found your gift, I see."

Maher jumped, cursing as he knocked his head against the side of the table, and scrambled to his feet.

Luthais, smug bastard that he was, leaned against the study doorway. Rubbing the side of his head, Maher started to demand an explanation, only to let out a frustrated huff as more of Lord Kingfisher's advisors arrived for the meeting.

Maher's disgruntled feelings towards Luthais evaporated the moment he sat in that godsbedamned chair.

He didn't really care what the other man's reasons or motivations were for this expensive purchase. Or that he was receiving a range of puzzled and envious looks from the rest of the table. They'd have to pry the chair from beneath Maher's corpse if they thought he'd part with it now.

Mrs. Thorley, the manor housekeeper, soon came into the study with three servants in tow. They'd brought hot tea and other refreshments. A young maid who must have been new, for Maher didn't recognize her, paused after filling his teacup.

"Beg pardon, Mister Villaon," she spoke so softly, lips hardly moving, that he nearly missed what was said. "A note arrived for you, sir, from them that minds the Bear's Den." She briefly rested the teapot against the table and a small roll of parchment slipped from between the handle and her palm. It rolled off the edge of the table and Maher deftly caught it while stirring milk into this tea with his other hand.

"Thank you," he nodded, catching her dark eyes for a moment. She bobbed a curtsy and moved on to the woman sitting on Maher's left.

Keeping the note in his lap, Maher broke the tiny dot of wax holding it together and unrolled the paper. With all the secrecy of the missive's delivery, he though its contents would have been more urgent. But Pimm was only requesting that he come to the Den earlier than they'd originally planned, if his schedule allowed.

With the scroll tucked into his vest pocket, Maher refocused on the meeting. Luckily, the current speaker was an older advisor who took ten minutes to complete one sentence. Glancing around, Maher caught Luthais eyeing him from across the table. He looked pointedly at the place where Maher'd concealed the note and then towards the head of the table where his father Gaius sat.

Maher shook his head. No, nothing for Lord Kingfisher to be concerned about right now.

Luthais nodded with his eyes, a trick Maher just couldn't seem to master, and cut into the conversation just as the long-winded advisor paused to take a breath.

The meeting finally ended and, for the first time, Maher found himself reluctant to leave the table. Luthais really had unearthed the most comfortable chair on the entire continent. That thought reminded him that he ought to demand an explanation for the extravagant gift, no matter how much he intended to keep it.

Maher looked up from his notes, expecting to find Luthais still in the room, but he was already gone. Perhaps he had some other Lord of Trade duties to attend. It wasn't as if he could avoid Maher for long, not when they lived in the same house.

Later, Maher told himself. *First see what Pimm wants, then you can track down a certain gift giving sailor.*

After a quick meal in his room and changing into a less conspicuous suit of clothes, Maher began the walk on the private path that led from the manor to the city. This was the earliest he'd gone to the Lantern in ages. He soon reached the one place where the path forked. The right side leading to the temple of the sea; the left continuing on into town. Head Priestess Esa crossed his mind every now and then. Ally's former tutor was bound to be missing her. Maher really ought to make a point to visit the temple soon, more than anything to ensure Esa knew Ally's first year as a mermaid was nearly at an end.

Maher took his time, a luxury he couldn't often afford anymore. Stopping where the path met the old Kingsport seawall, he stood near the edge of the ancient stack of gray stone and watched the waves steadily rolling in to break on the sand. While he knew the likelihood of seeing Ally out in the water was slim, the tiny hope that he'd catch a glimpse of her kept him in that spot for several minutes. He knew for certain which day she'd gone down to meet Pasha on the shore, but wasn't sure how long it had taken to *change* Ally into a mermaid. His only confirmation that the ritual was successful was the note left for him with the shark tooth, written in Pasha's stilted hand.

Nevertheless, Maher was resolved to be there when Al emerged from the sea. He'd start on the date she left last year, and come to the beach each day thereafter until they found each other.

Dusk was just beginning to fall by the time he reached the Den. Patrons weren't allowed in until after dark, but the barkeep was good enough to let Maher into the establishment.

"Alright?" he asked the burly, redheaded man from Swan Island.

"Can't complain," Barkeep jerked a thumb upwards. "Pimm's on the fourth floor."

"Many thanks." Maher wasted no time climbing the stairs. With any luck, this could be handled quickly and he could be in bed before midnight for once.

The fourth floor of the Bear's Den had once been a mystery. Off limits to both employees and patrons, on pain of facing Mama Bear's wrath. Now, after years of curiosity, he knew the true purpose of that floor. The Madam of the black lantern, coincidentally also Mama Bear's mother, used the top floor of her daughter's establishment to house her own guests. Those who traded the secrets of cruel Lantern owners or customers in exchange for safe haven and care. Once healed enough to travel, they'd come to the Den or Pimm's home in the northern district to stay until transportation was secured to take them wherever they wished to go.

Reaching the room reserved for Pimm's use, Maher raised a fist, only to find it knocking on air as Olga swung the door open.

"Mister Villaon!" the slip of a kitchen maid beamed at him. "My, you're here early, aren't you?"

"For once, yes." He winked. "Is Pimm here?"

"Aye, they're at their worktable."

"Maher?" Pimm's voice floated out. "Come on inside."

"Are you hungry?" Olga jostled the tray of cleared plates in her hands. "Pimm's finished their supper, but we'd be happy to bring up something else."

"I thank you, but I've already eaten." He paused. "We?"

"Good evening, Mr. Villaon." Another girl appeared behind Olga, holding an empty water pitcher. A matching white mop cap covered her brunette, chin-length hair.

The manor maid who'd delivered Pimm's message.

"You!"

"Pleased to meet you, sir." She cut him off with a short curtsy.

"This is Gertie," Olga went on, oblivious to his surprise. "I've been saying for years that we needed a second maid, and now it's finally happened!"

"Indeed." He stepped aside to let them pass. "Welcome, Gertie. I can see Olga is glad of the help."

One corner of her mouth tipped up as she followed Olga downstairs. Stepping into the room and shutting the door, Maher rounded on Pimm. They were still bent over one of the maps on the table.

Maher cleared his throat when they didn't look up. "Pimm?"

"Hmm?" they glanced at him, sandy hair falling into their eyes.

"Care to explain Gertie?"

"Ah, well," Pimm chuckled. "We really did need another maid, I told you, but I thought it would be best if we found one with skills outside of what the position required. The Madam recommended Gertie, and here she is."

"Very smart, though I take it Olga doesn't know about her additional duties?"

"It's safer that way." Pimm's expression darkened for a moment before returning to normal. "Come, sit."

"Where is young Kit? I didn't see him downstairs." Maher took the offered chair and instantly longed for the new green one sitting in Lord Kingfisher's study. How difficult would it be to cart that one with him everywhere he went?

"Kit's assisting Ms. Orel with a few errands, he'll be back later tonight." They pulled a smaller map from a nearby stack and spread it out. "Do you recognize this?"

Maher studied the illustration of a building that spanned two whole city blocks. A diagram of a massive rotunda took up the center. A wall was built around it, with only two entry points at the north and south ends. Maher actually knew this building quite well. He'd just never seen it from a bird's eye view.

"The Treasury."

"I've used every resource I have to determine who could possibly have the resources to mint their own Saprean coins with that stolen press," Pimm sighed, "and I've learned nothing except that wealth is a closely guarded thing. But someone inside the Kingsport Treasury offices might know, or at least have an idea of which nations could produce that much silver."

"It's possible..." Maher caught the pointed look Pimm gave him. "Oh no, I can't ask him for help, Pimm, you know that."

"You don't *have* to go through Khafra. Surely in all the time you've spent visiting the Treasury with him, you've met a contact or two."

"Not any who weren't likely to go squawking to my father the moment I left."

"Well we can't just send anyone there." They ran a hand through their hair.

"They'd need at least some credibility if they were questioned, and that place is a maze on the inside..."

"Maher," Pimm straightened in their seat. "We know the perfect person. Marielle."

Maher couldn't deny the gunfighter would be perfect for the job, but could he go to her directly again? He already owed both Marielle and the Madam significant debts after their help last year. Debts neither had come to collect, yet.

Shifting to a more comfortable position, Maher sighed heavily. "I'm going to owe Marielle my firstborn child at this rate."

Chapter Thirteen

Summer was passing quickly. Ally felt the subtle changes in the water, noticed which sea creatures were preparing to migrate to their winter homes and which would stay near the Isles through the colder seasons.

Her first year as a mermaid would be over soon too, though not before her twenty-third birthday had passed. They may not have marked the exact day Ally was changed, but there were still plans to make. According to the limited information left behind by Pasha's shoal, once the sun rose on that last day, she'd need to get to land as quickly as possible.

Pasha called it the *pull*. The innate need to leave the sea for just a while, to let her tail split for the first time and relearn how to use her legs. And there was something beginning to tug as the edges of her mind. It was just out of reach, like a fish darting away in her peripheral vision.

It was starting to affect Pasha as well. Though she'd once spent decades, centuries, beneath Kingfisher Island, never setting fin or foot on land, she was Ally's maker. The one who gave a scale of her own to be the seed from which all of Ally's scales would grow. And Ally was learning there was a fine balance between the time mermaids spent in each form.

Pasha had been having headaches of increasing intensity over the last several days. Ally couldn't help but feel partially responsible, it had to be related to the changes her own body was anticipating.

Ally swam lazily through the great cavern, with its many murals and towering carvings. Pasha was out on a hunt. She'd insisted on going, even though her head had bothered her all morning. Ally wanted to help, but she wasn't much of a hunter yet, and it did seem like some time alone might do Pasha good.

Something flitted through the edge of her vision. Ally stopped, moving her tail beneath her so she could float upright. Turning slowly, she tried to catch whatever it was that was hovering just outside the boundary of her mind. It flashed by again and Ally twisted towards the mouth of the nearest tunnel leading out of the cavern.

Is Pasha back from hunting already? Her stomach twisted. *Did her headache get worse and force her to return early?*

Ally moved closer to investigate. Surely if it was Pasha, the corals would be waking up to light her way. As if reading her mind, the corals around the mouth of the tunnel began blinking wildly on and off.

"What's wrong?" Ally tried to soothe them. "Pasha? Are you down there?"

The acrid scent of blood reached Ally's nose just as a cloud of red hit her face. She reeled back, gagging as a large shape came careening through the tunnel. It flailed violently, bounced off a stone wall, and tackled Ally to the ground.

Chapter Fourteen

Marielle was stationed in her usual post on the ground floor of the black lantern establishment. All the guests had been attended to for the time being and the Madam had retired early. So she settled into a chair by the entrance to the lounge and opened a book. Slower nights like this were something of a rarity and she intended to take advantage.

She'd gotten through the first two chapters of the novel when the lock on the front door turned sharply and Eustace's pale face appeared.

"Miss Marielle," the door guard looked and sounded especially put out.

"What is it?"

"Mr. Maher Villaon is here to see you. *Again.*"

By his tone, she would've guessed Eustace would rather have his teeth pulled than allow the Magpie inside without invitation.

"I knew this was too good to be true," she muttered and closed the book. "Please show him in, Eustace."

Looking very much like he'd just sucked a lemon, Eustace closed the black-painted door with a snap.

Marielle stood and stretched, fists pressed into her lower back. Hopefully, this was nothing they'd need to wake the Madam over. Adjusting the wide belt that holstered the two heavy pistols to her hips, she moved into the lounge and waited there.

Before too long, she heard the door open again and Maher thanking the door guard effusively for his kind assistance. She snorted, the Magpie definitely knew how to get under Eustace's skin.

"Good evening, Marielle." He strolled into the room.

"Maher," she shook his hand. "What brings you by tonight?"

"It's very simple." Pulling a folded sheet of parchment from his breast pocket, Maher held it out for her to take. "How familiar are you with the Kingsport Treasury?"

"Let me see if I rightly understand this," Marielle stared at the map now spread out on a side table in the lounge, "you want to know which nations could possibly have mined enough silver to print these damned coins." She flicked the Saprean coin he'd used to weigh the paper down. "But instead of walking into the Treasury and, I don't know, *asking* someone you might already be acquainted with, you want me to tuck up one of the most secure buildings in the Birde Isles and nim the information?"

"That about sums it up." He sipped the whiskey she'd poured for both of them when the conversation began.

Marielle's brow pinched. Her tongue pressed against her teeth, sliding over the gold caps scattered across them. Four in front, four in back. One of the last remnants of home she couldn't seem to let go. It'd been nigh on ten years since she left The Riddles, but the thought of removing the caps made her physically ill.

Buying more time to think, she pulled out the tin of mints she always kept in a pouch on her belt. With the tiny green sweet tucked into the pouch of her cheek, Marielle considered the many potential outcomes.

"My soul and body. This is cracked, Maher."

"I'm well aware," Maher agreed readily, as if they were only discussing the weather. "But I'm out of options. You are the only one I know who could get in and out without detection. I still haven't figured out how you do that, but I've decided to remain in blissful ignorance."

"Could you not simply ask one of the Kingfishers?"

"I thought of that too. There would still be some sort of official communication, and I don't yet know if anyone inside of the Isles is involved. I don't want the wrong person knowing that we've learned how these coins are being made."

Marielle sucked in a deep breath. "That I can understand. What I don't like is the idea of making another bargain without the Madam's blessing."

He considered that. "We could involve her, if you'd like. Though I would much rather owe you an additional debt, than your employer."

"I've heard that before," she smirked.

"We do what we must," Maher scrubbed a hand over his face. He looked more haggard every time they met. "Can I interest you in a firstborn child?"

Marielle choked on a laugh. "That won't be necessary." She coughed. "Earning the right to brag that I have the Magpie of Kingsport in my pocket will suffice."

"Does that mean you'll do it?"

"It's a good trade." Marielle raised her glass. "I'll see what I can do. In the off chance I can't get in, I won't hold you to this latest deal."

"To doing what we can."

They clinked glasses and drank. The liquor burned down her throat and warmed her belly.

To doing what we can.

PASHA

CHAPTER FIFTEEN

Pasha's hunting trip had been less than successful. A few meager fish waited in the net clutched in her hand. Hardly enough to feed one hungry mermaid, let alone two. But nearly every time she got close to a school of fish, pain would lance through her skull. By the time her vision cleared, they'd scattered.

She supposed she ought to teach Ally to hunt, she'd been asking, but Pasha liked that this was something she could do for her.

On the verge of vomiting from the pain in her head, and after losing yet another catch, Pasha gave in and turned back towards home. She swam as quickly as she dared, aware that moving too fast caused the discomfort to spike. The outline of the big island loomed ahead, the sun setting above the surface cast long shadows across the seafloor. Pausing, Pasha turned in a slow circle, something was missing. Where were the other sea creatures that made their homes around this edge of the island? There were none in sight, even the anemones clinging to the rocks seemed to have shrunken into themselves.

It was only after she drew closer to the nearest tunnel that Pasha felt the crackle of strange energy. Her fins flexed and her grip on the net tightened. This wasn't her or Ally's energy, it was sickly and tinged with terror. A faint trail led from the open ocean, straight towards the island.

No, not towards the island. *Beneath* the island.

Ally! Pasha shot for the tunnel. The smell of blood assaulted her senses and the ache in her head spiked again. Swimming faster, Pasha reached the mouth of the tunnel. The corals around the bottom edge were smeared with blood, their lights flickered weakly and a few had scorched completely out. Racing down the tunnel, Pasha felt a new flash of energy from somewhere ahead. Lights spiraled around her, the corals signaling their alarm.

The sounds of a scuffle and Ally's scream echoed from the great chamber. Pasha whipped her tail harder, nicking the edges of her fluke on the walls. She burst into the cavern and hit a blooming cloud of sand and blood.

On the floor of the cave, Ally was struggling against a creature that pinned her down. Pasha reached behind her for the spear she'd found in an old mermaid trove, then remembered it was in the tapestry cave. There was a sharp grunt and Ally cried out again.

"Ally!" Pasha dropped the net of fish and dove into the fray.

"Pasha? Pasha!" Ally coughed through the sand swirling around them.

Pasha lunged for them, electric charges building in her hands, and shocked the creature hard enough to send it flying across the cavern. She scooped Ally up and pulled her to safety, into clearer water. Ally was coated in grit and Pasha's stomach sank when she saw bloody claw marks running down her arm. She tucked Ally behind her and whirled around, teeth bared, new charges spiraling down her arms, ready for an attack.

But nothing happened.

They both were breathing heavily as the sand settled. Pasha glanced back, "Are you alright?"

"Yes," Ally coughed again. "Yes, I'm alright."

As the water finally cleared, they saw whatever it was that attacked Ally lying motionless against the opposite wall. It was curled inward, all either of them could see was a row of dark green spines on its back.

"Stay here."

"Are you serious?" Ally pushed herself up. "We go together."

"Now is not the time," Pasha started, but Ally was already past her. Growling, she grabbed Ally's fluke to slow her down. "At least stay behind me. Please?"

"Why?"

"Because you can't defend yourself yet!"

The intruder moaned, drawing their attention back across the cavern. They eased closer, Ally staying just behind Pasha's tail. Snuffing out the charges on one hand, Pasha kept the other ready to strike as she reached for the creature's side. Taking a quick breath, Pasha rolled it over and backed away.

Pasha's headache vanished so suddenly, her vision doubled. The white-hot currents running over her skin died.

"What is it?" Ally touched the small of Pasha's back and her spine went rigid.

She was still alive; the charge had only knocked her out. Lacerations and welts, some long healed over and some newer, dotted her stone-gray skin. A particularly nasty, half-healed gash was bleeding sluggishly from her abdomen. Her tail showed signs of past damage too, there were scattered patches of regrown scales and a worn indention just above her fluke. The silver hair that had once flowed down her back had been hacked short, and a long scar now marred her forehead, but Pasha *knew* her. She knew how this mermaid looked when she was happy, when she was upset, especially when she was angry. She knew her eyes, if they opened, would be like two shining copper coins looking up at them.

Ally pulled herself around Pasha's side. "Pasha, what's going on?" She gasped when she saw what – who – Pasha was staring at. "Is... is that a mermaid?"

Pasha nodded. The warm summer sea around them suddenly turned to ice. This wasn't possible. They were all gone, had been gone for centuries.

"Who is she?" Ally's hand twined with hers, a spot of warmth in the cold that had soaked into her core.

"That's Hama." Pasha barely got the words out.

"Hama?"

"My cousin."

CHAPTER SIXTEEN

Ally could scarcely believe her eyes. After centuries of silence, a member of Pasha's family was *here*. But what happened to her? Hama almost looked as if she'd been… tortured.

Who could have done this? Was she captured by humans? A chill crept up Ally's spine. Pasha hadn't moved or spoken in quite some time.

"We have to help her," Ally said gently. "I don't think she meant me any harm."

Pasha blinked once. Twice. Slowly, her head turned and she looked at Ally. "You have a cut here, too." Pasha touched a fingertip to Ally's temple.

"It'll heal. We should get Hama off the floor, see how badly she's wounded."

Saying the other mermaid's name a third time broke through the fog that had settled over Pasha the moment she recognized her cousin. "I should… I should heal her." Kneeling in the sand, Pasha screwed her eyes shut. When she opened them again, they were dry. "Why can't I cry? This would be the moment to cry!"

"You're still in shock, give it some time. It will probably hit you all at once and we'll have plenty of tears. I'd try it if I could."

The few tears Ally had shed over the last year, tears of joy, tears of frustration with herself, had been ordinary tears. They lacked the pearlescent magic that could heal wounds and burn away disease. Pasha believed Ally's tears would change once she could harness the energy around them. But Ally suspected it ran deeper than that. She wasn't born a mermaid and there had to be other differences they hadn't considered.

Hama moaned again. They turned to her just as the mermaid's hand flailed and wrapped around Pasha's arm. Hama's face twisted with agony and fear. She didn't seem to know where she was.

"Hama." Pasha pushed the words to her in mermaid language as she said them aloud. "Wake up, Hama. You're safe. You're *home*."

Ally felt the tremendous wave of energy that passed between them. Bitter electricity stung her nose and made her temples throb. Was this what had triggered Pasha's headaches? Had her cousin been calling for help? Hama's eyes flew open and Ally was struck by their burnished metal shade. She stared at Pasha and Ally without seeing them. Her cracked lips moved, but no sound came out.

"Hama? It's Pasha. Can you hear me?"

Those copper eyes rolled around the chamber, pausing briefly on Ally, before landing on Pasha.

"Si..." Hama tried to speak. Her voice was like two stones brushing against each other.

"You don't have to say anything yet." Pasha glanced at Ally, her brow knitted with worry. "We need something to dress that wound on your stomach –"

Hama surged upwards, her other hand gripped the back of Pasha's head. "*Sirens.*"

"What?" Pasha whispered.

"The sirens are coming."

CHAPTER SEVENTEEN

Sirens? Pasha tried to wrap her mind around what Hama was saying. She tried to talk to her, but the other mermaid only repeated, "The sirens are coming."

Ally retrieved long strips of seaweed to wrap over Hama's largest wound, but she wouldn't let them touch it. They needed a tear to start the healing, just *one*. Pasha willed herself to produce a tear and still nothing.

Do I have to hurt myself to get one damned tear?

"Don't do that," Ally said firmly. Pasha hadn't realized she'd pushed the thought out of her own head.

With no other option, Pasha would have to give Hama some of her own energy. Hopefully it would steady her enough so they could dress her wounds and move her somewhere more comfortable.

Laying one hand against Hama's reedy chest, Pasha cracked open the wellspring of her energy, allowing it to trickle through the connection. The spark inside of Hama, the place that should have responded right away, was a yawning pit. It drank greedily from the source that Pasha offered.

"Careful, Pasha," Ally cautioned. "Too much too quickly won't be good for either of you."

Pasha knew Ally was right. As much as she wanted to keep going, she slowly pulled back. Hama's coloring looked much improved, for a moment, before the last of the light sank into her skin. Her eyes fluttered open and she grabbed Pasha's arm again.

"The place where the seas meet."

"What does that mean?" asked Ally.

"I'm not sure." Pasha pushed Hama's ragged hair off her forehead. She still looked so scared, so full of anguish, it broke Pasha's heart. Finally, her eyes began to sting. If she could just get one tear...

"The place where the seas meet.... They were hiding, but..." Hama's chest heaved. "The rest, they're off the map."

"The rest of whom?" The urgency in Ally's question made Pasha look up. They locked eyes. The rest of Pasha's shoal? The rest of the mermaids?

Hama was talking faster, gasping between words. "Don't let them into... the islands. Don't let them call... A mermaid must always remain beneath the island."

"Hama, I don't understand what you're saying." Pasha finally felt pressure in the corner of her left eye. "Let us help you and then you can tell us everything."

Hama looked over at Ally, really focused on her for the first time. "I was so worried. Pasha, all alone." She reached out and, without any hesitation, Ally leaned closer. Hama touched a shaky hand to the pattern of blue-hued scales that wrapped over the front of Ally's shoulder. "So glad... glad she found you."

The tear slipped free and Pasha lowered her head to Hama's abdomen. She said something else to Ally that Pasha didn't catch. The fat, pearl-like tear soaked into the wide gash. Bubbles fizzed and popped as the wound sealed shut. When Pasha sat back up, tears were streaming down Ally's cheeks.

"What is it?" Pasha glanced at Hama as she sighed in relief, her body relaxed into the sand. "What did she say?"

"She said, it wouldn't be enough." Ally rasped, taking Hama's free hand. "She asked me to take care of you."

Pasha grabbed her cousin's face. "Hama! Don't give up now! It's healing, can't you feel it?"

"Better," Hama's voice was less strained, but smaller somehow. "But it's not enough." Pulling her close, Hama cupped Pasha's face and pressed a kiss to her brow.

"Please don't leave again," Pasha sobbed.

Hama's last words washed through Pasha's mind. "*Help the others. Protect our home. It's why they chose you.*" Her hand slipped from Pasha's cheek. "*Take care, little one.*"

Hama's eyes closed and her spark faded away.

And Ally was right, grief swept over Pasha like a rogue wave. She cried enough tears to heal every wound on Hama's skin, but none were enough to bring Hama back.

Chapter Eighteen

The memories came slowly at first. Scraps of the past floating by.

A favorite lost toy. Her cousin Johanna mocking her for being the only member of the family with a freckled face. The aftermath when she retaliated by slipping a pair of cockroaches into Johanna's bed while she slept. The look of fury on some rat-faced boy when she refused to dance with him at a ball, she hadn't bothered to remember his name.

Scenes of her life that held little or no consequence.

Then, they began to arrive in earnest. Full, vivid remembrances, both of the sort that once brought her joy and others that she'd wished to lose forever.

The day Jon asked her to leave everything behind to sail the world with him, played out with especially perfect clarity. They'd only spoken a handful of times, but each encounter had imprinted on her more than the hundreds of conversations she'd had with the children of her parents' friends. Her love for Jon had swept beneath her like an undertow and pulled her out to sea before she'd even realized her feet were no longer on land.

Jon was so alive, so open and unlike the stuffy people around her, so *free*. At twenty years old he'd already worked his way up to quartermaster of his father's crew. And thanks largely to a new privateering contract he'd secured with Meredia, the same government that had attempted to hang him only a few short months before, Jon would soon be made captain of the *Tide's Last Revenge.*

The news of this contract was enough of a surprise, she'd not thought of the Meredian lord provost as particularly forgiving, but then he asked Foraoise to join him. Not only as a shipmate and a lover, but as his bride.

They were sharing a rare moment alone on the beach when he asked her. How could he be so sure? He wasn't after her family's wealth, of that she was certain. The dowry her father had set aside most definitely wouldn't be coming with her if she chose this path. There would be no going back if she left Meredia to follow this frank, uninhibited man out to sea.

"But I know nothing about sailing!"

"Is that your answer?" Jon flashed that infuriatingly handsome grin, his silver tooth winking at her. "Don't worry, I'll teach you everything you need to know. Your first lesson, why do most sailors sport an earring or two?" He flicked the small gold hoop pierced through his earlobe.

"I don't know," she huffed. "A fashionable source of bribery?"

"Close!" Jon leaned in and whispered into her ear. "It's to buy our passage to the next world, should we die at sea. For a proper burial, a sailor should be sewn into their hammock, sent overboard with a bit of gold or silver to pay their way and a final stitch through the nose for good measure."

"Why through the nose?" Foraoise's head tilted and Jon's beard brushed her cheek.

"Firstly, to ensure the sailor is truly dead." He pulled back until they were eye-to-eye. "And secondly, to make sure they *stay* dead."

Jon ended the lesson with a kiss, their first, and Foraoise was only too happy to be swept away with the current.

CHAPTER NINETEEN

Ally sat alone in the tapestry chamber, staring at the painter's case that held the woven map she'd repaired for Pasha. Despite the extra protection that had been added to the fabric itself, she was reluctant to open it underwater.

Hama's words ran whirled through her mind.

The place where the seas meet.

What could that possibly mean? There were many points on the map where one sea blended into another, but those were imaginary lines drawn by humans to understand the limits of the world. There was nothing in those places but endless stretches of water.

"But maybe, underneath?" Ally chewed her lower lip, reached for the case, then changed her mind. The small map showed the last known locations of all the mermaid communities. Any groups of threads representing land lacked any real detail and were only meant to indicate where the seas ended.

That's why Ally wanted to study Pasha's map, it might show something none of the human maps had found.

Ally couldn't go onto land yet, but what were the rules about breaking through the surface? If not the surface of the sea itself, what about the hatching grounds? The mermaids' sacred place, hidden beneath Snake Island of all places, was an enclosed cavern with a crystal-clear lagoon inside. Could Ally swim there and hold the map open above the water, if she was careful not to touch the strip of beach that ran along one side?

Neither she nor Pasha were entirely sure what would happen to Ally if she touched land before the year was up, but they didn't want to find out either.

Twisting around, Ally paused in front of the largest tapestry left behind by Pasha's shoal. A group of mermaids holding baskets stuffed full of shells, woven into the baskets were names from their shoal and others in multiple human languages. It was preserved between two massive slabs of mottled glass. Pasha's name was the last one added, the reddish thread brighter than the rest.

Ally glanced at the doorway. "Is Pasha still with her?"

The corals glowed brighter for a moment, then dimmed again. Yes, Pasha was still standing vigil by her cousin's body.

Pasha was utterly inconsolable after Hama's death. At least Ally'd convinced her to move Hama to a better place for the rites that needed to be performed. Pasha would let Ally know when she was finished, but she'd wanted to be alone for what would come next.

PASHA

CHAPTER TWENTY

Hama's body lay on the raised slab of stone in the same chamber she'd once shared with one of her year mates. Pasha's sharp nails combed slowly through her hair, gently scratching her scalp as she worked out each knot and snarl.

As a child, she'd been jealous of Hama's hair. It shone and flashed like a sleek school of tarpon in the sunlight that filtered through the waves and trailed behind her like a silver mist. Knowing that someone had hacked it off above her shoulders, as if it were nothing, made Pasha's stomach burn. When each strand was smoothed back, Pasha took up a stalk of wide, flat kelp. Starting with Hama's face, Pasha carefully wiped away every speck of sand and streak of blood. She worked her way down Hama's neck and shoulders, lifted each arm to graze the kelp over her skin, between each finger, and across her palms.

Of course, they were creatures of the sea, the water washed away most things that would cling on land. But this wasn't really about cleansing Hama's skin, it was about giving her one last act of care. Mermaids were tactile. It wouldn't be right to not give Hama this last gift.

Pasha had only seen this ritual performed a few times in her life. The last was for Pallagia. She worked methodically, trying to remember everything that was supposed to be done.

After finishing with Hama's torso, Pasha traded the kelp for a hunk of sandstone. The chamber filled with the shushing of the stone rubbing over Hama's tail. Any loose or dead scales would slough off, leaving the rest of the dark green armor polished.

There were *so many* scars. A few had indeed healed when Pasha'd finally wept over her cousin's body, but there were still more.

"What happened to you?" Pasha whispered, knowing the other mermaid wouldn't answer. Her fingers traced the indentation just above Hama's fluke. It was as if something solid had been wrapped around her tail for *years*, compressing the scales down. Even the dark gray webbing of Hama's fins had been damaged and healed over.

Pasha lost herself in the motions of the ritual, neither knowing nor caring how long she tended to her cousin. The tombs were open and ready, she could take all the time she needed. Perhaps this was meant to help her as well. By the time she finished, a small piece of her grief broke apart and floated away.

Looking up at the corals watching from the walls, Pasha noticed the change in the light they provided. She'd been with Hama all night and well into the morning. Pasha folded Hama's hands across her stomach and placed a kiss on her forehead.

The wish Pasha'd carried deep in her heart for centuries had finally come true. For a brief moment, a member of her shoal had returned.

With one last look around the cave, Pasha went in search of Ally. She found her curled on the floor of the tapestry chamber, one arm tucked beneath her head as she slept. Stroking a finger down Ally's cheek, Pasha waited for her eyes to flutter open.

"Pasha?"

"I need your help."

ALLY

CHAPTER TWENTY-ONE

Ally's joints protested mightily when she rose from the sandy floor and followed Pasha down the tunnel. It was getting harder to move or swim without discomfort, something she worried was also becoming worse for Pasha.

They swam in silence back through the great cavern and down another tunnel lined with caves that had once served as bedrooms for the shoal. About halfway down they turned into the place where Hama rested. Ally could see the care Pasha had already given her cousin; she could almost believe Hama was just sleeping there on the stone bed.

"What can I do?"

"We have to wrap her before bringing her to the tombs." Pasha gestured towards the pile of kelp they'd gathered before Ally left her to perform the mermaids' death ritual in peace. "Will you help me? Please?"

"Of course." Ally gave Pasha a quick peck on the cheek and they began.

While Pasha handled the actual weaving of the seaweed around her cousin's body, Ally prepared each strip and helped to steady Hama when it was time to slide the makeshift shroud beneath her. When they were finished, the mermaid was wrapped from head to tail.

All that remained was to bring Hama to the tombs.

Ally was thankful Pasha had the presence of mind to break open the sealed tunnel leading down into the shoal's honeycomb of tombs before beginning the burial ritual. Using the green stone spear might have made the task easier, but it still required a tremendous amount of energy to force apart the door Pasha's kin put in place just before they left.

Pasha carried Hama while Ally held a ball of glowing electricity that Pasha had formed to light their way. Like the other caves they'd broken open while searching for the secret to change Ally into a mermaid, the corals in this place had long since gone dormant and fossilized. The tombs were carved three tall into either side of the tunnel. They didn't go too far before Pasha found the alcove she wanted. Few of the graves in this part of the tombs were occupied, that Ally could tell. Pasha placed Hama in an open middle one and they stacked rocks over the opening to cover her.

Ally'd half-expected some kind of ceremony, some words spoken or a prayer said for Hama's safe passage. The priestesses at the temple of the sea went through an intricate funeral process when a believer of the sea goddess required their services.

But Pasha only used a small charge to seal the tomb and said a final goodbye in mermaid language. Ally took a short moment of silence, grateful that Hama had made it home before succumbing to her injuries. As much as it hurt Pasha to lose her, this was the first proof they'd seen that the other mermaids were out there, somewhere.

The place where the seas meet.

As they made their way out, Pasha stopped to rest her hand on a sealed grave closer to the mouth of the tunnel. Ally knew, somehow, that this must belong to Pallagia. Pasha's older sister.

Moving next to her, Ally silently placed her hand over Pasha's as they paid their respects to another lost member of their family.

CHAPTER TWENTY-TWO

"**M**ister Villaon? Mister Villaon... Maher!"

Maher jolted awake to find himself slumped over Pimm's worktable at the Den. Kit was standing over him, blonde brows knitted together with concern.

"Are you alright?"

"I... what? Yes, I'm fine." Maher yawned wide, jaw creaking, and pushed himself upright in his chair.

"If you're sure," the lad clearly didn't believe him. "Pimm sent me up to tell you they'd be just a little longer with Mama Bear."

"Thank you, Kit." He stretched, wincing when his left shoulder gave a sharp twinge.

"How about a fresh pot of tea? Maybe something from the kitchen?"

Maher nearly declined, but he didn't have the energy to go through the rituals of polite refusal. Proper etiquette be damned. "That would be lovely, Kit, and much appreciated."

Blue eyes lighting up, Kit scurried from the room.

With a groan, Maher scrubbed a hand over his face and pulled out his pocket watch. "How long was I asleep?" The steadily ticking hands were nearly at midnight. "Fuck, nearly an hour."

His regular meeting with Pimm had been delayed for some reason or other. Inner workings of the Bear's Den that he wasn't privy to. Maher thought he'd just rest his eyes until Pimm appeared.

Some Intelligencer you are, Maher Villaon, drooling on Pimm's maps while a young lad tucks up on you.

"Fuck me," he swore again, pressing the heels of his hands against his dry, bleary eyes.

"I thought we agreed to keep our relationship professional?"

Maher startled for the second time that night. A smirking Pimm was standing in the doorway. Behind them, Kit tried unsuccessfully to hide his crimson face behind the teapot sitting on his tray.

"I'm too exhausted to come up with a response to that remark, try again tomorrow."

"Jackass," Pimm slid easily out of Kit's way so he could arrange the tea and plates of food on the one free corner on the table. After he'd gone, and Maher had wolfed down two whole sandwiches, Pimm broke the silence. "Kit said he found you passed out in here."

"Well you were late," he shrugged. "I thought I'd have a brief respite."

"Don't try to spin a yarn with me, Maher, I know you too well for that."

"Your point?"

"You're overextended, is my point. You're not sleeping or eating enough. And what's the meaning of this?" Pimm knocked their boot against his and a clump of sand broke off onto the floor.

"Ah, that, right." Maher sighed. "To the grave?"

"Of course."

"Ally's first year as a mermaid is nearly over. I've been staking the best possible points on the beach to spot her when she returns."

"Gods above and below," Pimm's gray eyes widened a fraction; he'd actually managed to stun them. "So, you've been running back and forth from the manor to town at all hours, *and* you've been walking the beach in-between? Maher, enough is enough."

Opening his mouth to argue, Maher caught the firm set of Pimm's jaw and his shoulders slumped. "You're right. I know you're right."

"I thought having one of Lord Kingfisher's sons back in the Isles meant that you'd finally have some help?"

Maher snorted. Even with Luthais back, he'd been immediately swamped by his own duties as Lord of Trade. The hardly saw each other outside of council meetings. It made Maher anxious in a way he couldn't describe. "Luthais has his own tasks to attend to, especially with Gai still on sabbatical."

"And when is the future Lord Kingfisher due back?" Pimm pushed a plate of fruit and cheese at him and crossed their arms.

"Soon, I think." he popped a few grapes into his mouth. Useful when one wished to avoid answering pointed questions.

"That's all you're going to tell me, isn't it?"

"For now." Maher placed a hand over his heart. "But I swear, I'll find a way to rest."

"Good. You won't be a very effective Intelligencer or Magpie if you work yourself to death." Pimm refilled their cups. "Have you gotten any word from Marielle?"

Maher was beginning to think he'd seen more dawns than any rooster in the Birde Isles. It was not a superlative he appreciated.

Yet again, Pimm had been right. If nothing changed, he was going to completely exhaust himself before the year was out.

After having the meeting he'd gone there for, Pimm insisted he rest at the Den before returning to Kingfisher manor. Any argument he might've made was nullified when Pimm threatened to tell Mama Bear about his current condition. So Maher collapsed onto the narrow bed in Pimm's room and was asleep before his friend left the room.

At six o'clock in the morning, Maher woke to a breakfast of sizzling ham, eggs, and fresh bread. Kit remained in the room until Maher ate every bite. Pimm's orders, he claimed. Not even the bawdiest joke Maher could come up with that early in the morning was enough to chase the lad away.

Olga arrived next with a fresh pitcher of water for the washbasin. Apparently all the employees at the Den were worried about him. It touched him, Maher couldn't deny that, and he left feeling more refreshed than he'd been in months.

With sunlight just starting to peek through the tall glass windows, Maher let himself into the house. A few servants were already up and going about their morning duties. They greeted him and kept moving, as they were now accustomed to his odd hours.

When the door to his rooms closed behind him, Maher let out a deep sigh. It felt good to be home. One of the servants must have run up ahead of him and stoked the fire. It burned cheerily in the hearth and warmed the room. Despite it being summer and hot as blazes before noon, Maher found he now needed the extra heat when he slept.

Rolling his shoulders, Maher sat on the edge of his bed to remove his boots. Next to the candle the servants must have also just lit, he found a small clay jar and a silk pouch of tea sachets. One whiff of pine and Maher recognized the same liniment Luthais had given him last winter. Beneath the pouch was a slip of paper that read: **Chamomile. For sleep.**

Warmth that had nothing to do with the fire, or the shark tooth around his neck, bloomed in Maher's chest. It appeared Luthais was thinking about him after all.

LUTHAIS

CHAPTER TWENTY-THREE

L uthais Kingfisher watched Maher trudge down the corridor leading to the guest wing. He was on his way to the kitchen, where the cook would have breakfast waiting, before leaving for the wharf. There were some jobs that demanded an early start.

He nearly spoke, but Maher was focused solely on returning to his room. Stopping a servant headed that direction, Luthais asked them to please tend to the fire in Maher's quarters.

Last night, Maher slipped away immediately after dinner. It seemed like a good time to leave the liniment and tea in his room. Luthais could scarcely believe how haggard Maher looked. When they'd met on the dock upon his return, he'd been so elated to see the other man that he hadn't noticed at first. Then Luthais got a better look at him over the following days.

This was an unfamiliar sensation, wanting to help someone and being unsure how to go about it. With Ally, the choice had been simple. Replenishing his sister's sewing basket was the easiest thing in the world. But Maher? Playing both roles as the Magpie, whatever all that entailed Luthais didn't know, and Intelligencer of the Birde Isles, a position he was more than familiar with, was clearly weighing him down. But what could Luthais really do about that? Maher was a grown man, surely he'd tell Lord Kingfisher if he was overwhelmed? And Luthais wouldn't insult the arrangement between Maher and Gaius by sticking his oar in.

Grunting in frustration, Luthais continued down to the kitchen. One thing he did know, the work at the wharf would wait for no one, not even the Lord of Trade.

The repairs needed on the docks were such that Luthais chose to stay the night in Harbormaster Heper's office and continue early the next morning. It was late afternoon by the time he felt enough had been done that he could return home for a bath and a hot meal.

When Luthais' horse trotted up the gravel path towards home, he found the house in a flurry of activity. Wagons loaded with goods were being directed around to the back entrance. Mrs. Thorley looked like a general commanding troops, giving orders and checking off a list as servants hurried to assist with the wagons or unload a separate carriage parked directly in front of the manor.

"Mrs. Thorley?" Luthais handed his horse off to a groom with his thanks. "What's happening?"

"Lord Luthais, you must join Lord and Lady Kingfisher in the drawing room. Your brother has returned from his travels!"

"Gai?" Luthais allowed himself to be shooed inside by the housekeeper. Boots thudding on the polished floorboards, he ran the short distance to the drawing room. The doors were wide open, Gai stood in the middle of the room with their father and Rochelle. His hair was lightened by the sun and grown over his ears, his skin was rosy, and he was sporting a pair of loose, wide-legged trousers like those who work in Teratsu. He looked lighter and livelier than Luthais had ever seen him.

"Luthais!" Gai smiled wide as he crossed the room. "Brother, I knew it was you the moment you crossed the threshold, like a bull stomping through the house!" They clasped hands and Gai pulled him into a rough embrace.

"I can be quiet when it matters." He chuckled, pounding his older brother twice on the back. "It's good to see you, Gai. How was the trip?"

Pulling back, Gai hooked an arm around Luthais' neck, dragging him over to Gaius and Rochelle. "I've seen something of the world and I'm a better man for it."

Rochelle giggled behind her hand, her dark eyes held a knowing look. "If you ask me, it sounds as if our Gai is in love."

"Oh?" Their father put an arm around her. "Is that what's happened, son?"

"In a way," Gai grinned, squeezing Luthais tighter. "I'm in love with life, my dear Rochelle, and I can't wait to share some of the things I've learned here at home."

Luthais huffed out a laugh and pushed him off. "I think you spent too much time on deck. The sun's baked your brain."

Dinner that night was a celebration of both Luthais and Gai returning home. Even Maher was in attendance and looking a bit more rested, Luthais was pleased to note. He watched as his once so reserved older brother regaled them with tales of his travels. Maher broke in when Gai got to the part of his trip spent in Saprea and the two bantered back and forth during the entire second course. Rochelle laughed so hard she had to put her fork down.

A strange, bitter thread of jealousy wormed its way into Luthais' gut. A ridiculous reaction, he knew. Gai and Maher had always been friendly, and Maher had always filled whatever room he occupied with his personality, but to see Gai respond so easily was putting him out of sorts.

Luthais had often struggled with carrying on conversations. Small talk and polite niceties bored him to tears. And after their mother passed so suddenly, he didn't feel much like speaking at all. Soon he was ducking his lessons at the manor and spending every spare moment by the shore. Then later, when he was older, at the wharf. The only time the tumbling thoughts in his mind quieted and gave him some peace was when he was at sea or putting his hands to work. No one spoke out of turn down there, no one forced him to chat about trivialities or express false sentiment. When the servants, and eventually the rest of

Kingsport, dubbed him the Pike, he'd embraced it. He wanted to be left to his boat and his work around the docks, and for years no one bothered him.

Until a gangly Saprean boy moved into their house with his ambassador father.

Luthais had never met anyone like Maher Villaon. Even at twelve years old, Maher was completely unbothered by Luthais' surly demeanor. If he refused to respond to any of the thousand things the boy had to say every day, Maher simply shrugged and carried on. Khafra forced his son out onto the water with the Kingfisher brothers a handful of times, which he clearly didn't enjoy. Then Maher made friends with Ally and the two became downright chummy. Then they only saw the younger boy when he and Ally were on their way to town or sitting together in Rochelle's parlor.

They all grew older. Luthais could only open up and be himself among his crew, but not Maher. Everything about him, from his quick wit to his clothes, grew louder and more vibrant. And Ally bloomed in his light like a daisy following the sun. Imagine his profound surprise when Luthais found himself turning towards that light as well.

Luthais glanced at the empty seat at the family dining table that belonged to Ally. The household staff were told she'd gone to stay with a friend for a while. Not exactly a lie, but Mrs. Thorley still kept a place set for her, as if she would walk through the door at any moment.

It was still hard to reconcile that his sister was now a *mermaid*, living somewhere in the sea around the Isles. Maher told the family as much as he could, and they all knew her first year was nearly at an end. Perhaps that was why Gai returned when he did? Luthais made a mental note to ask him.

Gai made some joke and Maher tossed his head back with laughter that echoed through the dining room. The long, brown column of his throat exposed over the collar of his shirt. Luthais' mouth went dry at the sight.

You are in such trouble.

After dinner finally wound down, when Gaius and Rochelle retired for the night and Maher disappeared with a promise to Gai to continue their chat later, Luthais stole his brother away.

"It's been ages since I've been up here." Gai sighed. They'd swiped a bottle of their father's best brandy and headed for the roof. In the center was a flat portion with the door leading down into the attic. Leaning against the gable that housed the stairwell, they passed the bottle beneath the stars.

This was the place they'd used as boys to escape their tutors and tailors, or the cries of their baby sister. Or sometimes, before he was old enough to join them, Cal. He pushed aside any thoughts of their younger brother before they could reach his mouth. This wasn't the time to have that conversation.

"Not since your twentieth birthday," Luthais chuckled.

"Right, nearly forgot about that." he coughed. They'd gotten into a bit of trouble that night. One of the brothers, there was still some debate as to which, had the drunken idea to perform a list of every prank they'd ever wanted to play on the household, including hanging Mrs. Thorley's petticoat from the roof like a flag.

The brothers drank in comfortable silence for a while before Luthais asked about Ally.

"Of course that's why I'm back now. I didn't want to miss her return." Gai smoothed his mustache and leaned his head back against the gable. "Maher made sure I marked the date before I left."

"I'm sure he did."

Gai took another swig and passed the bottle. When Luthais brought it to his lips, Gai asked, "How long have you been in love with Maher?"

Coughing and sputtering around a mouthful of brandy, Luthais wiped his mouth and glared at his brother. "What did you say?"

"It's obvious, Luthais." Gai gave him a sidelong look. "I heard about the very expensive chair you brought him from Zavatleo."

"I can't help the man who saved the lives of our stepmother and sister?"

"And his name has been creeping up in the few words you manage to say each day."

"Gai," he warned.

"And I saw the way you looked at him during dinner."

"How was that, exactly?"

"Like you wanted to have him for dessert."

Heat flooded Luthais' face and the image of Maher laughing at the table floated through his mind. "Bastard."

"Lucky for you, I'm not. Elsewise you'd be on your way to being Lord Kingfisher. Have you told him?" Gai reached for the bottle. Luthais held it out of his reach.

"I have not," he growled.

"Great goddess, why not? It's not because you think he's too young for you?"

"Of course not!"

"Good, because he's isn't. For the goddess' sake, he's closer in age to Cal than to Ally..." Gai cleared his throat.

Giving the brandy back just to shut him up, Luthais rested his forearms on his bent knees. Maybe it was the liquor warming his tongue, but Luthais found himself saying the words he'd long kept to himself aloud. "I want to tell him, but there's a way of doing things. I just wanted to go about this the right way."

"With Maher Villaon? Is there really a right or wrong way where that man is concerned? Just be honest with him."

"What if... damnit, what if he doesn't feel the same?"

"What makes you think he doesn't?"

Luthais shook his head. "I don't know. He treats everyone with equal enthusiasm, it's hard to tell."

"Maybe for some," he chuckled. "But I also saw the way *he* was looking at *you* during dinner."

Head slowly swiveling towards his brother, Luthais gripped his shoulder. "If you're lying to me, Gai, I swear by the goddess –"

"Would I do that?" He clapped Luthais on the back. "I'm pleased for you, little brother. I wasn't sure if you'd ever find someone, or even wanted to. There's nothing wrong with living an independent life, provided that's what makes you happy. But I never imagined that would be the best course for you."

I'll be damned and dusted, but he's eloquent when he drinks.

"So, you approve then?"

"Tell him, Luthais." Taking another sip from the bottle, Gai pressed the brandy into his hand. Luthais knocked it back, the expensive liquor went down smooth. "You're not getting any handsomer, you know."

CHAPTER TWENTY-FOUR

*O**ne breath, in and out.** That was what Marielle focused on as she watched the Kingsport Treasury from her perch on a neighboring roof.

One breath.

One step.

One movement at a time.

That was the only way this would possibly work.

Warm summer air ruffled the hood covering her head. Another hour or so until the sun went down, and then they could begin. Behind her, Jerd inspected the tools they'd brought specifically for their entrance into the Treasury building. They'd never worked a job this size together, but his knowledge of the layout of this place had already proved valuable. They were going to tuck up right under the guards' noses.

"Everything as it should be?"

"Aye," Jerd grunted, tugging sharply on the rope in his hands, "t'would be better if we knew what exactly we're looking to find."

"It would," she glanced over her shoulder, "but I suspect if our employer knew what it was, this job wouldn't even be necessary."

Of all the methods Marielle'd used in the past to enter places without invitation, and many had been unusual to be sure, this had to rank as one she'd prefer to never use again.

The breeze that'd felt so refreshing on the roof had become her enemy. Swaying her body to and fro while the cobblestones rolled like the swells of the sea a good three stories below. This contraption Jerd rigged together was meant to make the crossing from one roof to another an easier task. When this was over, they were going to have a long chat about the meaning of the word *easy*.

A section of knotted ship's rope was stretched between the two buildings. A row of fat knots spaced an arm's span apart ran down its length. Jerd had managed to get the end secured to a grappler anchored to the Treasury parapet on the first try, and it was holding. So far. He made the crossing first, and was using his leverage to weigh it down even more.

Secured around her waist was a thick leather strap. Through the front buckle was yet another belt that wrapped around the makeshift bridge. Marielle's legs were hooked over the rope, knees squeezing tightly as she moved her hands from one knot to the next. The purpose of the belt, according to Jerd, was to catch her if she lost her hold.

"I've tested this thrice now, Marielle," he'd assured her before they began. "Nothing to worry about."

"During one of these so-called tests, did you happen to strap a weight of some kind across your back? In case you've forgotten, I easily weigh one and a half of you, you pillock."

"Oh, erm... I'll go first and secure the far end, shall I?"

The distance was short, compared to any of the other nearby roofs, but Marielle still took the task slowly.

One breath. One movement. Take your time.

Her muscles were on fire by the time she reached the other side, sweat-soaked through her shirt. The heft of the pistols she carried had always been a source of comfort, but now Marielle wished she'd chosen a slimmer pair for this job. After all, they'd have to leave the same way they'd arrived.

Jerd helped her over the parapet. She tore the belt off and took a deep, rib-stretching breath.

"Not so bad, eh?" he whispered, clapping her softly on the shoulder.

"Never again," Marielle hissed. "Come on, we've a lot of ground to cover and not much time."

Breaking into the Treasury itself was a cinch compared to the rooftop journey. After confirming the time they were to meet again, they parted ways, each headed for one end of the building.

Marielle straightened the Kingfisher green jacket she'd thrown over her own clothes. It hung down far enough to cover her gunbelt and was similar enough to a guard's uniform to not arouse suspicion from a distance. Striding down the corridor as if she belonged there, Marielle located the maintenance stairwell from Jerd's diagram and made her way to the ground floor. The cellar of the Treasury housed the city vaults. There was no way they'd be able to search those sealed rooms without inside help. If nothing was found in the rest of the building, Maher would simply have to call on his contacts among the Kingfishers, whether he liked it or not.

Meanwhile, there were three other floors to search. Something Marielle'd learned a long time ago, spaces that were heavily guarded on the outside were often less secure on the inside. Though all the offices were empty this time of night, many were unlocked. And those that were locked had no more than a simple tumbler system to keep the doors closed. A lockpick's dream.

Marielle finished her search of the first floor, with little to note except there were several treasury employees who were particularly unorganized, and moved on to the second. Unless Jerd found something worth investigating, he should be in roughly the same position on the south end. She was halfway down the floor, when what sounded like a horde of voices echoed from the other end of the corridor. At least five guards, if she was any judge. A shift change? Marielle checked the watch she'd tucked into her vest pocket.

Damn, it is a shift change.

She'd been able to move freely without drawing notice from individual guards, but a whole squad? Eyes darting to the left and right, Marielle chose the nearest unmarked door and tried the handle. Locked. Of course. The voices drew closer as she knelt by the door and inserted her tools in the lock mechanism. Once they turned the corner ahead, there'd be nowhere to hide and no way to explain her current position on the floor.

She tried to rake all the tumblers in one go, but had to give that up. Switching to a finer pick, Marielle breathed deeply and focused on one section at a time. The first tumbler soon clicked open. Marielle kept her head at an angle that allowed her to see both the lock and the open corridor. There was a second, tell-tale click.

Two tumblers down, just one more.

Marielle's heart thumped so hard she wouldn't have been surprised if the noise gave her away.

The third tumbler clicked and she grabbed the knob again. Still locked.

Four fucking tumblers?

Even the offices only had three at the most. Holding her breath, Marielle felt for the last barrier to her freedom. Long shadows appeared on the far wall. As the guards began to round the corner, the last tumbler gave way and Marielle toppled into the room.

MARIELLE

CHAPTER TWENTY-FIVE

With the door shut as quickly and quietly as she could manage, Marielle pocketed the picks and slipped further into the darkened room. Breathing slowly through her nose, she paused to get a sense of where she was. The only light offered came from a row of high, narrow windows near the ceiling. Too small to squeeze through, even if she'd been able to reach them.

As her eyes adjusted, the outlines of rows of neatly stacked crates and neatly arranged shelves took shape.

A storage room. Why have a more secure lock on a giant closet than the Treasury officials' offices?

Marielle heard the faint tap of footsteps as the guards passed her hiding place. Ducking behind the nearest freestanding shelf, she crouched low until she was sure the corridor was empty again. Slipping a mint from her belt, Marielle tucked it inside of her cheek and mulled over her options.

It would be best to wait until the shift change was over to leave the storage room. Or at least until it seemed like most of the guards were back in their posts.

Unless there happens to be another way out of here, that might be your only choice. she snorted softly.

Jerd would be arriving at their meeting point on the third floor soon, assuming he wasn't also waylaid by the moving guards. She supposed she could use this time to search for another way out, unlikely as that was. Lighting a candle would be risky, lest someone see the light beneath the door but she was even more likely to draw unwanted attention if she knocked over a crate or sent a shelf crashing to the floor. From an inside pocket she withdrew a short beeswax candle and box of matches. She'd give herself until the candle ran out to explore the room, half an hour. After that, it would be time to leave.

Moving to the closest wall, Marielle lit the candle and began mapping the room. Many of the labels and stamps on the crates were in languages other than Trader's Tongue. Perhaps this was a place for confiscated goods. But why store them in the Treasury and not in one of the many warehouses under the harbormaster's jurisdiction?

The candle was nearly half-gone when Marielle made it to the back wall. Still no sign of another exit; the grates installed to allow air to flow throughout the building were too high to reach. Even if she climbed the tallest shelf, they'd still be at least ten feet away. As Marielle neared the third corner, the candlelight reflected off glittering specks scattered across the floor. Glass? Perhaps something had broken back here and no one noticed?

Kneeling, Marielle brought the light closer. Not glass after all, but a trail of sand. That wasn't so unusual on an island, sand tended to show up where one least expected, but there'd been none tracked anywhere else that she'd seen. Marielle sifted through the grains, rubbing a pinch between her fingers, and something snapped into place in the back of her mind. A sensation that triggered a flood of memories. This sand was too fine to be from the Birde Isles, or even the eastern shore of the continent. It was powdery, like baker's sugar against her skin. And she knew for certain, even before bringing the candle flush with the floor, that the sand would be a vibrant shade of pink.

I must be going mad. This cannot be real.

But it was. It was as real as the melted wax dripping onto her hand. She hadn't seen this kind of sand in ten years, and thought she might never again.

The trail led to a large crate as tall as her waist and twice as wide. There were no discernable markings, stamps, or writing on the outside. The wood was plain, roughhewn like the rest of them. Before she could change her mind, Marielle dripped a pool of wax on the next crate and stuck the candle there. Retrieving the knife tucked into her boot, Marielle wedged the point beneath the lid and twisted until she felt the nearest peg give. She repeated the process until sweat dripped down her temples and she was able to pry it open with her hands.

Marielle's breath caught, "Gods save me…"

Moonlight shone down from the high windows, illuminating a crate full of peony sand from The Riddles. Returning the knife to its place, Marielle dug into the mound and sifted the soft grains through her fingers. When her wrist bumped against something solid, she pulled the item free and held it up.

I really am going mad. Marielle turned the small toy drum towards the light. It was simple, carved of wood and covered in brightly dyed canvas. The sort of thing given to children during festivals. She'd owned a few herself at one time or another.

Who would go through all the trouble of shipping something like this? It's far from valuable, Marielle gave the toy an experimental shake, and something hard rattled inside.

With a sudden, sinking feeling in the pit of her stomach, she grabbed her knife again and sliced through the covering. Three shining silver coins fell out and landed in the sand with muffled thumps.

It can't be… not all this time. Pocketing the coins, Marielle began digging in earnest. More unassuming toys and trinkets rose to the surface. More coins rattled inside each of them.

How many more of these crates were stored here? Did the Treasury even know what they had sitting under their own roof? Surely if they did, these goods would be down in the vault. And Maher would've been informed by now.

Maher. The entire reason she was even there. *He needs to know about this, but what will he do once he learns where the coins are coming from?*

The candle was burning low, Jerd was waiting for her. Had he found anything else? She needed to find him, but she also needed more time to search the rest of the crates.

Burying everything back beneath the sand, Marielle picked up the lid. She'd leave a subtle mark to show this one had already, been opened. Turning it over, intending to carve a symbol along the edge, Marielle found two stamps on the inside panel.

The lid nearly slipped from her grasp. This was worse than she'd imagined. So much worse.

"That fucking idiot. What has he gotten himself into now?" she hissed.

CHAPTER TWENTY-SIX

Ally and Pasha swam together towards Snake Island. The map, in its protective case, was strapped across her back.

For twenty-two years, Ally believed the isolated spit of land sitting just inside Trader's Bay was as barren as it looked. A hunk of rock that her brothers would sail to on a whim, always without her. Who could have guessed such a beautiful, sacred place was hidden underneath?

Life was so different now, Ally sometimes forgot that she wasn't even allowed near the shore for her entire childhood. The one time she disobeyed, and nearly drowned in her seventh year, ensured she stayed away long after her parents might have relented.

It all seemed like a dream now, and to learn that Pasha was the one who saved her back then? Ally glanced at the mermaid swimming next to her. Shafts of sunlight broke through the murkiness of the sea and made her scales shine. While Ally hadn't expected to look exactly like Pasha as a mermaid, she still wasn't prepared for how different their appearances were. Pasha was sleek, beautiful but deadly like the foxgloves that grew across the Isles. She was made for slicing through the water and blending in among the predators of the sea. Ally was more akin to the decorative fish she'd once seen in a garden pond at an ambassador's house in Kingsport. They were larger than she'd expected, in colors ranging from dazzling white to bright orange, and deep red. Their tailfins trailed behind them like a gossamer train on a ballgown. Fascinating, but ornamental.

Sometimes Ally wondered if the kind of mermaid she turned out to be was connected to her inability to harness the natural energy resources around them. But, from what she'd heard from Pasha and seen in the countless murals decorating the sea caves, it appeared she was an oddity.

As the shadowy outline of Snake Island began to take shape, Ally drifted closer and brushed Pasha's mind. "Thank you for coming with me."

Pasha offered a weak smile. It'd been five days since they laid Hama to rest. Ally was relieved to see Pasha slowly coming back to herself.

Reaching the spired base of the island, they found the hidden entrance and slipped inside.

Up they went through the narrow tunnel and out into the warm, mirror-like water of the lagoon. A shiver ran down Ally's spine and her heart fluttered. This was the sacred place where Pasha performed the ancient ritual to transform her from a human into a mermaid.

"Ready?" Pasha took her hand. "If anything doesn't feel right when we surface, we'll leave."

"Ready," Ally nodded. Their tails propelled them upwards and then Ally was taking her first breath of air in nearly a year. The cave blurred around her and her grip on Pasha's hand tightened until her eyes adjusted.

The calm water hugged a band of white sand that backed up to the far wall. More of the luminescent corals and rare glowing plants clung to the edges cave walls, throwing the murals carved into the walls into sharp relief. In the roof of the cave was a crescent-shaped opening with a view of blue sky.

Spots of brilliant color winked at them like jewels in the sand, fragments of the mermaid eggs that had hatched over the centuries. Tucked against the wall that curved around the small stretch of beach, was a row of stone eggs. These eggs did not and would not hatch. Instead their sides had been carved with images showing the steps Pasha used to change Ally.

As she drank in their surroundings, Ally felt something that had been tightly wound within her begin to unravel. She felt better than she had in weeks, the pain in her muscles and joints melting away. It must be the magic in this place, calming her body and mind.

"Are you alright, Ally?"

"Amazingly enough, I'm fine. It was strange at first, I'm still a little lightheaded, but I feel great."

"The more you go between the sea and the land, the faster your senses will adapt."

"I hope so," Ally held the case between them. "Let's take a look at this map."

Each of them took an end of the map, holding it open above the water. The corals lining the hatching grounds cast a soothing glow over the tapestry. It looked as she remembered, but nothing stood out as being the place where the seas met. The five larger mermaid communities marked with green thread on a sea of blue, with several smaller ones scattered between. The largest shoal, Pasha's, was stitched next to three nameless hunks of land, ostensibly the Birde Isles, in an upper quadrant. There were brighter shades of red, blue, and green woven throughout, evidence where Ally had repaired what she could. A dark brown streak still marred the center, from when the glass slabs encasing it had cracked some time ago.

Ally used her other hand to trace the shapes embroidered into the map. It was wonderful to be handling thread and fabric again. She's been so busy learning how to be a mermaid, she hadn't realized how much she missed her needlework.

After a while, Pasha sighed, "Hama was in so much pain, maybe she wasn't talking about a real place."

Ally hummed in response. Her fingers skimmed around the edges of the small tapestry. Running along the bottom right corner, her thumb caught on a whorl in the fabric. A string of knots in the thread, their shape reminding her of a fishhook. She'd assumed it to be a flaw during the repairs and nearly pulled it out, then decided to leave it alone.

"I wish we could compare it to a human map. My father has an antique one in his study of the entire Known World. Maybe the old lines of the seas would match this more than a modern illustration."

"We only have a few more days before your first year ends," Pasha said as she carefully rolled the map back up and they locked it in the case. "Once you're able to walk on land again, maybe we can ask to borrow your father's map?"

"I like that idea," Ally smiled. "I'm sure Maher will help us."

MAHER

CHAPTER TWENTY-SEVEN

The lamp lighters had only just begun their work for the evening when Maher turned onto the high street that led into the Lantern district. True to his word, he'd pushed many of his regular appointments earlier into the day. Was he still not getting as much sleep as he ought? Of course not, but there was some improvement. He'd become quite adept at catnapping when possible.

Maher soon crossed into the Lantern square. A handful of musicians were tuning their instruments by the burbling fountain in the center. The poorly disguised Kingsport Guards, who'd been assigned to the area to monitor the street crew activity, were in their usual places. He nodded to one of them as he passed; the guard rolled her eyes.

Slowing as he neared the Whistle and Bells, Maher leaned on the iron gate and admired the work that had been done to restore the establishment. He'd first witnessed the damage upon his return to the Isles with Ally and Rochelle, a mark of how badly the street crew violence had grown in his absence. Several windows and the apricot panes of its lantern had been smashed. The lacquered sign with the club's carved tongue-in-cheek name had been torn off its hinges. Now a new, even larger sign, was hanging above the door. The destruction inside had been even worse, they'd had to commission all new fixtures and furnishings for the entire ground floor

Archie walked out the door, holding a polished new lantern with even brighter orange panes than the last one. He grinned when he spotted Maher.

"We've not reopened yet, good sir, but do come back in a week's time for the grand reveal."

Chuckling, Maher watched him hang the lamp to the right of the entrance. "You shouldn't tease a man like that, Archie."

He joined Maher at the gate, turning to take in the view for himself. One of the youngest establishment owners in the Lantern, Archie was only a year older than Maher. The stress of this last year had aged him, leaving behind a slight furrow mark in his brow and a few new lines around his eyes. But Archie still looked very much a lad with his cleanshaven face and easy smile. His vivid orange hair, that'd fallen to his shoulders when they'd first met, had been cropped short on the sides and left long enough to comb back on top. A style usually more popular with Char-range sailors.

"We're nearly there, my friend. I've truly appreciated your support with the owners' guild."

"Don't even mention it. Are many of your employees returning?"

"Oh yes, most of them are, but there are some who prefer the positions they took while we were closed. They'll be missed, but I'm happy for them just the same."

"Like Kit?" Maher couldn't help asking.

"Aye, like Kit." Archie looked at him. "Don't worry, I wouldn't dream of trying to tempt him away from the Bear's Den."

"They do like him very much over there."

"I know, that's why I wouldn't dare to offer his old job back. Kit fits better there anyway, I think. And I'm sure the patrons are more apt to leave him to his work."

"Indeed," Maher pushed off the gate. "Speaking of the Den, I'm headed there now. Shall I give Kit your regards?"

"If you would, thank you." Archie paused, then laid a tender hand on Maher's forearm. "Will you come, when we open again? I've missed seeing you pop in and out, collecting your trinkets. And," his pale blue eyes darted to Maher's mouth, "you never did take me up on my offer to stay the night whenever you'd like."

The old Maher would have made some ribald reply, or maybe implied he might just accept Archie's offer. Instead, his thoughts turned to Luthais and this new, tenuous relationship they were weaving.

"I'm afraid I won't be able to stay the night, Archie, though I do appreciate the invitation." Maher patted the top of his hand. "But I look forward to seeing the old place in full swing again."

Archie's expression shifted from hopeful to resigned as Maher's full meaning sank in. "So do I, Maher." His hand slid away.

He bade Archie goodnight and continued down the row of brownstones. With everything that had happened in the last year, he hadn't thought Archie was still interested. Best to end it before it began and not lead the other man on. There was a time when Maher might have gone to bed with Archie, or one of the other Lantern owners, without much care for the consequences. Gods knew, he'd shared a few nights with Mama Bear when he first started visiting the Bear's Den. But as he'd grown more entrenched in the work that'd earned him the Magpie name, he'd kept a more professional distance. And now there was a whole new element to consider: Luthais.

He'd nearly reached the Den, already contemplating a short nap in Pimm's room, when a pair of strong hands grabbed his shoulders, yanking him backwards into an alley.

Not again! Maher's mind raced, remembering with nauseating clarity the night he was ambushed in another alleyway by a street crew. Twisting in his captor's grip, Maher reached for the pistol secured beneath his jacket and shouted, "Guards! Gua—"

"Shut it!" One of the hands clapped over his mouth. "Are you trying to get us both arrested?"

"*Marielle?*" his voice was muffled against her palm. His eyes finally focused on her face and a gold tooth winked at him in the scant light from the square. Maher jerked himself free and righted his clothes. "Marielle! What in all the gods' names are you doing sneaking up on me like that?"

"Keep your voice down," she hissed, eyes darting past him to scan the people milling about the Lantern.

"I could have shot you!"

"Doubtful."

"Was that necessary? Why not approach me in the street or wait at the Den?"

"I didn't want to be seen."

A dreadful feeling settled deep in Maher's gut. "Why?"

Marielle squared her shoulders. "I need your help, Maher."

MAHER

CHAPTER TWENTY-EIGHT

Maher went into action. Taking her down the street that ran behind the Den, he let them in through the kitchen door and pushed the panel to reveal the back stairwell hidden in the pantry. They climbed quickly to the fourth floor and knocked softly on the door to Pimm's room.

Gertie walked out of an adjacent room, carrying an armful of sheets stripped from the bed. "Pimm is downstairs."

"Gertie!" Maher pasted on a smile and gave a short bow. "Lovely to see you again. Would you mind telling Pimm we've come to see them?"

"Of course, Mister Villaon." She eyed both warily before leaving down the main stairs.

When the door was shut securely behind them, Maher turned to get a better look at Marielle. Mud was splattered on her boots and her usually neat suit of clothes was disheveled. Most notably, one of the hefty pistols she carried on each hip was missing.

"Tell me *exactly* what happened."

"We made it into the Kingsport Treasury without a hitch," Marielle paced across the small room.

Maher leaned against the worktable, too anxious himself to sit down. "You took someone with you?"

"That building is massive. At the time it seemed like a good idea to bring a partner, split up, and start on each end. The plan was to meet in the middle."

"What went wrong?"

"That mutton-brained moron was careless and the guards knew someone was there who didn't belong." She ran a hand over her shorn hair and blew out a breath. "He got himself pinched."

Maher's stomach dropped. "Fuck."

"I knew I should've gone alone."

"Then why didn't you?" he snapped.

"Jerd used to be a Kingsport Guard recruit, he did part of his training at the Treasury. I thought he'd know his way around."

"Why didn't he become a full guard?"

Marielle huffed, "Discharged for pilfering the guard supplies."

"Fantastic."

"I know, believe me."

"I think I need a drink. When did all this happen?"

"Three nights ago," she winced.

"Three nights ago! And you waited until now to tell me?"

"I was trapped in there for two days, Maher! The entire place was locked tight, I barely made it out myself."

Pimm knocked on the door as they let themselves into the room. "I take it the Treasury job didn't go well?"

"Something like that. Hello, Pimm." She slumped against the wall, suddenly looking much younger. "The Madam won't even see me, I don't know what to do."

Pimm looked from Marielle to Maher. "Both of you stay here. I'll have refreshments sent up. As far as anyone else knows, this is just one of Maher's regular visits."

"Where are you going?" asked Maher.

"To pull a few strings of my own."

Kit came and went with whiskey and water for both of them. By then, Maher was too weary to stand any longer. He sank into one of the chairs and poured a dram for each of them. Marielle sat across from him and they drank in silence, waiting for Pimm's return. How had things gone so wrong? Marielle wasn't reckless. By the gods, she'd gotten in and out of more heavily guarded places than the Treasury without detection. But she'd always gone alone, far as he knew. The partner she'd brought this time must truly have been thoughtless. Where had she found him? Did he also work for the Madam?

Having collected himself, Maher remembered the reason he'd asked Marielle to steal into the Treasury in the first place. "Were you able to find anything of use before the mutton head fouled things up?"

Marielle looked up from studying the bottom of her glass. "I was just thinking of how best to tell you."

Maher straightened, ignoring the pull in his shoulder. "Why do I not find that reassuring?"

"I think I found where the Saprean coins are being made. Or, at the very least, where they're being shipped from."

"Why didn't you lead with that?" he slapped his drink down, whiskey sloshed over the rim. "Here I sat, thinking the entire endeavor was a failure. What did you find?"

Adjusting the gun on her hip, Marielle braced her elbows on her knees. "I was trying to think of how to tell you because you're not going to like it."

"Nothing will surprise me, unless you tell me they're being secretly minted in my closet. Where are they coming from, Marielle?"

"The Riddles."

"The... The Riddles? The same Riddles that are several weeks, if not months, journey by sea from here? The islands that are, quite literally, impossible to reach unless the islanders want you to set foot on the shore?"

"The very same."

"How?" he raked a hand through his hair.

"When Jerd drew the attention of the guards..."

"That's a polite way to say he royally fucked up," Maher snorted.

"Do you want to hear this or not? When the alarm was raised, I ducked into a storage room. And I found this leaking out of a crate,"

Reaching into a pouch on her gunbelt, Marielle sprinkled a small pile of pink grains onto the table.

Maher rubbed a few of the tiny grains between his fingers as Marielle recounted what happened in the Treasury. He'd always wondered if the stories about the vibrant shores of The Riddles were true. Or if the color was some trick of the eye played by nature. But the sand really was a bright shade of pink and fine as the sugar sprinkled on top of Mrs. Ekmekci's pastries.

Waiting until he was sure Marielle had finished her story, Maher knew what he wanted to ask next. "And you have the coins you found in the toy?"

From another pouch, Marielle pulled a few silver pieces and deposited them next to the sand. Maher picked one up. It was newly minted, shiny, and unblemished. Lacking the wear of a coin that had changed numerous hands.

Marielle's voice lowered, "Maher, I was able to dispose of the toy and get the crate back together. But as soon as whoever stored it there comes to claim it, they'll know someone found the coins. I'm sure they were expecting a specific number in each shipment."

"Gods save me," Maher paused when the door creaked open, only relaxing when Pimm and Mama Bear walked into the room.

"My dear little Magpie," Mama Bear bustled over and pulled him into a crushing hug.

"I'm fine, dear." Maher squeezed her waist. "It's Marielle there who needs your attention."

"Of course," Mama Bear released him and fluffed her skirts. "Pimm informed me of your predicament, Marielle. So I went to the black lantern,"

"You did?" she jumped to her feet. "What did the Madam say?"

"Mother is furious. She feels you've endangered her establishment's work by allowing that young man to be arrested."

"Allowing?" Maher scoffed. "That's hardly fair."

Mama Bear held up a hand for silence. "The fact of the matter is there's no guarantee this Jerd won't trade what little he knows to save himself. And because they were in the Treasury on your behalf, Maher," her blue eyes focused on him, "it's *you* who is responsible. The Madam is calling in her favor. It's your mess to clean up. Without her help."

CHAPTER TWENTY-NINE

Marielle felt as though all the air had been sucked out of the room. Her eyes darted from Mama Bear, to Maher, to where Pimm stood guard by the door.

She'd expected the Madam to be upset, to hold her responsible for the mayhem she'd left at the Treasury. Instead she was calling in Maher's account, making Marielle *his* problem to deal with. The Madam must've been well and truly incensed.

Pimm's head tilted thoughtfully, watching Maher absorb the edict delivered by their employer. They were one of the few fixtures in the Lantern who didn't owe some boon or another to the black lantern. It was smart of Pimm, really. For all the good the Madam did for Kingsport, she was not someone to be crossed.

"I'm sorry, darling," Mama Bear was saying to Maher. "I tried to reason with her, but Mother's mind is set."

Eventually, he spoke. "How the fuck am I supposed to fix this?"

"You're Intelligencer of the Birde Isles, are you not?" Pimm noted. "Surely you can pull some sway with the Kingfishers."

"You want me to bring Lord Kingfisher into this? Are you mad?"

A knock on the door stopped the conversation short. Pimm stuck their head into the hall, then opened the door to let Kit through.

"Begging your pardon, but you're needed downstairs, ma'am."

"Alright," Mama Bear sighed and kissed Maher's forehead, "don't leave without saying goodbye."

"Yes dear," Maher tugged roughly at his beard. When she was gone, he looked at Pimm. "Can Marielle stay here a few days? Until I cobble some kind of plan together?"

"Of course," Pimm nodded at her. "Is there anything you'd like retrieved from the black lantern?"

"Nothing, I thank you." Even though Pimm would be allowed in without any trouble, she didn't want any of the Madam's ire drawn Pimm's way. There was nothing in her room at the black lantern that she couldn't live without. Marielle didn't want anyone to set foot in there on her behalf until they could show this calamity had been handled.

"And I'm sorry, Marielle, for hooking you into this. I don't think I said that yet." Maher sighed.

She waved him off. "I agreed of my own free will. It wasn't as if we could have predicted every outcome of an operation of this scale."

"Alright," Maher stood and righted his black waistcoat. "I'll be back in a day or two, send word to me through Gertie if I'm needed sooner."

"I'll take care of things here." Pimm assured him.

"Thank you, my friend." They clasped hands and Maher's voice lowered. "Listen, I need a way to get to The Riddles."

"The Riddles?" Pimm's gaze cut to Marielle

"Marielle can explain everything she found, but we have sufficient reason to believe the Saprean coins are being smuggled from there at the very least. Possibly even minted there."

"Gods save me. How soon would you need to leave?"

"I'm not sure. I must stay in Kingsport until... my friend returns."

"Understood."

Marielle didn't bother to ask who they were discussing. She'd heard countless rumors about what had become of Lady Alphonsine Kingfisher. That she was a tamer of sea monsters, now residing on her own ship; that she'd made a deal with the goddess for power over the tides or betrothed herself to a sea witch, and was dragged to the depths after her mother's safe return; or possibly, Lady Alphonsine was herself a sea witch and had left the Birde Isles to break the long-held curse on the Kingfisher daughters.

Whatever the truth, it sounded as if she were due home soon.

Maher prepared to depart. She needed to call in her own favor before he was gone for who knew how long.

"There's more."

Pimm paused with their hand on the doorknob as Maher turned slowly on his heel.

"What else could there possibly be?"

"You need to take me with you to The Riddles."

"Marielle, I don't even know how I'm going to get there yet. It might be on a rowboat and a prayer, for all I know. I can't promise that."

She stood, hands braced on her gunbelt. Marielle'd half-hoped it wouldn't come to this, but clearly he needed a reminder. "I have two open boons from the Intelligencer of the Birde Isles. I'm calling one in. You owe me this, Maher."

"I... you just... *fuck*." Maher quickly composed himself. "I'll see what I can do."

"That's all I ask."

Once she was alone in the room, Marielle crossed back to the worktable and pulled out one of the maps of Kingsport. The sprawling city seemed much smaller now, considering how much her life had altered in the past few days.

She hadn't wanted to trigger the alarm that put Jerd in the hands of a squad of Kingsport Guards, but it couldn't be helped. Not now, not with what she'd found in that storage room.

Sorry Jerd, I'll make it up to you somehow.

For the first time in ten years, one way or another, Marielle was going home.

CHAPTER THIRTY

Ally's first year as a mermaid came crashing to an end.

Like a tidal wave slowly building out at sea, Ally became gradually weaker in the few days before. When she was too unsteady to sit up or eat on her own, Pasha knew they had to be close.

As sundown approached, Pasha lifted Ally from the floor of the great cavern. Using a line of rope they'd salvaged to secure Ally against her back. Ally's head lolled against her shoulder and her arms dangled limply by Pasha's sides. Grabbing the other supplies she'd prepared, Pasha began the journey through the tunnels.

Ally jostled against her and whimpered, "It hurts."

"I know, sweetheart, just hold on." Quickening her pace as much as she dared, Pasha swam out of the tunnel into the open ocean. She'd chosen the route that would put them closest to the shore, but they still had some distance to go.

"How much further?" Ally's voice was so thin.

"We're almost there." Pasha had to remind herself, no matter how distressing this was, it was normal. According to the carvings left in the hatching grounds, this would be the final stage in Ally's transformation. "I'm going to surface, Ally, you'll see we're getting close."

Propelling them upwards was harder than swimming in a straight line. The muscles in Pasha's tail and back were burning by the time they broke through into the soft twilight of the world above.

Blinking the water from her eyes, Pasha turned until they were facing the stretch of beach that bordered Ally's family home. "There it is, sweetheart. Do you see?"

"I see it. I can't believe –" Ally convulsed, the force plunging them back underwater. "Hurry!"

Pushing past the pain in her own body, Pasha made for the shore. The closer they got to land, the more Ally groaned and trembled, her tail dragging behind them like an anchor. When they were nearly to the shallows, Ally cried out. An even fiercer spasm jerked at the rope around them.

"Untie me!" she gasped. "Pasha, let me go!"

Fumbling for the slipknot she'd tied over her chest, Pasha gripped the free end and pulled it loose. Ally twisted, forcing them both into a spiral until she was floating on her own. She sagged in the gently rolling swells. Small tremors wracked through Ally as Pasha flexed her fins. She circled Ally, wary of what might happen next. In the quickly fading light, Pasha glimpsed the tell-tale thinning of the scales of Ally's tail. It was already trying to split and they hadn't even reached the land.

"Ally," Pasha took her hand. "Let's try to swim closer to shore."

Glazed eyes focused on her for a moment and Ally opened her mouth to reply, then doubled over again in pain. With no other options, Pasha towed her closer to shore. They reached the place where the waves started to crest and foam, when the seam appeared down the middle of her tail and Ally screamed.

"I've got you," Pasha wrapped her arms around Ally and held her up. The change from tail to legs was happening at an agonizing pace. Even Pasha's first change after spending more than a century asleep beneath the island hadn't been this bad.

Her own tail split quickly once they reached the shallows. Turning Ally onto her back, Pasha crooked her arms beneath Ally's and backed out of the surf. Small, sharp waves smacked against them and Pasha nearly lost her footing in the squishy sand at the water's edge. Finally Pasha laid Ally down on the beach. Feeling a slight glimmer of instinct, she set to work building the pebbly sand around Ally into a nest. Something to help her feel more secure in the open air. Then Pasha sat next to her, ready to provide whatever was needed.

Ally's breath came in pained, shallow gasps. Her eyes squeezed shut and she gripped Pasha's hand as her tail changed, scale by scale, inch by inch. The sunset bathed them in a warm glow, making the azure seed scale embedded in Ally's chest gleam. Slowly the outline of Ally's legs began to show, her beautiful fluke looked sad and shrunken.

Pasha soothed and coaxed Ally through her first shedding of her tail. This seemed nothing like when they'd performed the ritual to change her into a mermaid. Pasha desperately wanted to know what she was feeling. But Ally couldn't speak, she hardly knew Pasha was there.

The sun had set and the moon had long risen by the time Ally regained her legs. Stars twinkled down at them, reminding Pasha of the corals on the cavern ceilings. Taking one of the scraps of sail they'd brought, Pasha mopped the sweat from Ally's brow. When her eyes fluttered open, Ally stared at the night sky for a long moment before finding Pasha.

Relieved to see her out of pain, Pasha pressed a kiss to Ally's temple and murmured, "You did so well, sweetheart."

Leaning into the contact, Ally relaxed into the sand.

"How do you feel?"

"Like I've been chewed up and spat out by a snapjaw," she croaked. Her feet wiggled slightly. "How do they look?"

Pasha sat up. Ally's legs looked just as she remembered that night in the hatching grounds one year ago. Ribbons of scales wrapped over her round hips, down her thighs, and crossed over her knees before continuing all the way down to her toes. "They're beautiful."

"That's so specific."

"Care to see for yourself?"

"Not right now, I feel like a silk stocking someone left on the floor."

Pasha's head tilted, "What does that mean?"

"Stockings can't hold any shape on their own."

"Take all the time you need," Pasha grabbed their other supplies.

"How long will we stay on land?" Ally yawned.

"At least until morning. You should be able to walk by then." She covered them with a larger piece of sail and carefully pulled Ally into her arms. "Rest now. I'll keep watch."

"Are you sure?" She was already nodding off.

"Absolutely." Pasha tucked Ally's head beneath her chin. She spent the rest of the night feeling the subtle rise and fall of Ally's chest and counting the stars.

Pasha kept her promise, staying awake through the night and into the morning. The early, gray light of dawn soon melted into shades of pink and orange. Her back ached from laying on the dry sand for so long, but at least they'd made it far enough up the shore that the changing tides didn't bother them. Ally mumbled and stretched. Her feet brushed Pasha's and the sensation pulled her out of sleep.

"Good morning, Ally."

"G'morning," she muffled a yawn into Pasha's shoulder.

"How do you feel, now?"

Ally paused, taking stock of herself. "A little sore, but not nearly as uncomfortable as last night."

"I'm glad to hear it," Pasha sat up, reaching her arms overhead. The sun felt good on her shoulders. "Do you want to see your legs?"

"I'd nearly forgotten!" Shuffling into a seated position, Ally flung the sail off them and took in the sight. "They do look pretty," she admitted.

"I believe the word I used was, beautiful."

"Don't be so persnickety," Ally teased. "Come on, help me up."

Pasha rose first and planted her feet in the sand before taking Ally's hands. Together, they carefully maneuvered her until she was standing.

"This feels so strange," Ally tittered. "But so easy compared to changing from my tail."

"That will get easier too, and much faster than you'd expect."

Ally took an experimental step and her knee buckled. Catching herself on Pasha's shoulders, she held her lower lip between her teeth and concentrated on putting one foot in front of the other. After they'd made a small circle in the sand, Pasha insisted they take a break.

Sitting together with the canvas wrapped around their shoulders, Pasha took a few snacks from her bundle for them to share. One was a stalk-like plant that she rarely ate but apparently reminded Ally of a common vegetable that grew on land.

When they'd finished, Ally sighed and laid her head on Pasha's shoulder. "Thank you so much, Pasha. I couldn't have gotten through this without you."

"I'm happy I could help. Even knowing it wouldn't last forever, I hated seeing you in such pain." Pasha's throat tightened, the words she'd held back bubbled to the surface. "Ally, I want... I—"

"Ally!" A voice shouted from up the shore. "Ally, by all the gods and their grandmothers, is that really you?"

Ally's head popped off her shoulder. They both turned to see a tall, dark-haired man stumbling towards them through the sand.

"Maher?" Ally gasped.

"Of course," Pasha growled under her breath.

"Maher!" she waved.

Damn that man and his infernal timing.

CHAPTER THIRTY-ONE

"Maher!" Ally's heart was fit to burst. How had he known where to find them? "I can't believe it."

"Neither can I," Pasha grumbled.

Her focus drawn back to the mermaid at her side, Ally cupped Pasha's face and pressed a quick kiss to her lips. Pasha was still grieving the loss of her cousin, yet she carried Ally to shore and saw her through an excruciating and terrifying process. "Thank you."

It was nothing like when she first became a mermaid: That sense of finally coming into who she was meant to be. Last night was like shedding an old, too-tight skin that just wouldn't come free. Hopefully, Pasha was right and it wouldn't be like that again. But who knew what to expect really, for a made mermaid?

Maher had nearly reached them. Her heart swelled again when she realized he was wearing one of her favorite suits, cobalt blue with a daffodil yellow shirt and gold tulips that she'd embroidered on the front of the waistcoat. Pushing awkwardly to her feet, Ally took a few steps to steady herself. Maher slid to a stop, kicking up a spray of sand and nearly falling backwards onto his ass. His chestnut eyes widened, "Whoa, Al. You really have changed."

"Sweetheart," Pasha coughed into her fist to cover what Ally was certain was a laugh "I think you've forgotten something."

She looked at Pasha, then at herself. "Oh, right." Maher snorted back his own laugh and she glared at him, hands propped on her bare hips. "Is there a problem? I haven't worn clothes in a year, you know."

"No problem at all, Al," he chuckled. "I just wanted to make sure you were aware before I hugged you."

"Here, try this." Pasha quickly helped her fashion a short dress from scraps of sail and rope.

"There," she huffed. "Happy now?"

"Ecstatic," he grinned.

"Good. Now get over here."

In four long strides, Maher was sweeping her into his arms. An embrace that made all the pain of coming back onto land that much more worth it. She could feel his heart drumming through his reedy chest as Maher's signature pine and cardamom fragrance filled her nose. A spark of heat flared from the shark tooth hanging beneath his shirt. Ally knew that warmth as well as she knew her own name.

"I see you still have my gift."

Behind her, Pasha snorted, recognizing the same words she'd said to Ally the first night they met properly on this very beach.

"It's been an incredible help." Maher said, unaware of the silent exchange happening between Ally and Pasha. "I've missed you, Al," he rasped. "So much."

"I missed you too, Maher." A year's worth of pent-up emotion made her own voice catch. "You have no idea. How did you even find us?"

"I've spent the last fortnight walking the beach as often as I could. I wanted to be here when you came back to land the first time."

The tears Ally'd held back spilled down her cheeks and onto his jacket. And for the first time since she'd become a mermaid, it didn't bother her that there was no magic to them.

It was a long while before he released her. Back on her feet, Ally took Maher by the shoulders, careful of the left one, and held him at arm's length.

"You look exhausted, what's wrong?"

"Not everything has changed, I see." Maher shook his head and kissed her cheek.

"That's not an answer."

"I know. But first, hello Pasha."

"Maher," Pasha nodded from where she'd been standing quietly while they had their reunion.

"Now, let me have a look at *you*," he took Ally's hands and held them up. Sunlight glanced off the scales that capped her knuckles and Maher whistled. "I'm not quite sure what I expected but, excepting the added adornments, you still look like you Al."

"Wait until you see my tail." Ally smirked as the gears in Maher's mind began to turn. Then a shadow passed through his eyes and Maher drifted away for a moment. Ally didn't like how spent he looked. Was her father working him too hard?

Ally squeezed his hand. "Tell me, how are Mama and Father? Gai and Luthais? Mrs. Thorley?"

Blinking back into focus, Maher laughed, but he still looked troubled. "Slow down, Al; I'll tell you everything about everyone."

CHAPTER THIRTY-TWO

Maher couldn't stop staring at the kaleidoscope of scales that decorated Ally's skin. Each time she moved, the sun would catch on them and they'd sparkle like a thousand jewels. As they sat together on the beach, he gave her a brief report about each member of her family, including Cal's sentencing to lifetime imprisonment.

He left out the details of his evolving relationship with her brother. They'd save that for when they were next alone.

Seeing her naked wasn't what had stopped him mid-step, it was how stunning she looked. For the first time in months he felt the old urge to take up his brushes and capture the sight before him. The challenge of recreating the shine on her scales with paint was almost too much to resist. When Ally mentioned her tail, he'd immediately began planning how they could make that happen. Then he'd remembered the mess he had to contend with, and all those grand plans fell apart. The last thing Maher wanted was to burden Ally, or Pasha for that matter, with the river of shit he'd found himself swimming in. But he also remembered the last time he tried to hide his troubles from Ally and the disastrous results.

After he'd finished, Ally began to tell him about her life as a mermaid. She became so animated; he couldn't help but smile to see her so happy. Then he caught Pasha with a similar expression, as if she'd be content to sit and listen to Ally forever. Any lingering anxiety about her choice he'd held onto had lifted and he sank a little deeper into the sand.

Ally was trying to describe for him what it was like to swim with a tail, but found herself stymied.

"No, that's not right," she huffed, looking to Pasha for help.

"I'm not sure either," the mermaid shrugged. "I've always had a tail."

"You're no help," she flicked a pebble at Pasha. "Darling, you'll just have to see it for yourself. Now that the sea is warmer, we could... What's wrong, Maher?"

"I'm so sorry, Al," Maher sighed, rubbing the space between his eyes. "I want to see you as a mermaid more than anything, but I'm afraid it's going to have to wait."

"Wait for what?" Ally shot Pasha a worried look.

"Until I return."

Her brows pinched together. "Where are you going."

"The Riddles."

Silence stretched out between them. Ally's mouth opened and closed a few times. Maher chose not to tell her that action, combined with her new scales, made her look very much like a fish out of water.

"What are the Riddles?" Pasha's question drew their attention.

How could a mermaid, who'd lived as long as her, not know about The Riddles?

"They're a chain of islands past the Unending Sea. They're the most isolated nation in the Known World."

Pasha still looked puzzled. "None of our maps show any land in that sea. Are they very large?"

"They're easily as large as the Birde Isles and nearly as spread out as those around Nuvwaan. From the accounts we've had, anyway. It's a difficult journey, not one many would undertake."

"That's right!" Ally snapped out of her stupor. "So why do you have to go there?"

Maher sighed, "It's a long story, Al. I don't even know yet how I'm going to get reach them, but I have to go, nonetheless."

"Why are these islands so difficult to reach?" asked Pasha. "Human ships can sail very far, yes?"

"It's not only the distance," he glanced at Ally. She was looking out at the waves, gnawing on her lip. This was not something she was going to allow without further explanation. "The Riddles are surrounded by a water formation unlike anything else in the Known World."

Pasha leaned closer, dark eyes glittering with interest. "What sort of water is this?"

"I've not seen it myself, but those that have made the journey describe it as a swirling current that separates the islands and the waters around them from the Eastern and Unending Seas. The journey takes weeks and crossing the barrier is only possible if you have someone from The Riddles to guide the way."

The tip of Pasha's tongue ran across her upper row of shark-like teeth, and Maher realized he'd never really seen her this closely before. "So, The Riddles are between the two larger seas?"

"Almost exactly," he shrugged. "Although modern maps have the coordinates separating the seas noted much closer to the Birde Isles, historic maps tended to place the dividing line near The Riddles. Since few people travel to or from those islands, it's not been confirmed –"

"The place where the seas meet!"

"Um... what?" he looked to Ally for clarification. She'd fallen silent again while Maher was describing The Riddles to Pasha. Tracing her fingers over the rough fabric of her makeshift dress, she didn't seem to have heard either of them.

Ignoring him, Pasha laid a hand on her arm and squeezed. "Ally, the place where the seas meet. Just like Hama said."

"I beg your pardon, who's Hama?" Maher felt as if they'd lapsed into another language.

Eyes widening, Ally released her dress. "Maher, what shape do The Riddles form?"

"What?" He was well and truly lost now.

"The islands that make up The Riddles, what's their shape?"

"I'm not positive," Maher wracked his brain for the last time he'd seen an illustration of The Riddles. They were so remote they were left off most newer maps altogether. Only a single line in the legend indicating their direction.

But he *had* seen them recently. Where was that? He was sitting comfortably at the time, which didn't happen often these days except when he used the chair Luthais brought him from Zavatleo.

Lord Kingfisher's study!

The memory came back to him like the striking of a match. During a break in a recent council meeting, Maher'd had an opportunity to study the various maps and paintings lining the walls. Hanging just behind Luthais was an antique map of the world that spanned across every sea. In the bottom left corner, conveniently next to Luthais' face so Maher could observe both at the same time, were the islands labeled as The Riddles.

Smoothing a place on the sand, Maher drew a line of circles of increasing size. Smallest starting at the top, then curving out to the left from the largest one and growing smaller again.

"It's something like this," he tapped the space inside the curve. "There's at least a dozen tiny spits of land around it, but this is the shape of the main islands." Maher considered his work. "It sort of resembles..."

"A fishhook," Ally breathed. She and Pasha exchanged a look that made the hair on the back of Maher's neck stand up. "That's where Hama was, where the rest of them are. It must be."

"Who are you talking about, Al?"

Ally hesitated, but Pasha spoke for them. "The mermaids. All of them, except for us." One long, black nail traced the edge of the drawing. "We think they're trapped in this place."

CHAPTER THIRTY-THREE

Swain leaned against the railing of the quarterdeck, sweat trickled down his face in the sweltering noonday sun. There was shade to be found on land and belowdecks. But in the bowels of the ship the stench of the rotting crew was far worse. At least fresh air was offered on deck. Going onto land meant crossing waters infested with those serpent creatures and Swain was in no mood to deal with them. His skin still crawled when he remembered the slithery tail wrapped around his throat, the wretch's fetid breath in his face. And until all terms of their agreement were settled, she owned him.

After his last encounter on the beach with the creature who knew his name, he sent Smith and three others on a schooner, also stolen, towards Kharabo. They were to gather information and perhaps even some news of the outside world. The creatures took them across the whirling current surrounding The Riddles using the same magic they'd employed to get the warship into these waters without drawing the islanders' attention. A brunette with the tail of a python followed, to keep them from going astray.

Swain often wondered why the creatures didn't simply pick off the Riddles' inhabitants and take the islands for themselves. But they only hunted outsiders. What was it about the native islanders that warded those monsters off and how could Swain gain that knowledge for himself?

"Water, sir?" A wooden bucket and ladle were offered to him by a crewmember. Swain thanked him and downed a mouthful. The tepid liquid tasted of old metal, but at least the dryness in Swain's throat was eased.

"Thank ye," Swain declined to take any more. "See to it everyone gets a ration."

"Aye, sir." The sailor ambled off.

Swain cast another look towards the island. A trip onto land would become a necessity, sooner or later. He tried not to think too far into the future, only to whatever the next step was to move forward. The crew were restless, each wondering when they would set sail again. But they wouldn't be going anywhere until the creatures delivered on their promise. Swain didn't care how long it took. Though he wondered how many corpse crew members they'd have left by then. Enough to keep a ship of this size afloat?

He'd said as much to the redheaded creature once. Her answer had chilled him to the marrow, despite the oppressive tropical heat.

"Not to worry, we can always make more sailors." She grinned, showing too many teeth. "Just think of how many humans there are to choose from."

"Yet you never seem to pick from the people of these islands," he observed carefully.

Her smile shifted into a sneer. "*These* humans still remember the old ways."

"Old ways?"

"The humans who make their lives on the water know them as well. Though I doubt they recognize why. But the rest? They've all finally forgotten."

Swain took a chance, pressing for more. "I don't really understand."

"Think of your superstitions, Swain," she hissed. "They didn't appear out of nowhere."

He wanted to know more, but another creature called her away. Swain spent the rest of the night turning her words over in his mind. What superstitions did sailors hold that others did not? The most common practice that came to mind was putting a stitch through a dead crewmate's nose before burial at sea.

But that was to certify the sailor had really died, and...

To ensure they stay dead.

Was this creature truly saying anybody in the sea without a stitch could be raised again?

And how many people had gone into the sea without a stitch? Too many.

"Quartermaster! Ship off the bow!"

Jerked out of his thoughts, Swain strode across the deck, dodging living and dead crewmembers alike until he reached the nose of the ship. The same sailor who'd offered the water pointed out at the glassy sea stretching beyond their little secluded stretch of beach.

Squinting in the bright sunlight, Swain could just make out the distinct outline of a schooner. At last, Smith was back.

When the smaller vessel finally reached the bay, a rowboat was sent out to meet them. They'd also brought provisions from Utollmir, as much as the hold could carry.

"'Tis good to have you back, Smith," Swain clapped her on the back. She looked well, they all did. The benefits of the fresh food offered on land. He took her aside while the others unloaded the cargo. "What news from Kharabo?"

"The gods have smiled on us, Quartermaster." Smith drew a packet of papers secured in a leather sleeve from her jacket and handed them over. "Copies of the requisition from Kharabo to Utollmir. For a ship, crew, and soldiers to safeguard the delivery of something quite large."

Swain thumbed through the documents. It was all there as she said, but nothing specifying what was being delivered. "And you're sure it's for the turbine?"

"Without a doubt, sir."

"Where's the machine now?"

"On its way from the university at Botsa to Darajha in Utollmir, and then to the coast. It's to replace the one that never made it to Fraolland."

"You've done well, Smith. Better than I'd hoped." Swain shook his head. "How did you find this?"

She smirked, glancing back across the deck at her crewmates. "You can thank Alonso and their particular tastes."

"Come again?"

"They insisted we take rooms at an inn renowned for its location across the street from Utollmir's most famous brothel."

Swain grunted, "What does that have to do with it?"

"Alonso took up with one of the brothel workers. I wasn't going begrudge them a bit of fun, considering what was waiting for us back here."

Unable to argue with that, Swain nodded for her to go on.

"Well, this lady also happened to be a favorite of the Darajha trade commissioner. Care to wager how we were able to work that to our advantage?"

"Aye, I can imagine the rest from there. What did she want in return?"

Smith shrugged, "Only for that bastard to no longer darken her doorway."

"How resourceful." Swain turned back to the papers, not bothering to ask what had become of the Utollmir official.

"That she was, and she had a line into all the latest scuttlebutt from the continent."

Absorbed now in the plans laid out at his fingertips, Swain grumbled some noncommittal answer. What did he care for brothel gossip when their arrangement was finally coming to fruition?

"In fact," Smith snorted back a laugh, oblivious to his disinterest. "Shortly before we arrived in town, she'd entertained a trade captain assigned to the Birde Isles route. You'll not believe it."

"I doubt I will..."

"One of the Kingfishers is in prison!"

"Prison?"

"Aye, for high treason, no less!" she cackled. "I thought of you the moment I heard, after what that little chit put us all through."

"Smith!" Swain grabbed her shoulder. "Tell me exactly what you heard."

Sobering instantly, Smith shifted uncertainly. "I meant no disrespect, sir."

"Just, tell me."

"Word is, the youngest Kingfisher son, Calder, tried to murder his own sister or some such. The lady was foggy on the details. But, what the captain knew for sure, they caught Calder making his own deals with trade allies, especially the Meredians. Apparently, he spent a lot of time there when his father thought he was elsewhere. And he might've also been selling information about the Isles to Meredia, but it's not known exactly what."

"That's all of it?" When Smith nodded quickly, he sighed. "Good. You've earned yourself a reward, Smith. Give me some time to think on it."

"Aye, sir. Thank you, sir." As soon as he dismissed her, Smith hurried back to help the others.

Wrapping the papers back into the leather sleeve, Swain mulled over what Smith'd said about the Kingfisher son.

"Tried to kill his own sister. Made his own deals. Took stolen information of some kind to Meredia." Swain listed it all out again, searching for the thing itching at the back of his mind. "Meredia..."

Like a strong wind filling a slack sail, the answer came to him. "I'll be damned."

BEAR'S DEN

PIMM

Chapter Thirty-four

Pimm gathered a tray of food from the Bear's Den kitchen. Both Olga and Gertie offered to carry it upstairs for them, but they simply explained it was for a guest on the fourth floor and brooked no further argument. Next they stopped off at the bar to retrieve a mug of cider from the barkeep, then made their way upstairs.

Maher had been gone for two days, and still no word on if he'd managed to procure a ship. The whole thing didn't sit particularly well with Pimm. Certainly they understood the Madam's anger with Marielle for handling her own dealings on the black lantern's time. But they would've thought she'd also be impressed by such a breakthrough in their investigation into the false Saprean coins flooding the city. Apparently not, given her reaction to the method of Marielle's discovery.

Pimm was only slightly winded when they reached the top floor. A vast improvement, they were happy to note, after having their ribs cracked the year before. Marielle had been settled into the room next to theirs. Balancing the tray on one hip, Pimm knocked quickly and stepped back as the gunfighter answered the door.

"Good gods, Pimm, are you trying to fatten me up for the winter?"

"I wasn't sure what you'd like," Pimm stepped through and set the tray on a small table tucked into one corner, along with a single chair. These rooms, much like those Pimm kept available in their own building, weren't meant for extended occupancy. They were comfortable, but sparsely furnished. "Is there anything else you need?"

"No, thank you, Pimm. Mama Bear sent up some clean clothes, as you see," she gestured at herself and Pimm recognized the wine-red blouse as one belonging to their employer. They couldn't remember ever seeing Marielle in such an eye-catching color. She looked well in it, but not entirely comfortable.

"The offer still stands; we'll gladly send someone to collect your things."

"Not yet," Marielle sighed. "I appreciate all you've done, Pimm, truly. I honestly had nowhere else to go." Shaking out her shoulders, she reached for the cider and took a long pull. "Care to join me? Clearly, I have enough food for both of us."

"I have to get back to the door, but perhaps next time." Pimm turned to go, then paused. "Why do you need to go with Maher to The Riddles?"

"What?" Marielle lowered the pasty she'd just selected, her expression slipping into a carefully guarded mask. "What do you mean?"

"Only that it's going to be difficult for Maher to secure a ship and enough supplies to make this journey. The more passengers aboard, the more they'll need to bring." They lifted one shoulder. "I'd think you'd want to stay in Kingsport, in case the Madam changes her mind and wants to see you."

"I'm going because I want the chance to make this right. Besides, Maher will need someone who knows the waters around the islands."

"And that's all? That's the only reason you insisted on accompanying him?"

"That's all."

Back in the lounge once again, Pimm wove through the crowd of patrons, gray eyes scanning for anything out of the ordinary. Things had been fairly quiet as of late, a fact that did not ease Pimm's mind. The trouble with the street crews notwithstanding, the Lantern was not generally known for its tranquility. Long stretches without any disturbance always felt to Pimm like the calm before a storm swept in from the sea.

A lone, young patron sitting in the far corner caught Pimm's notice. He sat with his back to the wall, nursing an ale and avoiding eye contact with everyone else in the establishment. This wasn't one of their regulars, more likely someone who'd borrowed a token from a Bear's Den member. He shifted nervously and Pimm's steps slowed. It could be that he was simply new to this kind of place altogether and unsure of himself. On the other hand...

"Kit!" Barkeep bellowed loud enough to make the nearest patrons jump. "Where's that lad gotten to now?"

Pimm changed course and slid behind the bar. "Problem?"

"Aye, I sent Kit out to retrieve a few more bottles of wine from the cellar and he's still not back."

"How long ago was that?"

"Can't say for certain, s'been damned busy down here. I managed to pour another whole bottle since he's been gone."

"I'll find him." Pimm's pulse raced as they moved back into the crowd. Surely the lad was only having trouble finding what Barkeep needed, they told themself as they ducked back into the kitchen. But, in the back of Pimm's mind, lurked the ghost of Ezmira and the way she'd noted Kit's appearance.

It would be a shame to ruin such a pretty face. I could get a nice bit of coin for it.

When they didn't see Kit in the kitchen or the pantry, Pimm rushed out the back. The double doors leading to the cellar were set beneath a low stone alcove, secured by a padlock and chain. Hopping down the short set of steps leading into the alcove, Pimm found the doors locked tight, but the dirt around the threshold had been recently disturbed and a newly emptied crate sat off to the side. Pimm climbed back onto the street, eyes searching down either direction for some sign of Kit.

Faint music from the square wafted through the air and someone in a nearby building broke into drunken song. The nearest alleyway leading to the main street was a few buildings down from the Den. Flicking their wrist sharply to the left, Pimm released a knife from their sleeve into their palm and set off. They'd nearly reached the alley, when they heard a muffled thump up ahead and the sound of breaking glass.

"I said, *back off.*"

Kit! Pimm sprinted for the opening that led into the alleyway, knife at the ready. They rounded the corner and slid to a stop. Kit stood with a whole wine bottle in one hand and a broken bottle in the other. At his feet, a figure lay motionless on the cobblestones, a pool of red spreading beneath them.

Fuck, Pimm rushed to Kit's side. They spoke softly, careful not to startle him. "Kit, what happened?"

"Pimm?" Kit turned, seeming surprised to find them there. "I was coming out of the cellar and this one," he pointed at the body on the ground with the jagged bottleneck, "wouldn't leave me alone. He tried to follow me through the kitchen door, so I decided to go round front."

"Are you hurt?"

"I'm fine, Pimm, don't worry."

They glanced up and down the alley. "We should leave. We'll have to get someone to move the body."

"What?" Kit resisted when Pimm took his arm.

"You may have been defending yourself, but you can't be here if the Kingsport Guard come through on patrol."

Kit looked at the man on the ground, then at the bottle neck in his hand, and began to laugh.

Gods, he's in shock. They attempted to steer him away again and Kit shook his head.

"He's not dead, Pimm, he's drunk!"

"He's... what?"

"Soused as a sow in springtime. That's wine all over him, not blood." Kit regained his composure, somewhat. "I didn't even hit him, but I did push him off and when he went down, he knocked the bottle out of my hand."

Pimm frowned as, the man groaned, rolling onto his back in the puddle of wine. "What did he want?"

"He's a patron at the Den, I've seen him before. He kept asking why I didn't work *upstairs.*"

"s'too pretty to jus' be workin' the bar..." the man slurred.

Pimm's frown shifted into a scowl. Sidestepping Kit, they grabbed the man by his expensive lapels. "For a so-called patron, you seem to have a poor understanding of how the Lantern works." Pocketing their knife, Pimm rifled through his jacket pockets until they found his membership token for the Bear's Den. "You will never set foot into the Den again, nor will you speak to any employees. Is that understood?" Pimm jerked him upright until he muttered his assent, then let him flop back onto the ground. "Come on. We'll turn his token over to Mama Bear, and the guard will find him soon enough."

They walked around to the front of the row of brownstones. Pimm's fist clenched so tight around the confiscated token, the edges bit into their palm.

"Thank you, Pimm," Kit said as they reached the front gate. "Some establishments would've made excuses for him just because he was drunk."

"I know, but that's not how things are done at the Den."

"I'm glad. I don't know how to respond when people say such things when they're sober, let alone when drink is involved."

Pimm paused, one hand resting on the gate, and regarded Kit. "I've noticed you avoid such conversations, even with folk you know. You have no interest in physical affection, do you Kit?"

"Not especially."

"Does it bother you when Maher and Marielle flirt with you the way they do?"

"Not with them, I know they don't mean anything by it. I just can't ever come up with anything to say back." Color tinged the lad's cheeks, but he kept his gaze on Pimm. "Honestly, I'm not interested in anything from anyone, other than friendship."

Now it all made much more sense. It explained why Kit felt more comfortable in a green lantern establishment like the Den. He could do his work and, mostly, avoid unwanted attention from patrons. Working in a place like the Whistle and Bells must have been trying indeed, even with a kind employer like Archie.

"I understand," Pimm said softly.

Kit's brows rose. "You, as well?"

"Not entirely, but it takes a great deal of time and effort for me to become interested in another person in that way. Neither of which I have much of to spare at the moment."

One corner of Kit's mouth tipped up into a smile. "I understand, too."

"Good," Pimm ushered him through the gate. "And if anyone else here doesn't respect your wishes in that regard, you refer them to me."

CHAPTER THIRTY-FIVE

Ally could scarcely believe everything Maher'd told them that morning on the shore. There were so many details to be arranged if he was really going to take on this voyage to The Riddles. She could see Maher wrestling with himself, wanting to make the right decisions. They'd stayed on land until the sun reached its highest point in the sky.

By then, Ally'd begun to feel a deep-seated longing to return to the sea. It wasn't like the fishhook pull of being Sea Kissed, but it wasn't exactly pleasant either. Pasha sensed it as well and suggested they arrange a time to meet Maher the next day. As much as Ally wanted to stay a little longer, she knew Pasha was right.

Before they left, Ally and Maher took a moment to speak privately. Maher's most pressing concern was how he would actually reach The Riddles.

"What am I supposed to do, Al? Commandeer a ship? Hardly. I'm sure your father would eventually notice, if the harbormaster didn't catch me first. Agnes would just love that." He muttered, glancing over where Pasha was packing up their supplies.

"I doubt you'll have to resort to theft. Why not ask Kamharida or Luthais for advice? Surely one of them could get both you and Marielle on board some sort of vessel?"

A strange look had passed through Maher's eyes at the mention of her brother. Ally knew they'd formed a kind of friendship before she left with Pasha. Rather unexpected, but still it gratified Ally to know they'd both found that companionship in each other. Luthais had certainly never carried anyone else through the house before. Had that friendship flourished in her absence? Or were they back to the polite, tolerable acquaintanceship they'd formed when Maher first moved into the Kingfisher home?

"You have a point," he'd eventually agreed. "They've both proven they can keep secrets when needed."

"More so, they're your friends. Loyal ones, at that."

"You're right, Al." Maher'd wrapped her into one last hug. "I promise I'll talk to one of them."

Changing back to her tail wasn't nearly as painful as the first split to her legs. Nor as slow. Almost as soon as she plunged into the shallows, Ally's thighs began melting together. It was such a relief to be back in the sea, already it felt more like home than the land ever had. Ally questioned now what her years as a human would've been like without people like Maher or Priestess Esa in her life.

They swam at a leisurely pace back to the caves beneath Kingfisher Island, but Ally took off for the tapestry chamber as soon as they crossed the threshold of the great cavern.

"Ally?" Pasha followed, dropping the bundle onto the floor. "What are you doing?"

"I want to see that place on the map again," she flicked her tail harder. Pasha sputtered when one of Ally's long fins caught her in the face. "Sorry!"

"By the tides, *slow down.* We'll have to carry it back to the surface before you can open it anyway."

Ally veered into the cave, Pasha close behind her, and picked up the map case from where she'd left it next to Pasha's spear.

"This has to be what Hama was talking about." She held the map close, heart hammering in her chest. "How else could the other mermaids be so well concealed for all this time?"

"I don't know," Pasha admitted. "I was beginning to think Hama must have been delirious. All that talk about sirens and the place where the seas meet. Whatever happened to her, it all seemed impossible. What creature could possibly be strong enough to capture and keep every mermaid in the seas captive? Who could hate us this much?" Shimmering tears misted over her deep blue irises and Ally's heart ached for Pasha.

Placing the map aside, Ally took Pasha's hands in hers. The current of energy constantly running within Pasha thrummed beneath her skin. White arcs gathered to dance across her arms and wrap around their intertwined fingers.

Ally considered her next question carefully. "I thought the sirens were your distant relations, or something. Why would they want to harm the mermaids?"

"I don't know."

"There must have been something that happened to cause such a rift. You don't remember any stories about them from the elders? Anything besides them preferring warmer climates?"

Pasha frowned, "What?"

"It's what you told me that day we met the pod of whales. That they were the ones who sang, not mermaids, and that they lived in warmer waters."

"No, nothing else." She looked utterly helpless in the face of Ally's questions.

"You know, we could accompany Maher on his journey. We could stay beneath the ship or even ask Euphonia if she'd be willing to carry us."

"Ally..."

"Pasha. Don't you want to go look for the others?"

"I don't know!" Pasha's energy flared, sending a shock through Ally's palms. The spear leaning in the corner clattered to the floor. The green stone flickered.

Ally eyed the spear. "Maybe there's a way to find out what happened between the sirens and the merfolk. You said that spear was old, right?"

"Ancient," she sighed heavily.

"And it still has the last owner's energy inside it, yes? Could we, I don't know, channel it somehow?"

Pasha released Ally's hands and shook off the threads. "That spear isn't suddenly going to tell us a story, Ally."

"Maybe it will, if we know how to listen."

"What do you mean?"

Ally caught her bottom lip between her teeth and thought for a moment. "When you made me a mermaid, when we were in the hatching grounds, when my body and mind and soul were filled with the power you drew in from that space... I saw things. Heard sounds. Smelled scents that made no sense at the time. By the end they'd faded away, but when my first year was winding down and my body was changing again, they all came rushing back. And it was easier to focus on those memories than the pain. I think I was seeing flashes of other rituals and ceremonies from the past. They left trails of energy behind, and when you pulled them to us, I could experience what mermaids before us were doing there."

"Ally, why didn't you tell me this before?"

"It never occurred to me I might have seen or felt something you didn't. After they were gone, I was so caught up in learning how to be a mermaid, I didn't think much about it. Until now."

Pasha grabbed her face and kissed her. "You're brilliant. Forgetful, but brilliant."

MAHER

CHAPTER THIRTY-SIX

By the time he returned to the manor late that afternoon, Maher was practically asleep on his feet. His body might have been on the verge of collapse, and his mind weighed down like a ship anchored into the bay, but his heart was light. A small part of him had been terrified that Ally wouldn't return after all. Or he'd be forced to leave for The Riddles before she did and he'd miss her altogether. And so, despite everything else in his life that threatened to drown him, Maher thanked every deity who might've been listening for his good fortune that day.

Tripping his way through the front door, Maher bumped right into Mrs. Thorley.

"Maher!" She steadied him until she seemed satisfied that he could hold himself upright. "Are you quite well?"

"Never better," Maher attempted to grin, but suspected it was more of a grimace. "I was just..." he stopped short of telling her he'd seen Ally, remembering just in time that not everyone knew where she'd really gone, "just on my way to my room to lie down."

"I'm not certain you could make it up the stairs in your condition." The housekeeper caught his elbow, with a surprisingly strong grip, and towed him into Rochelle's parlor. "I want you to rest here for a while, before climbing those steps."

Maher found he had neither the strength, nor the inclination, to argue with her. Falling back onto a sofa, he allowed Mrs. Thorley to fuss and adjust him until there was a throw pillow beneath his head and quilt draped over his legs. Somewhere amid all this, she managed to remove his boots and loosen his collar.

"Thank you, Mrs. Thorley," he mumbled, already fighting to keep his eyes open. "You're a gem."

"Think nothing of it. You rest here as long as you need. Lady Kingfisher is out until dinner, so you won't be disturbed." She drew the curtains over the doors that led into the garden. "I'll send one of the footmen with a pitcher of water and a plate of sandwiches for when you wake."

Maher wanted to thank her, again, but words were quite impossible. There was a soft click as the door closed behind her, and then sleep carried Maher away.

Maher was not a man who dreamed very often. Not that he could remember, at any rate. But lying on that sofa in the darkened parlor, Maher fell into one of the most bizarre dreams of his life.

Clinging to a raft in a storm-tossed sea, Maher pressed his face into the rough, waterlogged boards and prayed for the downpour to end. Some goddess must have heard him. In the blink of an eye, the storm ceased and the skies cleared. Sitting up, Maher stared out at the calm water surrounding him on all sides. The raft bobbed along, caught in a random current, carrying him to an unknown destination. A sharp splash drew his attention and Maher caught a glimpse of a jeweled tail before it disappeared beneath the waves.

"Ally?" His throat was raw from the salt and sun.

Another splash, now there were two tails waving at him.

"Ally! Over here!"

A great swell shoved the raft and nearly flipped it over. Maher's nails dug into the wood as he held on with what little strength he had left. When the raft settled, there were two heads floating above the waves. Two pairs of eyes watching him with mild interest.

"Ally! Pasha!" Maher searched for a paddle and found nothing. "Pleases help me get to shore."

Ally looked to Pasha, but the mermaid shook her head. "He is of the land, we are of the sea. We cannot help."

"What?" His stomach dropped.

"I'm sorry, Maher," Ally gave him a small, regretful smile. "She's right. You must help yourself."

"No, wait!"

Pasha dove beneath the waves. With one last glance in his direction, Ally followed.

"Ally, don't do this, please." Hot tears stung his eyes and burned down the back of his throat.

The raft dipped and jerked beneath him. Maher twisted around to find a monstrous wave towering high enough to blot out the sun. He barely had time to suck in a breath before it came crashing down. Maher tumbled through the water. The sea around him pulsed once and searing pain lanced through his left shoulder.

Not again... Curling into himself, Maher grasped for the electrified hunk of metal he knew must be skewered through his shoulder. Try as he might, his fingers couldn't seem to find enough purchase to pull it out.

"Maher?" A muffled voice reached him through the cloying waves. "Maher, look at me."

When a strong, solid hand closed over his shoulder, the pain lifted. Maher's, eyes flew open. Sunlight filtered through the blessedly shallow water. A blurred face with moss green eyes peered at him from above the surface. The hand holding his shoulder gently lifted him and then Maher was blinking dazedly at Luthais Kingfisher.

"What... what happened?"

"You fell asleep in the bath, again," he chuckled, long blonde hair falling over his bare shoulder.

"Again?" Maher looked down, finding himself – as one expected for taking a bath – quite naked. And Luthais was kneeling next to the copper tub in nothing but a pair of breeches. There was something unusual about him, he seemed softer somehow. Relaxed.

"Mm-hmm," Luthais hooked a finger through the chain holding the shark tooth around his neck. "I think this is part of the problem. You'll have to ask Ally about it, next time we see her."

Forgetting entirely about their varying states of undress, Maher grabbed his wrist, sending water sloshing over the rim of the tub. "What are you talking about? Ally's *gone*."

Luthais gave him a puzzled look. "She comes back on land every month, around the full moon. How long were you underwater just now?"

Maher swallowed the panic and confusion that had been steadily building in his throat. "I don't know."

"Don't worry, we'll see her soon." Luthais cupped Maher's face, a calloused thumb brushed against his jaw. "Now, are you getting out of that tub, or do I have to get in there with you?"

CHAPTER THIRTY-SEVEN

"What happened?" A more familiar, gruff Luthais asked.

Well fuck. It was all a damn dream.

Mrs. Thorley answered, "Mister Villaon was so disoriented when he arrived home, I insisted that he lie down in the parlor for a while."

"How long has he been down here?"

"Since just after teatime," her tone grew stern. "He is working far too much. This is untenable, my lord."

"I know." Luthais sounded almost angry. At what? Surely not at him.

"If you want me to rest so badly, why are you being so godsbedamned loud?" Maher grumbled, pulling the quilt over his head.

Luthais snorted and asked the housekeeper to join him in the hall. The closed door muffled their conversation too much for Maher to understand any more. He thought to perhaps investigate the food Mrs. Thorley had promised, but the comfort of the sofa won out over his hunger. The clock ticking away on the mantle lulled him back to sleep. He'd just dozed off, wondering absently if dream Luthais would pay him another visit, when the real Luthais pushed the parlor doors open.

"Wake up, Maher."

With a groan, Maher peered out from beneath the quilt. Luthais strode across the room and stopped next to him, arms crossed over his barrel chest.

"Is your surly silence meant to convey something?"

"Come with me, Maher."

"Where?"

"To your room."

"My, what?" Maher's head popped up. Maybe this was another dream after all.

"You've slept the entire afternoon in here. The servants need to clean and you need to eat something. Then you can continue to rest in your own bed."

Perhaps not.

Knowing that arguing with that mulish set of Luthais' jaw would be pointless, Maher pushed himself up and rubbed the sleep from his eyes. "Luthais, just the man I wanted to see."

"Well," he smirked. "That was easier than I thought it would be."

Maher stood and stretched, sending cracks and pops through his joints. "What, were you planning to hoist me over your shoulder like a sack of grain? Again?"

"If it proved necessary."

Sniffing indignantly, Maher found his boots and tucked them beneath his arm. The food tray had already been removed, and hopefully carried to his room. "I want it understood, I'm only being this cooperative because I have something to tell you."

Luthais led the way out of the parlor. "What's that?"

Maher glanced around, ensuring there was no one else on the stairs with them, and murmured, "I saw Ally today."

"*What?*" Stopping mid-step, Luthais gripped Maher's good shoulder. "Her first year has ended? Where is she? By the goddess, why didn't you tell us?"

Wobbling under Luthais' hold, Maher nearly dropped his boots and huffed out a laugh. "I'll tell you everything, but let's get off the staircase before I add a broken skull to my growing list of injuries."

"Of course," he snatched his hand back. "I'm sorry, I was just, I can't believe you actually saw her."

"Trust me, I can't either." For the rest of the slow walk to the guest wing where Maher still kept his rooms, he relayed all that he could about Ally and how she'd spent the last year with Pasha.

"I was going to tell you all at dinner tonight, I didn't expect to sleep in Rochelle's parlor for so long."

Luthais grunted in reply as they turned down Maher's hallway. He seemed on the verge of saying something, but stopped himself each time he tried. Maher dug for his room keys in his waistcoat pocket. "What is it?"

Green eyes locked onto his and Maher stilled. Despite being a full head shorter than him, when Luthais turned such intense focus on Maher it suddenly felt as if the hallway was shrinking.

"Is there something I can do to help?"

Maher didn't need to ask what Luthais meant. By the gods, he was falling asleep all over the house at this point, even with the adjustments he'd made to his schedule. And, it just so happened, there was something Luthais could do for him.

"As a matter of fact, there is something I need."

Luthais blinked several times, as if he were surprised Maher had agreed so readily. Not that Maher could fault him for that.

"What's that?"

Maher took a deep breath and let it out. The worst Luthais could say was no, and Maher would be no more a beggar than he was at this very moment. "I need a ship."

Turned out, he'd managed to catch Luthais Kingfisher off guard twice in one evening. Thrice, if he counted the news about Ally.

Clearing his throat, Luthais asked, "Why do you need a ship?"

Maher chose his next words carefully. "I'm obligated to help a friend return home. Time is of the essence, I'm afraid, and we don't have long to set this voyage in motion. And what's more, I have to go with them."

"And where is their home?"

"Ah, yes, that's the more difficult aspect of our agreement."

"Maher," Luthais' brows knit together, "where do you have to take this friend?"

"The Riddles."

"Great gods, you can't be serious."

Well, that was a better response than I expected.

"I reacted much the same when I heard the news. But I am, most definitely, serious."

Luthais scrutinized him in silence, as unreadable as he ever was. Maher was beginning to feel that ever-constant veil of fatigue, his new companion, dropping over him again.

"I don't need an answer at this moment, but if you know of a trade ship traveling to Char-range that'd be willing to detour to The Riddles, or a captain who'd name a price to take us directly there, I'd greatly appreciate any advice or direction."

Luthais stood still as a statue. A slight, confused tilt of his head was Maher's only indication he was even listening.

"Right, well, you know where to find me." Maher sighed and unlocked his door. The clicking of the tumblers seemed to shock Luthais into motion. His hand closed over Maher's, warm and calloused, just like in his dream.

"I'll take you."

It was his turn to stare at the other man. "Come again?"

"I'll see you to The Riddles and back."

Chapter Thirty-eight

Luthais waited as Maher grasped what he'd just offered. The boots slipped from beneath his arm and clattered to the floor.

Goddess help him, Luthais had even surprised himself when the words first left his mouth.

"Are... are you sure?"

Luthais nodded, not quite trusting he wouldn't promise an entire fleet if it would make Maher's face light up like that again.

Maher propped one hand on his hip and ran the other through his hair. The action caused the scent of the pomade he used to waft in Luthais' direction. "I must still be dreaming," he muttered. "It can't have been that easy."

"What?"

"Nothing," Maher shook his head. "Aren't you needed here, or on another trade delegation, for your father?"

"Not now that Gai is back." He could feel Maher's lingering hesitation. "Maher, I wouldn't offer the use of my ship and crew if they were required elsewhere. You know that. Besides, no Birde Isles ship has made the voyage to The Riddles in recent memory. Establishing a trade route with them could only help repair our reputation with our allies."

"True enough," he chuckled. "Alright, I accept.

Luthais stopped short of taking the hand Maher offered. "I do have one condition."

"And what is that?"

The shift in Maher's demeanor was immediate, falling into place as if he'd simply donned a new shirt. Luthais suspected he was speaking with the Magpie of Kingsport for the first time. And there was something unsettling in this knowledge. A nagging kernel of apprehension at the back of his mind, that he couldn't readily identify.

"I want to meet this friend before any plans are made."

His head tilted, the new angle bringing their faces closer. "Why?"

"This will be a voyage unlike anything my crew have taken on before. I won't ask that of them without knowing exactly who we're transporting. And why."

From one breath to the next, the Magpie vanished and the Maher he knew was standing before him again. "That can be arranged. And I was going to tell you why we're sailing anyway, it's –" A wide yawn cut him off.

"You can give me the rest of the details tomorrow," Luthais pushed the door open, "when you aren't falling asleep in the middle of a conversation."

Maher snorted and stepped into his room, only to stop and give Luthais a look of utter bewilderment. "What's all this?"

"What does it look like?"

"If I answer, I'll only sound daft."

A short laugh escaped Luthais as he retrieved the boots from the hallway floor. Giving Maher a gentle nudge, Luthais steered him towards the full copper bathtub sitting by the fireplace. Steam rose in curling wisps from the lavender scented water. He'd asked the servants to draw the bath while he herded Maher from the parlor. Mrs. Thorley was happy to oblige. There was also a pot of freshly brewed tea and a plate of dinner waiting on a small table that had been placed by the bed.

"I'll be damned," Maher rubbed his left shoulder absently and Luthais knew he'd made the right choice. This would do him good.

When Maher looked back at him, Luthais caught the tinge of color rising on his cheeks. "You did this, didn't you?"

"Mrs. Thorley and the servants prepared everything."

"But you asked them to?"

Had he miscalculated after all? Crossed some boundary he hadn't been aware of? Slowly, he nodded. But then Maher smiled softly and shrugged out of his jacket.

"Thank you, Luthais. You're sweeter than you let on, you know."

Clearing his throat, he looked away before Maher could see the flush creeping up his own face.

"I'll leave you to it, then." Luthais placed the boots next to the closet. At least Maher'd finally had the two rooms connected. From the corner of his eye, he saw Maher's waistcoat hit the floor.

Not wasting any time, is he?

As Luthais crossed the room to leave, he heard Maher snicker to himself, "Really thought I was still dreaming, for a moment."

That was the second time he'd mentioned a dream. Luthais turned back to ask exactly what that meant, just as Maher's white shirt slipped from his shoulders to pool around his feet. Firelight from the hearth danced across his lean back, casting a bronze glow over deep brown skin. Long arms lifted as Maher stretched, and Luthais' mouth went dry. He found himself wanting to run his hands over every inch of sinewy muscle, to map out this body that was so different from his own. To know if Maher's skin was as soft as he'd imagined...

Maher twisted to grab the towel folded neatly on his dressing table and Luthais nearly swore aloud. The scarring on his back was minimal, but the thick starburst that marred the skin just outside of Maher's collar bone was impossible to miss. Faint lines spread out from the raised, rough tissue, a sign the shrapnel that pierced through had been electrified.

Seeing with his own eyes the damage done to Maher's shoulder during the downing of the *Pike*... if Foraoise Dare wasn't already dead Luthais would've hunted her down and wrung her neck himself. The heat that had begun to pool in his stomach shot straight up into his chest, a deep and gnawing ache.

What are you doing? Luthais backed out of the room and eased the door shut before Maher noticed he was staring at him like a damned pervert.

Stalking back through the house, Luthais berated himself for taking such liberties. Surprised or not by Maher's nonchalance about undressing in front of him, he'd had no right to linger like that.

In truth, he was anxious to know more about this friend and why they needed Maher's help to the extent that he'd grant them a favor of this scale. But he could wait until Maher'd had a decent night's sleep before learning more. Whatever the underlying motivations were, Luthais couldn't help but feel a swell of pride. Maher'd come to him for help. What he wouldn't abide was Maher being dragged into yet another mess of someone else's making.

MARIELLE

CHAPTER THIRTY-NINE

This must be what cabin fever is like, Marielle thought with a groan.

Splayed across the narrow bed in her hideout at the Bear's Den, she counted the whorls and grooves in the plaster ceiling. She knew the whole pattern by heart now.

Word had finally arrived that morning from Maher, he'd managed to secure a ship. But the captain wanted to meet her before they set sail. Marielle didn't particularly appreciate the vague composition of the letter; though, she supposed, the Magpie might've simply been erring on the side of caution.

Gods, she'd don a dress and take tea with Lady Kingfisher if it meant they'd agree to take her to The Riddles. She *had* to reach them before anyone else discovered how those coins were being smuggled into the Birde Isles. There wasn't exactly a plan of action for when they arrived, but she'd have the entire voyage to worry about that. The important thing was to get there before he got himself imprisoned. Or killed.

Marielle soon lost interest in the ceiling and began a routine of stretches and calisthenics. The open floor space left just enough room to move through each exercise. Boredom had initially led her to add this task to her day, once in the morning, at noon, and in the evening.

It had once been a daily part of her life when she first arrived in Kingsport.

The routine was nearly at its end when there was a sharp rap on the door. Righting herself with a huff, Marielle turned the knob, expecting to find Pimm, Kit, or even one of the maids. But she was quite wrong. Mama Bear herself was standing in the hallway, red painted lips pursed and hands propped on her hips.

"Ma'am?" Marielle's heart skipped. Had something happened? Had the Madam changed her mind?

"Feeling restless, are you dear?"

"Pardon?"

Mama Bear glanced around her at the empty room. "Well, based on the complaints I've received from patrons about excessive noise in the *attic*, I had to assume you were either dancing a reel or perhaps feeling a bit cooped up."

"Oh! Apologies ma'am, I was only... exercising."

"I thought as much," she turned, plum skirts swishing over Marielle's feet. "Come along."

Marielle hesitated for only a moment before grabbing her gunbelt from the bed and hurrying after the Den's proprietor. She'd take any excuse to get out of that blasted room.

Barkeep's pale blue eyes narrowed and his orange beard twitched as he gave Marielle a cursory inspection. "Ye want me to put her to work, then?"

"What am I, a mule?" Marielle snorted. "Perhaps you'd like to check my teeth?"

Next to the large man, Kit stifled a laugh before escaping with a tray of drinks to be delivered to patrons in the lounge.

"Marielle will be with us a few more days, yet," Mama Bear ignored the animosity already brewing between them, "and needs something to keep herself occupied. Surely there's something you could use assistance with, some task that's often overlooked?"

Kit darted back behind the bar with more orders from the lounge, effectively distracting the gruff Swan Islander from whatever argument he was about to make.

"Fine." He relented as the lad slid an array of glasses over to be filled. "We'll find something f'her to do."

"Thank you, dear." Mama Bear patted her shoulder. "Mind you, no venturing outside. We want to minimize the chance of anyone recognizing you."

Nodding, Marielle watched her move through the growing crowd of patrons. From the door, Pimm gave her the barest hint of a smile and a wink. She gave them a little salute, understanding they must have influenced Mama Bear's decision to allow her downstairs.

Turning back towards the bar Marielle clasped her hands behind her back. "What can I do to assist you, gentlemen?"

Kit ducked his head, hiding a grin, while the barkeep looked ready to spit nails.

CHAPTER FORTY

Pasha and Ally swam together towards the hatching grounds, each armed in their own way. Once again, the map case was strapped across Ally's back like a shield, while Pasha kept both hands wrapped tight around the spear. They'd not even reached the tiny island yet, and already Pasha could feel a faint spark beneath her fingertips.

Not that she'd doubted Ally's memory, but this would be yet another facet of Pasha's own kind that she'd hadn't known existed. How much more knowledge had she been denied by being the one left behind by her shoal? They were silent as they found the hidden opening in the island's base and swam up the coral-lined tunnel. Lights flashed around them and the spark within the spear became a veritable flame as they entered the lagoon and broke through the surface.

It was already agreed that Pasha would tap into the energy locked inside the spear alone. Ally would keep watch, ready to pull her out if needed. Besides, it was doubtful that Ally could connect to the energy on her own. Pasha just couldn't understand what they were missing, what trick or method would allow Ally to access the skills that came to Pasha as easily as breathing.

"Which should we do first?" Ally asked as they shed their tails and walked onto the soft strip of sand. The transition was already coming easier to her now, to Pasha's relief.

"Let's open the map. We know that won't take too long."

"Why are all mermaid rituals so arduous?" Ally whined as she opened the case and removed the map.

"Your guess is as good as mine. I'm sure it's to teach some vague lesson about patience." Pasha drove the metal-capped end of the spear into the sand until it stood upright on its own and helped her unroll the tapestry.

"Here," Ally's thumb brushed over a barely raised bunch of threads in the bottom right corner. "I mistook it for a flaw at first. Can you imagine if I'd pulled the knots out when I was repairing the map?"

Pasha squinted at the fabric, her own fingers followed the same path. A raised outline, very like a fishhook, took shape. All the years this tiny clue had been laying forgotten on the floor of the tapestry chamber. She supposed they were fortunate the elders hadn't sealed that tunnel along with the others that were closed off before the shoal left. Was that intentional? Had they meant for Pasha to find this? There were too many questions, too many possibilities hinged on this one artifact. Inside, it felt like a jellyfish had moved into Pasha's skull and couldn't decide where to settle.

"There's one thing I don't understand," Ally mused, pulling Pasha back from the mental spiral she'd been circling.

"Only one thing?"

"Only one about the map," she amended. "I know the land masses wouldn't have been as important to the mermaids who made this map, but there are things much closer together than they ought to be."

"Such as?"

"On our maps, for instance, the Split Sea is much wider at the base. And The Riddles are much farther from any other land."

"They could have moved," Pasha shrugged.

"You're joking!"

"I'm not! I remember once, when I was very small, a revered elder visited our shoal. Pallagia said she was so old she remembered a time when the seas were wider than they are now."

"Surely your sister was teasing you." Ally held the map closer, as if she were trying to divine the truth in the threads.

"You never know," Pasha glanced around the cavern, saturated with centuries of magic. "We might live long enough to see the seas change again."

Pasha stood at the edge of the lagoon, legs planted in the sand, jewel-toned shards of eggshells digging into the soles of her feet. The discomfort was good. It would help keep her grounded. With the spear held in front of her, Pasha dipped the tapered black blade into the water. Breathing deeply, Pasha opened a tentative bridge.

The spear responded immediately, drinking greedily from the power soaked into every surface of the hatching grounds. Pasha's knees nearly buckled with the effort to stem the flow. Bright arcs gathered around the pale green stone and traveled up Pasha's arms. She could taste electricity in the air of the cavern. Behind her, Ally gasped softly. She might've spoken, but Pasha couldn't hear over the hum of the energy being pulled into the spear.

Gritting her teeth, Pasha pushed back against the tide. She didn't want to fill the weapon with new energy, she wanted to draw out the signature of its previous owner. A growl built in her chest when the spear seemed to push *back* at her. As if to say its secrets wouldn't be so easy to unlock. Pasha bared down, the bones in her hands groaning with how tightly she held on. There was movement nearby, and then she felt the ghost of Ally's hand resting between her shoulder blades. No energy passed between them, but still Pasha felt bolstered by her presence.

Riding the waves of power rippling through the spear, Pasha slowed her breathing and waited for a break in the swells. When the next one came, she dove through, leaving her body there on the sand and spiraling into the life of the last mermaid to wield the spear.

Pasha opened her eyes. She was in a strange sea cavern, massive with sparkling crystals embedded into the rock. A dozen-odd mermaids were gathered, none of whom she recognized, save one. The mermaid warrior whose likeness was carved in a place of prominence in the great cavern. The portrait she'd slept beneath for years after Pallagia died and the rest of the shoal departed. She was even more magnificent than Pasha'd imagined.

A fanned, bony crest ran from the top of her brow to the base of her skull. Her skin was a similar shade to Pasha's, shark-like and sleek. Muscles shifted and bunched in her arms and shoulders as she shifted a spear, the same spear Pasha was holding in the hatching grounds, from one hand to another. She was quite sizable, for a mermaid. Her gray and black scaled tail was easily twice as long as Pasha's. The gathered mermaids were speaking, but Pasha heard nothing but the buzz of energy shifting around them. When one mermaid farther down the row said something and shook her head, the warrior banged the metal cap of the spear into the ground and gestured sharply. In answer, a collection of bones rose up from the cave floor and danced around her tail until she dismissed them with a wave of her hand. A sense of kinship, of belonging that Pasha'd never felt before, bloomed deep in her chest and she wished the warrior would call the bones up again.

Then Pasha glimpsed a long, thin scar on the inside of her forearm. One that matched the scar she carried in the same place. A phantom itch crawled over Pasha's skin and she resisted the urge to scratch. She wanted a better look at the warrior, but as she drifted closer the scene dissolved.

Pasha's vision cleared a second time, just as a massive bird with a human woman's head and torso dove from the sky. Beautiful face twisted with rage and taloned feet aimed for her throat. Stifling a scream, Pasha barely resisted ducking beneath the surface, remembering these were only shadows of what had been. Talons snatched at the air above her head and came up empty.

Everything around her was chaos, but still she heard nothing. In the distance, cannon fire launched from strange human ships, not unlike those they'd seen in the cave murals. They were closing in on a large and instantly, achingly familiar island. Dozens of bird-women soared above the land, screaming their fury and diving for the sailors on board. Others, perched in the rigging, appeared to be singing, their arms held out to sailors who tried to reach them but were held back by their crewmates.

More bird-women flew over the water, attacking the merfolk who bobbed above the surface. A pair of them worked to free another from a net weighted down with stones on each corner. Some dodged the electric charges hurled by the mermaids, others weren't so lucky. The same one who'd greeted Pasha upon her arrival took a full force shock to the chest and plummeted like a rock into the sea. Ducking beneath the swells, Pasha quickly lost sight of the bird-woman, but gasped at the battle taking also place beneath the water. More mermaids than she'd ever seen in her life fought alongside sharks, giant squid, and creatures like Euphonia. For all Pasha knew, one of them might've been the same ancient sea monster Ally'd befriended.

Charging at them were snapjaws, massive sea serpents with row upon row of needle teeth, and other creatures Pasha didn't even recognize. A strong current pushed her aside as a larger mermaid swam past at great speed.

The warrior! Pasha tore herself away from the sight and followed.

Spear already crackling with unspent energy, the warrior shot to the surface. When Pasha reached the open air, she found the mermaid locked in a fight with another bird-woman. The writhing tentacle stretched from the open gash in her arm to wrap around a feathered wing. A sphere of power gathered at the end of the spear until it was large enough to turn loose at her target. The struggling bird-woman saw the attack coming, twisted, screeched, and clawed at the tentacle around her wing. If the warrior felt the fresh gouges in the mottled purple flesh, she gave no indication. The sphere struck the bird-woman and she dropped. This time, Pasha looked carefully to see what happened while the creature sank into the depths. She half-expected another mermaid or one of their allies to finish the kill. Instead, three mermaids surrounded her, encasing her in a bubble of magic. A nearby shark began circling the group, guarding them as they worked.

Pasha felt a sudden, wrenching pull in her gut as a surge of energy was drawn in by the three mermaids. And she watched, transfixed, as the bird-woman changed. Wings, talons, and feathers were burned away. Gaping, ragged gills split through both sides of her ribcage.

Finally, shorter bird legs stretched and warped into a serpentine tail. When they were done, another mermaid pulled the newly made snake-woman away. One of the three who'd performed the magic was utterly spent and had to be helped to safety.

The truth of what Pasha was witnessing lodged in her throat like a fish bone. All the sealed-away carvings and scraps of stories she'd heard as a child, each a puzzle piece on its own, slotted into place. These creatures, *they were the sirens.* They'd once been predators of the air and land, and Pasha's kind had condemned them to a life in the sea. Working with *humans*, no less. That part was almost more amazing to Pasha than anything else.

This time, she was prepared when the scene began to change again.

The warrior's back was to her. Before them was a swirling wall of water that stretched in all directions, as far as Pasha could see.

More warriors were there, each holding weapons made of the same green stone and inky black metal as the spear. They were driving what remained of the sirens towards the wall, less than half of what she'd seen in the previous memory. The sirens hissed and shrieked, but they were weak and unused to their new forms. Pasha glanced around. There were other mermaids gathered but, like the sirens, many had been lost. Pasha wasn't sure how she knew this, but it was true just the same.

The warrior from Pasha's shoal swept her spear in a wide arc and an opening tore through the wall. As the sirens were forced through, the world dissolved one more time. Pasha followed as the warrior swam alone through the open ocean. She was exhausted, her well of energy drained. After some time, she came to another place that Pasha knew. A stone spire at the edge of a young kelp forest. But when Pasha tried to follow her into the mermaid trove, she was forced back by some unseen barrier. Growling in frustration, Pasha circled the rock formation, hunting for another way inside. No matter what she tried, the boundary denied her entry.

Waiting outside the trove, Pasha burned with curiosity. What could she have found inside that was worth leaving the spear behind?

But when the warrior emerged, she was empty handed. She stacked stones over the opening and, with one last look at the trove, swam slowly away.

"Wait!" Pasha called out, heart aching. But the warrior couldn't hear her. The moment the other mermaid was out of sight, everything shifted and Pasha sank into the darkness.

CHAPTER FORTY-ONE

Luthais dug through the dusty wardrobe that sat on the far side of his room. It was mostly used for storing the trappings he was expected to wear to formal functions or when representing the Birde Isles as Lord of Trade.

One benefit of traveling without Gai, or any high-ranking officials, was that Luthais could usually get away with wearing what he wanted. What foreign dignitary could argue with a Lord who also served as captain maintaining a more practical form of dress. It also allowed him to blend in, at least for a while, until Kamharida inevitably pointed him out to whoever'd been sent to receive them. He still didn't see eye-to-eye with his first mate on that little trick. As he'd said, many times, appearing as a common sailor gave Luthais the opportunity to observe their hosts' behavior towards those who worked for them without the veil of propriety. And, as she'd often countered, that was all well and good until some noble or ambassador arrived to greet him and he was nowhere to be found.

Once, he'd suggested she take his place, just to see if it worked.

"Do you honestly think," Kamharida had asked, in a tone one would use to speak to a child, "that anyone would believe I am Luthais Kingfisher, Lord of Trade of the Birde Isles?"

"Not with that attitude, they wouldn't."

In the end, she'd still refused to try the experiment.

Luthais finally found what he was looking for among the fripperies. The only garment he owned that'd been embroidered by Ally, one his father had passed down to him. He wasn't certain Ally knew he had it. A simple white shirt, with a circle of kingfisher feathers around each cuff.

Tomorrow, the family would see Ally again. Ally, who was now a mermaid. Maher had arranged everything, and the Kingfishers couldn't have been more grateful.

Maher had done his best to prepare them to reunite with Ally and to meet Pasha. Though the goddess only knew what would happen at the appointed hour. Not that Luthais foresaw any trouble, but how exactly was one supposed to greet the mermaid who saved your sister's life? They were fortunate this meeting could take place before they set sail for The Riddles. In truth, there were still several details to finalize for their voyage. Not the least of which being that Maher still hadn't told Lord Kingfisher their plan. There was no avoiding it. He suspected Maher planned to use the joy of Ally's return to lessen the shock of the request.

And Luthais still had to meet this friend of Maher's who'd made such a breakthrough with the origins of the false Saprean coins. The details of which Maher had been decidedly vague on, no matter how Luthais phrased the question he'd gotten yet another glimpse at what it was like talking to Maher as the Magpie. Luthais would meet them, and learn what he could from the source. That task, at least, would be completed soon. One of Maher's contacts in the city had agreed to give them a private place to meet.

Throughout all this time spent around each other, Luthais tried to keep in mind his conversation with Gai, but still found himself pulling back where Maher was concerned. One moment he could confidently express a deeper level of familiarity, and the next he was stepping back to a polite distance. Perhaps the most beneficial consequence of this journey would be the opportunity to spend time together, away from the manor and his family. Away from Kingsport and Maher's dual responsibilities as the Magpie and Intelligencer. They could simply *exist* for a time, two sailors working side-by-side. Luthais always felt more like himself at sea, maybe this would allow him to finally relax and take his brother's advice to heart.

Laying the shirt across his bed, Luthais sighed and scrubbed a hand over his face. "I can hear Gai now. '*You have bigger problems, Luthais, if you truly have to be out at sea to profess yourself to Maher Villaon.*'"

CHAPTER FORTY-TWO

Tapping into the history stored in the spear had to be the shortest mermaid ritual on record.

No sooner had Ally settled in to wait, when Pasha abruptly woke from the strange trance that'd settled over her. Letting the spear fall to the side, Pasha dropped to one knee and sucked in a ragged breath.

In an instant, Ally was by her side. Had something gone wrong?

"Pasha, are you alright?"

With a shaky nod, Pasha scooped a handful of water from the pool and splashed her face.

"What happened? What did you see?"

"It's *them*," she rasped. "The bird-women in the mural we found. They're the sirens."

Ally frowned, "I've never heard anything about sirens living on land, let alone having wings."

"Me either."

"But they became those serpentine creatures from the carvings?"

"They did. I saw so many things, I don't know where to begin." Pasha turned her face towards Ally, a shadow of sorrow passed through her deep blue eyes.

"At the beginning," Ally helped her ease into the water. The sea would enable her to recover faster. "And when you're done, we'll decide what to do together."

Back in their home, Pasha recounted all she'd seen and they discussed this new revelation well into the night, until Pasha could barely keep her eyes open. Now Ally sat with her back against a polished slab of stone and a sleeping Pasha's head nestled in her lap. Her fingers combed gently through Pasha's hair. Lifting a lock, she watched as the strands hung suspended in the water before settling back down.

Across the cavern was the carving of the mermaid warrior whose history was stored in Pasha's spear.

At least, Ally thought of it as Pasha's. She'd traded that jeweled necklace for it in the trove, fair and square. Ally wasn't certain how far the concept of ownership extended among mermaids. They seemed to share so much, living in close-knit communities and combining resources.

It had been one of the more serious discussions they'd had since before Ally became a mermaid. They'd gone over all their options, the potential outcomes, benefits, and dangers. But, in the end, there was really only one choice to be made.

They were going to accompany Maher to The Riddles. Even if they arrived to find the last of the merfolk weren't still located there, they were certain to find some sort of sign as to what'd happened to them and where they'd gone. Both recalled Hama's warning, the same one given by Elder Nerys to a young Pasha, *"A mermaid must always remain beneath this island."* They'd reasoned it had to be connected to the knowledge stored inside of the sealed caves they'd reopened. And certainly the hatching grounds were important enough to warrant guarding against outside threats.

But if the sirens were really trapped, as Pasha had seen, then surely they could leave for a short time. Pasha was gone for nearly a month when they journeyed to rescue Mama, and everything was just as it should have been when they returned.

Ally briefly considered staying behind, so a mermaid would technically be there, but she wouldn't let either Pasha or Maher face this journey without her there to support them. More than anything, Ally wanted to see her family before they left. And thankfully, there would be time. Maher and Luthais had come to an agreement for the use of her brother's ship and crew, but the details of the voyage itself needed to be arranged. Ally had to admit, she was cheered at the prospect of seeing Kamharida and Ga-Seung again. Not to mention Weams and Olebile.

But she still worried, *Would they want to see me?*

The following day and night passed in a blur. They'd met Maher on the shore in the morning and he confirmed the reunion with her family was set for the next afternoon. Maher would come to the appointed meeting place around midday with clothes for both Ally and Pasha, a detail Ally'd quite overlooked in her excitement. Again.

"I do love that you've become so comfortable not wearing clothes so quickly." Pasha remarked later that night, trailing her hand down Ally's arm.

"I'm sure you are." Ally snorted, even as gooseflesh rose across her skin. "Personally, I'm looking forward to seeing you dressed in something besides an old scrap of sail."

"I think you'd put a dress on a shark if it would only let you."

"Depends on the dress." She tapped one finger against her chin. "In Meredia they wear these magnificent brocade gowns with the most enormous ruffles you've ever seen." Ally examined Pasha, much like Maher would consider a blank canvas. "Yes, I think something in a nice lapis blue would do, with wrought silver wire for the ruffle structure. Oh and a row of tiny sapphires along the neckline..."

With a mock growl, Pasha tackled Ally to the floor as she shrieked. "That will be enough of that, Ally Kingfisher."

Sharp nails grazed her side and Ally gasped, "Spoilsport. I happen to think it would look beautiful on you. I think anything would look beautiful on you." Pasha nipped at her earlobe and she lost whatever else she'd been about to say.

Just as well, for then she was looking into Pasha's eyes as the mermaid angled her head for a kiss. Ally's arms slid around Pasha's neck, and soon clothes were the farthest thing from her mind.

# ALLY

CHAPTER FORTY-THREE

"This is ridiculous," Pasha held a stocking carefully between two fingers, as if it might turn on her at any moment.

"You don't have to wear them, you know," Ally giggled as they sorted through the bundle of clothes Maher'd left for them on the beach. He'd tucked them behind the same crop of large rocks where Ally used to hide her clothes when she met Pasha for swimming lessons.

How long ago that seemed now, almost like it'd happened to someone else.

"I'm sure those are for me anyway, in case I wanted to put on the boots."

"Don't know why you'd want to wear those either."

"You must admit, it was nice of him to bring all this down here... Oh! Hello, old friend." Ally held up her favorite periwinkle skirt.

All her clothing had been packed away with packets of dried herbs to help keep the fabric fresh and ward against moths. The scent of thyme and lavender filled her nose as she shook out a few wrinkles. Pasha looked utterly flummoxed. After Ally finished dressing in the skirt and matching cream shirt with periwinkle flowers embroidered on the collar and cuffs, she turned her attention to the mermaid next to her.

It took a bit of work, and more than a few curses from Pasha, but Ally was eventually able to help her into a simple, brown cotton dress that laced up the back. Maher'd also included another shirt and a pair of loose trousers, but Ally suspected Pasha wouldn't want her legs encased like that, unable to return to her tail at will. It was, in fact, strange to see Pasha clothed. The dress fit her well and Ally still maintained she'd look lovely in anything, but there was also something sort of off about the sight.

Ally had to admit, despite the outfit being something she'd worn countless times before and a beloved favorite, her own clothes now felt oddly restrictive. The fabric brushed over her scales in a way that wasn't entirely pleasant. Still, she found herself rubbing the different fabrics absently between her fingers, just as she'd always done. Some habits, it seemed, were impossible to break.

Wrestling her damp curls into a braid, Ally took a set of hair combs from the bundle and secured Pasha's long hair back from her face.

"There," tucking a stray strand behind a pointed ear, Ally smiled. "I believe you're ready."

Pasha caught her hand as she drew it away. "Are you?"

Taking a quick, shaky breath, Ally nodded. "I am. Thank you for being here with me, Pasha."

Kissing the top of her hand, Pasha glanced down at herself. "You're the only one I'd do this for."

"Meet my family?"

"Wear a dress."

Ally and Pasha sat together on the sand, toes dipped into the tiny wavelets washing ashore. The sun was just falling into its midafternoon path when Maher appeared at the top of the seawall. He called down to them and they waved back. Pasha helped Ally stand as he hurried back towards road, out of sight.

They walked halfway up the beach and stopped. Ally hadn't fully tested her limits yet, how far she could venture from the water before it would call her back. This was not the day she wanted to learn, either.

Soon Maher was back, making his way down the stone steps with four people close behind. Her parents, Gai, and Luthais bringing up the rear. Ally's breath caught, tears already threatening to spill down her face. A reassuring hand rested on her shoulder, Pasha's steady presence calming her mind even as her heart thrummed. This was it, the moment she'd dreamed of for a solid year. The four Kingfishers reached the sand. When Maher pointed out the two mermaids, there was a sudden pause.

I think I may pass out.

Rochelle broke into a run. Hiking her skirts up with both hands, she left the others behind and shouted Ally's name. Four dumbfounded men watched her dash across the sand, then they took off after her.

"Mama!" Ally ran to her, closing the distance between them that much sooner. She practically collided with her mother and Rochelle enveloped her in a breath-stealing embrace.

"Alphonsine, my Alphonsine," she murmured into Ally's hair. Tears landed on Ally's face and she choked back a joyful sob. The crunch of booted feet hammering towards them came to an abrupt stop near the women.

Slowly, Ally pulled back enough in her mother's arms to find her father, brothers, and Maher all standing around them. She held her breath as her family took in her new appearance. Mama was still too busy crying to look properly at her, but Ally could see the gears turning in her brothers' heads. Their father's face was an unreadable mask. What did they see when they looked at her? Did they still see a sister? A daughter?

Finally, Luthais snorted and shook his head. "I confess I was hoping for something a bit more exciting. Gills, or a dorsal fin or some such thing."

Maher rolled his eyes as Gai laughed. Rochelle released Ally enough to fully inspect the changes in her face. And Ally drank in her mother's appearance at the same time. Rochelle was the picture of health. The bruising on her face and dark circles beneath her eyes had finally faded, her dark brown eyes were bright, and she'd regained the weight lost while held captive on the pirate ship. But Rochelle's beautiful, rich brunette hair was still cropped short. Dare had hacked it off with a knife, in a fit of rage, before they were able to reach her.

Ally ran a gentle hand over one of the curls tucked behind her mother's ear. "Hello, Mama."

"Hello, my darling." Rochelle gave her a wobbly smile before stepping aside to let the rest of the family greet her. Before Ally could get out another hello, Gai and Luthais were squeezing the air out of her again.

PASHA

CHAPTER FORTY-FOUR

Pasha stayed back as Ally was embraced and welcomed by her family.

Of course, seeing Ally so happy made her happy in turn. But a small, still-grieving part of her heart ached to have such a reunion with her own kin. This was also the first time she'd met anyone in Ally's family, besides Rochelle, and it was disorienting how much Ally's father and brothers resembled Gaius I. Especially her father, with the Kingfisher crest embroidered on the front of his tunic. It was like she'd journeyed back in time to the night on this very beach when she'd made that desperate bargain with Ally's great-grandfather.

They're not the same people, Pasha reminded herself, trying to shake the growing sense of unease deep in her chest.

They were all speaking now. Asking Ally questions, examining the scales on her hands, arms, and face. Only her father seemed to be keeping his distance. Pasha couldn't interpret his expression, not that she was great at reading humans to begin with. Surely though, if Gaius was angry about his daughter's new life, he wouldn't have come here today.

The conversations faded when Ally turned at last to her father. For a moment, they merely studied each other. Then, tears sprang to the older man's eyes and he opened his arms. Ally folded into the embrace and Pasha could've sworn she heard him apologize.

Maher chose that moment to nod at Pasha and draw the others' attention her way. "Rochelle, I know you've already met. Gai, Luthais, this is Pasha, Ally's... companion...?"

Neither of the two men moved at first. Rochelle tsked at them, "Don't be rude, boys, Pasha is a member of the family now."

Pasha's eyes widened, "I'm... I am?"

"Of course, dear," Rochelle beckoned her closer, taking Pasha's hands, and bent to kiss her cheek.

From the corner of her eye, Pasha saw Maher nudge Luthais. Snapping out of whatever thoughts he'd been having, the long-haired man strode forward an held out a hand. "Pasha, I'm pleased to meet you."

The mermaid hesitated, remembering the last time she clasped hands with a Kingfisher lord. Pushing past the memory, she returned the gesture. His wide palm nearly engulfed hers. "I'm pleased to meet you, too."

Gai approached then, his posture more relaxed than his brother's. "We can't thank you enough for all you've done for Ally. I'm sure Maher has only recounted a fraction of your escapades."

"I'm sure," she smirked, clasping hands with the fourth Gaius.

"Tell us," Gai raised his voice to get his sister's attention, "is Ally behaving herself out there in the ocean? Luthais and I have a wager on the subject."

"You have *what?*" Ally piped up.

Pasha hid a smile behind her hand. She would always grieve the family she'd lost, but that Ally's people would welcome her so readily... That small gesture slowly began to heal something in her that she'd long tried to ignore.

CHAPTER FORTY-FIVE

S o much had happened in the lives of her family since she'd been away. Gai was full of stories about his experiences traveling abroad. It would probably take a year to hear all of them. He also cheekily hinted at a few gifts he'd brought back for Ally.

"Can't you tell me?" she'd needled.

"That would ruin the surprise," Gai's blonde mustache twitched as he tried, and failed, to keep a straight face. "Think of them as incentives to become stronger, so you can make it up to the house again."

Luthais had been on the move for much of the year as well. Though his purpose was to represent the trade interests of the Birde Isles, rather than pleasure. She was pleasantly surprised to note he'd even worn a shirt trimmed with her embroidery. A small, but much appreciated gesture.

As they talked, Ally couldn't ignore the way her brother's gaze kept wandering to where Maher stood conversing with Mama and Pasha. Luthais, who always kept his deepest thoughts and feelings to himself, was practically *staring*. As if he were dying of thirst and Maher were a glass of water. Ally made a mental note to ask Maher if he was aware of these attentions.

She was pleased to learn that Mama was getting out of the house and taking an active interest in the community again. Right now Rochelle was assisting those who'd been displaced by the events of the previous summer. Even working with the priestesses at the temple of the sea, supplementing the food resources for families of former fishers and sailors forced to find other work once the fishing trade dropped off so suddenly.

And her father... Ally'd been more nervous about seeing him again than anyone else. Though they'd reconciled before she left to join Pasha, there was still some of the old pain left when Ally thought of everything Gaius had kept from her. And, as it turned out, her father felt much the same. When they'd shared that first embrace, he'd apologized again for everything, and Ally felt that nugget of worry float away.

Dusk was soon upon them, and as each of her family members began discussing when and where they could next meet, Ally knew it was time to tell them about the voyage to The Riddles. At Pasha's request, Ally left out the part about Hama's return and her death shortly after. The loss was still too fresh to share, even with Ally's family.

This wasn't exactly the sort of news Gai or her parents had expected, and their concern was obvious even before the questions began in earnest.

"Please," Ally cut in gently, then took Pasha's hand. "This is a chance to find out what happened to Pasha's family. Perhaps we'll even find those who are left and bring them home."

"That's so far," Rochelle's brow knit with worry, "you've only just returned home."

Luthais looked to Ally, head tilted in question. When she nodded, he stepped forward. "Don't worry, Rochelle. I will be escorting Ally and Pasha to The Riddles."

"You will?" Gai gaped. "Since when?"

"Will you take your own ship?" asked their father.

"We're still working out the details, but yes."

Ally caught the slight tick in Maher's jaw as he waited for Lord Kingfisher to speak. His reaction would be a good indicator of what Maher could expect when he revealed the other reason for this voyage.

Rochelle took the opportunity to take Pasha and Ally's free hands in hers. "I don't presume to know what Gaius' opinion will be. But, though I would rather have you both safely here, I understand the urgency of why you must go. Just promise me you will take care of one another."

Pasha squeezed Ally's fingers tight. "We will, thank you."

Releasing Pasha, Ally hugged her mother again. She knew that couldn't have been easy, not after Rochelle's belief that she'd lost Ally last year. "Yes, thank you, Mama."

Finally, Gaius braced a hand on Luthais' shoulder. "Well, if this journey must take place, you are the only captain I'd trust to escort them." His green eyes narrowed. "But no jumping ship at the last moment."

"Again," Gai coughed.

Ally giggled and the tension broke. "You see, Gai? Now you really should tell me what you brought me from your travels. It will be some weeks before I can start working my way up to the manor."

With a put-upon sigh, "Fine, if you really must know,"

"I must."

Pasha snickered beside her.

"Among a few other things, I've found a bolt of Saprean silk in your favorite shade of blue," he gestured to her skirt.

"Oh!" Ally gripped Pasha's arm in her excitement and the mermaid smiled. "An entire bolt? That's too much!"

Maher cleared his throat, "Sorry to interrupt, Al, but, speaking of Saprea, your lordship..."

LUTHAIS

CHAPTER FORTY-SIX

"I still can't believe you chose that moment to tell them about the Saprean coins and your part in all of this."

"I thought it went quite well."

Luthais shook his head, shifting uncomfortably in the suit jacket Maher'd insisted he wear for their excursion into the Lantern. Something about blending in with the other patrons milling about the district. Just 'two gents out for the evening.' Luthais grudgingly changed into the forest green suit, but flatly refused to put on the matching waistcoat.

Maher, of course, had no such qualms. Sitting across from him in a hired carriage, the other man looked every inch the dandy in a suit of fine mustard yellow with rust-colored tulips embroidered along the waistcoat. No doubt, a gift from Ally. Maher was the picture of ease, one long leg crossed over the other, watching the city pass by through the window.

Meanwhile, Luthais felt constricted, like a bull in a too-small pen. The carriage bounced, and he swore as the jacket pulled across his shoulders.

"You know, you can have clothes tailored to fit as well as your own skin," Maher smirked.

"This *was* tailored."

"How long ago?"

"What does that matter?"

"How long?"

"Five years," he grunted.

"Therein lies your problem. You should have your entire wardrobe altered as needed each year."

"Gods, that sounds like a nightmare."

"Well, you're obviously bigger than you were five years ago."

Luthais raised a brow, "Bigger?"

"Through the shoulders, at least," Maher shrugged. "It's your choice if you would rather be uncomfortable than stand an hour for the tailor."

"It's never just an hour," Luthais muttered.

Maher snorted, "By the gods, or let someone else take your measurements once in a while."

"Are you offering to take the job?"

Chestnut eyes widened a fraction as one corner of Maher's mouth lifted. "Are you asking?"

Their knees brushed in the cramped space as Maher uncrossed his legs. Luthais suddenly felt the night could hinge on what he said next. He wanted to lean forward, to put himself into Maher's space and see if he was receptive. But the damned jacket kept him back against the seat.

Just as he was considering ripping the offensive garment off, Maher broke eye contact and glanced out the window.

"Driver," he knocked twice on the carriage ceiling, "we'll stop at this corner."

"Why here?" Luthais clambered after him, leaving behind the intimacy of the carriage for the open street.

"The outer streets will soon be too narrow for a coach to pass through. Best to continue on foot from here and blend into the flow of people." Maher paid the driver and started walking. He looked over his shoulder at Luthais. "Are you coming?"

The closer they got to the boundary of the Lantern district, the more crowded the streets became. During the summer, businesses from the market to the wharf would stay open late on the night of the full moon, taking advantage of the light and the balmy weather. Even the northern district participated, in their own way. Luthais was unsure at first, worried too many people would recognize him, but Maher felt it was a perfect opportunity to move through the Lantern without drawing much attention.

They soon crossed into the pleasure district, with its brightly colored lamps to indicate the offerings of each establishment. The central square teemed with activity while a band played a jaunty tune near the fountain. As they passed the first brownstone on the row, Maher's hands slid into his pockets. His posture relaxed, and his pace slowed. The Magpie was here again.

Despite Maher's wish to appear as nothing more than two patrons out for a night of fun, it was obvious just how attuned he was with this world. Luthais quickly lost count of the number of people who greeted him on the street. Lantern workers and patrons alike tried to chat or lure them into certain establishments.

They were passing an orange lantern establishment when a young man perched on the fence snagged Maher's sleeve, and Luthais' fists clenched. The knot of apprehension that had settled in his gut when they first arrived turned leaden.

"Well, if it isn't Maher Villaon," rouge was dusted across the tops of the man's tawny cheeks, and his white silk shirt was undone nearly to his navel. "We haven't seen you around here since the reopening. Archie's been wondering when you'll visit again."

Luthais finally noticed the name of the establishment, the Whistle and Bells. A displeased growl rose in his throat before he could stop it.

Maher deftly escaped his grasp. "When the interests I'm handling on behalf of the Birde Isles are settled, rest assured, I'll be visiting."

"If you say so," he sighed, then noticed Luthais standing just behind Maher, eyes raking over him. "Or, perhaps you'll be busy."

Maher waved him off and they continued down the row until they reached the Bear's Den. Bypassing the massive bear's head knocker on the door, Maher turned the knob and let them into the club.

Getting off the street did little to improve Luthais' increasingly sour mood. He'd known about Maher's status in the city, but he'd always assumed it was exaggerated, much like his own. Luthais had never *literally* thrown a captain off their own ship for abuse towards a crew, but that was the rumor. That kind of story about the Pike and His Temper was useful, it helped him in his work. He'd thought Maher's reputation in the Lantern served the same purpose, yet another layer to his role as the Magpie of Kingsport. Now, though, it appeared there was some truth to the rumors, and it made Luthais uncomfortable in a way he couldn't describe.

They'd no sooner crossed the threshold when yet another voice called out to them. "It's about time, Maher."

"Patience, my friend," Maher grinned. "Luthais, this is Pimm. They're door guard of the Bear's Den and an all-around brigand. Pimm, may I present Luthais Kingfisher."

Gray eyes rolled before the slender guard stood from a chair pushed against the entryway wall. They straightened a dark brown flat cap and extended a hand. "Pleasure to meet you, my lord."

"Luthais, please," he shook their hand. Luthais had never seen a guard, of any kind, so slight before. Pimm must've been very good at their job to hold the position at an establishment like this.

Maher observed the bustling lounge. "Is she upstairs?"

She? Luthais' head tilted. That was the first hint he'd gotten for the identity of this so-called friend they were there to meet.

Pimm smirked. "Not anymore. Mama Bear's put her to work."

"Of course she did."

Just then, a young lad with blonde curls and bright blue eyes emerged from the crowd. "Evening Mister Villaon, Sir," he greeted them both before turning to Pimm. "Barkeep says we're full up for now and not to let anyone else inside until the crowd thins."

Pimm nodded. "I thought as much. We should also go through and check any borrowed tokens again. There've been more than usual as of late."

"Won't that upset some people?"

"If it does, they can take it up with Mama Bear. Aye, Kit?"

The lad nodded, wished Maher and Luthais a pleasant evening, and was gone.

"Shall we wait here?" Maher asked. "I doubt we'll find an open seat."

"Mama Bear will take care of it. She knows you're here."

"How..." Luthais started, but Maher gave him a pointed look.

"Best not to ask."

At a loss for how to respond to that, Luthais turned his attention back to the Den's patrons. Some reclined on coaches or cushioned chairs, others drank around tables or leaned against the bar. Every so often, a woman would lead someone up the left staircase, while another woman would escort a different patron down the right staircase.

This was his first time inside the Bear's Den, or any Lantern establishment for that matter. Though he'd heard plenty of stories from other sailors and, occasionally, his own brothers. He'd never spent much time in the district until the need arose last year for a secluded meeting place. Disguising the series of rotating locations as a private, unknown Lantern establishment seemed like the perfect answer at the time. Luthais was by no means a blushing youth, this simply wasn't his preferred method of finding partners.

"My Magpie!" The sea of customers parted and a voluptuous woman in wide, carmine skirts approached them. "So sorry to keep you waiting." She took Maher's face in both hands and pressed her mouth to his.

Luthais had barely taken a step forward when she released him. Completely unfazed, Maher introduced them.

"You're very welcome to the Bear's Den, Lord Luthais." Mama Bear bobbed a perfunctory curtsy.

Luthais nodded curtly, hating the way she slipped her arm through Maher's as she led them into the lounge. He turned back to thank Pimm and found the door guard standing much closer than before. When had they moved?

Saying nothing, Pimm gestured for Luthais to follow Maher and returned to their chair.

"I've reserved a table for you, gentlemen." Mama Bear escorted them to a small table tucked into a back corner of the lounge on a low platform.

Heads turned as they passed. The unmistakable looks of curiosity and envy made the hair on the back of Luthais' neck stand up. He caught the eye of a patron who'd been particularly interested in Maher and scowled. The patron flushed and spun back around in their seat.

Mama Bear left them at the table, but not before giving Maher another, longer kiss. Sitting with his back to the wall, Maher waited until she was out of sight before using a handkerchief to check his lips for any trace of crimson.

Glancing up, he must have caught something off in Luthais' expression. "What? Did I miss a spot?"

"Maher," Luthais felt a sharp tug in his chest. The often-ignored voice in the back of his mind urged him to keep his mouth shut, but he had to know. "Have you been intimate with her?"

Maher cleared his throat, color rising on his cheekbones. "I have, but it's been a long time since then."

"Why is that?"

He blinked, as if the answer were obvious. "It wouldn't have been right to continue that sort of thing after establishing a business relationship. Besides, I'm not just running around here on my own trading secrets anymore. I have an official role within the Birde Isles and I'm not going to put her in a compromising position with the other Lantern owners."

"And the others?"

"What others?"

"The dozen other folk we passed on the way here who seem to know you far better than anyone else, except my sister."

Maher shook his head, tucking the handkerchief away. "With the exception of my friends here at the Den, no one in the Lantern really knows me at all."

They were interrupted when Mama Bear returned with another woman in tow. She was younger, around Maher's age if Luthais was any judge, with a strong jaw and black hair shorn close to her skull.

They assessed each other as Mama Bear bent to murmur something to Maher. The *friend* they'd come to meet hooked her thumbs into a wide leather belt and he clocked the revolver sitting towards the back of her hip.

Mama Bear patted Maher's shoulder. "Well, I'll leave you to it. No one should bother you here, but let me know if there's anything you need."

Maher thanked the proprietor, then gestured for his friend to sit. "Join us, please. Marielle of The Riddles, Luthais Kingfisher."

Surely he's getting tired of introducing me all over the damned Den. Luthais thought, not missing the wary look she was giving him from across the table.

"Luthais has agreed to ferry us to The Riddles."

Marielle's gaze shifted rapidly, flitting over the crowded club before resettling on them. *What was she looking for?*

"I'm pleased to hear it. How soon could we be ready to leave?"

"Well," Maher looked to Luthais, "that's down to the captain, here, really. He knows his ship's needs better than I do."

Now she addressed Luthais directly. "How much time do you need?"

"For a voyage of this magnitude? A few weeks, give or take."

"*Weeks*?" she huffed.

Luthais crossed his arms over the table. "When were you wanting to leave, then?"

She matched his posture dark eyes narrowing. "As soon as possible, *Captain*."

Luthais bristled, his back molars ground together. Next to him, Maher briefly rested his forehead in his hands before addressing them both. "Why don't I secure a round of drinks?" He pushed up from the table, adding under his breath, "Maybe it will help everyone relax a bit."

Luthais watched Maher weave his way towards the bar. It was the first time he'd observed their surroundings since their arrival. The crowd had thinned somewhat. Across the lounge, the lad Kit was going from table to table, checking patron tokens.

Turning back to Marielle, his voice hardened. "Why are you here?"

BEAR'S DEN

PIMM

CHAPTER FORTY-SEVEN

That is not going well. Pimm thought to themself as Maher escaped from Mama Bear's personal table and made a beeline for the bar. Though they'd never met Luthais Kingfisher before, the Pike's reputation most definitely preceded him. Even from across the room, they could see Marielle's hackles raise as soon as introductions were made.

Pimm had to admit, they were surprised as well. Not so much that Maher had turned to one of the Kingfishers for help, they were all practically raised together, after all. Rather, it amazed them Lord Luthais would be willing to offer up another ship after the last one was sunk not that long ago.

They turned their attention to Kit, making his round to check tokens and take new orders for drinks. A few patrons had grumbled about showing the stamped metal discs again, but so far it was nothing the lad couldn't handle. Though a handful of patrons had departed since Maher's arrival, Pimm would wait until Barkeep gave the signal to allow more inside. They'd already turned away a group of four, offering suggestions of other establishments that might have more room that night. The other members of the Lantern owners' guild always appreciated that.

Pimm was quite glad for the quiet moment by the door to look over the latest entries in their notebook. The assistance from Nitya's daughter, and her friends among Kingsport's original street crews, was approved by the owners' vote. Though Pimm still felt some trepidation about the plan, they had to acknowledge the addition made the search for Ezmira's lair much easier. Already they'd scoured the market district again and were reporting to Pimm regularly.

Barkeep's distinct, braying laugh made half the heads in the room turn. When Pimm looked up, he was slapping Maher on the back hard enough to rock him on his feet.

Must've been a good story, they chuckled softly. *I'll have to ask about that one.*

Doing a quick check of the floor before returning to their notes, Pimm observed that Marielle and Luthais hadn't reacted at all. It was like a cloud of unease hung over the lone table. Pimm searched for Kit once more. It took a moment, but they finally spied him by a table against the wall near the hearth. They remembered when the man sitting there arrived, about an hour ago. He'd visited the Den three times now on a borrowed token, but never ventured upstairs.

Pimm'd initially chalked it up to nervousness, but now the man was angrily shaking his head as Kit requested the token.

Slowly, Pimm stowed the notebook and slid from their chair. They kept one hand poised, ready to release a knife from its sheath if required. Kit frowned, placing his tray on the table and said something else to the man. Another patron a few tables down paused, ale suspended in mid-air, and watched.

That does it. Something's not right here. Pimm made it halfway across the room before the man surged up, pushed Kit roughly in the chest, and flipped the table.

CHAPTER FORTY-EIGHT

"**Y**ou'll have to be more specific." Marielle drawled. "Is *here* in this chair? This club? The district? The city? On this particular island? Or is it a more philosophical question? Why am I *here* as in, what's my purpose in the world?"

"You know very well what I mean," Luthais growled.

"Do I?"

"I know why Maher needs to reach The Riddles..."

"Thanks to information *I* found."

"But why is he adding the risk of bringing you? What do you hope to gain, I ask myself."

Marielle smiled tightly, nearly sneering, and he caught a flash of gold in her mouth. It was rare to come across sailors from The Riddles, but those he'd had the opportunity to meet sported several gold-capped teeth as well.

"Perhaps I'm looking forward to a long overdue family reunion," she said sweetly. "You know what that's like, don't you?"

"What I know," Luthais glanced pointedly towards the bar, "is that you're stalling."

"Is that so?"

"You won't answer any questions until Maher returns."

"Or your questions are too dull to answer."

An abrupt crash broke through the low buzz of conversation around them. Marielle jumped to her feet, hand already on the grip of her pistol. Luthais twisted in his chair, leaping up when he saw Kit sprawled on the floor and one of the lounge tables toppled onto its side.

"Now look what you've done!" Another man grabbed the one who'd upended the table and look a swing at him. Someone screamed, and the Den descended into madness.

The single fight that started between the two men spread like a plague, with more infections popping up around the room. Luthais backed up to the wall, ducking a flying tankard of ale. More screams echoed through the lounge as the patrons not engaged in the scuffle tried to escape. But two of the brawlers had rolled square into the entryway.

And where was Maher?

"Something's wrong!" Marielle shouted over the din.

"What gave you that idea?" he barked back.

"You don't understand! Bear's Den patrons know not to start fights here, they'll lose their tokens and be banned."

Pimm pushed through the throng of bodies, dragging a dazed Kit behind them. They shoved the lad through the door that must've led to the kitchen and slammed it shut. Dodging a fallen chair, they slid to a stop by Marielle.

"We have to break this up before someone gets killed!" A knife suddenly dropped into Pimm's hand.

"The pack by the door are preventing others from leaving," Marielle added, drawing her pistol.

"It's too close to fire that in here," Luthais warned.

"You haven't seen her shoot." said Pimm, eyes trained on the chaos.

"Where's Maher?" Marielle beat Luthais to the question racing through his mind.

"Don't worry, he's with –"

A bellow reverberated across the room as the barkeep leapt from behind the bar, brandishing a club. Behind him, Maher hopped onto the bar itself and searched until he found Pimm. They exchanged a quick flurry of hand gestures Luthais didn't recognize and Pimm turned back to them.

"Right. Maher will stay with Barkeep and guide people to safety. We need to clear the front door and kick these bastards out."

"Understood." Marielle checked the rotating chamber of the revolver and snapped it back into place. "Do you know who's behind this?"

Pimm pointed their knife at an impossibly large man who'd just thrown an entire sofa across the room. "See that one? He wasn't here before. I think someone else let him in after the fight started. He's with Ezmira."

"Fuck," she hissed.

Luthais would have to learn who this Ezmira was another time, Pimm and Marielle were already moving into the crowd.

# MARIELLE

CHAPTER FORTY-NINE

Any frightened employees or patrons they found were sent towards Maher. While the barkeep cleared a path with his sheer size and reach with that wooden club, Maher was hiding as many people as possible in the small room behind the bar.

More than a few had recovered themselves and, rather than retreating, had joined into the fray. Marielle was beginning to have trouble distinguishing between the real patrons and the ones planted to start this row. She kept her pistol by her shoulder, barrel pointed towards the ceiling. Accidentally shooting one of the Den's members would not improve her standing with either Mama Bear or the Madam.

One of the women in Mama Bear's employ was latched onto a brawler's back, gouging his face with her fingernails. Streaks of blood ran into his eyes and he spun wildly, trying to throw her off. If he backed up much further, he was going to throw them both into the fireplace. Wrapping one arm around the woman's waist, Marielle yanked her free. She cracked the man on the back of the skull with her pistol and he crumpled to the floor.

When a small fist nearly collided with Marielle's jaw, she shouted, "It's alright, I've got you!"

The moment the thrashing woman recognized the gunfighter, she went slack in Marielle's arms and burst into tears.

CHAPTER FIFTY

Luthais finally reached the fight blocking the front door. Grabbing one man by the back of his collar, Luthais hauled him out of the pile of bodies. His arms hung limp by his sides and his eyes were nearly swollen shut. Luthais pushed him towards the barkeep, who'd already collected a few incapacitated fighters in one corner.

Upon closer inspection, several of those he'd encountered had been thoroughly trounced, but showed little to no sign of defending themselves. They weren't trying to escape and they weren't fighting back. They were letting themselves be beaten. He'd had his share of breaking up altercations between sailors, this was not the same.

Marielle was right. This isn't a real brawl! Luthais' head snapped around as a sharp, earthy scent tickled his nose. A scent that could spell disaster aboard a ship.

He spun in place, searching for the source. Only then did he notice the faint haze hanging over the room. Smoke. But it wasn't from the hearth or any of the candles, those that'd been knocked over were snuffed out. The important thing was to keep calm and find the source before anyone else noticed.

"FIRE!" someone behind him shouted. "There's a fire!"

Fresh screams ripped through the air and the crowd surged. Swinging around, Luthais came face-to-grinning-face with the man Pimm had identified. The one who worked for Ezmira, whoever she was.

"Fire!" he called out again, using his bulk to block the closest way out.

Luthais charged, ducking low when he threw a punch and catching him around the waist. He might've been bigger, but over twenty years of hauling rope lines and wrestling sails had made Luthais stronger. Planting his feet, Luthais twisted his hip and pulled the man off balance. He swung around with all his might, aiming them away from the entrance. The man landed on his back, wheezing as the air was forced from his lungs.

Throwing open the front door, Luthais herded people out until the barkeep came to assist. Leaving him in charge, Luthais ran to where Maher was directing those who'd been hidden behind the bar.

"Maher!" Luthais grabbed his arm. "We have to get out of here."

"Not until they're all safe," Maher pulled away and helped the last terrified patron from the barkeep's room. He coughed as the smoke began to thicken near the ceiling. "Do we know where the fire started?"

Luthais shook his head. "I don't think it's down here, unless it's back in the kitchen."

"Wherever it is, we have to get everyone outside."

Luthais followed Maher back into the lounge. They stopped short as a wave of people streamed down both sets of stairs. "Fire upstairs!" an employee screamed as she helped another towards the door. Just as Luthais was determining how furious Maher would be if he tossed him over one shoulder and ran to safety, the kitchen door was thrown open. Pimm rushed through, cap askew and a tea towel clutched in one hand.

"Pimm!" Maher caught them by their jacket. "Where is everyone?"

"Marielle is helping folk go through the back way into the alley. I've sent Gertie and Kit for the fire brigade," they tied the towel over their mouth and nose, "but I don't think they'll make it in time."

"Why..." Maher trailed off, once again understanding something Luthais couldn't catch.

"Wool in the walls. Listen, I'm going to find Mama Bear, she's got to be upstairs. Get as many people outside as you can and then get the fuck out."

"Don't!" Maher started, but Pimm was already dashing up the stairs. In the space of one breath, Maher went after them.

"Maher!" Luthais lurched forward, reaching out to stop him.

There was a swift pain to the back of Luthais' head and a muffled ringing in his ears. Then, everything went dark.

BEAR'S DEN

PIMM

CHAPTER FIFTY-ONE

Pimm's lungs were already burning as they raced up the stairs. They knew Mama Bear had gone up after delivering Marielle, but hadn't seen her come back down.

Please, please, please. Pimm chanted to themself, beseeching every god they'd never believed in to keep her unharmed.

Ezmira had to be behind the chaos downstairs, they were sure of it. She'd made good on her promise to the Madam after all, sending her gonys to massacre the Den. Destroy everything Mama Bear had built. Ezmira's pinched, pale face flashed through their mind and Pimm felt a rage unlike any they'd experienced before settle deep into their gut.

Pimm reached the second floor. A gray haze hung in the air. All the bedroom doors appeared to be open.

"Hello!" Pimm coughed. "Anyone there?"

No answer. The fire didn't appear to have reached this level yet, but it was only a matter of time. Pushing past the pain in their chest, Pimm made for the third floor.

Pimm ran into a few more employees and patrons on the third-floor landing, trying to find a way down. The smoke on this level was even worse. Thick and black as it seeped into every crack and crevice.

It was noticeably warmer on this floor, but still no sign of flames. The fire had to be contained somehow on the fourth floor, but the longer Pimm delayed, the closer it would get.

Moving down the hallway, Pimm guided everyone they encountered towards the stairs. Finally they reached Mama Bear's room. The door was ajar. Pimm pushed inside.

"Mama Bear? Are you here?"

"Pimm?" Her hoarse voice floated from the other side of the bed. Mama Bear was on her knees, prying a floorboard loose. A thin silk scarf was tied over her face. Bloodshot eyes darted frantically and tears streamed down her cheeks as she twisted the board free. "What are you doing? Get yourself outside!"

"What are *you* doing?" They took her arm. "The fire is spreading, nothing can be so important!"

"No, I have to find it!" she pulled away and grabbed the next board. "If you're going to stay, then help me."

Heat from the floor above was radiating through the ceiling, quickly turning the room into an oven.

"Get back," Pimm knelt beside her. Pulling a short, wide knife from their boot, Pimm drove the blade into the seam between the boards.

CHAPTER FIFTY-TWO

Maher was almost at the stairs when Luthais called his name. There was a sharp grunt and the distinct thud of a body hitting the wooden floorboards. Spinning around, Maher saw one of the men who started the fight standing over an unconscious Luthais, a leatherbound blackjack in hand.

And he knew exactly which despicable wretch favored blackjacks. Fucking Ezmira.

"Luthais!" Maher changed course, darting back across the lounge. Pimm knew the building inside and out, they'd be alright until Maher could join them.

Luthais' assailant raised the weapon again. Drawing his pistol, Maher stopped and fired, clipping him in the shoulder. The blackjack clattered to the floor. Spewing a string of curses, the man slapped his other hand over the bleeding wound and stumbled towards the front door. Perhaps Barkeep would stop him, but Maher didn't have time to worry about that.

Kneeling on the floor, Maher checked Luthais over. A sizable goose egg was already forming on his head, but wasn't bleeding, thank the gods. Smoke continued to fill the room. Those who hadn't made it outside yet were panicking, trying to find their way to the door. Maher pulled out his handkerchief, hoping to get it secured around Luthais' nose and mouth.

Shots rang out. Maher's head swiveled until he found Marielle backed into a corner, fending off a group of her own attackers. One lay on the floor, felled by a bullet through the chest. Another tried to slow the blood leaking from her side. Three more kept Marielle boxed in, it appeared she was out of bullets.

"Fuck!" Fingers fumbling, he quickly covered Luthais' face with the cloth. Taking up his pistol and the discarded blackjack, Maher ran to Marielle's aid.

As he reached them, the leader grumbled, "Come on now, Ez said to get 'er in one piece. The boss is waiting."

"You'll have to disappoint her then," Maher said as he bashed the leader over the head with the blackjack. With a shriek, the other woman with them launched herself at Maher and his pistol flew from his hand. Tumbling backwards, he brought the blackjack up to block her and pain raked across his forearm.

"Damnit!" Maher shoved her off and caught a flash of metal against her hand. She was wearing a fucking cat's claw. An iron gauntlet with four curved blades mounted across the top.

Marielle was wrestling with the last one, Maher's dropped pistol clutched between them. Scrambling to his feet, Maher shoved the long blackjack in front of his neck and jerked hard. Marielle wrenched the gun free as he gasped and clawed at the weapon pressing down on his windpipe. Maher tightened his grip and threw his weight back against the wall. Sweat dripped down Maher's face and stung his eyes, but he held on until the attacker went slack.

Maher sagged against the wall, sucked in a breath, and hacked when all he pulled in was smoke. He took a step towards Marielle, then stopped when she raised his pistol.

"What –" Maher's heart stuttered when Marielle pulled the trigger. Behind him, the woman who'd tackled him lay on the floor. With the hand wearing the cat's claw frozen above her head and a bullet between her eyes.

"Thanks," Maher rasped.

"Your gun needs oiling," she said as she handed the pistol back.

"Right, right." Shaking himself once, Maher searched for Luthais. He was still laying where Maher'd left him. "Help me get him outside."

Together, Maher and Marielle hooked Luthais beneath the arms and dragged him through the kitchen and into the backstreet.

"Why is he so damned heavy?" Marielle growled through her teeth.

"If I find out, I'll let you know," he panted. The heels of Luthais' boots skidded over the cobblestones, his head lolled from side to side. With each passing minute, Maher grew more concerned with just how hard that bastard hit Luthais.

They passed Olga and the Den's cook, knocking on the back doors of the other establishments on the row, calling out the alarm. High above, glass popped and exploded out from the fourth-floor windows. They hauled Luthais farther down the street and propped him up against a building across the way. He couldn't stay there for long, but it would have to do for now.

Maher handed Marielle his pistol. "Stay with him, please. I'm going back in."

Another pane shattered and flames licked around the edges of the window. Marielle shook her head, even as she took the offered pistol. "Don't, Maher. The fire is only going to spread faster now that more air is feeding it."

"I can't just stand out here." Quickly he checked Luthais' head again and breathed a sigh of relief to find the other man was still breathing steadily. "If Pimm and Mama Bear come out the back before I return, fire two shots into the air."

"You might not hear them."

"I know." Taking his handkerchief back, Maher tied it over his own face. Before she could argue with him again, and before he could give in to his desire to stay with Luthais, Maher dashed back inside.

In the few minutes they'd been outside, visibility on the ground floor had grown even worse. He wrenched open the door to the pantry to find two Den employees cowering inside. Taking them each by the hand, Maher directed the women through the kitchen, to the back door. As soon as they were safely delivered into the cook's hands, he ran back to the pantry. Finding the right panel, Maher pushed until he heard a faint click and the entire back wall gave way. The hidden staircase, a holdover from when the Lantern was first established, was seldom used now. But it was empty and blessedly smoke free. The door swung shut, leaving Maher in near-total darkness. Taking advantage of the cleaner air, Maher took a few deep breaths before starting the climb.

BEAR'S DEN

PIMM

CHAPTER FIFTY-THREE

"I don't understand, it has to be here!"

Five floorboards and several tense minutes of searching later, they'd uncovered a small pirate's hoard of valuables, even a few documents and letters.

But apparently, not what Mama Bear wanted.

"There's no more time, ma'am," Pimm rasped. "We have to leave, now."

"I just don't understand..." Mama Bear swayed on her feet, hands clasped tightly against her chest. Sweat had drenched through her satin bodice.

"Ma'am, please," Pimm was at their wit's end. Somewhere above them, glass shattered and the building seemed to moan. Pimm grasped her arm, ready to drag her downstairs if need be.

"Pimm!"

Was that...

"Maher?" Pimm wheezed, their voice on the verge of giving out. "We're here!"

Through the thickening smoke, Maher appeared. He slid to a stop. "What are you still doing here?"

"I can't convince her to leave!"

"We can't find it!" she cried.

Maher took Mama Bear's masked face in both hands. "Listen, you have to leave it."

"But…"

"Everything here can be replaced, except for you. We're leaving. No arguments."

When she nodded weakly, Maher steered her towards the balcony. "Good. Can you climb down?"

Mama Bear's eyes cleared a bit as she looked over the edge. "Yes, I can."

"Why don't we just go back the way you came?" Pimm followed.

"I took the hidden stairs, but the door on this floor is halfway down the hall, the fire's too close now." From the balcony, Maher whistled to grab the attention of the people gathered below. He took Mama Bear's hand, "Time to go, dear."

Pimm joined them and they helped her climb over the railing.

"Just keep going until you touch the ground," Maher instructed. "Don't stop, don't look up or down. Just keep moving."

Mama Bear gripped the vined trellis tightly with both hands. "Aren't you coming?"

"We'll be right behind you," Pimm promised.

Lips pressed into a determined line, Mama Bear nodded once and started down the trellis.

"Your turn, Pimm."

Their bloodshot eyes narrowed. "What are you up to? And don't hedge, because we're literally out of time."

"When I came out of the pantry stairs, I heard shouting down the hall. I'm going back for them."

"Right." Pimm strode back into the bedroom.

"Pimm! Get back here!"

Not bothering to answer, Pimm grabbed two silk scarves from the vanity and soaked them in the washbasin. They tossed one to Maher and tied the other around the tea towel on the bottom half of their face. The rose-scented water barely broke through the acrid smell of smoke. For once, Maher didn't argue, silently tying the soaked scarf over the handkerchief already covering his face.

Pimm nodded. "Not much, but better than nothing."

CHAPTER FIFTY-FOUR

Smoke burned Maher's eyes and seared his lungs, making him cough more and more between breaths. Somewhere outside, he thought he heard the faint bells of the fire brigade.

About time.

Crouching low beneath the ribbon of smoke rapidly filling the hallway, Pimm and Maher stayed close together. More than one door was pushed open to reveal the occupants already dead from inhaling the smoke. One woman looked as if she were merely taking a nap in her bed. Had she been sleeping when the fire started?

Maher couldn't be sure where the shouts he'd heard before had come from. Were they on this floor or the one below?

What if we're too late?

They hadn't gone far when a scream came from one of the rooms at the far end. Pimm pointed at the door they thought it was and both tried to move faster. There was a loud, drawn-out groan and the building shuddered. Flames licked down the staircase leading to the main floor. Instantly, the framework began to warp, charred hunks of wood and carpet broke away.

Maher tried to move forward again, but the floor beneath them buckled, then snapped. A gaping hole yawned open down the middle of the hallway, destroying their path to the other rooms or to the door to the back pantry stairs. Pimm grabbed Maher's hand and they bolted back down the hall. Stumbling into Mama Bear's room, Maher slammed the door shut. As if a hunk of wood would do much to stop the fire. His eyes were watering so badly now that he could hardly see, and the precious water Pimm had soaked into the scarf had all but evaporated.

The world jerked suddenly when Pimm grabbed Maher by the shoulders and yanked him backwards. A beam from the ceiling came crashing down right where he'd been standing, bringing a cascade of fire down with it. They threw themselves onto the balcony, each grabbing one of the glass-paned doors and slamming them shut.

Maher practically tossed Pimm over the rail and followed swiftly after them. Half-climbing and half-falling down the trellis, Maher forgot his own advice and looked up. The upper floors of the Den were engulfed in flames. An unbearable heat hit his face and Maher forced himself to focus on the trembling vines in front of him. Gradually, he began to hear the shouts and encouragement from the people below.

As they neared the ground, the whole building tilted, giving a final death rattle. Maher locked eyes with Pimm when their makeshift ladder started to splinter, and they let themselves fall the rest of the way.

ALLY

Chapter Fifty-five

Pasha and Ally lay together on the narrow strip of beach inside the hatching grounds. Their torsos rested on the sand, tails still dipped into the lagoon. Pasha's arms were folded beneath her head, her eyes closed as she lazily tossed her fluke in the water.

Ally was pleased to see her so at ease. The last few weeks hadn't been easy for either of them, but Ally could practically feel the anxiety rolling off Pasha. Perhaps she was, in a way.

Before they met Maher again to discuss the plan for the voyage to The Riddles, Ally suggested they spend some time to themselves. That morning they swam out into the open ocean to visit with the whales and call on Euphonia. The sea monster, with her saber-like teeth and opaque eyes, had been eager to see them both, but especially Ally. Their unexpected friendship had become quite dear to Ally, she strongly suspected Euphonia was the last of her kind and perhaps a little lonely. Rather than returning to the place out at sea where they'd met, Euphonia had made a new home a mere day's swim from the Birde Isles.

Well, a day's swim for Euphonia. It would've taken the mermaids a bit longer if the sea monster hadn't met them halfway.

With Euphonia's aid secured, they bid her goodbye and took their time swimming back home. Pasha even attempted to give Ally her first hunting lesson, with middling results. Perhaps, if Ally'd been a hunter as a human, it would've come a little easier to her. But as it was, she apparently lacked any instinct for when to strike.

In the end, Pasha caught a meal for both of them. They ate their fill and left the rest for the scavengers waiting just out of sight for them to leave. It still surprised Ally that many sea creatures saw her as a predator. One just as fearsome as Euphonia, if not a good deal smaller.

Now they relaxed in the hatching grounds, the only place where they could nap on dry sand without the chance of being discovered by any humans. It was the first time they'd been here since Pasha drew out the memories of the warrior who once owned her spear. Late afternoon sunlight filtered through the hidden opening in the cave ceiling, reflecting off the corals that lined the edge of the lagoon. They'd talked a bit more about everything they'd learned from the spear. Pasha'd admitted to feeling foolish, knowing absolutely nothing about the war between the merfolk and the sirens.

"Why did I not ask more questions?"

"You had no reason to." Ally pointed out. "It's not as if they left any visible records of what happened. How could you ask about something you'd never once heard spoken?"

"Still," Pasha flopped back onto the sand. "there were plenty of other things I did hear that I should've questioned."

Laying down next to her, Ally sighed. "Sometimes, it's easier to go along and accept what you're told. How many years was I deliberately kept in the dark about the actions of my great-grandfather?"

"Twenty-two."

"That question was rhetorical, Pasha." Ally used her longer fluke to splash her lover. "What I meant was, for a long time I didn't question something that felt wrong because I was too afraid."

"I suppose I have to take some credit for you finally confronting your parents." Pasha smirked.

Ally splashed her again. "I suppose you could."

In the cozy warmth of the cave, Ally dozed off shortly after Pasha. Such a simple thing, but Ally wouldn't take it for granted. It would be many weeks before they could do something like this again.

The sun set and Ally slowly woke as the corals gradually glowed brighter. Pasha still slept, her beautiful face untroubled and lips slightly parted. Turning on one side, Ally propped her head in her hand and watched the subtle movement beneath Pasha's eyelids. She was dreaming. A thin line creased Pasha's brow and Ally smoothed it away, fingertips lingering for a moment on skin too soft to be real.

Pasha's eyes fluttered open and she turned her face into Ally's retreating palm.

"Hello," she whispered. "Did you sleep well?"

"Hmm, yes." Pasha mumbled. "Did you?"

Ally nodded, "I did. You were dreaming for a moment. Can I ask what it was about?"

Pasha blinked, focused on the cave surrounding them, the tip of her tongue resting on one sharp tooth. "I was here, alone, and I was tapping into the spear's past again."

"Did you see something different?"

"No, I wasn't doing it to watch the memories again. I... I think I wanted to *feel* it all again. You know," Pasha shifted her arms from beneath her head and stretched them towards the ceiling. "tapping into that energy reminded me of how I felt after we destroyed the turbine on Dare's ship."

Ally held her tongue, not wanting to interrupt the flow of Pasha's thoughts. They never really talked about that time on the *Maiden's Revenge,* both preferring to move on.

Pasha's hands dropped to her stomach. "The energy didn't feel *wrong* though, not like last time, but the sheer power of it was there. This feeling that, if I could only channel it, I could do anything."

"Anything?"

"Mm-hmm, anything."

"That must be quite a sensation."

"It is," Pasha's hand drifted up to caress her cheek. "I wish I could share it with you. It's incredible."

Ally's throat tightened, she'd likely never be able to access that kind of power the way Pasha could. It was beginning to feel like her old fear of water, something that was at once beyond her control but still a problem her brain told her she ought to be able to solve. Shifting closer, Ally leaned over Pasha and brushed a kiss across her brow. The hand that still cradled her face shifted beneath her hair and Pasha used that new hold to angle their lips together. Ally melted into Pasha, indulging in the softness of her skin. Loving the tingling sensation that spread across the back of her skull when Pasha's nails shifted against her scalp. Every soft word uttered between kisses sent shivers down her spine.

Lacing their fingers together, she pinned Pasha's free hand above her head, exposing one side of her face and neck for further exploration. When she reached a particularly sensitive spot beneath Pasha's ear, Ally felt the gentle but insistent nudge of Pasha's mind against hers.

As much as she wanted to give in to Pasha's unspoken request, Ally gave that spot one last nip and pulled herself away. A disappointed whine left Pasha's throat and she tried to pull Ally close again.

"Wouldn't it be blasphemous, or at least a little bit disrespectful, to do much more of that in this place?"

Pasha glanced around, genuine confusion written on her face. "Why would that be? This is where the eggs are laid."

"Are we about to lay an egg?" Ally chuckled, a little apprehensive of what the answer might be.

"Of course not," Pasha rolled her eyes. "Neither of us is old enough, nor strong enough, to do that anyway."

"Ah, good to know." Ally sighed. "I'm open to a conversation about children one day, just not to the idea of accidental egg laying."

"There are no accidental offspring among mermaids. It's a very deliberate decision."

"That's fascinating, what happens if –"

"Ally," Pasha hooked a finger beneath her chin, redirecting her from a litany of new questions. "My point was, no it's not disrespectful if we are intimate here. The cave might even benefit from the energy created."

"Is that right?" Ally grinned, squeezing the hand she still held down into the sand. "In that case," Pressing against Pasha, Ally whispered into her ear. "I wonder if you'll do something for me?"

"What's that?" Pasha gasped when Ally nibbled on the point of her ear, fins thrashing in the shallow water.

"Would you leave your tail for me?"

Some of the desire cleared from her eyes. "What for?"

"I want to show you how we make love on land."

Now Pasha's eyes grew wider than Ally'd ever seen. Blinking owlishly up at her, Pasha squeaked, "Really?"

Ally sat up, giving her some space. "If you have no interest, I understand. But if you do, I'd be honored to teach you, just as you taught me how merfolk love each other."

"I don't know why, I hadn't even considered..." Pasha sat up too, hands smoothing over the scales of her tail.

"We don't have to do anything that makes you uncomfortable, Pasha, nor do we have to try this today." Ally assured her, feeling now they should've had a proper conversation about this before Ally proposed such a thing. "I only wanted you to know it's an option, should you change your mind. I'm sorry for springing this on you."

"It's not that," Pasha looked at her, eyes bright with nervous curiosity. "I wouldn't know where to begin."

"We'd begin, by leaving our tails in the water."

Cupping Ally's face with both hands, Pasha kissed her forehead, then the crooked bridge of her nose, then finally her lips. A wave of different emotions rushed at her, all tumbling over top of one another, making it impossible for Ally to catch just one. Pasha was nervous, yes, but also excited, inquisitive, aroused, elated, and...

Pasha broke the kiss, quick panting breaths puffed against Ally's skin. "Show me."

LUTHAIS

CHAPTER FIFTY-SIX

Luthais awoke to cold water splashing him in the face. Blinking several times, he took stock of his surroundings. Above, distant stars winked in and out from behind thinning clouds. Beneath, the ground was cold and something solid was digging between his shoulder blades. Water burbled somewhere behind his head.

The location finally came to him. He was lying in the Lantern square, leaned haphazardly against the base of the fountain.

Marielle was sitting on the stone edge, just above him. She was covered in grime, soot, and blood. He couldn't tell if the blood was hers or not. She stared out into the square, gaze fixed straight ahead. Luthais slowly rotated his head, groggily taking in the aftermath.

The fire brigade was packing up their wagons. Why were they so small? Only a single copper tank each, and pulled by the puniest donkeys he'd ever seen. The fire brigade unit that served the wharf was massive, hitched to a team of six horses.

Oh, right, anything large enough to require a pair of horses wouldn't fit through the narrow streets surrounding the Lantern, let alone a half dozen.

All that remained of the Bear's Den was a smoldering, charred skeleton between the neighboring brown stones. Dozens of people, those who escaped from the fire and those who came to either aid or gawk, milled around the square. Some were crying, some were wounded, and some, like Marielle, simply stared off into space

A spike of panic hit Luthais right in the chest; he didn't see Maher anywhere. He looked back at Marielle, opened his mouth to demand an explanation, but she beat him to it.

"You're really fucking heavy, you know that?"

"What?" Luthais' throat was raw, his mouth tasted like ash.

She glanced down at him. "I had to drag you all the way around from the backstreet. You'd better be able to get your own carcass out of here."

Luthais' head was splitting, he winced when the lump throbbing on the back of his skull brushed against the fountain. "What happened?" he ground out.

"Someone set the Den on fire," she waved a hand at the place where the after-hours club used to be.

"I know that. I meant who did this?"

"Couldn't tell you if I wanted to."

Did this disaster have something to do with why Marielle needed to leave the Birde Isles? A low, simmering wave of fury rose like bile in Luthais' throat. How dare she involve Maher and, clearly, put so many others in danger. "Where's Maher?"

"After we got you outside, he went back in for Pimm and Mama Bear."

Luthais surged up, his head swimming and vision going double from the sudden movement.

Marielle put a hand on his shoulder and pushed him back down. "Maher's fine. He went with Mama Bear to talk to the fire brigade. I'm supposed to watch you."

Sagging against the fountain again, he nearly vomited when the back of his head touched stone. He waited for his head to clear a bit, then slowly pushed up to sit next to her. Cupping his filthy hands in the trickling water, Luthais scrubbed his face, rinsed out his mouth, and ran a few handfuls through his hair.

By the time he finished, the square had cleared a bit and the fire brigade wagon was rolling away. Now that he could focus, Luthais tried to find the damage done beyond the Bear's Den. But the fire had only scorched the outsides of the buildings on either side. How was that possible? More to the point, why wasn't there nothing but a gaping hole where the Den used to be? A blaze that size? None of it should still be standing.

"Does this have anything to do with why you need to leave the Birde Isles?"

Marielle swallowed hard, coughed, as if the words were stuck in her throat. "It's possible."

"What does that mean?"

"I... I made a mistake."

Before he could pry further, she was on her feet. "Here they come."

Luthais looked across the square and felt the tightness in his chest ease ever so slightly. Maher was escorting Mama Bear towards them, one arm wrapped around the older woman's waist. A blonde wisp of a girl was crying on Pimm's shoulder. The scorched edges of her long apron lifted in the breeze, scattering ashes at their feet.

He stood as well, despite the desperate, nauseating need to lay back down. When Maher finally looked up and caught Luthais' eye, relief flashed across his soot-stained face.

CHAPTER FIFTY-SEVEN

Mama Bear was utterly distraught. Maher stayed with her while she spoke to the fire brigade, their hands laced tightly together, answering questions when she wasn't able. Someone from another establishment, Maher couldn't even remember who, brought out a stack of blankets to pass around. He wrapped one of the soft, knitted mantles around Mama Bear's shoulders.

Pimm reached them as they were finishing, a tearful Olga tucked beneath their arm. Nearly a dozen of Mama Bear's employees were unaccounted for, whether they were still in the smoldering remains of the building or had fled the area was still undetermined.

Barkeep's body was found just inside the entryway, pinned beneath a fallen beam. He must have still been helping others escape when the building collapsed. Maher kept himself between Mama Bear and the stretcher they used to carry the brave Swan Islander's body away. He would be taken to the temple of the sea, to be cared for by the priestesses. And Maher made sure a special note was sent to Head Priestess Esa about his sacrifice. There were special rituals reserved for those who died in service of others. If anyone deserved such honors, it was that man.

The fire brigade concluded the first round of questions, there would likely be more as the investigation was carried out. Thanking them again for their assistance, their small group moved further into the square. During the chaos, Marielle had somehow moved Luthais to the fountain in the square. How she did that by herself, Maher wasn't sure, but he was glad she'd gotten him farther from danger. Doctor Tambara, the Den's resident physician, was there treating the worst injuries. He would ask her to check Luthais before they left.

As they approached, Maher felt the distinct prickle at the back of his neck of being watched. Taking his eyes off Mama Bear, he found Luthais finally awake and on his feet. One hand was braced against the side of the fountain, but he seemed alert. Relief swept over Maher like a fresh summer wave.

Maher and Pimm coaxed Mama Bear and Olga into resting on the stone base surrounding the pool. Both women were still in tears, Mama Bear clinging to Maher's hand as he stood beside her. No one said anything for several minutes, while Mama Bear collected herself.

"Where are Kit and Gertie?" Marielle asked eventually.

"They're alright," said Pimm. "They're fetching supplies for the physicians called in by the other owners."

"Oh good," She drew in a shuddering breath, before turning to Mama Bear. "I'm so sorry, ma'am. I'm sorry for all the trouble I've caused you. For the loss of your home, your business, everything. I should never have made myself so visible..."

"The building can be replaced," Mama Bear whispered. "The furniture, the fixtures, the dishes, and bedding. It can all be replaced. It's the lives lost that we are mourning."

Olga sniffled, "What are we gonna do?"

"Everything we can," said Pimm.

Mama Bear's blue, red-rimmed eyes focused on Pimm, as if she'd just realized they were sitting next to her. "There are so many things to do. Everyone must be accounted for, friends and families should be contacted, funeral arrangements made..."

Maher placed a hand on her shoulder. "We're going to find whoever did this, and they're going to pay for every life taken."

"What happens after you catch them that did this to us?" asked Olga.

"Careful what you promise," Pimm warned. "It won't bring any of them back."

Mama Bear patted Maher's hand, "Pimm is right, darling." She wrapped an arm around Olga as the girl pressed a tear-stained face into the blanket around her shoulders.

"What about the gonys that started the fight?" Marielle's gaze cut back and forth across the square. Maher had no doubt she'd be on a knife's edge as long as they stayed out here in the open.

Pimm shook their head, suddenly looking as if they were about to keel over into sleep. "We still don't know exactly who made it out and who didn't."

"The fire chief was amazed that more lives weren't lost," Maher added.

Luthais spoke for the first time, "What kept the building standing?"

Pimm sighed, "Wool in the walls, oddly enough."

Maher caught the confused tilt of Luthais' head and elaborated, "Contrary to what Pimm and I thought at first, the wool used to insulate the rooms acted as a buffer to the fire, for a short time. According to the fire brigade, at least, the slow burning rate is what kept the flames from spreading more quickly than they did."

"That's... unexpected," Luthais' eyes screwed shut and he swayed on his feet. Maher darted around the others and caught him under the arm.

"Steady there." He helped Luthais sit back down. "How are you feeling?"

"Like an anchor that's been cut loose."

Maher looked to the gunfighter, "Did anything else happen after I went back inside?"

"Nothing of note. He came to after Mama Bear climbed down."

Luthais cracked one eye open. "I did?"

"Aye, long enough to steer you out into the square. 'Course, he kept asking where you were, Maher." Marielle coughed into her fist. "It was all I could do to keep him from running back inside."

Luthais' head snapped up, his expression shifting as a memory came hurtling back to him. "You pointed a gun at me," he grunted.

Maher raised a brow at them.

Marielle shrugged, "Like I said, it was all I could do."

It was nearly three o'clock in the morning when Maher and Luthais dragged themselves back to the manor. Well, a carriage transported them back, but Maher felt as if he'd traveled the entire distance on foot.

Pimm had agreed to hide Marielle at their building in the northern district, provided she kept completely out of sight until they could leave for The Riddles. And Maher was more than grateful; he doubted he'd've been able to sneak her into the Kingfisher house without someone noticing.

Exhaustion settled over them both the moment the carriage door closed. Gazing to where Luthais sat on the seat opposite him, Maher tried – and failed – to come up with something to say. Some explanation of how the evening could have gone so spectacularly cocked up. Luthais' clothes were streaked with grime, the offending jacket torn at the shoulder, and half his hair had escaped from the braid it was in at the start of the evening. Maher didn't even want to know the state of his own clothing, he doubted very much the suit could be saved.

With his eyes closed and neck cradled against the seat, Luthais almost appeared to be sleeping. But every time the carriage wheels hit a particularly hard bump in the road, his head would roll and the slightest twitch of discomfort would flit across his face. Doctor Tambara spent a long time examined the sizable lump on his skull and Maher's apprehension about the injury's severity started afresh. In the end, she released him into Maher's care, with instructions to monitor Luthais for the next two days for any signs of nausea or confusion.

"That man may have the hardest skull I've ever encountered," she said privately to Maher. "I've never seen someone take a hit like that and be up on their feet so soon."

And yet, even after being caught up in the worst Lantern row in decades, Luthais was still willing to transport Maher and Marielle to The Riddles. Damned if Maher knew why, but he wasn't about to question a gift from the gods.

Perhaps that knock to the head did more damage than Tambara realized. Maher snorted.

One green eye squinted at him in the darkness of the carriage. "What's so funny?"

Unable to hold his own head up any longer, Maher rested against the seat as well. "Nothing in particular. Just reminiscing over our magical evening together in town."

There was a long pause, and then, Luthais laughed. This was the first time that Maher could recall, hearing this sound come from Luthais Kingfisher. Not the short huff he usually allowed himself in front of a select few, but a genuine, quite brash, laugh.

Maybe he really did hit his head too hard. A chuckle started low in Maher's throat and rolled up until they were both doubled over. Maher inhaled too hard and began to cough, his chest still ached from all the smoke.

"Oh fuck me," he wheezed. A strong fist pounded on his back a few times until Maher waved him off.

"Are nights out with you always this stimulating?"

Maher'd finally caught his breath, only to lose it again. The question had been spoken so softly, it would have been easy to miss. But he'd heard it. And now his mind scrambled for the right response.

"Not until recently, no." Their carriage rolled to a stop on the gravel drive in front of the manor. Lamplight flooded the interior and Maher gripped the edge of his seat. "What in blazes is going on here?"

Despite the early hour, the house and grounds were buzzing with activity. Every window as alight and guards stood at attention as far as Maher could see.

"Could it be because of the fire in town?"

"Possibly." Luthais frowned, scanning the scene. "But why are so many guards gathered here if help is needed elsewhere?"

When they climbed out, Luthais paid the driver and strode into the house, Maher hot on his heels. A servant carrying an armful of linens froze in place when she saw them, nearly dropping everything onto the floor. It reminded Maher how frightful they both must look.

"Apologies," Maher said gently. "Can you please tell us where we might find Lord and Lady Kingfisher?"

Recovering her voice, she directed both upstairs and scurried towards the kitchen. Maher could only guess what rumors would soon be spreading throughout the house.

They found Gai in Lord Kingfisher's study, speaking with the captains of both the Kingsport Guard and the Kingfisher Guard that served the manor. All three turned in surprise when Maher and Luthais entered the room.

"What in the goddess' name happened to the two of you?" Gai blurted out.

Luthais shook his head. "We'll tell you that story after you explain what's going on here."

"Where's Lord Kingfisher?" Maher took in the state of the study. It appeared there were more people in this meeting before they'd arrived. Empty glasses littered the table, as did several open pots of ink, pens, and discarded sheets of paper.

"Father's gone to speak to Rochelle." Gai dismissed the captains. "Thank you, that's all for now. We'll reconvene in the morning as Lord Kingfisher requested."

When it was just the three of them left in the room, Luthais turned to his brother. "Gai, tell us what's happened."

"It's Cal," a deep furrow creased the eldest Kingfisher brother's brow, "he's escaped from prison."

SWAIN

CHAPTER FIFTY-EIGHT

Swain paced restlessly on the deck of the massive Fraollish trader commandeered for them by the creatures. What remained of the crew from the *Maiden's Revenge*, barely a dozen sailors all told, huddled together on the foredeck by the helm. How many months had passed, and they were still just as terrified as the day they'd first come aboard.

For his part, Swain had come to largely ignore the rotting, reanimated corpses that made up the warship's crew. They paid no mind to the living, their sole focus to carry out the tasks they'd been given. Swain still wondered how the creatures were able to capture so many. Were some pulled from the depths, the unfortunate casualties of shipwrecks? Or were they all taken alive from vessels sailing their course, without thought or fear that anything so monstrous could be waiting for them beneath the sea?

He stepped aside as an undead sailor trudged past, rolling a barrel of freshwater towards the hold hatch. The man, or the thing that used to be a man, had a dark green stone embedded to the side of its face. It shone an unnatural light, whatever fiendish magic that filled it pulsing in rhythm with the corpse's slow, plodding steps.

They'd at least seen proof that, without those gems, the undead sailors lost all steam. Several had decayed beyond recognition in the humid Riddles air, too far gone to be useful any longer. When that happened, one of the creatures would rip out the gem, grinding it into dust, and the body would crumple to the ground.

Although, there was that one time a sailor's head rolled right off their shoulders and severed the magic on its own.

They were preparing to make way. Not that he'd had any indication of when they would be finished with their work. But they'd been told to prepare for a voyage and that's what was being done what else could they do but bide time?

"Swain?" the creature who'd laid claim to him called his name. The sound of her voice, that had once so captivated him, now made his teeth grind together. That mattered not, his feet were already carrying him to the portside railing without his permission. One day, after he'd gotten what he wanted, Swain hoped to put his sword through her wretched heart.

Reaching the rail, Swain looked down at the red-haired beauty floating below.

"Come down, Swain."

"What is it now?" he snapped.

She gave him a too-wide smile. "We must join the others. It's time."

Swain left the sailor who'd accompanied him to guard the rowboat, docked at the mouth of the inlet they'd taken into the island. Now he traveled on foot, following the riverbank as the creature swam next to him. Staying just beneath the surface, she led him to the lagoon where he'd seen them lure more than one soul to their deaths.

Deep in his gut, Swain now suspected he knew what these deadly creatures were, though he dared not speak the name aloud. Perhaps he'd spent too much time on the shores of Saprea in his younger days, but Swain had adopted the belief that repeating a story only gave it more power. Better for his crew to stay in the dark as long as possible, than to know what nightmare of the deep they'd allied themselves with – then the rumors and terror would truly spread.

Sweat was pouring down his back and dripping into his eyes by the time they reached the lagoon. Coming to a stop on the bank, Swain waited for her to appear again. When she surfaced and found him still on land, her full lips twisted into a sneer.

"Don't you want to come for a swim, Swain?"

His traitorous body leaned towards the water, but it wasn't quite an order. Swain ground his teeth and kept his feet planted. "I don't think so, not if there's another option."

Shoulders rising in an exaggerated sigh, she lifted an arm from the water. "My sisters might be right, perhaps I do spoil you."

Swain bit his tongue so hard he tasted blood.

Pressing one of the many scales embedded in her own flesh, she submerged her arm. Swain'd barely took another breath before the water of the lagoon began to roil and bubble. Violet light spread from the gem and sank to the bottom of the pool. For a moment, the water went still. Then the ground beneath Swain began to tremble as a row of large, rounded stones rose up to the surface. When it was over, a path leading into the cave at the back of the lagoon lay before him.

Swain gawked at the creature. How many different magics did they possess? Focusing on her face, he saw fresh lines carved around her eyes and mouth. Blue veins stood out on her neck and divided the creamy skin of her forehead, like rivers carving across a map.

So, this magic does cost her something.

"Come along pet," she purred. "else we'll late."

Swain's heart thudded as he followed her across the lagoon and into the cave. Cool, misty darkness enveloped him, chilling the sweat on his brow. The steppingstones soon ended, forcing Swain to hop onto the narrow ledge at the bottom of the cave wall.

Once the sun disappeared behind him, it took but a moment to detect the eerie green light glowing from deep within the flowing stream.

Time lost all meaning as they moved further into the cave. With only the sound of his boots on stone and the occasional splash from the stream to keep him company. Eventually, they reached a place where the stream curved sharply to the left and the creature surfaced again.

"Stay here. I'll inform the others of our arrival."

Swain nodded stiffly, keenly aware now that he was being led right into the snakes' nest. She disappeared around the bend, leaving Swain perched by the edge of the water. With his back pressed into the damp stone behind him, Swain peered as closely as he dared into the gently flowing stream. Even with the water as clear as crystal, he still couldn't make out the source of that green light. With his legs beginning to ache, Swain slowly slid down the wall until he was seated. For a long moment all he heard was the water and his own shallow breathing, until hissed words began floating up from the direction the creature had gone. While he could barely distinguish one voice from another, he sensed they were arguing about something.

Scooting onto his hands and knees, Swain crept forward until his head cleared the curve. The stream meandered a little further, then dropped out of sight.

"This has taken too long," one of them barked. Swain flinched but held his position, hard stone biting into his knees.

"It would have gone faster if you'd let us use one of the captives," another responded.

"The necessary energy expended would have drained all of us! Why not simply use enough to control her and be done?"

"We need her," Swain's creature hissed. "We need her whole and acting of her own free will, or the key will steal the life we worked to restore. Don't forget," her voice dipped lower and Swain strained to hear, "sailors will follow a captain. And only she can sound the call and give us our revenge."

PASHA

CHAPTER FIFTY-NINE

Maher was already waiting for them on the shore when Ally and Pasha emerged from the waves, two days later. He raised a hand in greeting, then turned to give them time to change into the clothes he'd brought from the house.

As keen as Pasha was to leave, she'd been glad of the extra day to rest. She and Ally stayed in the hatching grounds all night and into the next morning. Only returning to the sea when hunger drove them from the privacy of the lagoon.

Of course, Pasha'd always known what her body was capable of on land. Hadn't she heard countless cautionary tales of merfolk getting involved with humans? And witnessed Pallagia meeting her human lover on the beach? But not once, in over three hundred years, had she thought to explore her other form.

That was no longer the case. Now, she wanted to know *everything*. Ally'd already taught her so much - slowly, patiently, lovingly – working Pasha up until she felt as if she'd go mad. And then... as familiar as Pasha was with the pleasures that could be achieved through an energetic connection, that in no way prepared her for the ripple of bliss that rolled through her body, only leaving a faint sizzle in her head at the very last.

And there was more to learn. When Ally revealed that she'd only started with the basics of human lovemaking, Pasha nearly dragged her back into the hatching grounds.

It was good they'd taken that time to recover, though. As they joined Maher on the beach, Pasha quickly realized there was more danger to this voyage than they'd anticipated.

Ally sat with rapt attention as he recounted the destruction of a place in the city called the Bear's Den. "Oh darling, I'm so sorry." Ally held his hand, tears welling in her eyes.

"I won't even scold you right now for running into a burning building. But don't you *ever* do that again, Maher Villaon."

"Don't worry, Al," he gave a half-smile, "you're the fourth person to make me swear the same thing."

"What was your friend looking for?" asked Pasha. Her experience with fire was limited, but she knew well enough the damage it could do. Many of the ships she'd explored on the seafloor had been felled by flames gone out of control.

"Mama Bear was looking for a proclamation signed by Lord Gaius Kingfisher II. Your grandfather, Al."

The one Gaius that Pasha hadn't met. Ally'd said once that he'd died before her parents met.

"What sort of proclamation?" Ally frowned.

"Apparently, as a show of gratitude to the original founders of the Lantern Guild for bringing order to the district, Gaius II granted them ownership of their properties in perpetuity. Mama Bear inherited hers from her mother, and thought the document was in her room."

"But it wasn't," Ally mused. "What will she do now?"

Maher massaged his left shoulder, the one Pasha'd healed. "I told her I'd speak to Lord Kingfisher about reissuing the same proclamation. Try and use what little influence I have left before it's completely squandered."

"That's a wonderful idea, Maher." Ally patted his hand. "And if Father gives you any trouble, you refer him to me."

"Luthais said much the same."

"Did he, now?" Ally smirked.

"And even after I got him bashed over the head and nearly burned alive, he's still willing to ferry us to The Riddles."

"And we have everything worked out with Euphonia," said Pasha, sensing some particular mischief in Ally's tone.

Ally nodded, "Right, and she'll stay out of sight, so as not to frighten the crew. We don't want to alarm them either, so Pasha and I will remain beneath the ship."

Maher looked as if he would argue with Ally staying in the sea, but then he seemed to think better of it. "There's one more thing that I need to tell you, Al."

"What's that?"

"It's about Cal."

The news of Cal's escape from confinement instantly set Pasha's teeth on edge. She reached for Ally the same time as Maher, both supporting her on either side.

After a long, deep breath, Ally whispered, "Has there been any word of him since then?"

"None." Maher took a wine skin from his bag and offered it to her. "Gai reckons he would've left the island as soon as possible, but they've still increased the guards at the manor and the wharf."

"Alright," the knowledge seemed to soothe Ally some. "Alright. Please tell us if you learn anything more."

"Of course."

Pasha ground a handful of sand into her fist. If that man harmed one scale on Ally, she'd...

"Whoa!" Maher squawked.

"Pasha!"

"What?" The mermaid started. "Tides protect me..."

A small assortment of bones had wriggled from the pebbly sand. They spun aimlessly above their heads. Pasha was about to dismiss them when Ally pointed wordlessly. Following her direction, Pasha found what had captivated her. Among the scattered fish bones floated an intact skull. A bird's. A seagull, if Pasha had to guess. The skull tilted, as if the bird was looking down at them.

"Let them go now, Pasha." Ally nudged.

A quick flick of her wrist and the bones dropped onto the ground. Ally bent to study them more closely, while Maher simply stared open-mouthed at the pile. Heat spread across Pasha's face. She'd never done that in front of a human before. Or on land, for that matter.

Ally gently poked the bird skull. "Pasha,"

"By the gods and all their grandmothers!" Maher'd apparently found his voice. "What the fuck was that?"

"A trick." Pasha shifted uncomfortably.

"A *trick?* What –"

"Hush, Maher," Ally spoke over him. "Pasha, did you know you could do that on land?"

Shaking her head slowly, Pasha picked up the skull. "I had no idea."

"Well," her brows rose "that's interesting, isn't it?"

Once Maher'd recovered from the shock of seeing a collection of random bones dance through the air, Ally steered the conversation back to the topic at hand.

There were still a few details of the voyage that Luthais and Maher needed to finalize. Supplies, funds, the size of the crew. But they could be ready to sail in a matter of days, barring any complications.

"Speaking of rations, I have a surprise for you, Al." From the bottom of his bag Maher produced a small white box tied with brown string.

"You didn't!" Ally eyed the box with glee.

"Happy belated birthday, Ally." Untying the box, Maher opened the lid to reveal an assortment of baked treats.

Pasha's nose was overwhelmed by the pungent, sweet scents wafting out of the box. But Ally looked as if she could eat all of them in one sitting.

"Why don't I let you two visit alone while you have those?" Pasha offered.

Ally tore herself away from the pastries. "You don't have to leave, Pasha."

Was Pasha mistaken, or did Maher appear relieved at the prospect of having Ally to himself for a while?

"It's alright." Rising from her spot on the sand, Pasha kissed Ally's forehead. "I couldn't eat any of that anyway. You two enjoy. I'll go hunt for myself and return in an hour or two."

"Thank you," Ally murmured, capturing Pasha's hand and brushing her lips against the mermaid's palm.

Maher caught her eye and nodded his own thanks as she turned towards the sea. Without ceremony, Pasha made quick work of removing the dress. Tossing it over her shoulder, Pasha smirked when she earned a startled grunt from Maher and a smothered giggle from Ally.

Free from the stifling fabric, Pasha walked into the surf and dove beneath the waves.

CHAPTER SIXTY

Ally and Maher settled farther up the beach to avoid the incoming tide. In addition to the pastries from Mrs. Ekmekci's bakery, he'd also brought a flask of tea, cups, and a tiny pot of honey.

When their little picnic was ready, Maher smiled wistfully. "I've missed this."

"So have I."

Now that they were alone, Maher allowed himself to fully relax. Ally wondered just how guarded he had to be now around everyone. Keeping one mask or another on all day, every day? It was no wonder he was so tired. The physical demands of his positions aside, every part of him, his body, his mind, even his spirit, was wearing down.

Just like the old days, they drank tea and shared Mrs. Ekmekci's pastries. Talking about everything and nothing.

At a certain point though, the conversation shifted. There were so many things Maher'd been holding inside since she left. Feelings about his father. The tremendous amount of pressure he was under to finally uncover the source of the Saprean coins. Lingering guilt over what had happened to the Bear's Den. The pastries dwindled while Maher kept talking. And Ally listened, giving him the understanding and undivided attention he needed.

Ally could tell Maher hadn't had someone to talk this openly with since she left. Of course he and Pimm were good friends, but it wasn't the same type of relationship they shared. Part of her hoped he'd form new bonds in her absence, like this new friendship with Luthais.

When all the words Maher'd stored up were spent, they sat in a companionable, comfortable silence. Their hands were linked, resting on his lap.

"Sorry I rattled on like that, Al." Maher's thumb skimmed over the scales atop her hand.

"You, rattle on? No such thing." she pecked his cheek. "But I am worried about you. Is there no one else you can talk to when I'm not here?"

"I talk to people all day long."

"You know what I mean, Maher. Someone you can really confide in, like I can with Pasha."

"We can't all expect your good fortune," Maher deflected, draining the last of the tea from his cup.

"What about Luthais?"

Maher sputtered, dropping her hand as if it were a coal hot from the hearth. "What are you implying?"

Ally's head tilted. "You're friends now, aren't you? Certainly more so than when we were children."

"I mean, that is," Maher took a moment to collect himself. "Yes, we are, but I could hardly talk to Luthais the same way I do with you."

"Perhaps not right away."

Fiddling with a beach pebble, Maher looked everywhere except at Ally. "Why do you ask?"

"It was hard to miss the attention he paid to you when we were all together the other day," Ally shrugged. "I thought maybe you were spending more time together."

"I wouldn't exactly say that," he cleared his throat.

"Maher Villaon," she gasped. "Have you tumbled my brother?"

"What! No! Nothing's happened."

"But you want something to happen?"

Maher stared helplessly at her. "I don't know... maybe?"

"Maher."

"All right, yes!" He buried his face in his hands. "Although, after not seeing one another for months at a time, I don't know if anything will actually come of it. I'm sorry, Al. If this makes you uncomfortable..."

"Stop." She gently pulled his arms down. "I want you both to be happy. If your friendship develops into something more, then I'll wish you every joy. And if not, I hope at least you both will have someone you can trust in each other. Luthais has more depth than I realized."

"That he does. Thank you, Al." Maher moved to kiss her cheek, hesitated when he remembered the scales that decorated her face, then pressed on. "And are you happy? You still feel you made the right decision?"

"Yes, I am." Ally laid her head on his shoulder as he wrapped an arm around her. "I'm not saying everything is always roses, because nothing real is perfect. But I'm happy and... I think I'm in love."

CHAPTER SIXTY-ONE

*F*oraoise...

Screams filled her ears as the swinging blade came down hard on her own sword. She felt the resulting tremor deep in her bones.

Foraoise...

She blocked again and again as strikes rained down on her without mercy.

Foraoise.

The sword was knocked from her hand and she landed flat on her back against the deck. He stood over her, murder in the deep brown eyes that no longer saw her for who she was. He was going to kill her. The blade swung a wild arc through the air –

Foraoise!

The world came back to Foraoise Dare all at once. Loud and harsh and filled with a gnawing hunger that settled deep into her soul. What was left of it.

Fighting through the onslaught of smells, sounds, and colors crowding her senses, Foraoise took stock of herself. She was stretched out across something cold, hard, and a little damp. The air was cool, droplets of moisture fell indiscriminately from above. Some landing on her, others pinging off a nearby body of water. Breathing in deeply, Foraoise caught the scent of peat, damp earth and stone. But underneath ran a current of decay. Something sickly sweet, like fruit gone bad.

And beneath the echoing chorus of sprinkling droplets, lapping water, and her own erratic breathing, there was something else. Was it... music? A light, airy tune tunneled into her ears and dug up a treasure trove of memories.

Slowly blinking her eyes open, Foraoise waited in the dim light until she could see the cave ceiling above. Turning her head felt like an enormous task, but she had to find the source of that song. The bones in her neck protested, like rusted hinges on a gate, but eventually she could look out into the cavernous space stretching around her.

In the gloom, a pair of sapphire eyes gleamed. Water sluiced over her current resting place as the owner of the eyes moved closer. A face like a dream emerged from the shadows, attached to the body of a nightmare.

"Welcome back, Captain Dare."

SWAIN

CHAPTER SIXTY-TWO

S wain had no inkling of how long he waited in that cave.

A chill settled deep into his aging bones as he crouched against the wall. The gentle lap of the stream lulling him into a fitful doze. Too exhausted to keep his eyes open, but too wary of his precarious position by the water to sink fully into sleep.

Something heavy plunked into the water and Swain jerked awake. His legs were numb from huddling in the cold and he pitched forward.

"Careful, pet." The redheaded creature caught him by the shoulders.

Wrestling against the urge to lean into her touch, Swain ignored the thousand knives stabbing his legs and pulled away. "What's happening?" His throat was dry as sawdust, but he didn't dare to drink from the body of water she was currently occupying.

A slow smile spread across the creature's face, showing far too many teeth than she ought to have. "She's awake."

"What? Where?" Swain tried to stand, but his knees and ankles burned too much.

"Slow down. The others must speak to your captain first, then you can see her."

Swain didn't want a pit full of those things to be Foraoise's first sight upon returning to the world.

Shaking his head, Swain tried and failed to rise again. "But she won't know where she is or what's happened in her absence."

"My sisters will tell her everything," she tutted. "Besides, I suspect she already knows more than you think."

The toes of Swain's boots hung over the rock ledge running beside the stream. It continued to shrink the farther they went, until he was forced to press his back to the damp wall and shuffle sideways like a crab. Eventually they came to a place where the tunnel narrowed enough that he could almost straddle both sides. The rock walls squeezed in on either side until Swain feared he'd have to join the creature in the water after all. But then, the ground sloped down and Swain emerged into a new tunnel twice as wide as the last.

Gods be praised. He mopped the chilled sweat from his forehead.

The creature waited for him at the bottom of the slope, crossed arms resting on the ledge. "Don't tell me you need a rest, Swain," she purred. "We're nearly there."

"So ye say," he grumbled.

"I need you to listen very closely." The hint of command in her voice forced Swain to look her in the face. "When we join the others, you will not speak until spoken to, and you will not be drawn in by any of my sisters' wiles. Do you understand?"

"Aye," Swain ground out. As if he'd have any real control in a roomful of these wretches.

"Good." The tip of her tri-colored tail slid from the water and wrapped around his ankle. "Don't forget what I said."

Fighting the revulsion that crawled over his skin, Swain jerked his head into a nod. Satisfied, she released him and they resumed their trek through the cave.

Gods only know how far beneath the ground we are now. Swain regretted the thought the moment it appeared. The idea of being essentially buried alive didn't sit well with a man who'd spent most of his life in the open air of a ship's deck.

FORAOISE

CHAPTER SIXTY-THREE

"That is our story." One of the serpentine creatures crooned. "We only need this one small favor from you, and then you will be free to go with our blessing."

Foraoise eyed the half-dozen others just like the one who spoke, bobbing in the deep pool that surrounded the flat stretch of rock where she'd awoken. Once the initial shock of seeing these creatures, – *sirens*, they called themselves, though Foraoise couldn't recall any sailor's yarn that depicted them this way – the reality of her situation had slowly sunk in. It turned out she wasn't dead after all, but neither was she alive, either. After kissing that mermaid, the memory still coming back to her in scraps, Foraoise'd fallen into a half-life state. Doomed to endure the constant, crushing agony of the ocean floor. Until *they* found her, that is, and brought her back to some semblance of life. It would appear that she owed them, if not her life, then at least her freedom.

And now they wanted to collect on that debt. A task that only Foraoise could perform, in her current not-quite-dead state.

It would also seem that they had a common enemy. Mermaids.

Foraoise's mind was still a little sluggish as she considered everything the blue-eyed siren had said. Every splash of water or murmured word was like a trumpet blasting into her ear. The glowing balls of white light illuminating the space, produced and scattered around the cavern by a siren with hair and skin like polished ochre, were like tiny suns searing her vision.

Even the damp clothes clinging to her skin, what scraps remained of them, felt oppressive.

"We had to *enhance* your human body in order to bring you back, Captain," she'd leered. "Luckily, the mermaid you kissed wasn't aware of her own power. Your rage was like a beacon," The others all drifted closer at that, eyeing Foraoise like the last morsel at a banquet. "It called to us, made it much easier to find you."

Rage. Now there was a familiar sensation. It thrummed through her veins and bubbled at the back of her skull. It fueled her like never before. If these creatures were telling the truth, she'd use it to take revenge for them all in one fell swoop.

But first...

"Well, Captain?" The siren tilted her head, blonde hair spilling over her shoulder. Foraoise supposed the move was meant to entice, but she felt... nothing. "Do we have an agreement?"

"I'm not sure." Foraoise propped her elbow on a bent knee, trying to hold herself steady. The sirens glanced amongst themselves. They must not've been used to hearing such a ready counteroffer.

"What else is there to know?" The blonde siren smiled a predator's toothy grin.

"You say you've brought me a ship and crew, but I could have procured those myself. What good is allying with you, if I get nothing I couldn't already have?"

"You have your *life*," another hissed.

"Indeed," Foraoise licked her lips, tasted the salt of the sea. "Would you care to have it back? I know what awaits me if you do. But it would appear I'm the only one who can perform the task you need."

"What do you want?" Cold blue eyes scrutinized her.

After another flash of light faded from the edge of her vision, Foraoise showed her own grim smile. "I want the Birde Isles."

"Is that all?" The lead siren rose on the coils of her tail until they were eye-level with each other. "Then we have an agreement."

"Done," she offered a hand. The creature sneered at the human gesture, but then clasped Foraoise's arm near her elbow. Ragged nails dug into Foraoise's flesh, but she hardly felt it.

An antiquated way of sealing a deal, but it would do. "Tell me, how did you know I was the one you needed?"

The siren released her. "That reminds me, we have another surprise for you, Captain."

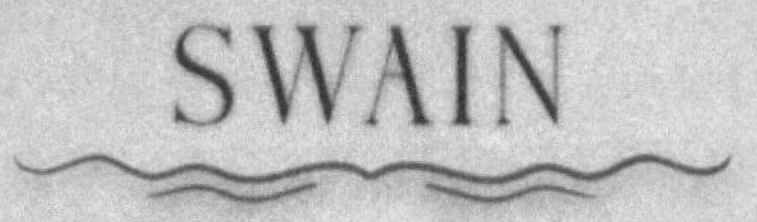

CHAPTER SIXTY-FOUR

Finally, the tunnel widened into a large cavern, the stream feeding into a pool of unknown depth. An underground lake. A scattering of lichen-coated stones formed a haphazard pathway to a wide boulder in the middle of the pool, worn flat and smooth over time.

It was too dim to make out much else, but he had the distinct, eerie sensation that they weren't alone. A dark shape shifted in the lake's center.

"So, you've finally arrived." A low, sultry voice spoke from the shadows.

"You said to give you time," Swain's creature replied.

Swain shielded his eyes as light blazed through every corner of the cavern. Several high voices cackled, the sound echoing off the curved walls. Carefully, he lowered his arm, spots dancing in his vision. Everything came back into focus, and Swain's heart fairly stopped in his chest.

Foraoise was standing on the rock in the lake. Her back was to him, but he'd've known her anywhere. While her red-stained hair was loose, hanging down her back in long waves, he could still make out the shaved side and the scar that wrapped around her skull. Her clothes were in tatters, her boots missing entirely. But, alive. She was *alive*. They'd really done it. Whatever witchcraft was used, whatever fate Swain had unleashed upon the world, Foraoise was here. He had her back. In the lake around her, more creatures waited, their hungry eyes trained on him. For the first time, Swain was glad for the protection the redhead's claim on him afforded.

"Don't just stand there," a blonde one chided, "greet your captain."

Swain's mouth opened without his permission and he clapped it shut. Hissing at her sister, his creature turned to him and nodded her approval. "Go ahead."

Fingers curling into fists, trying to hide the tremor that ran down his arms, Swain dared to step to the water's edge.

"Captain?" he croaked. "Foraoise?"

Slowly she turned, seeming not to mind the cold stone beneath her bare feet. Moss green eyes locked onto him, and Swain felt his legs might give out. Foraoise took him in, recognition flitting across her face. "So it is you, Swain."

Swain steeled his himself as Foraoise crossed the stone path to his side of the lake.

His last memory of her that day on the *Maiden's Revenge* had been forever etched into his brain. Body swollen and strangled, drowned from within. He'd tried to prepare himself to face that she may not look as she did before her death. But none of his imaginings had prepared him for the sight of the woman walking towards him now.

At first glance, Foraoise looked very much like her old self. But closer inspection revealed just how much the creatures had changed while bringing her back to life.

Foraoise's skin, once ruddy and sun-stained, was now only one shade past the pallor of death. Yet it also seemed to glow from within. Not outright, as if she were a living lamp. It was a sheen that only appeared in certain angles of light, like an eel. Her eyes were the same green they'd always been, but now a thin, black ring circled the irises. Dark gray stained her nails, spreading onto the tips of her fingers and toes.

And the scales. Unlike the corpse sailors with only a single scale to reanimate them, Foraoise was covered with the shining thumbprint-sized jewels.

They started at the middle of her forehead, curved-in a wide arc over one cheek, then down the column of her throat. More scales dotted her shoulders and spine, capped each elbow and knee. There were many colors, though the cooler tones were limited to her joints, blues, and greens, while the rest ranged in hues of orange, red, and gold. A single, violet scale was embedded in the center of her chest. They pulsed as she moved, only going still when she came to a stop in front of him.

"Swain." Her voice was even rougher than before. Black-rimmed eyes regarded him. This close, he could see the outlines of her veins beneath her skin, tainted with the same gray as her hands and feet.

"A-Aye," he swallowed thickly. A thin ribbon of fear snaked up his spine. "'Tis good to see you, Captain."

Lips the color of old, dried blood curved into a half-smile. "Is it?"

"Of course, it is!"

"In that case, it's good to see you, too."

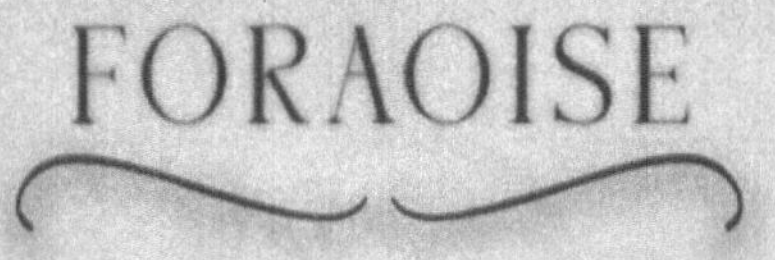

FORAOISE

CHAPTER SIXTY-FIVE

When Foraoise first stepped into the sunlight, the world exploded into a kaleidoscope of blurred colors and shapes. Following Swain out through the tunnel, she'd been able to adjust gradually to the growing light. Now, eyes squeezed shut, she stopped just outside the cave mouth.

The redheaded siren who'd tailed them from the water popped above the surface. "Give it time."

"How much time?" Foraoise hissed.

"The gifts will come faster than you think, if you are open to them."

Easing one eye open, then the other, Foraoise squinted at the lush forest surrounding the cave and the lagoon that flowed inside. Gradually, everything came into focus. A hazy mesh of greens became the grove of trees with canopies stretched far above her head. Branches stood out like cracks in a windowpane, and individual leaves crystalized until she found that she could count each one if she kept them in her sight long enough.

"You see?" The siren dove back into the water, shadowy silhouette aimed for where Swain stood on the bank. He said nothing, simply watched and waited for Foraoise to adjust.

Crossing the rest of the way, Foraoise clapped him on the shoulder. The barest twitch of discomfort vibrated beneath her palm. "Take me to my ship."

They trekked through the thick undergrowth, alongside the river where the siren still kept pace with them. The longer Foraoise watched her, the more detail she could make out beneath the water.

The gifts will come faster...

Swain glanced back at her. "There's something I should tell you, before we reach the ship."

"What's that?"

"About the crew, they're not... alive, so to speak."

Foraoise tore her gaze from the river. "They're *not alive?*"

"Aye. Those that're left from the *Maiden's Revenge* are, but the rest, them caught by the creatures? They're all dead."

"Swain," she stopped walking "you'd best explain better than that."

Turning back to look at her, he flicked a hand at the scales embedded into her skin. "They took dead sailors and used the same witchcraft to reanimate them. But they're not brought back to life, like you, they're puppets. Still rotting even as they carry out their work. A crew of corpses."

A corpse crew. Foraoise stared at the blue scales that topped each of her hands. A grin slowly across her face. "Wait until the Kingfishers see that."

She walked quicker now, keen to see this crew of the dead for herself. Swain rushed to catch up.

"She's impressive." Foraoise craned her neck to take in the massive Fraollish warship.

"Aye, that she is." The gangplank was already down. Swain stepped aside to let her climb aboard first. Their siren escort had finally departed, disappearing in the sea. But not before promising Swain she'd soon return. His barely concealed revulsion confirmed Foraoise's suspicions, the siren had her hooks in him.

They reached the main deck and Swain bellowed, "Captain on deck!"

Not that any of the crew in sight dropped their tasks, or even acknowledged that he'd spoken. Perhaps they couldn't.

Fascinated, Foraoise watched the corpse crew going about their business. They didn't stop, didn't show any signs of fatigue. Each with a single scale placed somewhere on their face or head.

A bitter, acrid scent hit her nose. Not death, in fact she didn't smell the rotting flesh of the crew at all. Following her nose, Foraoise turned towards the quarterdeck. Huddled there were the only living souls aboard the ship. They stared at her as if they were seeing a ghost. In a way, she supposed, they were.

Behind her, Swain barked, "I said, captain on deck! Fall in, ye wretched good-for-nothings!"

One sailor lurched forward, the rest following her like panicked ducklings.

"Quartermaster?" The lead sailor stopped a healthy distance from them. Her eyes darted over Foraoise, as if she was unsure where would be safest to look.

"Aye, Smith. Captain Dare's as alive as you and me. The creatures kept their word, and now we keep ours."

Smith. Now Foraoise could place the young sailor. She'd started out on the *Maiden's Revenge* as Swain's steward, a slip of a girl who'd scurried around doing the quartermaster's bidding.

"Aye, sir." Smith stood a little straighter. "Orders, Captain?"

Two little words, but music to Dare's ears all the same. They solidified the deck boards beneath her feet, made the ship take shape in her mind as well as to her eye.

"All hands," the words rolled off her tongue, "prepare to make way."

Smith turned to the miniscule crew, all that was left from Dare's burgeoning fleet. "You lot heard the captain. Move!"

CHAPTER SIXTY-SIX

With the living crew scrambling into action, Swain escorted Foraoise to the captain's quarters.

Twice the size of those she'd had on the *Maiden's Revenge*. Swain had inspected the contents when the ship was procured by the creatures and left it exactly as it was. Waiting to be occupied by their captain.

"There are plenty of clothes in the trunk and the wardrobe, boots too." Pulling open the double doors, Swain stepped aside. "It appears the last captain was of a similar size to you."

"How fortunate." She withdrew a white shirt with several ruffles at the collar and cuffs. "If not slightly more flamboyant."

"Aye, that they were." He cleared his throat. "I'll just leave you to settle in." Swain nearly made it to the door when she stopped him.

"Wait. Stay, Swain."

"Captain?" He looked back. "I won't be long, and we have more to discuss."

"Aye, I suppose we do." Swain turned his back to Dare again as she continued to rummage through the previous captain's belongings. While not entirely sure what had become of many of the Fraollish crew that once occupied this ship, he could plainly see they'd spared no expense in its design and furnishing. The wood was sturdy white oak, the most expensive shipbuilding material on the market, likely harvested from Teratsu. Every possible fitting in the captain an d officers' quarters gleamed with polished brass. The rooms boasted feather beds instead of straw or rope, and the captain's bed sitting to his left had a canopy with heavy red curtains. And the crew's quarters belowdecks were well-appointed, if much simpler. Gods, even the brig was nicer than many places he'd rested his carcass in years past.

"You can turn around now, Swain."

The sight of her fully dressed now, comforted him more than he'd expected. Something about the way she'd first appeared in the underground caverns – tattered clothes barely hanging on to her frame, feet bare on the stone and hair wild – combined with the alterations made by the creatures' magic, gave the impression she was positively inhuman.

Now she stood before him looking more like herself. A maroon shirt was tucked into the brown, slightly too-big trousers she'd cinched tight with a wide belt. Dark brown leather boots already covered her feet.

As Foraoise worked her hair into a braid, she leveled her gaze at him. "Now that we're away from prying eyes and ears. Tell me why I'm here, Swain."

"What?"

"Why make such a deal with those things, just to bring me back?" Digging through a small drawer set into the wardrobe, she found a strip of leather and secured her hair.

Tugging roughly on his mustache, Swain crossed the cabin and braced a hand on her shoulder. "I couldn't save my boy, but I could save you."

"Jon."

Something tightened in his chest. "Aye, Jon. I couldn't lose my last link to him, not like that. And when those creatures appeared…"

"Sirens. You can call them what they are. I think we're past the point of disbelief."

He forced the word out as if it left a bad taste in his mouth. "*Sirens.* When I saw what they could do, that they could bring you back, I'd've promised. anything. I'd've given them every soul that sailed the sea."

Foraoise held his gaze, her strange new eyes unblinking as she mirrored his stance. She was so still, for a moment he couldn't tell if she was even breathing.

One corner of her mouth twitched up. "Has anyone ever had such a father-in-law?"

"I'd wager not," Swain huffed. They released each other and he stepped back. Foraoise turned and selected a long, black coat from the collection hanging behind her. Swain clasped his hands behind his back, the rare acknowledgement of their connection beyond that of captain and quartermaster already feeling like it'd only happened in his mind. "What's our next move, Captain?"

"As you said, the sirens have held up their end of this bargain, so we must keep ours." Crossing to the rack of weapons mounted on the far wall, Foraoise chose a sword and strapped the scabbard around her waist. A high-priced six-shot revolver was tucked beneath the jacket at the small of her back.

"We know when the new turbine will be sent from Kharabo to Fraolland."

Foraoise braced a hand on the sword's hilt. "Then it appears we have another machine to commandeer."

MAHER

CHAPTER SIXTY-SEVEN

Dawn was just peeking over the city rooftops when Maher's carriage rumbled into the northern district. He was developing a true appreciation for this form of transportation. After spending much of the last decade traversing Kingsport on foot.

Soon the carriage driver, one employed solely by the Kingfishers and therefore more discrete than a city driver, brought them to a stop in front of Pimm's building. Maher used his copy of the keys to let himself inside. The stairs creaked and groaned as he climbed to the top floor. Though he was sure the other residents were used to the noise, Maher winced as each footstep announced his presence. One particularly sharp pop sent him leaping from the offending board. Memories of the Bear's Den floor snapping beneath his feet were still fresh.

At least he was able to have an audience with Lord Kingfisher about the Lantern property proclamations granted by Gaius II. The conversation went smoother than he'd expected; it wasn't even necessary to draw upon Luthais or Ally for assistance. New documents were already being drawn up to be delivered to both Mama Bear and the Madam. Gai even offered to deliver them personally, once he heard about the Lantern fire.

So Maher would undertake this next journey with his heart a little lighter than before. Gods be praised for that.

Knocking softly outside the room Pimm had leant out as Marielle's provisional home, Maher listened as faint footsteps moved within the room. They paused on the other side of the door.

"Marielle, it's Maher."

The lock clicked and the door swung open. "Pimm really ought to install eyelets on these doors."

"I'll mention that to them." He stepped aside as she left the room, one small pack strapped across her back. "Is that all you're bringing?"

"It's all I have to bring." Marielle locked the door behind her. On the way back down the hall, she stopped to slide the key beneath the door to Pimm's rooms. They descended the stairs as quietly as possible. As they passed the second-floor landing, Maher caught a whiff of pipe smoke. One of Pimm's elderly tenants already up for the day.

Back in the carriage, Marielle seated across from him, Maher took a leatherbound case from the place beside him and handed it to her.

"What's this?" Marielle asked, brows raising as she felt the substantial weight of the case.

"Open it."

As the lid lifted with hardly a sound, Marielle gasped. Nestled into the red velvet lining were two new revolvers.

"They're the latest issue from the Kingfishers' gunsmith. Everything you'll need to care for them, and a supply of bullets, will be waiting on the ship."

Lifting one out, she admired the detailed scrollwork on the barrel. The metal was polished to a high shine. "Maher, this is too much."

"It isn't nearly enough, not after everything you've done, and lost, on my behalf."

"But I couldn't..." she started to protest.

"If you try to give them back, it won't work. They aren't my style, and I can't return them. I doubt you'd want pistols that fine in the possession of someone who'd never use them."

"If you put it that way," Marielle flipped the cylinder open, eyes widening at the ease with which each piece moved together. "Thank you, Maher."

"I've never been on a ship this large before." Marielle gazed up at the vessel that would carry them back to her homeland.

Maher, for his part, was too busy stifling a laugh to reply. It was his first time seeing Luthais' new ship up close and he'd apparently learned nothing from his experience with the last one. Pressing his knuckles to his mouth, Maher failed to hold back a loud snort.

"What's so funny?" she gave him a skewed glance.

"Nothing," he choked up again. "Our captain has a penchant for unusual ship names."

Marielle read the word carved into the bow. "The *Foxglove?* I'll admit it's more... whimsical than I expected, but not all that unusual."

Maher finally composed himself. "I'll tell you a story sometime."

The crew of the *Foxglove* hurried about their tasks, preparing the ship to make way. Maher'd caught a glimpse of Luthais as he and Marielle boarded. But the captain had been on the move, striding quickly across the deck while in conversation with the bosun, Ga-Seung. Maher hadn't seen the Char-range man in months, not since they'd returned Rochelle safely home to the Isles, but his presence on the vessel was strangely heartening.

In fact, he recognized several of the sailors. And it was hard to miss Kamharida, towering over many of them as she did. He made a mental note to introduce Marielle to the first mate once they were underway. The two women had much in common. Both making their lives on the Birde Isles, far from their places of birth. Both extremely skilled in their professions. And both had managed to scare him at one time or another.

"G'morning, Mister Villaon!" A lanky young man with wild, orange curls tipped his cap as he passed, a small cask tucked under one arm.

"Weams! Good to see you." He scanned the decks for Weams' partner. "Is Olebile on board as well?"

"Aye, they're 'round here somewhere. I'll pass along your greetings when I see them, if you like."

"If you would, thank you." Maher bid Weams good day so he could get back to his duties.

"Do you know the entire crew?" Marielle asked.

Shaking his head, Maher declined to answer. There were many members of Luthais' former crew who never made it back from the downing of the *Pike*. While Weams and Olebile had once been part of the crew on Cal's ship, the *Wave Skipper*, they weren't involved in his plot against his family. Maher was glad to find them part of the *Foxglove* crew, they were good sailors and loyal friends of Ally's.

Thoughts of Ally drew Maher's eye out to sea. She and Pasha would be waiting for the ship to clear Trader's Bay before joining them. Along with the sea monster, Euphonia. He simply could not grasp the reasoning behind that name. Well, as long as Maher didn't have to make her acquaintance, the sea monster could go by whatever she liked.

Lord and Lady Kingfisher arrived later that morning with Gai to see the *Foxglove* off. There were additional guards stationed around the dock, and a thorough search had been done to ensure there were no stowaways aboard. Maher suspected that last detail had more to do with him than any credible threat from Cal. Of course, the person who'd secreted him aboard the *Pike* last year was standing right next to him, but he'd decided to keep that tidbit to himself.

"Prepare to bring in the gangway." Kamharida instructed the appointed crew members and they divided up to loosen the latches holding the structure in place.

"Wait!" A voice called from below.

"Who goes there?" Kamharida demanded.

"A late passenger!" One of the dock workers shouted. "Should we let up 'em up?"

Hastening to the rail, Maher peered down to find a familiar face looking back up at him.

"Pimm! What are you doing?" He turned to the first mate, "Let them up, please."

When Pimm set foot on the deck, Maher and Marielle drew them out of the crew's way.

"What's wrong?" Maher's heart pounded as he imagined some new madness that had befallen the Lantern. Then he noticed the travel pack strapped across their chest. "Pimm, you're not serious."

"Mama Bear's orders. Someone has to keep an eye on you. Both."

Marielle snorted. "Is that so?"

Lowering his voice, Maher asked, "What about rebuilding the Den? What about the search for Ezmira?"

"Kit will watch over Mama Bear and aid her with the rebuild in my place. And every owner in the Lantern is hunting Ezmira now, after what she did to the Den."

"But Pimm, we will be gone for weeks!" Maher sputtered.

"I have to go, Mama Bear will never forgive me if anything else happens to you."

"That's unlikely," he sighed.

"At the very least, she'll sack me." One of the massive sails connected to the foremast snapped open and Pimm jumped.

"Have you ever been on a ship before?" asked Marielle.

"I have not." Pimm straightened their flat cap. "But I'm staying. There's no time like the present to get my sea legs."

"I give up." Maher suddenly felt a headache brewing. "Welcome aboard, Pimm."

MARIELLE

CHAPTER SIXTY-EIGHT

Marielle joined Maher on the forecastle of the ship. They were well and truly underway now. The skies were clear and a strong wind billowed the sails, allowing them to clear the bay in record time. Marielle breathed deep, filling her lungs with salt air. So long since she'd been on the water, and yet it felt just the same.

"I don't know how well Pimm is going to fare on this voyage."

"Why do you say that?" Maher gave her a sidelong look.

"Because they're currently shut up in their cabin, becoming intimately acquainted with a sick bucket."

"We're barely out to sea! I should take them a remedy."

"I already left a packet of ginger for Pimm, for when they're able to chew something again."

"Thank you, Marielle." He massaged his temples.

"When Pimm is ready, we should find them a task," she suggested. "Give them something to concentrate on besides the rocking of the ship."

Though she would admit it to only herself, Pimm's unexpected presence on board troubled Marielle. As well as she thought of Pimm, and considered them a friend, they were more capable than most of ferreting out things about Marielle she wasn't ready to reveal. And the closer they got to The Riddles, the more likely those things were to make themselves known. A small part of her hoped Pimm would remain too sick to be their usual observant self.

"That's not a bad idea. In fact, you've reminded me, there's someone you should meet." Maher led the way back to the helm. Luthais Kingfisher was there, leaning over a map table that had been brought out to the quarterdeck. To his right was the woman Maher'd identified earlier as the first mate. She stepped aside to speak to the helmsman as they approached.

"Captain," Maher nodded.

Luthais cocked a brow at him. "Yes?"

"I'd like to introduce Marielle to your first mate. I'm sure she'll be invaluable as we approach The Riddles."

"And to the barriers surrounding them." The first mate rejoined them. Easily Maher's height, she strode back to the table in a few steps. Long, carefully arranged braids hung down her back, the ends secured with red and green enamel cuffs. Russet eyes set into deep sockets assessed her as Maher made the introductions.

"Kamharida Anyanwu, first mate of the *Pi...* the *Foxglove*," he corrected himself, "this is Marielle. Our resident guide to The Riddles and all parts thereabout."

"You enjoy doing that, don't you?" the captain muttered. Maher said something back, too low for Marielle to catch, as Kamharida offered her hand.

"We'll need all of the guidance we can get." Her palm was warm and well-calloused from the years at sea.

"I'll do what I can." Marielle caught the way the first mate's faint Utollmir accent rounded out her words, giving the way she spoke a soothing, musical quality. "It's been a long time since I was last there."

"Still," Kamharida released her hand, glancing to where Maher and Luthais continued to speak in hushed tones, "you are the only one aboard who has seen those islands at all. That will be more gainful than you might realize just now."

Despite her own misgivings, the surety in Kamharida's voice calmed Marielle a great deal. "Maybe you're right."

BEAR'S DEN

PIMM

CHAPTER SIXTY-NINE

Pimm had never felt so miserable in their entire life. Enduring bed rest for a broken rib felt like a country outing compared to the never-ending, roiling waves of nausea.

Why did I agree to join this voyage in the first place?

The tiny cabin around them lurched and Pimm dove for the fresh bucket that was just delivered a little while ago.

When the sickness faded, Pimm slumped back against the wall. *There couldn't possibly be anything left in my stomach.*

The slices of dried ginger Marielle'd brought them sat on a little table bolted to the floor. Pimm crawled across the cabin floor and snagged a piece from the paper wrapping. The sharp, spiced flavor exploded inside their mouth, nearly strong enough to burn. Chewing slowly, Pimm used the table to pull themself to their feet. Hands braced, Pimm stood as still as the rocking ship allowed and focused on squeezing every last drop of relief from the ginger.

How many days had the *Foxglove* been at sea now? Two? Three or more? They'd quickly lost count. Perhaps it had only been one long, nauseating day and Pimm had exhausted their ability to tell time. The stories of sailors going mad while stuck out at sea suddenly made all the sense in the world.

Feeling marginally steadier on their feet, Pimm wobbled over to the bed while the last of the ginger dissolved on their tongue. As soon as their head hit the pillow, Pimm's eyelids grew heavy. This couldn't possibly last much longer. How was Pimm supposed to keep watch over Maher if they could barely keep themself upright?

A soft knock roused Pimm from sleep. Faint, pink light filled the cabin, as the morning sun peeked through the only window.

"Pimm?" The door creaked open and Maher crept into the room. "You alive in here?"

"Barely," they croaked, throat raw and dry.

"Here, have a sip of this." He handed over a waterskin before placing a small basket on the table. Tilting their head back, Pimm tried to swallow too much at once and promptly began coughing. "Drink slowly."

A few sips later, Pimm sighed as the soreness in their throat eased. "Thank you."

"Don't mention it." Maher took the waterskin back and replaced it with a stoneware mug of warm tea. "Careful with that, I raided the officers' stash of tea leaves in the galley."

"You are a gift from the gods."

"Glad you can finally see that," he chuckled, leaning against the edge of the table. "Who would've thought the mercurial Pimm could be felled by a bout of seasickness."

Pimm glowered at him over the rim of the mug. "Jackass."

"Am I a gift or a jackass? Surely I can't be both."

"The two titles are not independent of one another."

"Point well taken." Maher snorted. From the basket he pulled a pewter bowl and spoon. Sitting on the edge of Pimm's bed, Maher offered to swap for the mug. "You should try to eat."

"What is it?" They peered warily into the bowl.

"Barley porridge."

Pimm's stomach flipped. "I don't know..."

"It's the gentlest option on board. Recovering from seasickness won't do you much good if you're too weak from hunger."

Pimm sighed and took the bowl. The first spoonful of bland, beige mash reminded them of paste, but it went down easily enough. If only it would stay down.

"Have you ever noticed that much of our friendship revolves around one of us bringing the other food?"

"Well, it is how we met."

After a few more bites, Pimm paused to ask, "How long have we been at sea, anyway?"

"This is day three."

"Only day three?" They forced down another mouthful of porridge. "Gods, take me now."

"Nonsense. You'll be up and about before you know it."

"How can you be so disgustingly cheerful?"

"Gift of nature."

Pimm held their tongue and made it halfway through the bowl before their stomach decided it'd had enough.

"Tell me, Maher," they sipped more of the tea, now gone cold, "do you think Marielle is only on this ship to repair things with the Madam?"

"Why do you ask?"

"It feels as though something is missing. Some motivation for her presence beyond what we've been told."

Maher shifted on the bed, considering Pimm's question. "You think she's lying? Truly?"

They lifted one shoulder. "I'm not sure. Call it intuition, if you like."

"Pimm, you're the one who first insisted I could trust Marielle, what's changed?"

"I'm not saying I distrust her, but neither do I think she's told us the whole story."

The ship listed to the side. Maher moved with it, like a rider on a horse. Pimm's stomach rebelled and they clapped a hand over their mouth.

"Shall I fetch the bucket?"

Waiting a few breaths for the rolling to subside, and for the porridge to settle back down into their stomach, Pimm shook their head. "Not yet."

"Perhaps the sea gods are testing your mettle or they think you should be more trusting of your friends," Maher smirked.

"Perhaps, when I'm no longer sick, I'll convince the crew to tie you to the mainmast for the rest of the voyage."

PASHA

CHAPTER SEVENTY

Pasha and Ally drifted along beneath the bulk of the massive ship. They'd kept a solid pace since leaving the islands, swimming on their own during the day and taking refuge on Euphonia's back at night. The spear stayed strapped across Pasha's back. As they moved further into the depths, the energy trapped inside the spear sparked to life, like it had done in the hatching grounds. On the third day of the journey, Euphonia veered off to hunt away from the ship, leaving the mermaids to swim alone in its long shadow.

"I'm still amazed you found her," Pasha remarked. "Let alone befriended her."

"I'm still amazed you can't remember what sort of creature she is," Ally snorted.

"You still haven't grasped how old Euphonia is, have you, sweetheart?"

"Apparently not." With a flick of her tail, Ally flipped over and coasted on her back. An easier position to hold with her longer fluke.

"Showing off now, are we?"

"You have to admit, it's much easier than towing me across an ocean."

Pasha smiled at her lover's antics. "You know I'd gladly tow you anywhere."

"How gallant," Ally pretended to swoon, one arm thrown across her face. Gathering a tiny electric charge between her fingers, Pasha aimed it at Ally's rump and let go.

"Hey!" Ally flailed, losing her balance and sinking a tail's length before righting herself. The glower she shot Pasha's way when she caught back up was impressive. "You damned cheater."

"Never let your guard down." Pasha drifted closer. "Maybe we should use this journey to practice your skills."

"What skills?" she huffed. "I think we'd have better luck teaching me to speak to a jellyfish."

Pasha touched Ally's arm. "I know you're frustrated, Ally. Perhaps, if we find the others, they'll know of better teaching methods, something I've missed."

"Or perhaps," Ally's teeth dug into her lower lip, "It's not something I'm able to learn."

Pasha found that hard to believe, even as she knew it was a possibility. The thought of Ally not being able to defend herself sent an unbidden shiver down her spine. "I'm sure they'll be able to help," Pasha cut off. A sharp pulse from the spear sent a shock rippling through her body.

"Pasha? What's wrong?"

"The spear," she grunted as an aftershock chased the first. All her fins flexed involuntarily and Ally caught her by the arm before she careened off into the sea.

"Are you alright?" Ally squeezed her bicep. "I can feel your skin buzzing."

When the spear didn't jolt her again, Pasha forced her twitching fins to still. "I think so, something set off the energy stored inside the spear."

"What could've done that?"

"Wait." While Ally kept her in the wake of the ship, Pasha sent out a handful of searching tendrils from her own energy well. They spiraled outwards in all directions, though Pasha wasn't certain what she ought to look for.

When nothing of note came back to her, Pasha prepared to reel them back. Then, something plucked at the tendril reaching behind them. Something strong and ancient that didn't belong there.

Pasha gasped, yanked her energy back into herself. "Did you feel that?"

"Feel what? Is something out there? Is it…" Ally's eyes widened. "Is it the snapjaws?"

"No, no, it's not them," Pasha rushed to reassure her. "But there's something out there, it feels so old that it's almost wrong."

Ally glanced behind them, but of course there was nothing there to see. Her brows knit together. "Pasha, is this the same presence you felt beneath our island last year?"

"I hadn't thought of that. But no, I don't think so. It's similar, that same feeling of *need*, but it's also different."

"Does your head hurt?"

Pasha checked in with herself. "My skull feels tight, but I haven't had that kind of headache since…" she met Ally's concerned gaze, "since Hama died."

Sliding her hand down to Pasha's, Ally laced their fingers together and squeezed hard. "If you feel anything else, I want you to tell me. Alright?" When Pasha nodded, Ally looked at the hull floating above them. "Should we warn Maher and Luthais?"

"Let's wait and see if it happens again, then we'll tell them."

CHAPTER SEVENTY-ONE

Luthais was beginning to doubt his instincts when it came to courting Maher Villaon.

His older brother's insistence on being straightforward was all well and good, and Luthais had truly believed his trepidation would ease once they were out at sea. Yet without fail, Luthais found himself returning to the respectful, but detached distance that'd existed between them for most of their lives.

As much as he wanted to have a real conversation with Maher about this shift happening between them, there never seemed to be a right time or place to bring it up. There'd been some small hope that their excursion into the city would've yielded the opportunity to let his walls down. Instead they'd landed in the dead center of a brawl. And a fire that could've destroyed a district. And returned home safe, only to learn of Cal's escape.

Worse still, he couldn't quite shake the uncertainty that'd taken hold since that night in the Lantern. Witnessing how easily Maher switched between identities was unnerving. When they were alone, Luthais could say whatever thoughts popped into his mind as they came. He could laugh, and allow himself to simply enjoy the other man's company. With no one else around, Luthais felt he was with the real Maher. Out in the world, he wasn't always sure which Maher was before him. Was it the Birde Isles Intelligencer? The Magpie of Kingsport? Or someone else entirely? And if Luthais couldn't tell, how could he be forthcoming about his intentions?

Getting Maher alone long enough to talk was the first challenge. And the odds of them being alone for long anywhere on his ship were incredibly bleak.

"Captain?" Kamharida was abruptly in front of him, concern creasing her brow. How long had he been standing there on the deck like a statue? Glancing around to ensure he hadn't attracted an audience, Luthais relaxed when he saw the crew going about their evening tasks.

"Aye, First Mate?"

"There's something I think you should see."

"What's wrong?" Luthais frowned. Nothing around them appeared amiss. The sea was calm, the sails were full, they'd made excellent time in the five days they'd been at sea.

Kamharida shook her head, the cuffs adorning her braids clicked softly. "I'm not sure what it is, but it's not natural. That much I know."

Luthais followed his first mate to the aft end the ship. He couldn't make head or tail of what she wanted to show him. Something unnatural was behind the ship? In the sea? Falling from the sky? If it'd been anyone else, he'd've demanded an explanation, but Kamharida was not given to flights of fancy. And so, he accompanied her without question.

Maher and Marielle were already there, passing a spyglass between them. Luthais could plainly see the rigid set of Maher's shoulders and the way Marielle kept fiddling with her gunbelt. Scanning the wake of the ship, Luthais saw nothing out of the ordinary.

"Is it still there?" Kamharida asked as they approached.

The gunfighter's chin jerked into a nod, hands drifting down to touch the pistols hanging off either hip. "Sure as the sky is still above us."

"What are you talking about?" Luthais was in no mood for puzzles.

Maher offered him the spyglass. A deep furrow ran between his dark brows. "See for yourself."

The metal casing was warm to the touch, as if they'd been using it for some time. Stepping to the edge of the deck, Luthais lifted the glass to his eye. The distant, rolling swells and endless horizon came into focus, but naught else. "I see nothing," he snapped. "Someone'd better explain."

"Here," Maher moved closer. One hand rested on Luthais' lower back, while the other guided his arms. "Stand at an angle, now tilt the glass down slightly. Try to catch the sunlight at the edge of the lens."

Doing as he was bid, Luthais shifted his stance and allowed Maher to adjust the position of the spyglass. The hand pressed against his back might as well have been a branding iron, for how aware Luthais was of its presence. One of those slender fingers brushed the skin of his wrist and Luthais forced himself to pay attention to what Maher said next.

"Now, look straight at the horizon line." Maher's soft words burrowed into his ear. "Do you see it?"

Squinting into the eyepiece, Luthais caught a glimpse of something out on the water. A hazy outline, no more than a prism reflected through glass. At first glance, it would be easy enough to mistake it for a trick of the light, a natural reflection of the setting sun on the water. But the longer Luthais looked, the more the outline took shape.

"Is that... a ship?"

"Seems to be," Maher murmured next to him.

"And it appears to be following us," Kamharida added.

Luthais lowered the spyglass and Maher's hands fell away. A brief sensation of loss rolled over his skin like gooseflesh. "How did you even spot this?"

"It was Marielle," Maher nodded at the young woman.

"I was trying to gauge where we were on the map when I saw it," she offered. "Thought my eyes were cheating at first."

"Captain," Kamharida closed the four of them into a circle, her voice lowering to just above a whisper. "I suggest we draw no attention to this until we learn more. The crew will surely panic if they hear rumors of some ghost ship chasing the *Foxglove*."

"Agreed, First Mate." Luthais collapsed the spyglass. "But how do we determine its purpose?"

"Maybe Ally and Pasha can help," Maher suggested.

"How can you ask someone who isn't here?" Marielle frowned.

"Oh, right, did I not mention they're both swimming beneath the ship?"

Marielle's mouth opened and closed like a fish caught on a hook, though nothing came out.

"It would appear you did forget that little detail," Kamharida smirked. Taking the other woman gently by the elbow, she steered Marielle away. "Come, I'll explain it to you while we go over the route in the chart room."

When they were alone, well as alone as they could be with half the crew still moving about the deck, Luthais turned to Maher. "How can we communicate with them? I thought they meant to stay off the ship."

Maher thought for a moment, lips pursed and fingers tapping out a random beat against his sternum. Something flashed across his face and Maher began to unbutton his shirt.

"What are you doing?" Luthais gawked, unable to look away. After the first few buttons were freed, Maher withdrew a braided silver chain. Hanging from the end was a sizable, fossilized shark tooth. The polished black surface gleamed in the fading light. Luthais knew it well, his sister had worn it around her neck for nigh on twenty years.

"Wait, isn't that Ally's?"

"It was, yes."

"Why do you have it?"

"Remember the little package addressed to me and left in your cabin last winter?"

Luthais nodded slowly, already guessing where this was heading.

"Ally didn't need it anymore after becoming a mermaid."

"So she gifted it to you." Luthais reached out to touch it, then hesitated. The worst tongue lashing he'd ever received from their father was the result of touching this necklace without permission. "May I?"

"Of course." Maher dropped the shark tooth into his palm, the chain pooled around it. "I'll be damned and dusted," Luthais breathed. "This is... it's..."

"Warm, isn't it?" Fascination shined in Maher's eyes. "It's been a great help for my shoulder. Bless Al and Pasha every day for leaving it to me."

Brushing a thumb over the fossil, Luthais felt the otherworldly heat transfer into his skin. "How?"

"Infused with mermaid magic," he grinned. "And now I finally understand what the note meant."

"What are you talking about?"

Plucking the shark tooth up by its chain, Maher slipped it back over his head. "*If you're ever in trouble, just bring the tooth home.*"

"What does that mean?"

Maher looked across the deck, where lanterns were being lit to combat the growing darkness.

"I know it's too late to try today but, first thing in the morning, I'm going to need a longboat."

CHAPTER SEVENTY-TWO

Ally woke as shafts of morning light filtered through the surface. It wasn't quite the same as feeling the warmth of the sun on her face, but still pleasant in its own way.

Beneath her cheek, Euphonia's eel-like body rocked with each deliberate undulation of her tail. It was decidedly easier to stay on her back as a mermaid, than it'd been as a human. Something about her new skin and scales allowed her to sprawl out against Euphonia's sandy hide and stay there. So long as there were no sudden movements. They were following just behind the ship. Still deep enough not to be noticed, but far enough back to enjoy the sunshine.

Sitting up carefully, tail still tucked beneath her, Ally yawned and stretched her arms overhead. "Is it my imagination, or is the water getting warmer?"

"It is, actually." Pasha swam up beside her and Ally jumped.

"Good morning, Ally."

"Good morning," She swatted half-heartedly at Pasha. "How long have you been awake?"

"Not very long. Are you hungry?"

Before Ally could answer, her stomach rumbled loud enough to be heard.

"I thought you might be." Pasha lifted the small hunting net they'd brought along. Six fat bluefish wriggled inside. "Shall we?"

Mouth already watering, Ally slid from Euphonia's back. "I think you were up and about earlier than you let on, but I'm too hungry to mind."

When there was nothing left of the fish but bones, Ally and Pasha caught up with the ship. Euphonia'd left to hunt her own food the moment she smelled blood in the water.

It felt good to spread out and really stretch her fins. They raced each other beneath the hull, turning flips and cutting back at sharp angles. Pasha was still faster, her sleek form slicing through the water like a bird through the air. But at least Ally could now give proper chase. As a human she'd been about as useful in the sea as a stray buoy.

Pasha was catching up to her as she crossed from port to starboard side. While diving down, Ally flicked her longer copper fins upwards at the last moment. Leaving Pasha to follow in the opposite direction.

"You sneak!"

Chuckling to herself, Ally slowed and curved back, ready to be caught by Pasha with open arms. But the mermaid was frozen in place, one hand braced on the ship's hull.

"Pasha?" Ally swam towards her, only to be pushed back as a sharp pulse rippled through the water. There was a bright, iridescent flash and spots danced in her vision.

When Ally finally recovered, she found a golden ribbon of energy piercing through the sea. It split in two and wrapped around each of their wrists.

"What is this?"

"The shark tooth, it's touched the sea." Pasha pointed to where the beacon curved beneath the ship and up out of the sea.

"Maher!" Ally shot towards the surface.

"Ally, wait!" Pasha scrambled after her.

The glowing ribbon led straight to a smaller shape floating next to Luthais' ship. A longboat? Swimming just past it, Ally paused long enough for Pasha to reach her.

"Ally!" she hissed. "You can't just surface without making sure it's safe."

"What if Maher's in trouble?"

"What if Maher's not the one holding the tooth right now?" Pasha countered. "I'll look first, I blend in more than you do."

"Fine!" Ally huffed. "Just look quickly, please."

Pasha's head disappeared above the surface. A string of words, distorted by the separation between water and air and sounding very much like a curse, left Pasha before she ducked back under.

"It's him." she muttered.

"Is he alright?" Ally's tail twitched with the urge to see for herself.

"Of course, he only wants to speak with us."

"Oh, for the goddess' sake," Ally sighed and pressed a quick kiss to Pasha's lips. "Let's go see what he wants."

Together, they swam up to the smaller boat that was tethered to the ship. Maher smiled as soon as he saw them. "Al! How goes the journey so far?"

"Maher, darling," Ally's fingers curled over the rowlock holding the oar in place, "did we not mention that call was for emergencies?"

"Er... I seem to remember something along those lines, yes."

"And are you in trouble?"

"Well, not exactly."

Ally shook the rowboat. "I ought to capsize you! Do you know how worried I was just now?"

"I'll help you," Pasha grumbled.

"Wait!" Maher clung to the bench beneath him. "It might be an emergency."

Ally exchanged a puzzled glance with Pasha before asking Maher, "How so?"

"There's something odd following us."

Pasha's ears perked up. "What do you mean?"

"It's a ship, I think, but also not a ship."

"If you were speaking Saprean I couldn't understand you less." Ally shook her head.

"We can only get a glimpse of it at dawn or dusk, when the sun hits the horizon. This is going to sound mad." Maher scrubbed both hands over his beard. "There's an invisible ship following this one, Al. I have no idea how they're doing it or what they want, but I doubt it's to invite us over for tea."

Ally looked to Pasha, the mermaid's brow ridges wrinkled and she ran her tongue over her teeth. "Do you think it's the same thing you felt the other night?"

"It could be." Pasha's gaze traveled the long way up to the masts of the ship. "You can see it at sundown?"

"That's right," said Maher. "Do you know what it is?"

When Pasha didn't respond right away, Ally brushed their tail fins together. "Perhaps if we can take a look ourselves?"

"Yes, that would help."

"We'll come aboard at dusk."

CHAPTER SEVENTY-THREE

Maher had the window to his cabin open and waiting for them as the daylight waned. The climb up the side of the ship was more grueling than Ally'd anticipated. How had Pasha done this so many times on their journey back to the Isles last year after they took over Dare's ship? Twice, she had to let Pasha boost her over a particularly steep slope in the stern.

Finally, they made it into Maher's cabin. It didn't escape Ally's notice that it was directly below the captain's quarters. Maybe it was a coincidence but, then again, maybe her brother was keeping Maher close.

Sprawled against the cabin wall, Ally panted while Pasha examined the clothes Maher'd laid out across his narrow bed.

"How are you not the least bit winded?" Ally wheezed.

"You've only been a mermaid for a year, sweetheart, you'll grow stronger over time." Pasha held up a pair of trousers, distaste clearly written on her face. "Do we really have to put these on?"

"We weren't planning to come aboard, remember?" Pulling herself to her feet, Ally crossed the room on wobbly legs. "Which makes us beggars, and therefore, we cannot expect too much."

"I prefer ingenuity over begging." Snatching up the blanket from Maher's bed, Pasha wrapped it around herself. Much like the scraps of sail she'd worn when they first met.

With a wry smile, Ally selected a shirt from the pile and pulled it over her head. Next, she found the loosest trousers available. They obviously weren't Maher's, she'd have barely been able to fit a calf into anything of his. There was a soft knock on the door as Ally finished buttoning up.

"Ally? Pasha?" Maher whispered.

"We're here." Ally lifted the latch and his head poked into the room.

"Are you ready? Ga-Seung has most of the crew gathered at the forecastle, but we should move quickly." He took a second look at Pasha. "Is that my bedding?"

"No time to explain" Ally said as she shooed him out.

He passed each of them a rough rain cloak, the kind that could be worn on deck during a storm. Hoods drawn over their heads, they followed Maher up one set of steep steps, keeping back in the shadows while he knocked on Luthais' door. Kamharida answered and ushered the three of them inside.

"Oh my..." Ally took Pasha's hand, startled by the number of people waiting inside.

While Kamharida wasn't exactly a surprise, Ally'd only really been expecting Luthais. But there were two others standing with her brother by a map table. A curvy young woman with shorn black hair and another person whose face was shadowed by a dark brown flat cap.

"Ally," Luthais greeted them, "and Pasha, welcome."

Ally reached for her hood, then hesitated. She hadn't seen Kamharida since becoming a mermaid, and these other people she didn't know at all.

"It's okay, Al," Maher encouraged. "This is Pimm, the door guard from the Bear's Den. I've told you about them."

Pimm lifted their cap, revealing a tapered face and gray eyes. "Pleased to make your acquaintance, Lady Alphonsine."

"Just Ally is fine, please." The tension in her shoulders eased a bit. "Of course, I've heard much about you, Pimm."

"And I you." They gave her a kind smile.

"This is Marielle," said Maher, "our guide to The Riddles."

"Hello, Marielle," said Ally. Something was oddly familiar about her.

Pasha had remained quiet up until then. Nodding at her, Ally pulled her hood back and Pasha did the same.

"Sea spirits save me." Kamharida's gaze locked on the spear still strapped to Pasha's back.

"Come, the light will pass quickly." Luthais beckoned them to the large window at the back of his cabin. Two sets of saucer-like eyes followed them around the room. Ally could've sworn she heard Marielle recite some sort of prayer under her breath, even if she couldn't catch the meaning.

Kamharida handed over two spyglasses to Ally and Pasha, while Pimm and Marielle merely watched in stunned silence. Apparently, Maher hadn't prepared them very well for the sight of two mermaids walking around the ship.

Standing as Luthais and Maher instructed, Ally put her eye to the glass and focused on the horizon. At first, all she saw was sea and sky. "I'm not sure I see anything unusual…"

"There!" Pasha stepped closer to the open window, nearly sticking her spyglass outside. "I can just make it out."

As she tried to copy Pasha's stance, Ally glimpsed a faint, shimmering shape some distance behind the ship. Whatever it was, it was massive. A ship made the most sense, as much sense as an invisible ship made to begin with.

"Do you have any idea what could produce such an illusion, Pasha?" Maher asked.

Lowering the spyglass, Pasha hissed through her teeth. "Not from this distance. But it feels like the same presence from the other night. Something very old."

"You can sense that from here?" Ally handed her glass to Luthais. "How?"

Reaching over her shoulder, Pasha touched the green stone shaft of the spear. Ally understood then, whatever was out there, it was speaking to the energy the mermaid warrior left behind.

"How do we make sure?" asked Kamharida.

Ally gauged the distance once more. "We could swim towards it and investigate."

"We?" Maher screeched.

"Pasha and I."

"Al, I'm not so sure that's a good idea."

Ally rolled her eyes. "We can make that distance in half the time it would take to send a boat, and we're far less likely to be caught."

"Absolutely not." Luthais' voice boomed through the cabin, making everyone except Kamharida startle. "We don't even know what's hidden behind that godsbedamned thing. I will not allow you to put yourselves in unnecessary danger."

"*Allow* us?" Ally glared at her brother.

"Thank you!" said Maher.

"Don't you start!"

"Captain," Kamharida stepped calmly between Luthais and Ally, "you must concede their point. They have a greater chance of learning what this is, who or what is behind it, and if they mean us any harm."

"See?" said Ally. "Your first mate agrees, Luthais."

"I have a solution." Pasha squeezed Ally's shoulder. Everyone turned their attention to the mermaid wearing Maher's bedspread. "The best option will be to wait until dark and then swim out to investigate. But I will go alone."

MARIELLE

CHAPTER SEVENTY-FOUR

Silence filled the cabin following the mermaid's suggestion.

Maher edged towards Lady Alphonsine like a hostler approaching a skittish horse. "Perhaps Pasha is right, eh?"

"What do you mean, you'll go alone?" Ally demanded, shaking Pasha's hand off.

Eyes like two black mirrors focused on Ally and Marielle did not know how she could stare so confidently back into those depths.

A mermaid. A *real mermaid* was standing in the room, arguing with another mermaid who'd once been human. Every story her grandparents had ever told came flooding back to Marielle. But she reminded herself, these weren't the same monsters she'd been taught to fear. Things of nightmares, who could ensnare you if they learned your name. It was why children in The Riddles were forbidden from saying each other's names near the water.

Pimm hadn't uttered another word since greeting the mermaids. Glancing over, she found they still looked a little green around the gills.

"Ally," Pasha attempted to reason with her, "it will be safer if I go and you stay here on the ship."

"But what if something happens to you?"

"Please, Ally."

"She's right," the captain said at last. "It will be far less noticeable if only one of you goes. And Pasha has more experience with defending herself, if it comes to that." He eyed the long, wicked spear strapped to the mermaid's back.

Maher spoke up again, "It's for the best."

Ally rounded on him. "The *best?*"

Wincing, Maher held up his hands in surrender. "Poor choice of words, Al. I'm sorry."

Why would that be a poor choice of words? Marielle tried to catch Maher's eye, but he was focused on Ally.

"I'll send a signal if I run into trouble," Pasha offered. "You will be the only one who could understand it, if needed."

"I know," Ally whispered, and Marielle suddenly felt she was witnessing something intimate that she really shouldn't. "I just hate that I can't help you. Please, be careful."

Unconcerned about their audience, Pasha pulled Ally into an embrace. Marielle's throat tightened and, next to her, Pimm averted their gaze.

"I promise," Pasha said. When they parted, she turned to Luthais. "When night has fallen, I will try to learn who exactly has been following us."

PASHA

CHAPTER SEVENTY-FIVE

True to her word Pasha waited until full dark settled around the ship before diving from the cabin window.

Ally'd finally agreed to stay on board with her brother and Maher. Though a small part of Pasha still worried she'd try to follow, and was sorely tempted to warn Euphonia of the situation. But the sea monster was nowhere to be seen below the ship.

Moonlight flitted between the waves as Pasha swam. Trying to conserve her energy, she let the current carry her as much as possible. Pasha knew she was getting closer when she began to notice a heaviness to the water. It clung to her in a cloying film, oily and unnatural against her skin. The spines of her pelvic fins flexed, trying to escape the sensation.

Any sea creatures that might've been nearby had all fled. Whatever this thing was, it had warded off every living thing in the area. Just as the miasma was making it difficult for her to breathe, Pasha came upon some kind of unseen barrier. It stretched as far as she could sense without tapping into her well. Placing a hand against it, Pasha half-expected a solid resistance. Instead, her fingers sank in, like grabbing a sea sponge. A shiver of revulsion crawled over her skin and scales. But, beneath the discomfort, there was something familiar here.

Teeth clenched, Pasha forced her way past the barrier. The crossing was torturously slow, but when she emerged on the other side, the sickly film was gone and daylight stabbed at her eyes. And before her was one of the largest ships Pasha had ever seen.

Easily twice the size of Luthais' ship, the hulking vessel hardly stirred the water as it sailed along the current. Shielding her eyes, Pasha tried to locate the source of the light that surrounded the hull. As she adjusted to the sudden flip from night to day, the answer made itself known. Energy, harnessed and imbued into the ship until every board and nail radiated with a sickly glow in shades of yellow and green. It shimmered in the water, hanging in ribbons like seaweed. A twisted version of her own power, contorted to the point that it made her physically ill.

Swimming as close as she dared, Pasha floated slowly towards the surface. It truly was like daylight had cocooned the entire ship. But the added light also made it easy to see the ornate carvings decorating the outside. Perfect for climbing.

Gouging her nails into the wood, Pasha split her tail and made her way up the side of the bow. Dozens of closed gunports lined the hull to her right. What kind of ship had a need for so many weapons?

As she neared the deck that sat atop the bow, Pasha paused to listen for any humans that might be above. But she heard very little. In fact, for a ship that size, it was eerily quiet. Closing the remaining distance, Pasha slowly raised her head until she could see between the split posts of the rail.

What is wrong with those humans?

The crew moving about the ship appeared to be human, but there was something decidedly off about them. Their motions were slow and irregular, limbs not in use dangling as if they didn't know how to use them. A sailor hauling a coil of rope passed near Pasha's hiding place, and the stench hit her nose.

Tides protect me, they're dead!

Ducking out of sight, Pasha pressed her face to the wood and breathed in the scent of damp earth and lacquer. None of this made sense. The magical curtain hiding an entire ship from view. The raw energy filling every nook and cranny. The crew of humans that were not human, dead but not dead.

"You're certain 'tis a Birde Isles ship we're chasing, Quartermaster?"

Pasha shot up. *That* human didn't sound dead. Peering onto the deck once more, she saw two live humans walking in her direction. A woman and an older man Pasha thought she recognized. His stone-gray mustache trailed down the sides of his face and hung below his chin. Where had Pasha seen him before?

"Aye, Smith," the man said gruffly, "the captain saw the Kingfisher flag right enough."

"But how, sir?" she asked, glancing around uncertainly. "We're still at least a league too far back to make that from the crow's nest."

"I think you already know the answer without my havin' to say it."

Pasha held her breath as another dead sailor passed by. Something green winked at her from the walking corpse's face and Pasha nearly lost her grip.

They couldn't have...

"Is there a problem here?" A new voice joined the others.

"N-not at all, Captain," the woman, Smith, stammered. Pasha craned her neck to see who'd had made all the color drain from Smith's face. But the damned sailors were blocking her view.

"Then I expect you have work to do, don't you sailor?"

"Aye, Captain!" Smith made her escape.

The man – what had they just called him? – turned to the captain. "What's our aim in trailing this other ship now that we have the machine?"

"I haven't decided yet." Heavy boots thudded closer to him, but Pasha still couldn't see clearly. "Perhaps we'll just scare them a bit, if they have nothing of value. Or perhaps we'll put the guns through an exercise and send them to the depths."

Pasha's nails scored the side of the ship. Something about this captain's voice grated on her nerves and made her scales itch.

"If you wish, Captain. As long as we can keep to our arrangement."

"We will, Swain," The captain finally stepped into Pasha's line of sight. "Don't you fret about that."

No! It can't be. She can't be here. She's supposed to be dead!

Waves roared in Pasha's ears and all her senses focused on the creature standing just across the deck.

So is everyone else on this ship. A small voice whispered in the back of Pasha's mind. *What have you done?*

Climbing back down the ship, Pasha made it about halfway before the urge to jump overwhelmed her and she dove back into the sea.

Fins unfurling as her legs fused together, Pasha started swimming before her tail was fully formed. She had to get back to Ally, had to warn everyone about what she'd seen and heard. Abandoning all pretense of stealth, Pasha shot for the filmy curtain surrounding the cursed ship. Arms stretched out, Pasha braced herself to dive through.

A head-splitting screech struck her and Pasha clapped her hands over her ears.

Something tackled her from the side, sending them both spiraling through the water. Twisting hard, Pasha raked her nails into her attacker and pulled free. As she spun around, Pasha reached around her back for the spear. Only to remember she'd left it with Ally.

Another scream drew Pasha's attention and she came face-to-face with one of the snake women from the cave murals. A siren.

Red hair swirled wildly around the siren's head. She shoved it back and emerald eyes burned into Pasha. Four, angry gashes carved across her beautiful face and her full lips curled to bare her teeth.

"What have we here?" she snarled. "The last of the mermaids, come to surrender?"

Pasha's eyes widened a fraction and her hands curled into fists. The last? How could she possibly know that unless... They really had captured all the others. Had this siren been one to hunt down Pasha's kin? Had she tortured Hama until Pasha's cousin could hardly speak?

Thick, white-hot charges gathered unbidden around Pasha's arms and flowed down into her clenched fists.

"Where are they?" Pasha growled.

A tri-colored serpent's tail coiled beneath the siren as she hissed, "You'll know soon enough, when you join them."

Almost too fast for Pasha to catch, the siren struck. Their hands locked together just as Pasha brought her arms up. Long, spindly fingers curled around and jagged nails dug into Pasha's wrists. Bright scales in shades of blue and green stood out on the siren's forearm. Mermaid scales. That's how they were doing all his. Must have even been how they...

Shaking off the wild whirlpool of thoughts before they could consume her, Pasha harnessed the grief and rage that'd settled into her since the day Hama died. With a roar, Pasha thrust the charges from her hands into the siren's. There was a blinding flash and the smell of sizzled flesh. The force blew them apart. Sending the siren back towards the ship and Pasha through the barrier, out into the sea.

CHAPTER SEVENTY-SIX

Ally paced across Luthais' cabin. Every trip around the room brought her back to the open window, where she scanned the swells for any sign of Pasha.

There'd been a brief attempt by Maher to distract her, drawing her into a conversation with Marielle. As they talked, Ally truly got the sense that she'd met the Riddle Islander before. But that was highly unlikely. Surely she'd have remembered encountering someone like Marielle, no matter how much time had passed.

They were interrupted when Kamharida requested Marielle's assistance on deck. Now Ally prowled the cabin like a caged bear. Maher'd offered food and drink, but her stomach was too knotted to accept. Luthais had gone above as well, going through his evening rounds and getting updates from the officers.

Pasha's spear leaned against a nearby wall. Whatever energy was stored in the green stone had gone quiet since Pasha left. Had it ever been out of the sea before? Was it anything beyond a simple weapon without a mermaid to wield it?

"She should be back by now." Ally gripped the windowsill after yet another turn around the cabin.

"Give her time, Al," said Maher. "It's not even midnight and we don't yet know how far she had to swim."

"Exactly, what if she hasn't even reached this damned invisible ship yet? What if the power concealing it has clouded her senses and now she's lost?"

"I'm sure Pasha's on her way back now. She said there'd be a signal if she was in danger."

Before Ally could list all the possible ways Pasha could be unable to signal them, the cabin door opened.

"Any word?" Luthais strode into the room and tossed his jacket over a chair.

"Not yet." Maher sighed. "But your sister has worn an impressive groove into the floor."

"Funny," she snapped. "Here's another for you. If Pasha isn't back in the next hour, I'm going after her."

"You promised Pasha you'd stay here!" Maher protested.

"You're not going back on your word, are you?" Luthais added.

Slowly, Ally turned on her bare heel to face both of them. They knew better than to order her to stay, but this synchronicity was new.

If she was forced to wait and worry until Pasha's return, perhaps she could have a bit of fun.

"My my, don't you two sound just like Mama and Father."

Maher sputtered, turning a shade of red Ally hadn't thought him capable. Luthais' jaw worked back and forth, his wide chest puffing out until he resembled a bull about to charge.

Satisfied with her petty moment of meddling, Ally turned back to the window. A cool breeze swept up from the waves to kiss her brow.

Please, she begged the sea, *keep Pasha safe.*

CHAPTER SEVENTY-SEVEN

Every muscle in Pasha's tail screamed for rest. Ignoring the burn traveling steadily up her spine, Pasha only beat her tail harder.

The force of the shock she'd thrown at the siren was enough to put considerable distance between them. But Pasha had no way of knowing how quickly she'd recover, or how many more of her ilk were in the water around that ship.

Don't look back. Don't slow down. Make it back to Ally. Pasha repeated those words to herself as she swam. A mantra to combat the ache spreading through her body. Finally, the shadow of Luthais' ship began to take. Pasha nearly cried with relief, but she couldn't rest yet. Not until she was back by Ally's side.

The foul odor reached her before she saw them. Death, decay, and despair. Then came the low rumble of a creature with far too many teeth.

Two snapjaws swept in from either side. Their eyes glowed blood red in the murky water. Pasha did the only thing she could, she stopped swimming and curled into a ball. The sudden lack of movement sent her sinking fast.

The snapjaws collided in a tangle of snarls, tough hides, and teeth. While they fought, Pasha made for the ship. A harsh growl that rattled her bones was her only warning before a long snout struck from behind. Pasha spun through the water until she no longer knew which way was up.

When she finally slowed to a stop, the snapjaws were circling her and steadily drifting closer.

"Hello again, little mermaid," one of them hissed.

"Did you miss us?" The other took a toying swipe at her with a wide, webbed foot.

Pasha's heart hammered in her chest. "Why are you here?"

"We've made some new friends," the first one answered smugly.

"But we do have to thank you." The second's teeth flashed in the moonlight. "If not for you, we'd still be bound to that trench."

Bound? Dizziness washed over Pasha as she tried to keep them both in sight.

"If you're so grateful, then let me pass."

"But our new friends want a word with you, mermaid!" They stopped circling, red eyes locked on Pasha. "More than a word, in fact."

Calling on the last of her strength, Pasha gathered charges into her palms. She knew, deep down, if they handed her over to the sirens, Pasha would never make it back to Ally.

The snapjaws closed in and Pasha raised her arms, electricity crackled.

Like a rogue wave, a creature much larger and with even sharper teeth rammed into the nearest snapjaw.

Euphonia! Pasha had never been so happy to see the sea monster. There was a distinct crunch as Euphonia's teeth closed around the snapjaw. Searching for the other one, Pasha threw the charges at it and scrambled out of Euphonia's way. Howling, the free snapjaw fled as blood clouded the water and Pasha swam hard in the other direction.

Ally cried out when Pasha pulled herself through the cabin window. She hit the floor, shaken, bleeding, and exhausted.

"Pasha!" Ally rushed to her side, knees hitting the wooden floorboards with a thud.

"It's... they're..." Panting through the burn in her lungs, Pasha sucked in a gulp of air and choked on it.

"Easy, pace yourself, Pasha." Ally laid a hand over Pasha's hammering heart and opened a link between them.

Pasha's depleted well pulled greedily from Ally's energy. When the trembling in her limbs subsided, Pasha pulled back. "That's enough for now, thank you Ally."

"You're sure?" Hazel eyes searched her face.

"I don't want to weaken you too, sweetheart."

"Here, Pasha." Maher approached carefully and wrapped a blanket around her shoulders. Pasha hadn't even realized he was in the room. Her only thoughts since Euphonia came to her rescue had been for Ally. Now she saw Luthais was there as well. Watching them warily, keeping his distance.

"Would a drink of water help?" Maher asked softly.

"I think so, thank you." Ally smoothed the wet tendrils stuck to Pasha's forehead. Working down, she checked Pasha over. "Oh, Pasha," Ally spotted the wounds atop her hands and wrists. "What happened?"

Maher returned with a pitcher, cup, and clean cloth. Passing the cloth to Ally, he poured Pasha a drink. The water soothed her throat while Ally cleaned her other hand. Though Pasha's heart still pounded steadily in her chest, the care they showed helped calm her considerably. It was surprising how concerned Maher appeared to be. Though they'd moved past their rocky start, Pasha'd still considered him Ally's friend. But now, she supposed, perhaps he was hers as well.

Ally's touch was gentle as she examined the punctures in Pasha's hands, but a storm raged in her eyes. "Who did this?"

"And what did you find?" Maher added, refilling Pasha's cup again.

"A siren." Pasha's voice caught and she drank a bit more. "I was attacked by a siren on my way back." Looking at her hands, she wondered absently if they would scar.

Pressing a hand to her mouth, Ally looked at the others.

"*Sirens?*" Maher yelped. "When were sirens ever part of this arrangement?"

"We think they're the ones holding Pasha's family hostage." said Ally.

"I'm sure of it now," Pasha bared her teeth and the two men shrank back. "And there were snapjaws. They've formed some alliance."

A gray tinge crept over Maher's face. "Al, is that one of the monsters you dredged up from only the gods know where?"

"It is," she whispered.

Luthais rose from his seat across the room. "What exactly are snapjaws?"

"How would you describe them, Al?" Maher's voice cracked. "Nightmare crocodiles?"

"Intelligent nightmare crocodiles," said Ally.

"Fuck," Luthais ran a hand through his hair.

"Listen, there's more." Pasha rasped.

"Of course there is," Maher muttered.

"You were right, there is a ship behind this one. A massive ship, with more guns than I've ever seen. The sirens must be the ones disguising it. They have..." throat burning, Pasha's eyes squeezed shut.

"What is it, Pasha?" Ally rubbed her back.

"I don't know how, but they're using mermaid powers. The siren I saw had scales embedded to her skin. They *stole* them." When Pasha's eyes opened, two pearly tears slid down her face. She would've probably tried harder to stop them before they fell, but she was beyond caring now if Ally's kin saw her cry.

"I'm so sorry, Pasha." Catching the tears on her finger, Ally dropped them onto Pasha's hands. There was a tell-tale sizzle and the wounds knit together.

"So, that's how you did it," Maher murmured, rubbing his shoulder almost unconsciously. Luthais looked from Pasha to Maher until realization dawned on him and his green eyes widened.

"They've taken my people's power and twisted it into something vile," Pasha spat. "What they've done to the humans on that ship,"

"What did they do?" asked Luthais.

"They're... the crew, they're dead. But not still. They move around the ship as if they were alive, but they aren't."

"A dead crew?" Maher walked shakily to the table. "How is that possible?"

"The scales," Ally answered for her. "They're using the mermaid scales, aren't they?"

Pasha nodded. "And there's more."

"Dear gods, what else can there be?" Maher exclaimed. Luthais placed a steadying hand on his shoulder.

"Ally," Pasha took both her hands. "It's Dare. She's on the ship."

Every drop of color drained from Ally's face. "*What?*"

"Captain Dare. She's alive. Or at the very least, she's not dead."

"Pasha, that's not possible. We both saw her drown."

"We did, sweetheart, but the sirens must have brought her back. I don't know why."

Time froze as Ally came to terms with what she'd heard. Maher slowly sank into a chair, brow creased, gaze fixed on the far wall.

After a while, Luthais' gruff voice cut through the quiet. "Is it the same as the crew? Just going through the motions?"

"No, the crew may be moving but they're still dead."

"Like puppets," Ally breathed.

Pasha squeezed her hands. "But Dare is different. She doesn't appear to be human any longer, but she's definitely not dead either."

A shudder rolled through Ally. "What could the sirens possibly want with her?"

Maher's palm struck the table. "This can't be right."

"Are you calling me a liar?" Pasha growled.

"Maher," Ally frowned. "What are you saying?"

He stood again, scrubbing a hand roughly over his beard. "I'm not denying you saw something, Pasha. But you said yourself the sirens have corrupted the mermaids' power. If they can hide an entire ship, couldn't they also make you see a person who wasn't really there? Or make someone else look like Dare?"

"So you don't believe it's also possible they could do all that, but couldn't have raised someone from the dead?" Luthais asked.

"I can't believe it, not until I see the proof for myself."

With Ally's help, Pasha rose to her feet, the blanket clutched around her shoulders. "Well, they plan to attack as soon as they're close enough. I've no doubt you'll get your wish."

FORAOISE

CHAPTER SEVENTY-EIGHT

A longboat was lowered over the starboard side, delivering Swain to where the fire-haired siren waited. She'd burst from the waves, screeching for Swain's attention. It was the first time Foraoise had witnessed the extent of the hold she held over her quartermaster. Instantly, Swain dropped everything, his body taking him across the deck. Even as he swore and protested, his face contorted at his inability to disobey.

The sirens had quickly learned that Foraoise could not be summoned at will, no matter how many of them knew her name. So they spoke through Swain since the sirens couldn't come aboard and the captain couldn't be compelled to come down. A burden he bore well, but Foraoise would not tolerate Swain being whistled for like an old dog much longer.

This will not do, not at all. Foraoise watched, stone-faced as Swain reached the water.

The siren hauled herself onto the nose of the boat, rocking it and Swain violently. Narrowing her gaze, Foraoise could just make out the siren's face in the light of Swain's lamp. Four swollen scratches pulsed against her alabaster cheek.

What sort of creature could have done that? Leaning against the railing, Foraoise tried to block out the noise of the ship and focus on the heated conversation happening below. Slowly, scraps of words began to take shape. It was as if she were underwater, listening to someone speaking from above the surface.

"We should... islands as agreed. Not... some ship." The siren hissed.

The last of the distance melted away, and Foraoise could hear everything, clear as day.

Swain appeared at a loss. "The machine is not yet operational, which is why we set a course for open water." He stared openly at her face. "What in the gods' names happened?"

"A *mermaid,* that's what happened!"

"Mermaid?" Swain glanced up to where the captain waited. "What sort of mermaid?"

"Does it matter?" she screeched, high enough to break glass. "There's a mermaid roaming free out there, the only one we failed to capture. And when I catch that shark-faced bitch..."

Foraoise lost her hold on the conversation. The sounds of the ship came rushing back and she clutched the rail as her mind reeled.

A mermaid, the last mermaid according to Swain's captor, with the face of a shark? The same mermaid that tricked Foraoise into drowning herself on the deck of her own ship?

That little monster was nearby, in the waters around this very ship. And the siren *lost* her?

The sirens wanted them to sail immediately for the Birde Isles once the turbine was retrieved. But Swain was right, they'd needed the time away from land to get it working.

And when the barrelman spotted an Utollmir vessel flying the Kingfisher flag nearby, Foraoise allowed herself a little detour. Now it appeared this ship was sailing straight for The Riddles.

And if her murderous mermaid was also nearby, did that mean her niece was as well?

"Captain?"

Everything around Foraoise contracted until she found Swain standing beside her on the deck. Was he back on board already?

"Captain," he tried again, "I assume you heard some of what was said?"

"Aye, Swain, that I did."

"And? Do you think it's her?"

"I'd stake the crew's lives on it."

Swain's mustache twitched. "The crew's lives?"

"Well, I've only just gotten mine back. I'm in no rush to wager it."

They stood in silence for a while. The briny sea air ruffled Foraoise's hair. She barely felt it. A thread of irritation curled in her gut over the mermaid being so close and slipping their grasp.

But it was nothing like what she'd've felt before she died. The simmering layer of rage was still present, but it was something that kept her in motion more than something to be felt. A distant part of Foraoise's mind wondered if it would always be like this from now on. Every emotion living and dying beneath a thick blanket of fog. Another, even more remote part of her, asked if she even cared?

Swain cleared his throat. "What're your orders, Captain?"

"We catch up with the Kingfisher ship, as planned."

"The sirens won't take kindly to another delay."

Foraoise's gaze dropped to the black, churning swells surrounding the ship. If no other person could've told Captain Foraoise Dare how to write her own story, then no creatures out of a fishwife's tale would either. "They'll get what they want soon enough."

"Aye, Captain," he grunted before departing to relay her orders to the crew.

Foraoise stared at the waves long after Swain left. Might've stood in that spot until dawn if one of the corpse sailors hadn't bumped into her, lugging a role of canvas.

Spinning in place, Foraoise stared them down. "Watch that drag sailor!"

The walking corpse ground to a stop. A violet scale embedded into their forehead glowed and Foraoise felt a scorching pain on her chest. Like being branded by a hot iron.

With the grating crack of bones grinding together, the sailor fixed its dead eyes on Foraoise, then on the canvas. Gathering it into both arms, the corpse lifted it clear of the deck and continued on their way. None of the other dead sailors paid the interaction any mind.

"That was educational." Foraoise touched the scale that had cooled once again. Turning back to the railing, she found a set of handprints pressed into the wood, where hers had been moments before. "Very educational, indeed."

CHAPTER SEVENTY-NINE

Maher paced the *Foxglove's* deck, unable to be still. With every step, his thoughts tumbled over each other, all vying for attention. Even though Euphonia was beneath the ship, he still hadn't felt comfortable with Ally and Pasha returning to the sea for the night. Gods be praised, they both agreed. He'd gladly given them his cabin, so they'd have somewhere private to rest. And it was just as well, because Maher wouldn't be sleeping tonight.

After his third or fourth lap around the mainmast, Maher paused to check his pocket watch. It was just past midnight. They had another six hours 'til dawn at least, when the ghost ship would be visible again. But then what? How could they possibly prepare to face an enemy they couldn't see? Luthais and Kamharida were off somewhere, strategizing that very quandary. They'd have to inform the other officers at least, before too long. A ship could hardly mount an attack without the bosun and gunner involved. Even the purser would have to be brought into the discussion at some point.

A scattering of laughter echoed up the stairs leading to the crew's quarters in the forecastle. Maher wandered that direction, reminded that the crew were still blissfully unaware of their situation. Descending far enough to peer inside, he found a spirited game of queens and bones underway. The four current players included Weams' partner, Olebile, Marielle, a sailor Maher didn't know offhand, and another, unexpected face.

"Anya?" Maher blurted.

Twisting her thin frame in her seat, Anya gave him a small salute. "Aye, present and accounted for, sir."

Stepping fully into the space, Maher got a better look at her in the lamplight. Formerly the barrelman of the *Pike,* and one of the handful of surviving crew members of that ship, Anya looked much as he remembered. Same wide, blue eyes and fair hair, but her face had taken on a sharp edge that was hard to miss. And no wonder, considering her brother Grant was one of their shipmates murdered by Dare.

Maher'd been in and out of consciousness by then, but he'd heard later how Dare drove her sword through the young helmsman's gut right in front of the others. Thoughts of Dare made his insides clench and he shook himself out of that mental fog, before any of the crew noticed.

"By the gods," Maher shook her hand, "I didn't expect to find you on this vessel."

"Aye, I'll sail under Captain Kingfisher as long as he'll have me." She tossed one card aside and pulled another from the deck.

"Still up in the crow's nest?"

"Nowhere else I'd rather be." Anya moved a white vertebrae the size of a plum onto the pile in the middle of the table. "Ready."

Marielle took no cards, but placed a barracuda's jawbone next to the others. "Ready."

Olebile and the fourth player took new cards but played no bones. Both indicated they were ready to show their hands. Maher'd never heard of this game until he and Khafra first sailed from Meredia to the Birde Isles. It wasn't common on the continent because there were other things to gamble with, but out at sea there was always a guarantee of acquiring the bones of various ocean-dwelling creatures.

"Aright, cards down," said Olebile.

Four sets of cards hit the table with faint slaps. Maher was no expert, but he was fairly certain Anya won. Two of her seven cards were queens, and she even had cards from each of those queen's suits. Hearts and spades.

"Gods be damned, Maher," Marielle said good naturedly. "I was on a lucky streak until you showed up."

"Where did you get the bones to play with, anyway?" He cocked a brow at her.

"I took Weams' place." The gunfighter grinned. "He had to go on watch."

"You did well by him," Olebile chuckled, a low, rumbling sound. "Better than he would've played for himself." The Kharaboan sailor gathered their and Weams' remaining bones and bowed out of the game.

"Care to play?" asked Anya.

"I thank you, but no." The possibility of what awaited them all come the morning came rushing back and Maher found he could hardly look at her. "Maybe next time."

After watching a few more hands of the game, Maher bid the crew goodnight and headed back above decks.

The moon had descended farther towards the horizon and the constellations shifted their positions. Time often passed quickly when cards were involved. Not that Maher was one for table gambling. He much preferred placing a friendly wager on the outcome of an event completely out of his control.

The sailors on watch changed shifts as he walked the length of the ship. A few greeted him, others were too tired to notice the Intelligencer among their ranks. Or was he the Magpie on this voyage? For the first time in weeks, months really, Maher wasn't constantly switching between roles. Out at sea, he was pleasantly surprised at how little anyone cared about which title he used in that moment. It was... refreshing to simply be himself for a while.

Reaching the stern, Maher squinted into the dark. It was maddening, trying to see something he knew was there, yet remained indistinguishable from the night behind them.

"Where are you?" he muttered.

"Looking for ghost ships?" A deep voice asked softly.

Whipping around, Maher relaxed when he saw it was only Ga-Seung. "What do you mean?" he asked carefully.

The bosun stood next to him, dark eyes trained on the horizon. "The captain and first mate have informed me of our... follower. Though I suppose it isn't really a ghost ship. That appears to be a phenomenon all its own."

"True," Maher sighed. "But I'm beginning to suspect the two are more connected than we thought."

Ga-Seung hummed in answer, but didn't ask him to elaborate. After a moment of comfortable silence, the bosun said, "I hope I'm not disturbing your privacy."

"Not at all. In fact, I'm glad you're here."

Oh? Why is that?"

"I wanted to thank you."

Now Ga-Seung looked genuinely curious. "What for?"

"You saved my life, you and Kamharida. And I've never really expressed my gratitude to either of you."

Shifting his feet, Ga-Seung smoothed his hands over the shaved sides of his head. A cut popular among sailors, the rest was left to grow on top until it was long enough to slick back down the center of the skull. "I'd rather think the mermaid currently concealed in your cabin is more responsible for saving your life."

Maher snorted. "True enough, but you kept me alive until she could work her magic. So I, most sincerely, thank you."

Ga-Seung's expression softened. "Well then, you're welcome."

Chapter Eighty

They talked a while longer, at ease in each other's company. Maher was curious to learn more about the bosun's life before he came to the Birde Isles and joined Luthais' crew. Reaching into his jacket, Ga-Seung produced a silver flask stamped with the Char-range mortar and pestle.

"To talk about those years requires fortification."

Brows raised, a wide grin spread across Maher's face. "I didn't think proper Char-range Naval officers drank while on duty."

After taking the first sip, he offered the flask to Maher. "Who said I was a proper officer? And I'm not on duty right now."

Intrigued now, Maher had a drink and nodded his approval at the quality of the liquor inside. "Do tell."

"Let's just say, there's a reason I left the Char-range Navy." Ga-Seung smirked, an expression Maher'd not seen on him before. "They're not anxious to see my return."

Chuckling deep in his chest, Maher had another swig before passing the flask back. "That's a story I'd love to hear."

"Not even the captain has heard the entire story," he mused. "Tell you what, if we live through tomorrow, I'll tell you on the journey back."

"Very well," Maher thought for a moment of what he could offer in return. It was bad luck not to trade a story for a story. "And I'll tell you how I stowed away on the *Pike* without being discovered. Until I walked right in front of Kamharida, that is."

Ga-Seung nearly spat out the mouthful of liquor he'd just taken. He let out a roar of laughter and clapped Maher on the back. "It's a good trade."

Wobbling from the impact, Maher slung an arm around Ga-Seung's broad shoulders. "It is indeed a good trade. But you must keep the secret to yourself. A tale for a tale."

"Aye, a tale for a tale," Ga-Seung toasted him with the flask and passed it over to seal the trade.

The liquor warmed Maher's throat in the way that all good drinks were wont to do. All the brief scraps of normalcy he'd encountered tonight – shipmates playing cards, the crew going about their nightly duties, sharing a drink and a chat with a friend – helped to quiet the noise inside his head.

Bidding Ga-Seung goodnight, Maher descended the short set of steps to the main deck. He felt well enough that he might even try to rest during the bit of time left before dawn. Assuming he could find a spare hammock.

"I wasn't aware drinking with my officers was one of your tasks on board."

"Gah!" Maher yelped, feet landing hard on the deck. Luthais stood a few feet away, burly arms crossed as he leaned against his cabin door

"Luthais! What have I said about sneaking up on me like that?" Maher slapped a hand over his racing heart. "Between you and your sister, I swear I'm going to go gray before my time."

His last comment was meant in jest, but Luthais wasn't smiling. Sobering instantly, Maher walked into the shadow cast by the quarterdeck's overhang. Luthais was rigid, breathing shallowly through his nose. He was angry?

"What's happened? Are Ally and Pasha alright?"

"They're fine." His clipped tone confirmed what Maher already suspected. Luthais was distressed. But why?

"Then what's wrong, Luthais?" Maher stepped closer. The only light in the alcove came from a lantern hanging from the far wall. He blinked, eyes adjusting, trying to get a better look at Luthais' face. If it was possible, the captain stiffened even more.

He's going to turn into a statue and become part of the ship at this rate.

"Talk to me," Maher murmured. "What's got you in high dudgeon like that?"

Jaw nearly cracking with how hard it was clenched, Luthais met his eye. "I saw," he ground out.

"You saw what? I can't help unless you can be more specific."

All at once, the fight seemed to leak out of him and Luthais deflated. "Nothing. It's not important."

"It obviously *is* important," Maher argued.

Turning away, Luthais opened the door to his cabin. His next words were so soft spoken, Maher nearly missed them. "I saw you with Ga-Seung."

"You saw what with me and Ga-Seung?"

His grip on the door latch tightened, the curved metal creaking on its mount. "I saw you together."

More confused than ever, Maher tried to lay a hand on his arm. "And? Why shouldn't I share a drink with a man who saved my life?"

"Forget it, Maher." Shaking him off, Luthais went into his cabin and shut the door with a snap.

Dumbfounded, Maher stared at the closed door and replayed the brief conversation over in his mind. He'd spoken to the bosun, all the ship's officers, countless times by now. Why had this instance caused such a fuss? They weren't even discussing anything important, it was all friendly...

"By all the gods and their grandmothers!" Maher pushed into the captain's quarters.

Said captain was currently bent over the map table. His head snapped up when Maher barged inside.

"Luthais!" Maher shut the door. "We are not done discussing this."

Scowling, Luthais shook his head. "I'll not argue with you when you've been drinking."

"Three sips from a flask?" he scoffed. "I've had more liquor during one of your stepmother's dinner parties."

"Very well," Luthais circled the table. "You want to have this out right now?"

"Yes, if I actually knew what we were talking about! You'd make an excellent spy, Luthais, no one would get a word out of you."

"Do you honestly think it's appropriate to consort with a ship's officer with an enemy hot on our heels?"

"*Consort?*"

"You were hanging all over each other!"

"For the gods' sake!" Maher huffed. "Ga-Seung was like to knock me down. The man is built like a bull, you know."

Luthais' nostrils flared, green eyes snapping.

"Not that I owe you any kind of explanation, either way."

"Is he? I'm sure you'll enjoy that immensely."

His gaze narrowed and Maher stalked across the room. It gave him no small amount of satisfaction when Luthais Kingfisher retreated a step.

"Don't tell me, after all the opportunities you've had to speak out, it's a stroke of jealousy that finally lights a fire beneath your ass?"

"Jealousy?" Luthais sneered.

"What else do you call taking a friendly drink between comrades and turning it into some sort of tryst?"

"What was I supposed to think? Your preferences aren't much of a secret, Magpie."

"Yours are, Pike. Who knows what you want, Luthais?" They'd drifted closer as they argued, pulled by an undertow until they were sharing each other's air. "Do *you* even know?"

Luthais' heaving chest brushed against his with each breath. Maher wanted to move even closer, to fulfill the desire that had taken hold of him for so long he couldn't pinpoint when it started. But he waited. He could see the conflict raging behind Luthais' eyes. If Luthais wasn't ready for this, if he told Maher to leave, then Maher would. No matter how desperately he wanted to stay.

Swallowing hard, Luthais whispered, "I want you."

"Come again?"

"I want *you*," he said a little louder.

"Just once more?" Maher grinned, sliding a hand behind his neck.

Luthais huffed. "I said, *I want you,* Maher. You maddening Saprean bastard–"

Dipping his head, Maher silenced Luthais with a kiss. He only meant for it to be a short one, but when Maher tried to break away,

Luthais gripped the back of his head in one large hand and pulled him back down.

How demanding, Maher smirked to himself.

Backing them onto the edge of the map table, Maher cupped Luthais' face in both hands and teased his mouth open, deepening the kiss. Luthais moaned and Maher swallowed the sound, thumbs brushing against the coarse stubble on his jaw. Snaking his free arm around Maher's waist, Luthais pulled them even closer together.

Gods, he really is solid as a fucking tree. Maher wasn't even certain he could lift Luthais but, by the gods, he wanted to try. He wanted to hoist Luthais onto that table, step between his spread thighs, and...

"Captain!" There was a sharp knock on the door. Kamharida. They froze mid-kiss and listened. "Captain, we have roughly half an hour before dawn. We should prepare to address the crew, as discussed."

Luthais cleared his throat. "Aye, First Mate. I'll be there directly."

When her booted steps faded away, Maher pressed their foreheads together. "How did she know?" he muttered. "Must be some sort of divine retribution."

"What are you talking about?" The arm around Maher's waist pulled them flush against each other again.

Maher chuckled as he grazed his lips across Luthais' cheek. "Ah, I interrupted Ally and Pasha's first kiss in much the same way."

Soft laughter rumbled against Maher's chest. "Of course, you did."

ALLY

CHAPTER EIGHTY-ONE

Whispers rippled through the crew gathered on the deck of the *Foxglove*. Dawn was just starting to break on the horizon and Kamharida had disclosed the news about the enemy closing in on them from behind. It was also now known that Ally and Pasha were on board and if any sailor had a problem with that, they could keep it to themselves or deal with the first mate.

Standing near the helm with Luthais, Maher, Marielle, Pimm, and the ship's officers, Ally scanned the gathered sailors until she spotted Weams and Olebile. Her tentative smile widened when Weams waved enthusiastically over Olebile's head. The Kharaboan sailor elbowed him in the ribs and gave her a more reserved greeting.

"Friends of yours?" Pasha asked softly.

"They taught me to sail. They were very kind to me."

Having finished speaking to the crew, Kamharida turned to the others on the quarterdeck. "Bosun, please relay any concerns from the crew as we prepare to meet the other ship." Ga-Seung nodded and stepped down where a group of sailors were already waiting for him. "Gunner, prepare the cannon teams. We'll also need a count of all weapons, shot, and powder."

"Aye, First Mate." The gunner, a middle-aged Swan Islander Ally hadn't met before, started calling the gun teams to ranks.

"We should check the other ship's position before the window of light passes." Luthais handed Pasha a spyglass, then turned to Marielle. "And we need to know how much distance still lies between us and

The Riddles. If we can risk trying I outrun them, or if we must turn and fight."

"Right." Marielle looked out into the horizon. She'd been very quiet that morning, but Ally didn't know her well enough to read her mood.

"Marielle, what are you thinking?" asked Pimm.

"I think," she frowned, then strode for the navigation table, "I need to see the map."

Pimm and Maher hurried after the gunfighter. Turning to where Pasha was watching the ship through the spyglass, Ally spoke softly, so as not to startle her.

"What do you see?"

"Something's different," Pasha adjusted her stance. "The curtain is still there but, if you observe closely, it's becoming warped. Take a look."

Ally accepted the spyglass and peered through the lens. Pasha was right, the faint outline of the ship was the same, but the middle portion had taken on the appearance of slowly melting wax. It twisted the clouds and distorted the color of the water. "Luthais," Ally called, "come and see this."

Luthais did as she asked. "What the... I'll be godsdamned." He looked at Pasha. "Is it possible they're losing the illusion?"

"I suppose it's possible. The siren who attacked me was injured too. Maybe she's having trouble holding it up now."

"Captain!" Kamharida had joined the others around the map. "You're needed here."

"What now?" Ally wondered as she and Pasha trailed him across the deck.

"I can't imagine," said Pasha.

"Listen to this," the first mate directed their attention to Marielle.

Fidgeting slightly, Marielle braced her hands on her gunbelt. "If my calculations are right, we're already close to The Riddles. We could reach them by day's end, with a good wind and no slatting of the sails."

"How is that possible?" Ally spoke first. "We've been at sea for, what, a week? According to every map I've ever seen, The Riddles are at least two- or three-weeks' sail from any other land."

"Not every map," Pasha murmured. Ally gasped softly. The woven mermaid map. Of course.

"In fact," Marielle continued, a pained expression creeping onto her face. "We should be seeing signs of the water barrier soon."

"But why are the maps wrong?" asked Pimm.

"Let's worry about that when there's not a ship full of dead sailors chasing us," Maher cut in. "What should we do first?"

"Send one of the ship's birds ahead to notify them we're here," said Marielle. "I'll write it, and hopefully they'll send someone out quickly."

"Do that, there's stationery in the chart room." said Luthais. "Will we be able to cross the barrier in this ship, or will we have to rely on someone from the islands?"

Before Marielle could answer, the air around them seemed to tighten. Ally covered her ears as pain lanced through her head. The pressure built and built, until it ended as quickly as it began.

Pimm gave their head a rough shake. "What the fuck was that?"

Maher and Kamharida shared an apprehensive look. "Did that feel familiar to you?" he asked.

"Aye, it did." Kamharida spared a glance behind them. Whipping back around, she bellowed, "Hold on!"

A monstrous swell came rolling towards them. It never crested into a wave, but it struck the of the *Foxglove* full force. Ally pitched off her feet, collided with Pasha, taking them both down. The ship rolled and listed sharply portside. Looking up, Ally saw Kamharida with Marielle caged between her arms against the table. Maher had caught Pimm when they slid past him, and Luthais was supporting their combined weight against the helm.

The ship held suspended in air for a breath and then, inch by inch, she rolled back onto her keel, the ballast in the hold pulling her back upright.

"Great goddess," Ally whispered. "Is everyone alright?"

Luthais grunted in answer as Maher and Pimm climbed off of him.

"I think so," Marielle looked back at Kamharida. "Are you?"

"Aye," the first mate eased off the table, freeing Marielle, "lucky this thing is bolted down."

"What was that?" Pasha asked, helping Ally to her feet.

"If I didn't know any better," Maher straightened his vest, "I'd say it was a turbine charging up."

"The turbine on Dare's ship was destroyed," Pasha protested.

"That doesn't mean someone couldn't have built another."

"Look!" Pimm pointed behind the *Foxglove*. Everyone turned, in the distance, the very air shimmered and bulged. Like a vessel looming out of the mist, a massive ship emerged from the fading mirage.

Maher braced a hand on the helm. "Fuck. Me."

"It's a Fraollish warship," said Luthais.

"Have any gone missing recently?" asked Kamharida.

"Last autumn," Pimm answered, surprising Ally. "When the ghost ship sightings were at their peak."

"Right." The captain moved into action. "Marielle, prepare the letter to send ahead to the islands. Kamharida will show you where the birds are kept. In fact, send two or three. Then come back here to guide the helmsman towards The Riddles."

"What can we do?" asked Ally. If Luthais told her to take shelter belowdecks, she was going to push him overboard.

"You and Pasha keep watch on the ship." He found where the spyglass had rolled across the deck and handed it to her. "See if you can recognize anyone on board or any other attempts to hide the ship."

"We will," Pasha took the glass when Ally was too stunned to react. He'd actually given them a real job.

Luthais moved on. "Maher and Pimm, will you check in with the other officers and report back anything of importance?"

"Leave it to us, Captain," said Maher, without a trace of sarcasm. As they passed, Maher paused to whisper something into Luthais' ear. The backs of their hands brushed together and color tinged her brother's cheeks.

Ally wondered what might've happened after she and Pasha retired the night before. But now was not the time to ask. She could wheedle it out of Maher later, when they weren't fighting for their lives.

Nearly an hour passed with no other activity from the Fraollish ship. Ally still couldn't bring herself to name the captain. She believed Pasha, yet at the same time hoped they'd somehow been tricked, as Maher suggested.

"Let me spell you for a while," Ally offered.

Pasha handed her the glass and stretched out her arms. "We will need to return to the sea soon. I'm amazed you're not feeling the call yet."

"I feel it, well enough," she snorted. "It just so happens this is sufficiently distracting."

"You always talk like that when you're weary," Pasha said fondly.

"Hush." Ally trained the spyglass on the other ship. The sails hardly flattered, yet they were gaining steadily on the *Foxglove*. Had they transferred the energy used to hide the vessel into pushing it to go faster? Ally was about to pose the question to Pasha, when she caught movement on the deck and in the rigging. Her eyesight was sharper as a mermaid, she'd never have been able to pick out sailors from this distance before. Ally lowered the glass a moment, as what she saw became clear. "Those poor people."

"The crew?" asked Pasha.

She nodded, taking a deep breath and looking again. What sort of heartless ghouls would do something like this?

What sort of person would ally themselves with such ghouls?

Something drew her attention to the bow and she adjusted the lens. A man, very much alive, with a long gray mustache. In the next breath, his name came to her. Swain.

Dear gods, Pasha was right. Her grip on the spyglass tightened. Swain, quartermaster of the *Maiden's Revenge*. The man who'd held a knife to Ally's throat in front of her mother. *But, if Swain is on board, then did Pasha really see...*

Captain Foraoise Dare, or at least something who used to be her, appeared next to him and Ally's heart leapt into her throat. She was just as Pasha described, changed but not dead.

The more she stared, Ally could almost feel Dare looking back at her through the glass. Foraoise's half-shaved head turned slightly. Kingfisher green eyes fixed onto Ally, and the captain smirked.

Stumbling backwards, Ally tripped over her own feet and the spyglass landed on the deck with crack of glass.

Chapter Eighty-two

*T*hat was fun.

Foraoise's field of vision narrowed until she caught her *dear* niece watching them. A wave of satisfaction warmed her bones when the little chit realized Foraoise could see her. And she wasn't the only Kingfisher aboard, a nephew was present if Foraoise wasn't mistaken. What a nice little family reunion they could have together. There was movement on deck as someone rushed to Ally's side.

The mermaid! Foraoise sucked a steadying breath through her nose. Now she really wanted to take this ship. The sirens could wait.

"Captain," Swain's voice sounded as if he were very far away, not standing a few feet to her right. Tapping into the abilities given to her by the sirens had been a slow process. But now she was picking them up more quickly. Often Foraoise wondered how they could best be used to exact revenge on her niece and the mermaid who killed her. Well, almost killed her.

"Yes, Swain?" she pulled back enough to focus on the quartermaster.

"Now they can see us, what're your orders?"

Foraoise glanced up at the morning sun. They'd catch up before noon if the sirens kept up this pace. "Make ready the guns."

CHAPTER EIGHTY-THREE

The current surrounding The Riddles stretched as far as the eye could see in either direction. Marielle had navigated the ship to this point on a twisting route that made sense to only herself. It was something she could sense in the currents, ingrained into her from a young age. The helmsman quickly relinquished the wheel when her directions became too complicated.

Contrary to what Maher'd learned in school, the quickest path to The Riddles was not a straight line. His Meredian mathematics teacher would be horrified.

Yet it explained why the journey to these islands was supposed to take so long. Why The Riddles were set so far apart from all other land on any modern map. Well, on any human map. Ally and Pasha had explained their odd exchange from earlier that morning. The map Ally'd repaired for Pasha put the islands much closer to the rest of the Known World. And why not, when merfolk traveled beneath the sea rather than atop it?

When Kamharida asked why the waters around The Riddles were like this, Marielle claimed not to know. But it explained why she was so reluctant to admit they were closer than anyone else knew. There was no hiding it now, though. More importantly, how was the ship crewed by the dead keeping up with them through the maze of currents?

Maher had to admit at last, Pasha hadn't been fooled by some trickery. Ally'd seen Swain, Dare, and the dead crew with her own eyes. Upon looking for himself, Maher couldn't see Dare, but he saw a damned corpse climbing the rigging and that was more than enough.

"We're coming up on the barrier," Marielle spun the wheel to veer around another unseen obstacle. "We'll have to skirt the waterline until help arrives."

"How long will that take?" asked Kamharida. She'd watched the gunfighter closely for the last hour. Maher assumed it was an attempt to memorize the route Marielle took, though how the first mate could possibly understand the haphazard path escaped him.

"We're going to give them our broadside?" Ga-Seung had rejoined them on the quarterdeck.

"It's our only option. If we try to sail over, we could capsize. Even if we made it across, a ship this size could scuttle within minutes," Marielle grunted, practically hanging all her weight on the helm. "Godsdamnit, Riddles-made boats are so much easier to sail."

"What say you, Captain?" Kamharida moved out of her way as the ship made another sharp turn.

"Whether we follow the channel or turn back out to sea, we'll still be presenting our side." Luthais looked back at the encroaching Fraollish ship, then at Marielle. "Port or starboard?"

"Hard to starboard." She paused, ready to make the turn.

"Hard to starboard!" Luthais bellowed. Kamharida jumped down to the main deck. The order was repeated and carried down the line. Marielle spun the wheel, sending the *Foxglove* careening into a wide right turn and putting the barrier on their left.

"Gunner!" Luthais barked.

"Aye, Captain!" The Swan Islander pushed their way forward.

"Make ready the starboard guns. All portside teams to assist with powder transfer and loading." The gunner took off, calling for any gun teams still on deck. Every sailor had a job to do, even Pimm was belowdecks tallying supplies with the ship's purser.

Gooseflesh raced over Maher's skin. He'd not seen this side of Luthais in action yet. It was no small wonder he had such a renowned reputation as a captain.

As the *Foxglove* straightened out, Maher looked down into the bottomless rift in the seas. There really wasn't much else they could do until aid arrived from The Riddles. Except wait for Dare's ship to get within firing range.

CHAPTER EIGHTY-FOUR

"They're broadsiding." Swain frowned as the Kingfisher ship pulled hard to starboard and hugged the barrier. "They know they can't cross the barrier."

"I'd wager they have someone at the helm who's been to The Riddles before," said Captain Dare.

"Aye," Swain grunted. He didn't give a rat's furry ass if they had the queen of The Riddles on board, the longer Foraoise toyed with that ship, the more agitated the sirens would become. Playing along was all well and good when Swain thought the captain only wanted to scare them. But now there were corpse sailors manning the guns. With some of the live crew minding them, on pain of death. That threat was beginning to lose its power. He was going to have to start promising to let the sirens make them into rotting puppets.

There was no way 'round it, Swain had to get Foraoise on track. She had to complete the task set by the sirens and soon, before they lost all patience.

Foraoise might've thought she could handle them putting her back where they found her, dead or otherwise. But Swain refused to lose her again, and he wasn't about to be eaten by a damned siren either. The rest of their crew would be doomed in the bargain. All his planning, all that work, would've amounted to nothing.

"Foraoise," he cleared his throat when her black-rimmed eyes cut over to him. "Captain. We shouldn't delay much longer. I know you want this prize, but the sooner we hold up our end of the bargain with the sirens, the sooner we'll be rid of them. Then we can sail anywhere and take any prize you want. You'll control the Birde Isles and all the seas."

Gripping the hilt of her sword, Foraoise's head tilted. "Why are you pushing so hard, Swain? We'll free you from the hold of that siren, I promise you that."

"'Tis not only that, Captain." Swain smoothed his mustache, trying to choose the right words to sway her. "Truth is, I've a surprise waiting for you in Kingsport."

"A surprise?" Her brows shot up. "What sort of surprise?"

Leaning close, Swain whispered the secret he'd been carrying into her ear.

The captain stiffened, her breath quickening. "It's true?"

"Sure as I'm standing here, Captain. I'd wanted to wait until we reached the Isles, but I don't know how long we have to act."

Not a complete lie. Swain really didn't know how long the surprise would remain in its current location.

"Shall we set a new course?" he asked cautiously.

The smile she gave him would've made any other man's blood run cold. But Swain breathed a sigh of relief. This was more important to her, his instincts had led him true.

"Set a course for the Birde Isles, Swain," Foraoise ordered. "I can deal with my niece and her pet mermaid afterwards."

"Aye, aye, Captain!" He turned to gladly carry out the order, but she stopped him.

"Let's have a bit more fun before we're on our way."

LUTHAIS

CHAPTER EIGHTY-FIVE

The *Foxglove* cut across the current, the helmsman steering the ship as directed by Marielle. Still no response from The Riddles. No boats sent to aid them or birds arrived with instructions tied to their legs. And Dare's ship would be upon them soon. Like any captain, Luthais thought the pirates would pull alongside to fire on them. They were well outgunned, even with every spare sailor supporting the starboard teams and with every cannon loaded.

But now Luthais questioned whether Dare intended to turn at all. If their course didn't alter soon, they'd ram the *Foxglove* head-on.

"She's not turning, Captain," Kamharida voiced his own concerns. "Do they intend to plow us into the barrier, you think?"

"I wouldn't rule it out."

"They're nearly in range," Ga-Seung noted and the gunner agreed. "If we target the forecastle and aim beneath the water line, could we sink them?"

"Those Fraollish ships are damned thick," said the gunner. "But it's possible."

"I say it's worth the attempt," Kamharida chimed in. "Captain?"

Luthais looked out across the deck, every soul on board relying on his decision.

"Ready on the guns."

"Aye, Captain!" The gunner took off for the gun deck. Ga-Seung followed to be ready to relay any orders down the hatch.

"All hands to station!" Kamharida shouted.

"What's going on?" Ally approached him as the officers scattered.

"We're going to try to sink their ship."

"Should I fetch the others from the chart room?"

"Not yet," he glanced back where Kamharida waited on the main deck. "They'll have heard the firing orders soon enough."

"Please tell me if there's anything we can do." Ally briefly laid a hand on his arm. Then she crossed back to where Pasha was watching for any change in the energy around the ship.

There was something Luthais wanted, but he'd be asking the impossible. He wanted Ally and Pasha to take Maher from the ship and swim to safety.

Never mind that Maher would never agree to it. Even if the fall from the ship didn't injure him, how could he possibly survive crossing the barrier?

"Ready, Captain!" Kamharida called out.

"Await orders!" Luthais grabbed the nearest spyglass and focused on Dare's ship. "Just a little bit further," he muttered.

Minutes crawled by until the prow of the Fraollish ship came into range. Lowering the glass, he saw Ally and Pasha braced against the starboard railing.

"Hold her steady," he told the helmsman, then cupped one hand around his mouth. "Fire all!"

"Fire all!" Kamharida echoed.

The order traveled throughout the ship until dozens of voices took up the cry, "FIRE ALL!"

Cannon fire erupted from the *Foxglove* like fireworks at the end of a festival. The ship shuddered in its braces and the acrid stench of black powder filled the air. Some artillery sailed wide, but the rest stayed true. Luthais lunged for the railing. He wanted to make sure Dare returned to her watery grave.

"Something's wrong," Pasha's voice carried over the smoke-filled air.

"Luthais!" Ally pointed towards the ship. Luthais' hands tightened on the rail when he saw what had his sister and Pasha so agitated. As they approached the other ship, the cannon balls seemed to slow down, as if they were traveling through molasses. Just before they reached their target, they glanced off and dropped into the sea.

"The curtain's still there, it just isn't hiding the ship anymore," Pasha hissed. "That's why we never felt any change."

"Tell them to stop!" Ally exclaimed. "We're wasting our ammunition."

"Godsbedamned pirates!" Luthais spun towards the main deck. "Cease fire!"

"Cease fire!" Kamharida echoed. Within moments, the air around the ship was still.

"What now?" Ally asked softly. "They didn't even slow."

Maher and Marielle came running up to the quarterdeck, Kamharida and Ga-Seung not far behind them.

"What in the gods' names is going on?" Maher skidded to a stop next to him.

"We're in deep trouble, that's what," said Pasha.

"Where's Pimm?" Ally looked around.

"Hurling in the chart room," Marielle answered. "All of the twists and turns and gun smoke have made them sick again."

The officers bounded up the steps from the main deck. "What trickery have they pulled now?" Ga-Seung demanded.

"The shield of magic that concealed them is still there, cannon fire is useless." Luthais turned to the two mermaids. "Ally, Pasha, can you swim out and find the Riddles boats? Can you lead them to us?"

MAHER

Chapter Eighty-six

There was a moment of pause while Pasha and Ally considered Luthais' request quickly between themselves.

While he was somewhat surprised by the decision, Maher sensed this was motivated by Luthais' instincts as a leader. Use every available resource, even if it meant involving his sister.

"We can try," Pasha said carefully. "But why would the humans of these islands believe two mermaids who appeared out of nowhere?"

"You could mention the three letters sent earlier from the ship," Maher suggested. "Say they were written by one of their own. Right, Marielle?" He looked to the gunfighter for confirmation, but she was staring out at the water, eyes unfocused and gunbelt gripped tightly in her hands.

Luthais went on, addressing the ship's officers. "While they go for help, we must prepare for the possibility that we might have to abandon ship."

Kamharida fixed wide, russet eyes on him. "Captain, you would abandon another ship to that wretch Dare?"

"We may have to," Luthais said firmly. "I won't lose another life from this crew, especially not to fucking Foraoise Dare."

Ga-Seung added, "We can't follow the water line forever. Dare's ship will either strike us head-on, or she'll pull alone side and pummel us with cannon fire that we can't hope to return."

Taking a steadying breath, Kamharida nodded. "I know you're right. I just hate to see another good ship taken."

Maher hummed in agreement. Putting the lives of the crew first was the right thing to do. As the discussion continued, he pulled Marielle aside. "Listen, Ally and Pasha are going to need advice on which direction to swim in search of the boats." He took in the tense set of her shoulders. "What is it?"

"Maher," her eyes darted to the sea, then to where Luthais stood, "I have to get to the islands."

"We all do, remember? The sooner we get Pasha and Ally on their way, the –"

"You're not hearing me." Marielle gripped his arm. "I must make it to land. I can't have come this far only to be shot down by a mad pirate and turned into a member of her corpse crew!"

"Marielle!" Maher hissed. "I swear, I'll do everything I can to get you there, but you must comport yourself."

The gunfighter's tough and unbothered mask slipped completely away. For a moment he saw how panicked she truly was. Then, Marielle blinked and the mask was back.

"I'll hold you to that, Maher. Remember, this is the debt you owe me."

"Of course." Maher held her shoulders. "Just promise me not to do anything rash in the meantime."

CHAPTER EIGHTY-SEVEN

The pirates were closing in, pushing everyone into action. The ship's crew scattered as new orders were relayed and the longboats prepared. Maher and Marielle were locked in a heated, hushed discussion. Normally Pasha wouldn't interrupt, but they were running out of time and the mermaids needed some sense of direction. As she approached, Maher shook Marielle by the shoulders. Pasha's sharp hearing caught the words "promise" and "rash." The Riddles Islander nodded curtly and he released her.

"May I speak with you?" Pasha spoke up, startling them. "Ally and I must leave as soon as possible."

"Of course," Marielle gave Maher a pointed look.

"I'll leave you to it, then." He joined Ally portside, where she was watching the swirling barrier carving through the sea.

"Which way should we swim once we cross the current?" asked Pasha.

Hesitating for a moment, Marielle turned so her back was to Maher and Ally. "Instead of telling you, why don't I show you?"

"Pardon me?"

"Take me with you."

"What! I can't do that."

"Please," Marielle checked over her shoulder, possibly to ensure Maher hadn't heard. "I have to get to the islands."

Pasha shook her head. "It's too dangerous. You'll come across with the others on the boats."

"What if the boats are too late? Pasha, *please*," she begged. "I must find my family. Their lives depend on it."

"But... I can't..." Pasha sputtered. "You'll likely drown before we make it through the current!"

"There must be something you can do! Are the tales of saving sailors from drowning all just codswallop?"

Pasha's throat constricted, Marielle's pleas to reach her family striking a similar chord deep within. Was this not her own reason for taking this journey? "Wait here, I have to speak with Ally."

"But..."

"I won't attempt this without her input, understand?"

"Yes," Marielle relented. "Please hurry."

Pasha walked back across the deck, thoughts churning with what she could possibly do to help Marielle. There was something, but even Pasha didn't know for sure if it was true or just a story her sister used to tell.

"Do you have what you need?" asked Maher.

"Almost. I need to talk to Ally, first"

"Why?" He frowned. "What's Marielle up to?"

"It's not my place to say. You should ask her, yourself," said Pasha. Lips pursed in a tight line, Maher hurried over to Marielle.

"What's going on?" asked Ally. "We haven't much time."

Moving close and speaking low, Pasha said, "Marielle wants to come with us."

"What, why?" Ally yelped and Pasha shushed her gently.

"Her family is in some kind of danger; she's here to help them, Ally."

"But what if we have to swim through the barrier? No human can hold their breath that long."

"There might be a way,"

Hazel eyes growing impossibly wide, Ally hissed, "The mermaid's gift? You'd give her that?"

Behind them, Maher shouted, "Have you lost your mind?"

Pasha spoke quickly. "Not that, but something else. I've never attempted it, but there might be a way to keep Marielle alive for a while beneath the water. Without giving her the mermaid's gift."

Chapter Eighty-Eight

"Have you lost your mind?"

"Say it a little louder, I don't think Anya heard you in the crow's nest," Marielle hissed.

"Even if you survived that jump without breaking something or getting yourself keelhauled, you'd drown before you reach land," Maher tried to reason with her. "Besides, you think the captain wants the crew to witness you throwing yourself overboard?"

"The mermaids are jumping," said Marielle.

"Yes, the key word there being *mermaids*. They can actually breathe underwater!"

"Maher, calm down darling," Ally said as she and Pasha approached.

"Have you heard this mad plan?" he demanded.

"I have, and Pasha says she can get Marielle to shore safely."

"She can?" Maher felt his argument quickly losing steam. "But how?"

"There's not enough time to explain now," said Pasha. "There's still a great deal of risk, but it might work long enough to reach land."

"Thank you!" Marielle grabbed Pasha's hand, took in the look of shock on the mermaid's face, and promptly released it. "Thank you, Pasha. What do I need to do?"

"First, show me the direction we should take once we're clear of the current." They crossed the quarterdeck yet again, with Marielle sketching out a route in the air.

Ally took Maher's hand in hers. "Maher, please, come with us."

"Al…"

"We can keep you safe."

Indecision choked Maher as he looked into her earnest hazel eyes. The thought of undergoing another attack by any pirate ship, let alone this pirate ship, sent phantom bouts of pain shooting through his shoulder and down his back. But the thought of abandoning Luthais to potentially fall into the hands of Foraoise fucking Dare without him, felt as though someone'd driven a knife through his heart.

Maher swallowed against the lump in his throat. "Al, I just don't know."

Understanding dawned on Ally and her expression shifted. "You don't want to leave Luthais."

"I'm sorry, Al." Maher rasped, eyes burning with unshed tears.

"It's alright, Maher, I understand." Lifting onto her toes, she kissed his cheek. "We'll retrieve the boats and you keep an eye on my brother"

"Someone has to." He laughed weakly.

"Exactly." Blinking back tears of her own, Ally let her hand slip from his. "Tell Luthais we've taken Marielle with us, will you?"

She walked away before he could reply, and all the chaos of the ship came back into stark relief. Searching the decks for Luthais, Maher spotted him near the capstan. The captain was striding right towards him.

"Luthais!" Maher met him halfway. "You need to know Marielle is going ashore with Ally and Pasha."

Luthais ground to a stop. "Does she have such a strong desire to meet her gods?"

"I know, it sounds mad." Maher followed as he started walking again. "But Ally says Pasha can keep her alive, even crossing the barrier."

"She can?" His gaze cut to where the two mermaids and the gunfighter had gathered midship. Pasha was pointing over the portside railing, no doubt explaining how Marielle was to jump.

There's a joke here, somewhere. Maher thought, feeling a little delirious. *Two mermaids and a gunfighter walk into a pub...*

"Maher!" Luthais snapped. "I said, can Ally perform this feat as well?"

"I don't know," he answered truthfully.

"Let's find out." He reversed course and made a beeline for midship.

Dodging crew members and ducking beneath a low sail line, Maher caught up to the captain. "Why? What good is that going to do? They can't possibly get everyone off this ship."

"It's worth knowing." His tone brooked no argument.

Huffing out a noise of frustration, Maher trailed Luthais back across the ship. As they neared, Maher became suspicious. Why would Luthais waste precious time asking, unless he had someone else in mind to go with the mermaids.

Pimm! Maher's stomach dropped. *Where is Pimm?*

Were they still holed up in the chart room? If Ally confirmed she could do the same trick as Pasha and get a human through the barrier, Maher was going to get Pimm off this ship. Even if he had to carry his friend abovedecks himself.

"Are you prepared to leave?" Luthais was already asking.

"We are," said Ally. "And you know Marielle is with us?"

"Aye, but the only reason I'm allowing it is because of Pasha's assurance she won't drown."

"I can't guarantee anything else," Pasha said carefully.

"Understood." Luthais turned to his sister. "Ally, can you do the same? Could you keep someone alive underwater?"

"Honestly, I don't know," Ally winced when the captain frowned. "There are many things Pasha can do that I can't. We're still figuring it out."

"Al, it's alright, just get Marielle to shore."

"Ship ahoy!" Anya sounded the alarm from the crow's nest. "Closing in fast, starboard side!"

Kamharida raced to the quarterdeck and helped the helmsman brace the wheel. "Swells incoming! Hang on!"

Before the first mate finished the warning, the *Foxglove* tilted violently to the left. The barrier loomed closer; their ship bobbed like a buoy pushed about by a storm.

"Go!" Luthais shouted, as they all tried to regain their footing.

"Ally, now!" Pasha tore off her makeshift dress, secured the spear, and took Ally's hand. They climbed atop the railing as the ship leveled out between swells. Ally spared one last glance at Maher and Luthais, and then the mermaids dove into the sea.

Struggling to his feet, Maher started when Marielle caught him by the elbow.

"Come with us!" she yelled over the cacophony swirling around them. "I need your help!"

"I told Ally, I'm staying here."

"Fuck!" Marielle released him, moving to make the jump. "Come on land as soon as you can."

"I will –"

Another, even larger swell hit the hull. The deck lurched and groaned beneath their boots. Maher lost his balance, the force flinging him half over the rail. With the air knocked out of him, he struggled to straighten. The edges of his vision went dark.

"Maher!" Luthais called his name, but Maher couldn't tell where he was.

The *Foxglove* pitched and yawed, the water rushing up to meet them. There was a rough tug at his waist.

"You can forgive me later!" Marielle hooked her arm around Maher and tumbled them both overboard.

CHAPTER EIGHTY-NINE

What Ally failed to realize, as she and Pasha dove from the ship, was how difficult it would be to get her clothes off once they were in the sea. They hit the choppy water and the fabric clung to her in heavy folds. The urge to release her tail was so strong Ally feared she might pass out. Then Pasha was in front of her, sharp black nails ripping her shirt down the middle. Ally sighed as Pasha also made quick work of the sodden trousers.

"I told you clothes were overrated," Pasha's voice tickled inside of head.

Ally was too focused on with her tail to retort. As her fluke unfurled, Pasha towed them further away from the ship.

"Where's Euphonia?" Ally scanned the rolling water, but saw no sign of the sea monster. "Do you think she's alright?"

"She has a taste for snapjaw now, maybe she's off hunting the other one that followed the pirates here." Pasha frowned up at the surface. "And where's Marielle?"

"I don't know, she was just behind us." Ally spun in place, stopping when she got her first look at the famed Riddles barrier from beneath the waves. It truly was a wall of roiling water, stretching down to the seafloor and in either direction around the islands.

"It looks just like it did in the warrior's memories," Pasha murmured. The spear strapped to her back pulsed, a faint spark returned to the stone shaft.

Above them, the *Foxglove* shuddered and swayed at a severe angle. Dare's ship was barreling down on them, the swells still pummeling the hull. This far below, the effects were much gentler. Ally and Pasha were buffeted by the strong current, but the barrier seemed to absorb much of the impact.

"There!" Pasha pointed as two tangled bodies hit the water, rolling into the depths. "Is there someone with her?"

"It's Maher!" Ally cried. They shot upwards, where the two humans floated. Marielle squinted blearily into the water, but Maher was unconscious. Ally grabbed him around the waist, while Pasha took Marielle. The gunfighter struggled at first, until Pasha ordered her to be still.

"What do I do?" Ally held Maher close. "He needs to breathe!"

"Watch me." Pasha gripped Marielle's chin and blew a puff of air directly into her mouth. She'd explained before they'd been forced to leave the ship; a breath from a mermaid wouldn't grant a permanent ability to breathe, but would keep a human alive underwater for several minutes. Despite being forewarned, Marielle's eyes still widened as her lungs filled with borrowed air.

Moving quickly, Ally did the same for Maher. She didn't know if it would work. If not, Pasha would have to breathe for them both. But Maher's chest inflated just as Marielle's had, and continued to rise shallowly and fall as if he were breathing on his own.

Nodding in approval, Pasha shifted Marielle until the gunfighter was held against her front. Copying Pasha again, Ally slipped her arms beneath Maher's shoulders, pulling him in tight so his back was against her chest.

"Ready?" Pasha asked as they drifted closer to the whirling wall of water.

"As ready as I'm going to be." Ally checked Maher once more, then followed Pasha and Marielle into the barrier.

Ally'd half expected crossing the barrier to be like passing through a waterfall. All harsh noise and punishing deluge of water. Only a couple of years ago, this would've been akin to her worst nightmare.

But as they crossed from the sea into this strange anomaly in the tide, everything went calm and still. Ally wasn't even certain she was still swimming, or if they'd somehow been suspended like dried flowers in a glass paperweight.

And was it her imagination, or did the barrier seem to *recognize* them as mermaids. There was an initial feeling of uncertainty. A conflicted reaction to their presence by the energy that flowed through this place. Then it seemed to realize they were mermaids and Ally got the distinct feeling it was happy to see them.

Or maybe it had nothing to do with them at all, and it was the spear Pasha carried that elicited this response. Whatever the reason, Ally was grateful for the respite. Maher was totally weightless in her arms, even more so than in the sea, where she could still feel some drag from his body. His heartbeat was steady beneath her hand. Thank the gods for that. Thinking back to the day Pasha gave her the gift to breathe underwater, Ally found new meaning in the way she'd offered it.

Don't fret, it doesn't have to be on the lips. Unless you asked me to.

What Ally'd taken as teasing, or possibly even an unusual method of flirting, had in fact also been a way she could've breathed beneath the surface. However temporary. And really, Pasha had been right at the time to brush off her own words as a joke. Ally wouldn't have been comfortable at all back then with this other method.

Her period of calm reminiscing ended as they neared the other side of the barrier. Ally wasn't so sure now if it really qualified as a barrier, more like a current as Pasha called it, but it did strongly resemble one from above. That would have to do for now. Just ahead, Pasha began to pass through into the sea again. Ally felt the pressure of the water slowly returning. In the off chance the barrier really was sentient on some level, Ally bid it farewell. Perhaps it was only her imagination again, but she could've sworn the energy surrounding them waved goodbye.

Chapter Ninety

Marielle would always remember leaping from the *Foxglove*, dragging a half-conscious Maher with her. She'd recall landing in the water hard enough to cause a tremor in her muscles. And she'd forever retain the memory of the blurred shapes of the mermaids emerging through the shadows of the sea.

Finally, she'd never shake the memory of Pasha's mouth covering hers, not quite a kiss. A stream of warm air filling her up and erasing the pressure building in her lungs. But after that, everything went hazy.

Going through the barrier, rather than over top of it as she was accustomed, was like being squeezed through a keyhole. The roar of the water and the constriction around her entire body was too much. They'd barely entered the barrier itself before Marielle passed out, and remembered nothing else.

PASHA

CHAPTER NINETY-ONE

The sheer contrast between the seas on either side of the current was enough to send Pasha reeling. While the waters had gradually grown warmer and less murky the closer they got to the islands, they were nothing like the impossibly clear, temperate sea that now enveloped them. Far below, on the ocean floor, shocking pink sand winked at them between white coral reefs teeming with life.

Looking back to ensure Ally and Maher made it through, Pasha couldn't help smiling when she caught the look of wonder on Ally's face.

"It's so beautiful," Ally murmured, hoisting Maher higher in her arms. His head lolled to the side, tiny bubbles escaped from between his lips.

Both humans were unconscious now. Checking Marielle's breathing, Pasha tilted her chin towards the surface.

"Let's get them above the water and see how close we are to land."

Ally nodded and they canted upwards. Bright sunlight rippled around them as they climbed. A school of curious fish with shimmering scales in blues and pinks circled them once, their vibrant colors flashing.

When they broke through the surface, Pasha felt Marielle take a deep, full breath. But she didn't wake. Passing through the current had been interesting, though not unpleasant, for Pasha. She wondered if it was the same for the humans. Scanning the horizon, Pasha found a thin stretch of beach in the distance.

"We'd better start swimming, it will take a while to reach the islands with these two unable to help."

"Pasha, I can't see the ship."

Following Ally's line of sight, Pasha saw the churning current, the darker waters and sky behind it, but nothing beyond.

Ally frowned, "We can't have swum that far off from the crossing."

"Perhaps the current hides whatever is on the other side. We couldn't see this land from the ship." A bead of pain pinched appeared right between Pasha's eyes.

Not again, she tried to feel if the spear was awake, but it had gone dormant again.

"Come on, let's get these two to land. We need Marielle to tell us where we are."

ALLY

Chapter Ninety-Two

Ally towed Maher towards the shore, taking in their new surroundings as much as she could. The waters surrounding The Riddles were a stark difference from those just on the other side of the barrier. Like swimming through liquid glass.

She was reminded of her childhood, all the times she pestered Priestess Esa for stories about this place. None of the tales had really done it justice. Even the sky seemed a more brilliant shade of blue here.

Are we really in the same part of the world that we were this morning?

The trouble with swimming through water so clear, was that Ally struggled to judge how far they'd gone. Which only served to make Maher seem heavier the farther they went. The tropical sun was high in the sky, not a cloud in sight. Ally could feel her curls expanding from the heat.

When they came upon a sandbar that'd been revealed by the changing tide, Ally insisted they stop to rest. "We should check on Maher and Marielle, anyway." she added.

The sandbar was a splash of pink in the glassy sea. After they settled their passengers on the soft sand, Ally took a handful and sifted the fine powder through her fingers.

"It's like pink sugar," she marveled. "Have you ever seen such a thing?"

"I haven't," said Pasha. "None of our histories mention anything about these islands."

Brushing Maher's dark hair from his forehead, Ally assured herself he was breathing normally. Then she checked the pulse point on his wrist.

"Could you see to her too?" asked Pasha. "I'm not sure what's normal for a human heartbeat."

Chuckling softly, Ally shifted closer on the sand, rolling her fluke to keep her balance. Neither of them had wished to lose their tails again so soon. She lifted Marielle's limp wrist and pushed her wet shirtsleeve up her arm. The gunfighter's pulse was strong, thankfully, but something else caught Ally's eye.

"Oh dear." Turning Marielle's Forearm this way and that, Ally examined an untold number of healed nicks and cuts. The scars were scattered across her bronze skin without rhyme or reason, some were even deep in the webbing between her fingers.

Ally hissed in sympathy. What could her work in the Lantern be like, that she was injured so often?

Maher groaned and rolled onto his side in the sand. Gently replacing Marielle's arm, Ally turned back towards him.

"Maher? It's alright darling, you're safe."

The furrow across his brow relaxed at her words. Chestnut-brown eyes blinked open and squinted up at her in the midday sun.

"Al?" With a grunt, Maher pushed himself into a sitting position. "What in the gods' names happened?" He listed to one side.

"You went overboard with Marielle," Pasha said as Ally steadied him. "You don't remember?"

"I remember the *Foxglove* rocking like a clock pendulum."

Ally snorted. "Is that what Luthais named his ship? I hadn't even noticed."

"What's so funny about that?" asked Pasha.

"I'll explain later, I promise. Go on, Maher."

"And Marielle," he looked to where she still lay, passed out. "Godsdamnit, she pulled me over!"

"Why would she do that?" Ally asked.

"I don't know, but I intend to find out." Maher cleared his throat, the sound like stone mortar grinding against a pestle.

"Fuck me, I'd give my father's fortune for a drink right now."

Ally's head tilted. "I thought your father disowned you?"

"Not in writing. If I want to trade all his money for a single glass of water, I will."

CHAPTER NINETY-THREE

Marielle stretched, feeling the soft, sun-warmed sand shift beneath her.

Must've fallen asleep on the beach again. She thought lazily. Sunlight painted the insides of her eyelids with streaks of orange and red. *Have I slept long enough to lose the shade? Mam will be upset, maybe Costan can cover for me.*

The gentle lapping of the sea would lull her back to sleep if she didn't move soon. Sighing, Marielle lifted her hands to block the sun and forced her eyes open.

A cloudless expanse of blue hung above her, the kind of sky that could only be found in The Riddles. Gods, she'd missed this.

Wait, Marielle's sluggish brain latched onto one word. *Missed?*

"Nice of you to join us, Marielle."

Head twisting to the side, Marielle found Maher Villaon sitting next to her on the beach. He did not look pleased. Everything came rushing back.

"Maher?" She struggled to sit up, the weight of her waterlogged gunbelt fought against her. Fully awake now, Marielle realized they weren't on the island at all. Just a spit of sand out in the sea. "What happened?"

"That's what we need to discuss." He crossed his arms, looking rather haughty for a man currently marooned on a sandbar.

Marielle's stomach sank. "Where are Ally and Pasha?"

"They should be back any moment." There was a light splash nearby. "Ah, perfect timing."

Through the smooth surface, two long shapes swam towards them. Vibrant hues of blue, green, silver, and copper flashed from beneath the sea. Then, two heads emerged, one brunette and the other a dark blue. Ally's pupils, blown wide while underwater, contracted swiftly in the sunlight into something slightly more human. But Pasha's stayed as two inky pools. Marielle felt she was really seeing the pair for the first time.

The two mermaids didn't join them on the sandbar. Rather, they kept their torsos and tails in the water, leaning on their elbows in the shallows.

"Are you alright, Marielle?" Ally asked.

"I am, thank you." Marielle licked her dry, salt-crusted lips. All three watched her keenly. What were they waiting for? "Shouldn't we get moving?"

"We should," Maher said. "But first, I have a few questions."

"Such as?"

"Why are you really here, Marielle? True, you might be trying to salvage your position with the Madam, but I highly doubt that's all. Furthermore, why did you pull me overboard, when I told you I was staying with the ship?"

"Y-you were about to fall over the railing."

At least that was partially true.

"Yes, and you could've pushed me farther onto the ship instead of dragging me off of it," he snapped.

"It was a split-second decision," Marielle protested.

"Let me put it this way," Maher's tone shifted into one she'd never heard from him before. "We aren't going anywhere, until you tell the truth."

CHAPTER NINETY-FOUR

The pirates were bearing down on them. Great swells from the larger warship tossed the *Foxglove* about, like a ship's cat toying with a rat. Giving it just enough space to hope for freedom, until right before it was eaten.

Another swell hit their hull and Luthais was thrown back against the mainmast. Stars danced in his vision when the still-tender back of his head hit solid wood.

A cannon broke free from its restraints, sending the hunk of iron rolling down the deck. Luthais lunged, caught the trailing rope, and braced against the mast for the weight to catch up. The rope twisted in his hands and Luthais thought his arm might be pulled from its socket. Three crewmates stumbled to their captain's aid. Sharing the burden between them, they lashed the errant cannon to the mast.

"Alright, Captain?" one of the sailors, Olebile, panted.

"Aye, thank you."

Olebile nodded and ran back to their station at midship.

Across the deck, Maher and Marielle held onto whatever part of the ship they could for dear life. The ship yawed at a sharp angle, throwing Maher hard against the ship's railing.

"Maher!" Luthais shouted, instincts screaming to help him.

But Marielle was closer. She pulled herself to Maher's side as the very boards of the deck continued to rattle. Wrapping an arm around his waist, Marielle hauled his limp body up.

No! Goddess, please, this can't be happening.

Just as Luthais moved in their direction, Marielle backed against the rail. Casting an eye to the churning depths, Marielle fell back, pulling Maher with her into the sea.

Two thoughts kept Luthais from diving in after them, the moment Maher and Marielle went over the rail.

The knowledge that Ally and Pasha were already in the sea, and would have a better chance to save Maher than he was.

And the absolute truth that, as Captain, he could never abandon his crew to an enemy.

It was those thoughts, and those thoughts alone, that kept his boots on the deck and his focus on the fight at hand. He refused to consider anything else. Maher wasn't condemned to death by Marielle's rash actions. Luthais wasn't right, in that he never should have trusted the gunfighter. They would both be kept safe by the mermaids. Gods, that's why he'd wanted to know if Ally could keep a human underwater. So the pair could take Maher with them, should he choose to go. Except he hadn't chosen to go, Marielle pulled him overboard.

"Captain!" Kamharida shouted from the starboard side. When he managed to cross the creaking deck to reach her, the first mate pointed past the swells battering their hull, at the pirates' vessel. "Sea spirits, protect us."

The blood in his veins turned to ice. Corpse sailors. Clearly visible now on the approaching ship. A wave of panic spread through the *Foxglove*. Some sailors beseeched their gods or called upon ancestors for aid.

Ga-Seung came bounding up from the hold, a short ax in one hand. When he saw what was nearly upon them, the bosun swore under his breath. "What're your orders, Captain? The longboats are prepped with what few supplies we could fit and still hold the crew."

As Ga-Seung was speaking, Dare appeared on the bow of the Fraollish ship. Or, at least, the woman who had once been Foraoise Dare now stood on the bow. He'd heard enough about her to recognize the pirate captain, but Luthais understood now what Pasha'd meant when she called this a distorted version of her own power. While the mermaids' appearances were unlike a human's, it was obvious they were in their natural state. But Dare looked little better than the dead sailors that made up her new crew. It was all so deeply *wrong*.

Luthais' fists clenched tight. "Abandon ship."

"You're sure, Captain?" Kamharida asked.

"Aye, before it's too late. We might even be able to cross the trench in the smaller boats."

"ABANDON SHIP!" The first mate's booming voice echoed down the length of the ship and the call was taken up amongst the crew. The sailors assigned to secure the longboats on their pulleys hustled to their posts.

Luthais stayed in place, mentally calculating for the hundredth time how many people would fit into each boat. There should be just enough room for every soul aboard.

Bending his knees as the deck lurched again, Luthais grabbed the rail. He'd be damned if Dare thought she was going to frighten him.

The crew rushed to fill the boats and Luthais overheard Kamharida order someone to check all the cabins.

Pimm! Luthais tore his eyes from the oncoming ship with its dead crew. "First mate!"

"Aye, sir?" She ran over. "Send someone to the chart room for Pimm, they might be too ill to come abovedecks themself."

Kamharida opened her mouth to reply, then her russet eyes strayed past him. "What are they doing now?"

Twisting back around, Luthais' heart fell into his stomach. The warship was turning. "Broadside! She's going to fire on us." He started to warn the crew boarding the starboard side longboats, but Kamharida caught his arm.

"Wait. They're pulling hard to port. They'll barely get a target."

Pausing long enough to confirm she was right, Luthais ran for the stern. On the way, he borrowed the barrelman's spyglass. She'd just climbed down from the crow's nest

The Fraollish ship continued its sharp turn, the resulting swells tossed the *Foxglove* about even more. When they reached the quarterdeck, Kamharida took over for the exhausted helmsman. At the stern, Luthais trained the glass on Dare's ship. A handful of living sailors were scattered throughout the walking corpses. Though they all watched the *Foxglove* with interest, none moved to ready the cannons or brandished other weapons.

He spotted Dare, still standing on the bow like some kind of figurehead. At the last moment, she turned her head and Luthais felt as if she were looking down the glass at him. Dare winked, and the hair on the back of his neck stood up. Then the pirate ship turned completely away.

"What made them swerve?" asked Ga-Seung as he appeared by Luthais' side.

"I've not a damn clue."

"The old Dare wouldn't have just faked on us and turned around." The bosun rumbled. "Something had to have happened, something more important that taking this ship."

"He's right," Kamharida said from the helm. "We are too good a prize to just give up. Not unless a better one came along."

"What in the gods' names is going on?" A hoarse voice drew their attention. Pimm dragged themself onto the quarterdeck, a trembling pigeon tucked against their side.

"Where did that come from?" Luthais frowned.

"My guess is from the ship that nearly rammed into us." They held out the bird so he could take the tiny scroll of paper tied to its leg. Unrolling the note, Luthais recognized the same fine penmanship that'd written the letter for Rochelle's ransom.

See you at home, nephew.

"What does it say?" asked Ga-Seung.

Luthais watched the departing pirate ship shrink into the distance. "We need to get across that trench, find the others, and get back to the Isles."

BEAR'S DEN

PIMM

CHAPTER NINETY-FIVE

Pimm stumbled from the gloom belowdecks into the sunlight, and was immediately accosted by a pigeon.

After securing the flapping bird, Pimm stood for a moment on the blessedly calmed deck and looked around. Half the longboats were loaded and ready to be lowered into the sea, but the crew only stared in confusion while the larger, menacing ship that'd been stalking them across the sea sailed away.

Voices drifted down from the helm, and Pimm slowly made their way in that direction.

Gods take me, I've been sicker and more injured in the past year than the twenty-seven preceding it. The pigeon cooed softly in their arms. *Maybe Maher is bad luck after all.*

After delivering the message to the captain, Pimm found they were reluctant to release the bird. As it calmed down, its delicate little heart beating against their palm was oddly comforting.

As Luthais read the note, his face shifted into a stony mask. And while Pimm agreed getting to land was the best plan, the captain's final words gave them pause.

"Wait, what happened to Maher?" Pimm demanded.

The bosun was equally puzzled. "Yes, where is he?"

"He's..." Luthais cleared his throat, rolling up the paper. "He's with Ally, Pasha, and Marielle."

Pimm glanced around. "And where is that?"

"In the sea. They've gone for help from The Riddles."

Pimm felt what little color that hadn't been claimed by seasickness drain from their face. The pigeon cooed in a way that almost sounded concerned. "Why did I assume it would be easier to keep an eye on both of them if we were all on a ship?"

MAHER

Chapter Ninety-six

Perhaps it was the salt that coated every inch of his skin, or the heat from the sun shining mercilessly down onto them, but Maher found himself unable to tell if Marielle was holding anything else back.

"That's all of it?" he shielded his eyes with his palm.

Marielle, on the other hand, gazed back at him with very little trouble. "That's everything. I wanted to come, in part, to make amends with the Madam. But more importantly, I must find my brother before anyone else does."

"You're sure it was his stamp on the crate?" Ally asked, fins swishing in the slowly rising tide. Maher was glad he'd had time to admire her tail before Marielle woke. The movement was almost hypnotic.

"Positive," Marielle sighed. "But I can't believe he knows these coins aren't really being made for Saprea. He's too kind a person for that,"

"But someone might've taken advantage of his kindness?" Pasha offered.

Maher mopped the sweat from his brow. "Why not tell me this from the start, Marielle?"

"I didn't want anyone to know. At least not until I found who's gotten him tangled in this mess." Marielle looked down at the fuchsia sand, sinking her fingers into the soft grains. "I'm sorry I pulled you over without warning. I know my brother, he won't want to believe that he's involved in something shady. Having the Intelligencer of the Birde Isles with me will save countless hours of convincing on my part."

"That may be, but again, you could've told me why you needed my help." There was a pause as he thought over all she'd said. "And you intentionally got Jerd pinched at the Treasury so you could travel to The Riddles without the Madam questioning anything?"

"I'll admit, I didn't expect her to be quite so angry, but yes. I'll make it up to him."

He snorted. "Assuming Jerd hasn't already given you up."

"We'll see."

Pasha fidgeted, the wicked black blade of the spear she'd brought caught the light, reminding Maher there was more than one purpose to this voyage. But Pimm's earlier suspicions still plagued him.

Was Marielle hiding something else?

PASHA

Chapter Ninety-seven

Pasha fought to remain still as Maher questioned Marielle. They were *so close* to finding the mermaids left from her shoal, from all the shoals, yet they dawdled here on a sandbar.

As the discussion continued, Pasha tried to send out a tendril of energy, searching for any traces of the other merfolk. But she was still recovering from the encounter with the siren and her well of energy hadn't truly begun to replenish until they returned to the sea. The tendrils faded before they could get close to the island and the incessant throbbing that'd started between her eyes was spreading around her skull. The pressure would soon drown out her ability to discern another mermaid's energy from her own.

Maher asked Marielle yet another question and Pasha's teeth ground together. She was ready to leave this human behind altogether to fare on her own. It would take time and strength to carry the humans to the nearest island, and Pasha didn't have much left of either.

Shifting in the shallows, Pasha tried to draw enough charges from the water to make a new tendril. The slender threads crawled towards her, binding together. Just when Pasha thought she had enough the charges twisted and collided with each other, fizzling out and escaping back into the sea.

BEAR'S DEN

PIMM

Chapter Ninety-eight

B y some trick of the gods, Pimm was no longer seasick. Though they doubted triggering swells violent enough to nearly capsize one's ship would make for a good remedy for everyone. It had, against all odds and common sense, worked for Pimm.

At least now they felt they could actually be of some use aboard the ship. The first mate quickly enlisted Pimm to assist with running updates to the captain and other officers as the ship was put back to rights.

Luthais was obviously worried about Maher, even if the words were never spoken aloud. It made Pimm curious about what all had happened while they were sick for the first half of the journey. Certainly the two men had become closer in the last year. Now Pimm wondered exact how close that was. They might not be well acquainted with Luthais Kingfisher, but they knew Maher's ways well enough to develop a few theories. Maher may not've been self-aware enough to realize it, but the man was often drawn to distinct personalities. And the Pike was most distinctive.

Not that Pimm wasn't concerned about Maher themself, he'd had some abysmal luck when it came to sailing. But they'd also heard enough about Ally to know she'd do everything in her power to keep him safe. And when they reached The Riddles, assuming Pimm was right about Marielle, they'd have a most welcome reception.

For now Pimm calmly went about the tasks asked of them by the ship's officers. While it was still uncertain when help would arrive from the islands, they were well stocked to see the wait through. Pimm even volunteered to assist the captain with charting the route they'd taken to reach this point. Of course it would be impossible to plot the twists and turns Marielle had taken them on, but at least they could try to get an idea of where they were at sea.

The only decision Pimm still hadn't settled on, was what to do with his suspicions about Marielle. While waiting for a tally of their remaining artillery from the gunner, Pimm rolled their first cigarette in days. They took it as a good sign when their stomach only rolled slightly at the initial pull of smoke. The trouble was, even if Pimm was right about the gunfighter and her real motives for making this journey, what would they do with the information? It wasn't even something they'd caught on their own, but an observation made by Olga.

Mama Bear sent the kitchen maid into Marielle's quarters at the black lantern to ensure there was nothing she'd need for the journey to her homeland. While sorting through her belongings, Olga came across a circlet of carved wood, polished smooth and studded with raw stones. Pimm only heard about it by chance, when they were preparing to leave to pick up Marielle from their own building. They weren't sure what the headpiece symbolized, but it was a safe assumption it placed Marielle in some position of importance.

And, even if proved to be true, what effect would it really have on the outcome? It made perfect sense to Pimm, Marielle discovered the false provenance Saprean coins were being minted in The Riddles and wanted to protect her family. Pimm would've likely done the same, if they'd found one of their tenants was caught in the middle of something untoward.

"I wouldn't smoke that too close to the hatch." The gunner emerged with the new inventory in hand. "A bit lost in thought, were ya?"

Smoke curled from Pimm's nose as they took a final drag and stubbed the ember out against the heel of their boot. "Lost is certainly one way to put it."

CHAPTER NINETY-NINE

Ally was torn between her concern for both Pasha and Maher. She could sense the impatience and unease radiating from Pasha. But if the sirens were as dangerous as the one that attacked Pasha, they couldn't just go bursting into a nest of them.

Try as she might, Ally couldn't shake the guilt over not being there for Pasha when she was attacked beneath Dare's ship. Unable to help protect her, as Pasha had protected Ally so many times.

Even if Ally *had* been there, what could she have done in that moment besides provide another target for the sirens and snapjaws? The fact that she'd been able to share a prolonged breath with Maher had given Ally a spark of hope that she might one day tap into the ability to harness energy from the sea, and be of some use as a mermaid.

But what if, even after this new development, that never happened? Ally worried, despite Pasha's assurances, that eventually she'd become frustrated or resent Ally for not being able to do the things that came naturally to mermaids. Pasha shifted restlessly next to her and Ally snuck a glance at the mermaid's sharp profile.

I'd rather have no mermaid talents at all, than hold onto false hope.

It was midafternoon by the time they reached the shore of the nearest island. Ally towed Maher into the shallows, feeling a new appreciation for all the times Pasha'd ferried her out to sea and back.

Pasha released Marielle the moment she insisted she could swim. And Marielle was indeed a strong swimmer, no surprise given that she'd grown up in this place.

"Any idea where we are?" Maher wrung the seawater from the hem of his shirt before tucking it back into his trousers. The silver chain holding the shark tooth was barely visible beneath his collar. Ally'd taken the time to check it before they left the sandbar. The smooth, black fossil still burned steadily with the energy she'd fed into it, with Pasha's help.

Scanning the beach, Marielle turned back to them with a relieved half smile. "I think we're on the main island. We should be able to walk to the capital fairly easily."

"How can you tell?" he asked.

"The smaller islands all have flags posted to warn of hidden shallows. With the water so clear, it creates a mirror at certain times of day. Even our boats can become stuck if they're not careful."

Ally walked stiffly out of the water, her tail had been reluctant to split back into legs again. Fatigue settled over her like a heavy cloak as they discussed the best way to reach the nearest city on foot. Looking over her shoulder, Ally found Pasha moving even slower than she was. A pained expression flashed across her face.

"*Pasha?*" Ally tried to speak through her mind. It should work, since they were both still standing in the sea. "*Are you alright?*"

Pasha flinched, hard, and shook her head. Had Pasha's headaches returned now that they were on the other side of the barrier? And if so, did that mean they were close to finding the other mermaids?

CHAPTER ONE HUNDRED

Now that they had a reasonable idea which island they'd landed on, Marielle was impatient to press on. Maher understood her motivations far better now. Naturally, she didn't want her brother to sink any further into the muck than he already had. But Maher had to think of Ally and Pasha as well, two naked mermaids couldn't exactly go waltzing into town with them.

Perhaps it was the excitement of being home, or the need to find her brother, but Marielle appeared not to have noticed Ally and Pasha had shed their clothes altogether.

"We should be on our way." Marielle said as she finished checking the contents of her gun belt. The new pistols had, amazingly, stayed put during their fall from the ship and underwater journey. "It will be faster to walk to the city than search the water for the boats, especially if they've already crossed the current."

Maher turned to Ally and Pasha, still standing in the small wavelets washing ashore. "Al, why don't you two rest here and watch for a sign of Luthais and the others from the *Foxglove?*"

"Wait here?" The ridges above Pasha's eyes snapped together.

While he wasn't surprised by Pasha's response, Maher hated the idea of no one being here in case they'd made it across the trench, with or without help from The Riddles. It ate at him, not knowing what'd happened to the ship, to the crew and Pimm. To Luthais.

"Even if they cross the current, there's no guarantee they'll come near this stretch of beach," Pasha argued.

"I know, but…"

"The longer we wait, the more the others could suffer!" she snapped.

Laying a soothing hand on Pasha's arm, Ally turned to Maher. "I know you're worried about what happened to Luthais, Pimm, and the crew. We all are, especially after what happened to the *Pike*. But Pasha's right, they could land anywhere on any one of these islands."

Maher's stomach turned to lead at the reminder of the *Pike*. A phantom itch started in his shoulder and he clenched his fists to stop himself from scratching. "Please Al, just for a little while."

The mermaids looked at each other, sharing some unspoken communication. Next to him, Marielle was peering into the trees beyond the beach, probably scouting for a path.

Ally's hand trailed down Pasha's arm to wrap around her fingers. "We'll wait until the sun hits the tree line. But then we'll have to go and search for Pasha's family."

PASHA

CHAPTER ONE HUNDRED-ONE

Pasha watched the two humans disappear into the trees, growing more frustrated and miserable by the second. What good would it do to spend an hour or more waiting here on this beach, with her captive kin right under her nose?

She knew Ally was only trying to do what was best for everyone – Pasha, Maher, her brother – and Pasha didn't blame her for that. But now her head was pounding nearly as badly as it had before Hama found her way home. What if it was a sign the others were closer than they realized? Pressing the heels of her hands against her eyes, Pasha squatted in the surf and breathed deeply. Ally'd suggested using this time to actually rest and for Pasha to restore her well of energy. And she'd tried, but the charges eluded her like they'd done out at sea. Was it something about this place that prevented Pasha from healing?

Neither knowing nor caring how long she stayed in that position, Pasha tried, and failed, to encourage her well to fill itself. A rope of panic knotted around her heart when nothing happened.

What if I don't have the strength to help them?

"Pasha?" Ally knelt beside her. "Is there something I can do?"

"No..." Pasha's head snapped up. "Maybe. Yes. I don't know why, but I can't seem to hold onto any charges from this sea long enough to fill my well again. Could I try..."

"Of course!" Reading her mind, Ally took Pasha's hand, pressed it against her chest and easily opened a bridge between them.

A wave of fresh energy washed over Pasha. By the tides, Ally's well had already replenished itself when not even a full day had passed. How was that possible? Even at her strongest, it would've taken Pasha a day or two in the sea to recover so quickly.

"Is this helping?" Ally asked, a little breathless.

Slowly, Pasha withdrew from the connection. She did feel somewhat better, but not nearly as much as she should. It was as if the energy was burning off faster than she could take it in. Ally looked at her expectantly, unaware of how little Pasha'd been able to hold onto in the exchange. They stood together, Pasha took the spear in hand.

"Yes, it did. Thank you, sweetheart." Pasha glanced at the sun, there was still some time before it reached the forest canopy. What if the little bit of energy she'd managed to gain was gone by then? "Ally, I can't just sit here any longer. Why don't you stay, while I search for some sign of the remaining shoals?"

Ally's response was immediate, visceral, amplified into mermaid language by the remnants of their link before she even opened her mouth. She would *not* be separated from Pasha.

"Absolutely not," she said aloud.

"I only want to find a trail, some hint as to where they're hidden. I'll come back to get you, by then the sun will have set enough that you'll have fulfilled the agreement with Maher."

With a small, sad smile, Ally shook her head. "No you won't. I know you, Pasha. The moment you find the trail of the others, you'll be compelled to follow it."

Pasha didn't bother to argue, Ally was right.

"And I couldn't possibly let you go alone. I promised to help find your shoal, and that's what I'm going to do."

In that moment, Pasha was keenly aware of the weight of the spear in her hands. A reminder that, should something happen to her, Ally wouldn't be able to wield it. With or without accessing the energy inside. "It's going to be dangerous, Ally. I couldn't live with myself either if something happened to you."

"Is this because I can't fight or harness energy the way a mermaid should?" Ally's teeth sank into her lower lip. "Do you think I'll only be a hindrance? Am I really so helpless?"

"That's not it at all, Ally, I swear. You're the strongest person I know. Look at what you've overcome since we met." Pasha grasped for the right thing to say. "But this is going to be very different from anything we've faced before. You weren't there when that siren attacked, you don't know how strong they are. I don't know where she'd gone by the time we returned to the sea, why there were no others nearby, but I was so relieved. I don't want them anywhere near you, I –" Pasha cut herself off. The panic began to rise again, trying to force out the words she'd been holding back at precisely the wrong time.

Ally stepped closer. The sea lapped around their ankles as those hazel eyes searched her face. "Be honest with me, Pasha. You're afraid you'll have to choose between rescuing your family, and protecting me, aren't you?"

BEAR'S DEN

PIMM

Chapter One Hundred-Two

One of the messenger birds sent to The Riddles finally returned to the *Foxglove* with a reply. Help was on the way, but it might take time to locate them as they continued to sail around the edge of the trench. With luck and the tides on their side, the Riddles boats should reach them by the next morning.

Pimm offered to return the bird to the cages that held the rest of the ship's messengers. It gave them a chance to check on the pigeon from Dare's ship. The poor thing seemed in no hurry to return; Pimm imagined its life on a pirate ship was anything but peaceful. Let alone one crewed by a hoard of dead sailors.

Shaking off the thought, Pimm gave each of the birds a treat from the supplies kept for them and made their way back above decks. Now that the seasickness had passed, they found they preferred the fresh air to being cooped up in a cabin.

News that The Riddles would soon send help had traveled fast, no surprise aboard a ship, and seemed to give the crew the motivation to return the *Foxglove* to rights in record time. One could hardly tell they'd been in distress, not so long ago.

After indulging in another smoke, Pimm joined the captain and first mate in the chart room. A long table was pushed against one wall, strewn with papers, weights, and cartography tools. Mounted on the wall behind it was a huge map of the Known World. They were tracing their route from the Birde Isles to The Riddles.

"How goes it?" Pimm asked.

"We've found the point where we believe Marielle took the helm," said Kamharida. "But anything beyond that would be a guess without her here to confirm it."

"If she'd even be so forthcoming," they mused.

"Meaning?" Luthais paused, an instrument of measurement poised in front of the map.

"Only that the people of The Riddles have kept this secret for a reason."

"They make a good point." Kamharida studied the expanse of blue that everyone had believed separated The Riddles from the rest of the world. "But why continue to allow the belief that they were so far removed? Why isolate themselves so completely?"

Pimm shrugged. "Perhaps we'll learn the answer while we're here."

Kamharida was eventually called away by the bosun. Soon after, the captain's steward brought bread, cheese, and a draught of ale for each of them. Pimm was a little surprised when Luthais invited them to join him at the small table where the food and drink waited, but they accepted.

Who'd've thought I'd be breaking bread with the Lord of Trade, they thought wryly. Then again, Luthais Kingfisher wasn't exactly what one imagined when picturing nobility.

"I hadn't realized how much time had passed." Pimm checked their pocket watch.

"Neither had I," the captain granted, fingers drumming on the table next to his ale.

Pimm felt no pressure to make idle conversation, they'd been working on the map routes mostly in silence up to that point anyway. So they carved a hunk of bread; might as well enjoy it before the inevitable switch to hardtack.

The longer they sat there, the more Luthais fidgeted, until Pimm began to wonder if they should excuse themself. When Luthais brought his fist down onto the table, Pimm nearly dropped the sandwich they'd just made.

"Why've they only sent one reply when we sent three missives for help?"

"You're upset they haven't sent all three birds back?" Pimm coughed around a mouthful of bread and cheese.

Luthais peered at Pimm, as if he'd forgotten they were there. "Of course not, but," he took a sudden interest in his ale, "there was no mention of Maher, or Marielle, in their reply. If they'd made it safely to land, I'd think we would've received word by now."

"You're worried about Maher," Pimm ventured a guess.

"Are you not?"

"It's not that I'm not worried. It's just that I've seen Maher extricate himself from far less certain circumstances. And this time, he has Ally to watch out for him."

"What circumstances would those be?"

"Where do I start?" They shook their head. "In the last year, Maher Villaon has survived the explosion of a ship, being skewered like a roast for the spit, and being held captive by pirates afterwards. Before that, he came to my own rescue, I'm glad to say, and fought off the three street crew gonys trying to crack my head open in an alley." They paused to take a sip of ale. "And let us not forget the street crew he held off by himself not long before that, until I arrived to help."

Luthais stared wide-eyed at them from across the table. "I'll be damned and dusted, what exactly has he been doing in the Lantern to draw such trouble?"

"You've been at sea for different periods of time, it's not unexpected to be somewhat removed from what's happening on land. As for Maher, he's only doing what's needed. That's what he's always done, it's who he is."

A muscle in the captain's jaw twitched. "Is it? How do you know?"

"Don't you?" Pimm's head tilted. "You practically grew up together in the same house. A rather large house, but together just the same. You truly believe you don't know Maher?"

Luthais' grip tightened around his cup. "I lived with Cal in the same house since I was three years old, and it turned out I didn't even know my own brother. How can I possibly know the real Maher when he switches between masks as often as he changes clothes?"

"Maher is very good at wearing those masks, I grant you."

"Why? I want to understand."

Pimm studied him for a moment. The answer had always been obvious to them but, then again, people often didn't bother to look for answers until they were needed. "Because of his father."

"Khafra?" Luthais blinked at them.

"Maher has always had to wear a different face around his father. As far back as he can remember, who Maher is as a person has never been what Khafra wanted him to be." They sighed. "But think about who Maher is when he's not being the Magpie of Kingsport or the Intelligencer of the Birde Isles, or dealing with Khafra. Think of the man who loves your sister more than his own life, who'd stride right into danger to help a friend. The Maher who tried to save as many souls as possible during the Bear's Den fire. The artist who fusses endlessly over his wardrobe." Pimm cracked a smile when Luthais snorted a laugh. "That's the real Maher, there's no mask. But I think perhaps you already knew that. And do you not do something similar, if less marked, when you must act as a captain or Lord of Trade?"

Pimm sat quietly while Luthais considered all they'd said. It was likely the longest conversation they'd ever have, and something told Pimm it was important for Luthais to hear this from someone close to Maher.

"I think you're right. Thank you, Pimm." Luthais said after a while. "And you truly believe they've reached land by now?"

"I do, and I expect they'll be very well-treated once they find her people."

Cocking a brow at them, Luthais lifted his ale. "Why do you say that?"

"I suspect Marielle is a bit more important than she's let on."

CHAPTER ONE HUNDRED-THREE

The Fraollish warship cut a path through the sea, speed held steady by the sirens that swam beneath it. Not for the first time, Foraoise contemplated harnessing that very skill for herself.

Sitting in the lavishly appointed captain's quarters, she felt the slightest twinge of longing for her cabin aboard the *Maiden's Revenge*. Smaller though it had been, the floor stained with the bloodlike concoction she'd poured over her head before taking a prize. But that cabin had also borne witness to some of the happiest moments of her life, and some of the most tragic. It was the one place she and Jon could be alone, to lay side-by-side in the bed they'd shared for many years. It was also in that room that Foraoise came to realize the Jon she'd known and loved was gone, and would never return. Where she'd spoken with Swain in hushed tones about what could be done. And where she'd sat after running her blade through Jon's heart, to cry the last tears she'd ever shed.

The ornate little clock next to the bed chimed the hour. Foraoise ran a hand over her face, brushing away the cobwebs. Several hours had passed since she'd come into this room. That happened, she'd found, if she thought too long about the past. Her body simply settled, like driftwood on the shore. And it was becoming more difficult each time to break away. Even the surge of rage she'd felt upon awakening in the cave, surrounded by sirens, had just... faded. Only rising again if there was a focus for her ire.

As Foraoise contemplated standing up, there was a knock at the door.

"Yes, Swain?" There was no one else who'd dare approach her on this ship.

"Afternoon, Captain." He came in and placed a tray of assorted foods on the table where she sat. "Thought we could share a bite."

"I'm not hungry."

"Captain, you've hardly eaten since we set sail to retrieve the turbine."

"My statement still stands. I don't seem to have much need for sustenance like this anymore." She gestured at the empty chair. "Sit. You should still keep up your strength."

Lowering stiffly into the offered seat, Swain chose not to press the matter. Digging into his meal, he said, "I expect we'll reach the Birde Isles within a week."

The captain nodded. "Aye, it appears The Riddles aren't as cut off from the rest of the world as we'd thought. Even less so with the sirens propelling us forward."

"Have to say, I'm still staggered they agreed to give you the Isles so readily."

"Because those islands once belonged to them?"

"Aye, exactly."

Foraoise plucked a grape from the tray and examined it in the light from the table lamp. "I'll admit now, after hearing their story, I expected them to say no or renegotiate. But then, it shows how much they need our help to take their revenge."

"That it does," Swain belched into his fist. "T'was the right idea either way, speaking of revenge."

"Mmhmm," She popped the grape into her mouth, out of habit rather than a desire to eat it. The fruit burst between her teeth. She felt the juice inside slide down her throat, could identify the texture of the skin against her tongue, but Foraoise might as well have been chewing on air. There was simply nothing there, not even a signal from her stomach that something now rested inside of it.

Were it not for Swain's reminder of their own purpose in sailing for the Isles, she might've slipped away into thought again. More driftwood on the beach. But the prospect of Swain's surprise was too enticing. And oh, did Foraoise have plans once she and her letter writing friend finally met.

CHAPTER ONE HUNDRED-FOUR

"Tell me, Swain, how did you manage to find my anonymous friend?"

Seeing a familiar glint in the captain's eyes, Swain was only too glad to tell her. He first relayed the story told by Smith, how a son of the Kingfisher family had been imprisoned for treason. It hadn't taken long to fit the pieces together. All the state information contained within the letters. How most of the birds sent to the *Maiden's Revenge* had borne Meredian tags on their legs. There was no way of knowing Calder Kingfisher's travel itinerary during that time, but the rumors of trade secrets sold to Meredia couldn't be a mere coincidence.

From there, Swain'd kept his plans to himself. Smith knew he'd sent a few sailors from their crew on another task, but even she didn't know the where or why. Of course one of the sirens accompanied them.

"The sirens were more willing to assist than I anticipated," Swain admitted.

"No doubt the prospect of catching a glimpse of their former domain was too good to resist."

"Indeed." What Swain left out of the story, was the reason he'd given the sirens for sending any of his crew out on their own again. That the thought of taking vengeance on Cal might be a way to get Foraoise to the Birde Isles quickly. Too good to resist. "But damned if they didn't arrive to find someone'd already nicked him from his cell."

Foraoise leaned one elbow on the table, black-rimmed eyes alight with interest. "And who else wanted to get their hands on him? For I doubt there was a crowd of supporters beating the doors down."

"Still don't know." Swain pushed his empty plate aside. "But the siren with 'em kept entrancing guards by the docks until one said he knew where Cal might be hiding."

"And they found him."

"Aye, that they did."

"Where is he now?" Foraoise picked up a hunk of bread, examined it, but never took a bite.

Much as he wished she'd eat, Swain knew there was no use in suggesting it a second time. "Tucked away, nice and safe, on the schooner. They'll circle the Isles and make port again when we arrive."

Dropping the bread back onto the plate, Foraoise dusted the crumbs from her fingers. "Swain, you truly have outdone yourself."

MAHER

CHAPTER ONE HUNDRED-FIVE

Marielle led the way as they picked out a path through the dense forest. They came upon a few clearings where homes were built or even crops planted, but she skirted all of them. Not that Maher was in the mood to stand about and gab over the fence, but surely they could've asked how far they were from the city.

When this question was voiced, though, Marielle insisted she knew exactly where they were. The city, she explained as they climbed over a fallen tree trunk wide enough to be a ship's mast, was almost exactly in the center of the island. They could start on any coast and reach it within three to four hours by the roads.

"Far be it for me to point this out," he'd panted, ducking beneath a cluster of flowering vines. "But we aren't *on* a road."

"Look, just trust me. I know this land as well as I know how to hit a target."

Too tired to argue with her any further, Maher concentrated on putting one foot in front of the other.

If Marielle's not been here in nigh on a decade, I wonder that she knows this island as well as she thinks.

As the afternoon shadows grew long around them, they burst through a break in the trees and stepped onto a wide, brick-paved road. A young boy pushing a small cart yelped, then stared at them with wide eyes.

"Apologies," Marielle smiled, showing her gold teeth. "Be on your way, friend."

The boy took off at a much faster pace than he'd been on before. Clearing the hill ahead and disappearing over the other side before Maher had time to acknowledge he'd even been there.

"This way, we're nearly there." she walked in the same direction.

Maher followed, grateful their destination was finally within reach. They crested the hill shortly after the boy, and Maher got his first glimpse of the Riddles capital city. It wasn't as large as Kingsport, or Laleseir in Saprea, but it was impressive.

The brown clay bricks of the forest road blended into streets of deep fuchsia, obviously made with the pink sands surrounding the islands. None of the buildings were more than three floors tall, but all were constructed of gleaming white stone. Polished wooden shutters were thrown open to let in the light and fresh air. Colorful curtains from open terraces flapped in the breeze.

To Maher, it almost seemed like something out of a fairytale. Any moment he expected some mythical creature to pop out and challenge him to a game of words.

As they passed through the outer streets and into the city proper, he did get the feeling they were being watched. Of course, visitors were uncommon. But hadn't a few nations on the continent been sending trade delegates in recent years? Surely Maher's presence wasn't wholly unexpected.

"It's not you." Marielle seemed to read his mind.

"What was that?"

"They're not staring at you."

They passed a small market that made Maher ache for the Birde Isles in a way he'd never experienced before. A woman at a fruit stall watched them pass, then grabbed her companion's arm and pointed. But not at Maher, at Marielle.

"It's her!" she whispered at a volume easily heard across the street.

"Can't be," the other squinted at them.

"I swear it, she's back!"

"Marielle," he glanced behind them, a small crowd now watched their progress "what is this?"

Fingers wrapped tightly around her gunbelt, Marielle winced, "I'm... very recognizable at home."

"Recognizable? What in all the gods' names is that supposed to mean?"

"You'll see soon enough."

Maher thought back to Pimm cautioning him on board the *Foxglove*. How they suspected Marielle wasn't telling them the whole story. Maher'd hoped he'd gotten it all from her on the sandbar, but now he wasn't so sure.

They soon reached a sprawling villa, the only building that stood a floor taller than those around it. Two guards stood at the front gate. There were no weapons in sight, but Maher knew that meant nothing. When they were halted just outside the entrance, Marielle's posture shifted. Shoulders pushed back and sharp chin lifted.

"Please tell my parents their daughter desires an audience."

As astonished as the boy from the road, one guard gave a short bow and disappeared inside. In a matter of moments, she returned with a tall, imposing man who was clearly their superior. Long, black hair hung down his back, bound every few inches with dyed strips of leather. A leather breastplate was strapped across his chest, embossed with a curled wave. He gave Marielle a quick once over, spared an even shorter glance for Maher, then bowed deeply.

When he straightened again, a smile split his handsome face, showing even more gold-capped teeth than Marielle. "Welcome home, princess."

MARIELLE

Chapter One Hundred-six

Marielle wanted to push her cousin into the nearest river.

"You know I could have you exiled, don't you Vas?"

His grin only widened. "You've been saying that since you were eight years old, and I've yet to see it happen."

"Today just might be that day," she muttered. Chancing a look back at Maher, she found the Magpie had curbed his reaction. But the calculated look in his eye made her curious. *What is he thinking?*

"Their majesties are eager to see you." Vas swept an arm out, ushering them through the gate. Maher fell in step beside Marielle as they followed her cousin around the front garden.

"It would seem we have a few things to discuss, your *highness*," he murmured.

Rolling her eyes, Marielle snorted, "I have no idea what you're talking about."

"I thought you'd told me everything."

"And I don't see how knowing my title has anything to do with why we're here."

"A *princess*, Marielle?" Maher hissed. "I'd say that could have a great effect on the success of this mission. At the very least, I hope your influence will ensure help is dispatched quickly to Luthais' ship." His voice caught. "Or what might be left of it."

"Maher..."

Vas halted at the edge of a sun-filled courtyard. Light, almost sheer curtains hung suspended from a vine- covered archway, giving the impression of a door. "You two aren't as quiet as you think." His smirk dropped when he addressed Maher. "Help has already been sent to your ship. The boats were dispatched as soon as Marielle's letters arrived. They might already have found the *Foxglove* by now."

"Thank the gods," Maher sighed.

Marielle hardly recognized this responsible, well-mannered version of her cousin. Vas looked much the same, except now he towered over her and had apparently worked his way up through the guard ranks.

"Are you ready?"

"Not at all."

"That's the Marielle I know," Vas chuckled. Then he pulled the pale green curtain aside, and Marielle steeled herself to face her parents.

If she were honest, the last thing Marielle expected was to be swept into a bone-crushing embrace by her mother. Yet here she was, being smothered in the bosom of the woman who gave birth to her.

"Marielle, my Marielle." Mother rocked gently as she'd done when Marielle was small, running a hand over her shorn hair. "Look at how much you've grown!"

"Let her breath, my dear." Mam's voice broke the spell. Extracting herself from her mother's arms, Marielle turned to face Mam.

Vas stepped into his official role. "Presenting their majesties, Queen Sefina and Queen Maeva, rulers of The Riddles and all islands contained therein."

Mam and Mother, the Queens of The Riddles. They stood next to each other, looking at their daughter with very different expressions. Not knowing what else to do, Marielle bowed low, until she could only see the sandals on her parents' feet.

"Sefina, Maeva, thank you for seeing me."

"Of course, sweetling." Mother took her hand, motioning to stand.

"And who is this you've brought with you?" Mam's sharp eyes cut to Maher.

"Maher Villaon, Intelligencer of the Birde Isles." He stepped forward and introduced himself with a well-practiced bow. "At your service, Your Majesties."

"Intelligencer?" Mam raised a brow. "I thought there must have been something of great importance to bring you home, Marielle."

Heat flooded Marielle's face and she might as well've been a child again.

"Oh, Sefina!" Maeva swatted her wife's arm. "Enough of that, you've proved your point. Now, hug your daughter so we can learn why she's finally home."

Face softening ever so slightly, Mam opened her arms. Marielle stepped into a more careful embrace this time. Mam's hard, muscled frame a world away from the round curves she'd inherited from Mother. But that didn't make the welcome any less wanted.

When Mam released her, they were invited to sit in the circle of woven courtyard chairs, while Cousin Vas went to stand guard at the archway.

Marielle glanced around. "Where are Father and Costan?"

"Your father left to fetch your brother not long after we received your letters." Mother poured each a cup of water laced with fruit juice and they drank gratefully. They'd been so focused on reaching the city, Marielle'd forgotten how thirsty she was and Maher must've been.

"But where was Costan that father's been gone this long?"

"On the north side of the island. He volunteered to oversee a new farm there," said Sefina. "Now, what is this all about?"

Marielle drained a second cup of water. "I'm not sure how else to say this, but we've come here to warn you."

"Warn us?" Maeva eyed the pistols hanging from her belt.

"Yes, there's something hiding in the waters around these islands. The monsters in the stories you told us as children, they're real."

Maeva and Sefina looked at each other, their expressions unreadable. Then Mother took Mam's hand and sighed deeply. "We know, Marielle."

CHAPTER ONE HUNDRED-SEVEN

While Marielle gawked at her parents in stunned silence, Maher cleared his throat. "You already know of the sirens' existence?"

Queen Sefina nodded, "Yes, we've always known. It is the duty of the royal family to keep our people safe from those creatures."

"How could you not tell me?" Marielle sputtered.

"We would have done, had you not run away, Marielle." The taller of the two queens snapped. With her quick tongue and jet-black hair pulled into an intricate knot at the back of her head, Sefina reminded Maher of a bird of prey.

"Run away?" he glanced at Marielle.

"It isn't running away when your family knows exactly where you're going and why," she shot at him.

"But not what's become of you since then," Queen Maeva said pointedly, fluttering a hand at her daughter's gun belt. "I sincerely doubt you are still living and working with the divers. Not unless oysters have grown too dangerous to harvest by hand."

"The *selkies?*" Maher gaped at her.

"Not now." Marielle moved them back on topic. "I don't even care right now that you kept the sirens' existence a secret all this time. We have bigger problems."

"Marielle's right," said Maher. "You may have known about the sirens, but did you know they'd resurrected a dead pirate captain set on destroying everyone and everything that gets in her way?"

The queens gave him their full attention. "We did not know they were capable of such a thing," said Sefina.

"They are, we only just learned that on the voyage here."

Maeva frowned, her wavy, chin-length hair swinging forward. "If that's not the purpose for your journey, then why are you here?"

Maher straightened his vest, the salt-crusted material crackled. "We're here, because we believe your islands are being used to mint and ship false Saprean currency to the Birde Isles."

"How could such an operation even be constructed here with no one noticing?" Sefina demanded.

Marielle held her gaze. "That's why I need to speak to Costan."

As if saying her brother's name again was some sort of incantation, the courtyard curtain flicked open and two men walked through the archway.

"Marielle!" the younger one cried, dashing across the flagstones. Maher was struck by how much they resembled each other. It was no small wonder the people in the city recognized her so quickly. Costan yanked Marielle out of her chair, and spun her around.

Following at a more reserved pace was an older man, a silver streak ran through the hair framing the left side of his face. As Maher stood to greet him, Vas joined them in the courtyard as well to make the introductions.

"Teva, Queens' consort, I present our guest. Maher Villaon, Intelligencer of the Birde Isles." He sighed. "And the horse's ass currently making his sister seasick is Prince Costan."

"How dare you!" Costan came to an abrupt stop, leaving Marielle's legs to swing like a rag doll.

"Put me down!" she wheezed, kicking at his shin. "When did you become such a giant?" As soon as she was released, Marielle greeted her father with the same enthusiasm she'd shown for the rest of her family. Throwing her arms around his neck and nearly knocking him over in the process.

Coming to stand at Maher's side, Vas crossed his arms over his breastplate. "Quite the family reunion, isn't it?"

Marielle wasted no time taking her brother aside. She dragged him across the courtyard, leaving Maher to entertain the rest of her family.

"Your Majesties," he slipped fully into his Intelligencer role. Leaning back in his chair with as much grace as he could muster, while still coated in salt and the remnants of the trek through the forest. "I'd dearly love to know how your people became isolated on these islands with creatures such as the sirens?"

Queen Sefina gave him a long, shrewd look. Maher suspected she saw right through his performance. "We knew this day would come eventually. Word would inevitably spread after the first sirens escaped. That was just over a year ago."

"So, you knew some of them had left The Riddles?"

"Of course we knew," said Sefina. "Our ancestors made a bargain with the sirens' only natural enemies, to keep the creatures imprisoned for all time."

Maher felt as if someone had lit a candle in his mind. "The mermaids."

The taller queen's brows rose. Whether she was surprised or impressed, Maher couldn't say. "Yes, the mermaids. They wanted the sirens gone for their own peoples' sake, and they had no quarrel with humanity back then. It was a mutually beneficial alliance. We allowed the sirens to be trapped here, with no escape, and the ancient mermaids used their power to ensure these islands would always flourish. The currents that seal the creatures in also draw every resource from the sea. We have little need for trade with the outside world. Perhaps this is difficult to understand."

"On the contrary," Maher smirked. "I've met a mermaid who used a similar trick to draw fish to the Birde Isles."

"There are still mermaids, then?" Vas chimed in. "I'd often wondered."

"Well, just the one. There are two, if you count my friend Ally. She was made into a mermaid." He took advantage of their stunned silence to ask, "Forgive me, Your Majesties, but why did The Riddles not warn anyone?"

"In a world where such predators were not meant to exist, who would have believed us?" Queen Maeva asked. "We did what we thought was best and sent more of our boats out under the guise of trade, to search for any trace of the sirens."

"Little was found," Teva added, "until the reports of totally abandoned ships found floating at sea began to spread."

"The ghost ships?" Maher's reticence slipped. "The sirens were the cause? Does that mean every soul on board those ships is now..."

"Dead." Sefina nodded. "Some may have still carried protections against a siren's song, but would then have likely been killed by those who'd succumbed."

"Protections?" Maher leaned forward, elbows propped on his knees. "What protections?"

"The origins may be lost to time, but we understand many sailors from every corner of the world still hold the same traditions," Maeva explained. "Sirens have only one use for humans, to hunt us for food."

"Their song is hypnotic, but the real danger starts if they learn your name," said Vas. "We learn at a young age not to speak names near the water."

Sefina nodded solemnly. "This is true, though there is a very slim chance to escape, even if they learn your name. It's a siren's kiss that seals your fate. Theirs is a kiss of death, but precious metal wards them away. Silver will suffice, but gold is the most effective."

Maher thought of the metal tooth caps common among sailors and the practice of wearing a single earring to trade to the sea deities should they die away from land. The gold decorating the teeth of everyone around him no longer appeared as a cultural practice or popular fashion. It was a defense. They wore it nowhere else, all their jewelry was wooden with stones or shells.

"The ancient mermaids ensured we have more gold than we could ever need, so long as it's used for its intended purpose," said Teva.

"But where did they get so much?"

"From the sea, Mister Villaon."

MARIELLE

CHAPTER ONE HUNDRED-EIGHT

Marielle towed her brother across the courtyard first chance she got; Maher was more than capable of holding his own with her family.

"Slow down, Mari!" he laughed. "What's this all about?"

"It's about this." She retrieved one of the coins she'd confiscated from the crate in the Treasury and held it between her thumb and forefinger. Sunlight glinted off the polished silver image of the Saprean queen.

Marielle watched her twin's face carefully as he recognized what she was holding. His smile dropped, replaced by a puzzled frown.

"Where did you get that?"

"So you do recognize it?" Marielle kept her voice low. "Costan, how could you get mixed up in something like this?"

"Like what?" Now his dark brows snapped together, no doubt mirroring her own. "What's so wrong with it? You think you're the only one who can make a life of your own?"

"Do you have any idea what this is?" she hissed.

"What does it look like, Marielle?" Costan bristled.

Taking a deep breath, Marielle reminded herself this was not the best way to communicate with her brother. Neither of them appreciated vague accusations.

"Please, Costan, I need to know where these coins are being minted and who approached you with this."

"But, why? I don't even understand how you know they weren't minted in Saprea." Costan's gaze wandered to where Maher was deep in conversation with their parents. "Wait, is this why you've come home after all this time?"

"It is," she sighed, pocketing the coin. "I found them in a crate shipped to the Birde Isles. Your seal was on the lid, Costan."

"Of course it was! How else would the Sapreans know what was in the shipment?"

"The Saprean government doesn't know anything about it; that's what I'm trying to tell you. The press you're using was stolen and the minting of these coins is *not* sanctioned by Saprea."

Costan stared down at her, mouth hanging open, as if the words had all been sucked out of him.

"Costan..."

"You can't be serious!" He found his words again, at a much higher volume. "How can you just show up here, without word or warning, and accuse me of, of..."

"I'm not accusing you of anything. I know you, we shared a womb for the gods' sake, I know you wouldn't intentionally become involved with something shady like this." Marielle saw Maher watching them and waved him over. "But the fact remains that someone has deceived you, Costan. And I won't allow it."

Maher crossed the courtyard. "You called?"

"I wondered why an Intelligencer would be traveling with you, Mari." Costan shook his head. "I suppose you're here to help convince me what a fool I've been?"

"I wouldn't quite put it that way..." Maher said diplomatically. "But the coins have been flooding the Birde Isles for over a year, so I have a special interest in the matter."

"That's official talk for yes."

"Please, tell us what happened." Marielle asked.

Running his hand over his hair, Costan gripped a handful and tugged once before letting go.

He still does that when he's nervous. She felt a twinge in her chest.

"I swear, I didn't know this wasn't a legitimate opportunity. Almost three years ago now, a small group arrived claiming to be a Saprean trade delegation. They had the coin press and a source of silver." The more he talked, Costan's shoulders drooped as he spoke. "They said their government was looking for a secure place to mint additional currency, to build up their treasury and prepare for the expenses of their queen's fiftieth birthday celebration."

"That's still a few years off," said Maher, "but a plausible excuse. The festivities will last at least a month."

"That's what I thought, but our mothers turned them down."

"They did?" Maher glanced back where they still sat. "Your parents didn't mention anything when we told them our suspicions."

"No, they wouldn't," Marielle muttered. "Go on, Costan."

"After Mam and Mother refused the deal, they came to me separately. They had documents with their queen's seal, everything I requested. I thought, if I could make this work on my own, it would open up more opportunities for The Riddles. Sefina and Maeva are content with how things are, but..."

"I know," Marielle said gently. "You wanted something different."

"Right. I didn't have the shells to just up and leave like my sister," he snorted as Marielle rolled her eyes, "but this seemed like something I could do."

"May we see the documents they provided?" asked Maher.

Costan hesitated a moment, then nodded. "Of course."

Inside the villa, Costan led the way to his room. Marielle's was just down the hall. She wanted desperately to open the door, to see if it was still the way she'd left it or if everything had changed.

Costan rummaged through a deep drawer in his desk until he found a thick stack of papers dripping with official seals and ribbons. Handing them over to Maher, he sank heavily into a chair.

"I'm so sorry, Mari. I can't imagine all the damage I've caused."

Perching on the arm of the chair, she wrapped an arm around his shoulders and kissed his brow. "What matters is that it was caught early. Thanks to Maher and a few friends of ours, we were able to reach you before anything worse happened."

"Don't let her pretend she wasn't integral to the investigation as well," Maher commented, nose buried in the documents. He flipped another page and stopped, squinting at the text.

"What is it?" Marielle stood. "Do you recognize something there?"

"I'm afraid I do."

PASHA

Chapter One Hundred-nine

Pasha was done waiting.

The moment the sun's rays touched the top of the tree canopy, they set off from the shore. Ally insisted they stay together, so they swam side-by-side through the shallows, following the trail of twisted energy that both repulsed Pasha and drew her closer.

Circling the island, Pasha let the energy pull her along. It was as if she'd been caught in an undertow of suffering. And the closer they got to the source, the more Pasha's head pounded. Even Ally started to feel it on some level. She described the water as oily against her skin, not unlike what Pasha felt beneath the pirate ship.

They swam for a long time, only adjusting their course when the trail shifted. It took them on a wide curve around the island, until they reached a small, secluded cove. This was where the sickening trail was leaking into the sea.

"Why are there no humans here?" Ally wondered. "It's beautiful."

"Perhaps they know it's not safe." Pasha winced as the throbbing in her head spiked.

Ally cast a concerned look in her direction. "Do you need to rest?" When Pasha declined, she didn't argue. "Where to from here?"

Scanning the water, Pasha spotted an estuary, "We follow the river."

The river wound through a thick swath of trees, with no sign of humans, before narrowing into a stream. And the further they swam down the stream, the more the number of water-dwelling creatures dwindled.

Soon they reached a clearing that circled a secluded, tranquil lagoon. Surfacing enough to take in their surroundings, Pasha noted the total absence of wildlife around the water. This should be a teeming source of water, yet it was completely deserted. But it had to be the right place, the water practically bubbled with suppressed energy.

"It's like plate glass," Ally whispered. "It's so still, like a…"

"It's too still. Too quiet."

Carefully, they crossed the lagoon to the open cave waiting on the other side. The water fed into the cave mouth, sounds of a rushing stream echoed out. Along with a current of energy so strong Pasha nearly blacked out. "I think I'm going to be sick," Pasha gulped. "It's too much."

Ally, on the other hand, appeared uncomfortable, but otherwise unaffected.

"Channel it through the spear."

"Why didn't I think of that?" Pasha's stomach rolled and she took the spear off her back.

The green stone of the shaft instantly flared to life. Pasha nearly sobbed with relief when she let the charges flow through her and into the spear.

"Does that help?" asked Ally.

"Immensely." Feeling a little lightheaded now, Pasha took another minute to adjust. The sheer amount of energy transferring from the water to herself to the spear was staggering. A nagging voice in the back of her mind, reminded her again of the way she'd felt on Dare's ship after destroying the turbine. Like anything was possible.

ALLY

CHAPTER ONE HUNDRED TEN

Deeper and deeper they swam into the cave. When the last of the sunlight was gone, Ally noticed the spear wasn't the only source of light. The very water around them glowed, whether from the energy manipulated by the sirens or something else, she didn't know. Ally had no idea how far they'd gone or how deep beneath the ground this stream went. She prayed they'd find the other mermaids in this place or, at the very least, a clear sign of where they'd been taken. It would crush Pasha if they'd gone through all this only to end up with nothing.

A sharp turn in the streambed took them to an open cave with an underground pool. In the center, a large, flat rock sat like some kind of altar.

"Why do I have the feeling something terrible happened here?" Ally shuddered.

"I'm not sure, but I feel it too." Angling the spear in front of herself, Pasha went first into the pool. Ally could see the tremor that ran through her fins.

"Do you think this is where the sirens were living?" She followed closely.

"I'd say I'm certain of it. Look." Pasha pointed down.

Ally gasped, a flurry of bubbles escaping before she covered her mouth with both hands. The bottom of the pool was littered with human skeletons. Stomach clenching, Ally squeezed her eyes shut.

"Come on, Ally." Pasha gently grasped her arm and towed her towards the far side of the pool.

"Where are we going now?" she asked, once she was certain her last meal would stay down.

"The trail leads to that tunnel." Gesturing with the tip of the spear, Pasha kept them as far above the boneyard as possible until they reached the opening. It would be a tight fit, but Ally could squeeze through.

"We've come this far." Ally breathed deeply. "Let's go."

The tunnel twisted and wound its way deeper beneath the island. It became very evident that Ally wouldn't have been able to withstand the pressure, had she still been human.

"We're almost there," Pasha assured her. "I can see something up ahead."

"Since all I can see right now is your fluke, I'll take your word for it." Ally tried to focus on the graceful rise and fall of Pasha's tail fins, and not on the increasingly narrow tunnel walls scraping her shoulders.

"It's just here…" Without warning, Pasha stopped and Ally got a face full of fin.

"Pasha!" she sputtered. "What is it?"

"It's…" Pasha's voice caught. "It's them."

"What?" Ally struggled against the sensation of being cracked open like a walnut. "Let me out, Pasha! Now!"

Surging forward, Pasha slipped from the tunnel, leaving Ally to tumble out after her. When she righted herself, Ally's breath caught.

"Goddess save me."

A shimmering, crackling cage of electric energy cut the underwater cave in half. Inside of the cage, were mermaids. Mermaids of every shape, size, and color, lying strewn across the sand floor or floating listlessly in place. Like Hama, their bodies were battered and scarred. Patches of scales were missing from each of their tails.

Ally felt her heart would split in two. Not only because of the sight before them, but because, deep in her soul, she knew these were the last mermaids in all the seas. There were at least three dozen trapped down here, but from everything she'd seen in the murals beneath Kingfisher Island, there should be more. So many more.

Next to her, the spear in Pasha's hands pulsed. Taking in the rigid set of Pasha's shoulders, the threads of electricity beginning to circle her hands, Ally worried she'd draw attention to them.

But we've encountered no one since we left the beach, Ally thought uneasily. *This was too easy. Even if most of the sirens were with Dare's ship, they wouldn't leave the mermaids completely unguarded.* Pasha's grip on the spear tightened and a charge sparked from her hands to the blade.

"Pasha, be careful."

One of the nearer floating mermaids stirred. Her skin was pale pink, her tail a mosaic of pinks, reds, and purples. Head lifting, she pushed her silver hair back and peered dazedly at them.

"Who..." Her voice was rough, as if it'd been a long time since she'd used it. Red eyes, finally focused on them, snapped wide open. "Pasha? Pasha!"

Ally nearly cried out when the mermaid rushed to the edge of the cage, but she stopped just short of touching the sizzling bars.

"Pasha. You've grown up, but it is you, isn't it?"

"V-Vesi?" Pasha's arms went lax. The movement caught the other mermaid's attention.

"You've come to set us free?" Vesi's voice cracked. She finally noticed Ally. "And who is this?"

More mermaids woke as Vesi spoke. A handful swam closer, but many were too weak to move. Soon they were all talking at once.

"How did you find us?"

"Where are the sirens?"

"How long have we been here?"

Pasha tried to answer their questions, while Ally examined the cage. It was impossible to tell what kept the bars in place.

"Wait, wait!" Vesi spoke over the others. "If you're here, then who is guarding our home?"

"No one, only Ally and I live there."

Vesi focused on Ally again, squinting through the bars. "Oh? Ohh, I understand. You *made* this one." The others whispered and flitted amongst themselves. "But, if you're both here..." Vesi's pupils contracted and her hands trembled. "No, there must always be a mermaid beneath the island!"

"If we'd stayed, we would've never found you!" Pasha protested.

"That's why they met no sirens here." An elderly mermaid with violet skin and scales approached. When she turned towards them, Ally saw she was missing an eye. "They'll have felt it and gone for the bell."

"What bell?" Ally asked.

"The bell," the elder rasped, "is the key to their freedom. If the island goes a full lunar cycle without a mermaid beneath it, the bell will awaken."

"I don't understand." Pasha shook her head. "I've never seen a bell in our home."

"It rests beneath the tombs. The ancients forged it to steal the sirens' wings and bind them to the sea. The bell sealed them in their prison and only the bell can release them."

"Release the sirens?" Ally's head was spinning. "But they've already escaped the barrier around these islands. Pasha was attacked by one on our journey here."

The elder leaned on Vesi for support. "Once the bell was awakened, the currents would not be able to hold the strongest of them back. And their prison is not just these islands, it is the sea itself. Rung once, the bell will be released from its resting place and the tides will rise with it. Rung twice, it will set loose every predator of the sea that sided with the sirens during the war."

"What predators?" Ally suddenly thought of the snapjaws. What other sea monsters would have been with the sirens?

"There are things in the deep, creatures you cannot imagine. Creatures that are waiting for their time to rise to the surface," Vesi answered.

"Rung three times," the elder continued, "and the bell will return their wings."

"Then there will be no stopping them," another mermaid said. "We've not the numbers or the strength to bind them again."

"Then we have to stop them before they can ring it," Ally said and then looked at Pasha. "We have to warn Maher and the others."

"They may be able to find the bell, but would they even find a human to ring it for them?" Vesi asked the elder.

"It will be difficult," she conceded.

"A human has to ring the bell?" asked Ally.

"A human must, of their own free will, ring the bell to raise it and then twice more to break the enchantment."

"Then, we might have a chance," said Pasha. "What human would willingly help the sirens? What's more, no human could hold their breath long enough to reach it."

Ally's spirits lifted with every word. Then they came crashing down when she remembered there was a human who could possibly breathe underwater.

"Wait, what about Dare? Could they have made it so she could reach the bell for them?"

"Of course, we did." A low, throaty laugh reverberated through the tunnel.

Ally and Pasha spun around, backs to the cage, as five sirens slithered into the cave with them.

PASHA

CHAPTER ONE HUNDRED-ELEVEN

The sirens spread throughout the cavern, trapping them against the cage bars. A blonde with a mottled green tail seemed to be the leader. She moved closer while the others stayed back, watching. "This must be the young mermaid left behind to guard the bell. We've waited ages for you to leave. But you," blue eyes locked into Ally, "you are different. You were not born a mermaid. How fascinating. What is your name, sweet?" She lifted her nose, as if scenting the water, and the fury simmering inside Pasha boiled over.

Lifting the spear, Pasha put herself between Ally and the sirens. A few of the snake-tailed creatures hissed when the green stone blazed, feeding off Pasha's anger.

"Where did you find that?" the leader snarled.

"Don't tell them your names!" Vesi shouted.

"Silence!" The blonde backed up until she was with the rest.

"Listen to me," Pasha spoke over her shoulder without taking her eyes off the sirens. "I will hold them off, you try to break the cage."

"But I can't wield that kind of energy!" came Ally's panicked whisper into her ear.

"You can still interact with it." Pasha adjusted her grip as the sirens spread farther apart.

"What if it doesn't work?"

"You have to try."

ALLY

CHAPTER ONE HUNDRED-TWELVE

The captive mermaids watched Ally through the crackling bars. Their hollow, haunted eyes pleading with her to help them.

If she was going to do this, she'd have to block out everything else and trust that Pasha would hold her own. All the bars ran from the ceiling of the cave to the floor, but the middle bar appeared thicker than the rest.

Steeling herself for the shock, Ally grasped the bar with both hands. The initial jolt nearly sent her flying into Pasha. But the longer she held on, the more the current coursed through and the more she adjusted to it until the twisting, writhing band of charges solidified beneath her fingers. With a groan, Ally pulled with all her might, but the bar wouldn't budge. Something struck the cage to her right and shattered, sending shards in all directions.

I don't want to know. Ally kept her eyes forward. She tried twisting the bar, but it only made her slide towards the floor. Another projectile landed and Ally flinched when a piece of it nicked her arm.

The sounds of struggle behind her intensified, while the mermaids who could move began urging Pasha on and throwing jeers at the sirens. All without saying any names. What would happen if the sirens learned their names?

Ally threw her shoulder into the cage. The impact reverberated up her neck and made her teeth ache, but the force of the electric charge had dulled to a mere sting. Through the noise and the pandemonium, Ally could've sworn she heard singing. Movement in the corner of her eye made her pause. On her left, a siren with brown hair and a brown speckled tail crept closer along the floor. Vesi and another mermaid thrust their arms between the bars, raking their nails down her side. With a screech, the siren backed away. But now that Ally was looking at her, she began to sing again.

Ally supposed the song was somewhat familiar, but not in a way that made her feel wistful or romantic, or even happy. It was damned annoying, a fly buzzing around her head.

Shaking herself off, Ally turned back to the task at hand. Somewhere off to the side, the siren shrieked. Vesi grabbed Ally's arm and yanked her down as a skull came flying right at them. It hit the bars and shards rained onto them.

Bones. They were throwing the bones of their victims.

The siren started singing again, louder, to Ally the sound was like an out of tune violin.

Whipping around, she screamed, "Shut up already, you overgrown earthworm!"

Several mermaids cackled from inside the cage. Furious, the siren shouted something Ally couldn't understand, and another abandoned the fight with Pasha. They sang together, and pain like a knife between her eyes forced Ally to cover her ears. Another skull struck the bars above her head. Ally ducked to protect her face. She needed to work to free the mermaids, but...

"You must move!" Vesi urged.

"No! Ally!" Pasha shouted. Ally looked up in time to dodge a heavy rock lobbed at her head. It bounced off the cage and flew clear back across the cavern. The sirens abruptly stopped singing, and the horror of what Pasha'd done slowly spread across her face.

"No. No, no, no."

"Ally, was it?" The green- tailed siren grinned nastily.

Vesi reached for Ally. "Don't listen!"

"Ally," the siren crooned. "What a lovely name."

A strange haze settled over her, and Ally briefly forgot what she was meant to be doing.

"Ally!" Pasha's voice broke through the fog. "Look at me!"

"No," a hand closed around Ally's forearm. She blinked and then the siren was right in front of her. "Look at me."

BEAR'S DEN

PIMM

CHAPTER ONE HUNDRED-THIRTEEN

Pimm watched the approach of the three vessels sent by The Riddles with some trepidation. They skated across the top of the waves. Their long, narrow hulls suspended half-out of the water by two hollow wooden structures bolted to the keel. With only a single mast at midship, Pimm was amazed at how quickly they traveled.

"Quite something, aren't they?" Kamharida commented as they drew closer to the *Foxglove*. One boat caught the crest of a wave head-on, the prow bounced high and soared over the ridge before landing back into the water on the other side.

"Indeed," Pimm pressed a hand to their belly. "I only hope I don't embarrass myself in front of our hosts."

As uncertain as Pimm was about riding on one of the Riddles boats, they had to admit it was indeed fascinating to watch them cross the barrier.

Once Anya spotted aid approaching, the *Foxglove* turned farther out to sea and dropped sail. This position offered a clear portside view and the crew took advantage.

As they neared the barrier, each boat ran out several pairs of sweeps, long enough to reach past the bottom supports, into the sea. Combined with the wind already filling their sails, the boats were soon flying across the surface like stones skipping on a pond. As each boat reached and crossed the barrier, Pimm realized the swing of the oars was timed to lift the moment they touched the edge. Then held up until they'd crossed safely to the other side.

Whoops and hollers echoed from the *Foxglove* crew. Several arguments ignited over who would accompany the captain and Pimm to shore, but were quickly shut down by Kamharida. She would take charge of the ship, while Ga-Seung, Weams, and Olebile would go ashore with them. The two sailors had already made their case the night before. They had an interest in Ally's welfare, which Luthais appreciated.

Representatives from The Riddles came aboard to meet their captain, and soon it was time to disembark onto the smaller vessels. Kamharida was on hand to see them off.

"Here, Pimm." The first mate passed them a small hunk of dried ginger wrapped in paper. "Just in case."

"Bless you." They quickly pocketed the ginger. "I thought I'd used up the entire supply on board."

"I always keep a bit extra put by," she chuckled. "When you reach the islands, do send word of Maher... and Marielle. T'would be a relief to know they made it safely to shore."

"Of course," Pimm promised. "I'll send word as soon as I can."

CHAPTER ONE HUNDRED-FOURTEEN

Luthais had heard much about the unique, but rarely seen, boats of The Riddles. He never expected to see them in person, let alone have the chance to ride one. Yet here he was sailing across the famed barrier where the Eastern and Unending seas met.

Even as his seafarer's spirit lifted with each wave they created as the boat flew towards the islands, there was a twisted knot in the pit of his stomach. The unexpected conversation with Pimm had eased his fears for Maher's safety somewhat. But the fears were now replaced with guilt over questioning Maher's motives and not trusting he was being himself with Luthais.

Twisting in the seat provided to him by the boat's crew, Luthais checked on the two vessels behind them. Weams appeared to be having the time of his life. He stood, one arm around the mast, with the other thrown above his head. Seated nearby, Olebile was more composed. Though a smile spread across the Kharaboan's face as they held Weams steady by the tail of his jacket.

Bringing up the rear were Ga-Seung and Pimm in the third boat. The bosun appeared to be deep in conversation with one of the Riddles sailors, paying little attention to the jostle and bump of the boat. Like Weams, Pimm was becoming well acquainted with the mast. Their forehead was pressed against the polished wood, but they didn't appear to be ill.

As if sensing they were being watched, Pimm's head raised and swiveled until they saw Luthais

When Luthais lifted a hand in greeting, Pimm tried to return the gesture. Then promptly returned to embracing the mast.

A delegation was waiting for them when they docked in a small fishing village on the main island. The leader, a captain of the guard judging by his breastplate, stepped forward to greet them the moment they stepped onto the shockingly pink sand of the beach.

"Welcome," he clasped Luthais' hand. "My name is Vas, captain of the royal guard. I've been sent by their majesties to escort you the capital."

"Well met, Captain. Luthais Kingfisher. Before we depart," heart hammering, Luthais asked, "there were two members of our party sent ashore yesterday. Have you had any word of them?"

"We have," Vas nodded said and Luthais nearly hugged him. "Both Mister Villaon and Princess Marielle reached the city safely and are resting at their majesties' villa."

"Thank the goddess." A mighty weight lifted from Luthais' shoulders. "Did you just say, *Princess* Marielle?"

One corner of the guard captain's mouth quirked. "That's correct."

Behind him, Pimm huffed and muttered under their breath. "I fucking knew it."

PASHA

CHAPTER ONE HUNDRED-FIFTEEN

"Ally!" Dismay nearly choked Pasha when the siren snatched Ally's wrist.

The four remaining sirens circled Pasha, driving her against the cage. She couldn't drop the spear, it was the only thing keeping them at a distance. But her arms were beginning to ache, the moment Pasha lowered her weapon they'd be on her.

At her back, the mermaids begged Pasha not to give up. They hurled curses and insults at the siren holding Ally captive. Vesi scrounged the cave floor for a stone and took aim, but the snake pulled Ally between herself and the cage like a shield. An icy trail of helplessness crawled up Pasha's spine. There was nothing she could do, no way to reach Ally with the other snakes blocking her path.

"Ally," the green-tailed siren purred. "Ally, Ally, Ally."

"Get away from her!" Pasha snarled. A surge of energy sparked from the spear's blade. The other sirens shrank back, but only a little.

"Put down your weapon," the blonde siren said, "and my sister will release your pretty pet."

"Lies!" Vesi sneered.

Ally! Pasha threw her thoughts at Ally. *Listen to me, please! You must resist.*

Snapping out of her trance, Ally struggled against the siren holding her. "Unhand me!"

"Ally," the siren crooned. "Don't you want to stay with me?" When Ally's struggles lessened, the siren grabbed her other wrist, pulling her closer. "Ally..."

"No!" Pasha swung the spear in a wide arc, pushing the others back even further and catching one on the shoulder. She howled, blood from the wound clouding in the water. White hot charges collected around Pasha's arms, feeding into the spear along with the energy she'd already been channeling.

A tremor shook the cave around them. Pebbles and flakes of sediment broke loose to trickle down the walls. Was too much energy being pulled into an enclosed space?

Tides, am I going to bring the cave down onto our heads? Pasha tried to reel in her charges. How was she even pulling them when her own well was sputtering and nearly spent?

"Ally, Ally, Ally," the siren started again. "Won't you kiss me?"

ALLY

CHAPTER ONE HUNDRED-SIXTEEN

The siren's words enveloped Ally, burrowing into her ears and making everything hazy again. Every time the siren said her name, Ally would forget for a moment where she was and what she was supposed to be doing. But, almost immediately afterwards, she'd realize how ridiculous that was. The cavern shook as she tried to pull out of the siren's grip. Ally desperately wanted to see Pasha, to know she was alright, but her captor kept her in place.

"Ally, Ally, Ally. Won't you kiss me?"

The shock of the question shook Ally out of any trance she might've been in from the siren saying her name.

"Absolutely not!" Ally spat.

Face twisted in annoyance, the siren regained her composure. She breathed into Ally's ear, "*Please*, Ally? Please kiss me."

Ally's skin crawled when that serpentine tail slithered around her waist. "I'd rather kiss a jellyfish!"

Somewhere behind her, Vesi cackled. "How long has it been since you've been refused three times?"

"You'll pay for that," she snarled, tail tightening painfully against Ally's ribs.

Three times? Ally thought dazedly. *Can she no longer hold if I refuse three times?*

"Ally!" The siren snarled, the command strong enough to snap Ally's head around. "You will kiss me, won't you? Just one kiss?"

Ally relaxed in the siren's hold, eyelids heavy and lips parted. "Just one?"

"That's it," she cast a triumphant look over Ally's shoulder. "All I want is one kiss."

"Ally! Don't!" Pasha cried. Her voice slammed into Ally's head. "*Wake up, Ally! Please, don't kiss her!*"

"*I'm sorry, Pasha.*" Ally thought sluggishly. Lifting her hands to the siren's beautiful face, her wrists were released. "Just one…"

"ALLY!" The cave walls shuddered again, debris skittered to the cave floor.

Cupping the siren's cheeks, Ally pulled her close.

"Yesss," the siren breathed, eyes fluttering shut. "Kiss me, Ally."

Slanting her head until their lips were nearly touching, Ally sighed and whispered softly, "No."

"What?" The confused siren's eyes blinked open.

"No," Ally's grip on her face tightened. "I will *never* kiss you."

Something new sparked deep in Ally's chest. The scale Pasha'd given to be the seed from which all of Ally's would grow was hot against her breastbone. This wasn't the inner well of energy that came with being a mermaid, made or born, that replenished itself naturally over time. This was something fiercer, primal. And hungry. But tapping into that hunger was easy as breathing. Once it was free, it prowled through Ally's body until it found the siren still held in her grasp. Ally could feel the energy pulsing within the siren, like blood pumping through her veins. She could feel every life the siren had taken. A thought occurred to her as the hunger continued its appraisal.

Do sirens have to feed on humans, or was their choice a matter of cruelty?

Terror slowly crept over the siren's face. Scrabbling at Ally's arms, she tried to free herself. But Ally hardly felt the nails scratching her skin. The tail around Ally's waist tried to throw her away, but her hands around the siren's face kept them locked together.

"What's wrong?" Ally's voice sounded strange in her mind, as if someone else was speaking with her in unison. "I thought you wanted a kiss?"

The siren shrieked for her sisters, but they were too distracted. Ally still couldn't see Pasha, but the sirens couldn't seem to take their eyes off her. A pop of energy lit up their faces. The siren's tail released Ally, lashing out as she made a last attempt to escape.

The hunger was gnawing at her chest now. Acting on instinct, Ally brought the siren close again. Lips parting, Ally leaned in and *inhaled*.

At first, Ally only felt a slight, warm tingling in her fingertips. Then, it was like the siren's life was laid out before her like a tapestry. Glowing threads of green and gold, woven together in a colossal embroidery that expanded for centuries.

As each event of the siren's life passed, one thing became apparent. It wasn't only the humans' flesh that fed the sirens, it was their fear. Food kept them alive, but the terror of their victims kept them young. Even before the mermaids made them into what they were now, the sirens would soar above the land, reveling as humans scattered in their wake.

A small, logical voice in the back of Ally's mind questioned what cruel twist of fate would cause such creatures to exist. A shark was a predator, but they didn't torture their prey for the joy of causing pain. Ally wanted to dig deeper, to search for more, but the hunger was stronger. In her mind's eye, Ally plucked at a thread until it came loose. The hunger latched onto it and fed. It devoured every strand until the last of the tapestry was gone, the light gone out.

Ally opened her eyes to the sight of the siren rapidly aging in her grasp. Every year she'd stolen bled away. Smooth skin shriveled. Lustrous brown hair turned gray, then white, then began to fall out. Teeth loosened and eyes clouded. By the time the hunger was sated, the siren had wasted away.

Ally released the husk. It hit the cave floor and crumbled into dust.

CHAPTER ONE HUNDRED-SEVENTEEN

"A lly! Don't!" Pasha tried desperately to reach her. "*Wake up, Ally! Please, don't kiss her!*"

"*I'm sorry, Pasha.*" Ally broke the connection. She cupped the siren's face and bile surged in Pasha's throat. This was all Pasha's fault. Like a fool, she gave the sirens Ally's name and there was nothing she could do to help.

"ALLY!" Pasha cried. Tears burned behind her eyes and the spear ignited in her hands. Energy flared in the water around her, filling Pasha up until every scale, every strand of hair on her head, burned from within.

The cave groaned, layers of rock grinding together as chunks broke free to land on the floor. Smaller pieces popped from the walls and drove up from the sand. Pasha tried to pull back again, but the spear latched onto the intensified current flowing through her, unwilling to let go now with so much power feeding into the stone. Something small and white whizzed by Pasha's head. Not another human skull thrown by the sirens, but the curved jawbone of a large fish. Next came what remained of its body, until it was whole again. The fish circled her once before hovering between Pasha and the sirens.

More bones came to swirl around her, more than she'd ever called at one time. They encircled Pasha until she could hardly see anything else.

One by one, the bones peeled off to form their skeletons. But these weren't only sea or freshwater creatures. There were humans

Mermaids. Those killed by the sirens over the centuries. Not many were truly whole, but the energy surging through them filled in the gaps. They arranged themselves in front of Pasha, her own skeletal army. Empty eye sockets trained on the sirens, now flattened against the far wall. Time suspended in the cave as the sirens took in their reanimated foes and the mermaids locked in the cage waited with bated breath for what would come next.

Pasha heard nothing but the click of bones and her own labored breathing. Then, a bloodcurdling scream ripped through the cave.

Pasha spun around, somehow knowing the bones would protect her, and the spear nearly slipped from her grasp.

The siren still in Ally's hold was wasting away before Pasha's eyes. A lifetime leeching away in mere moments. And it was Ally pulling the life out of her. What could've possibly happened in the time Pasha's attention was diverted by the bones?

Ally dropped the siren and her body disintegrated into the sand. The cage bars flashed brightly, then faded back to normal.

"What have you done!" the blonde siren shrieked. Another shot through the water towards Ally, arms outstretched and fingers curled into claws.

Before she could even get close, two mermaid skeletons broke from the ranks. They fell upon the siren with such ferocity, she had almost no time to react. Breaking free, the siren scrambled back to the others, a trail of blood following behind. The blonde siren let out an ear-splitting screech. Within moments, more sirens spilled from the tunnel. At least a dozen, all told, now crowded into the cave. Another cry from their leader, and they charged.

Pasha's army rammed into the advancing sirens. Teeth and claws ripped into flesh. Skeletal hands grabbed for arms, legs, and throats. Bones that were split apart collected themselves, more energy filling in for the ones that were missing.

When a second siren was felled, her body torn apart by the same mermaid skeleton pair that'd attacked first, the bars flashed again.

Does... does killing them weaken the cage? Pasha searched frantically for Ally. She was dodging the flying bones of a human that'd been knocked apart. Spotting Pasha, Ally made a break for her side of the cave.

A siren came screaming after her from behind. Without even thinking, Pasha raised the spear. A ball of energy gathered around the blade. When Pasha released it, the ball stretched and expanded into a shield, covering Ally as she reached Pasha's side.

The siren chasing Ally hit the shield and burst in a shower of crackling threads.

"Great goddess," Ally panted. "How did you do that?"

"I don't know." Pasha swung the spear around, bringing the shield to protect both of them. "How did you suck the life out of that siren?"

"I have no idea." Ally ducked as an eel skeleton came sailing through the shield to hit the cage bars. It reformed, shook itself off, and dove back into the fray.

"We'll figure it out later." Pasha pushed a fresh stream of energy into the shield. A human and a mermaid skeleton took a siren by the arms and threw her into it; she too disintegrated with a flash. The shimmering bars holding the mermaids captive dimmed further.

Those who were strong enough gathered close, eagerly watching the battle between the sirens and Pasha's bone soldiers. The mermaids who were too weak to move had been carried to the back of the cave.

"The cage weakens with each siren that dies," Pasha said quickly.

"How is that possible?" Ally asked.

"They took our power into themselves when they stole our scales," Vesi rasped through the bars. "But they can't pull more energy to sustain it, they have to use their own life force."

"They're part of the cage?" Ally touched a bar. "It is weaker than before."

"Not enough of them are dead to break it, though," Pasha grunted, fighting to keep the spear level.

"If you let us out, we can help," said Vesi as another siren hit the shield.

"I can't go out there and hold this at the same time."

Ally's hands closed around Pasha's. "Give it to me."

CHAPTER ONE HUNDRED-EIGHTEEN

"Ally," Pasha shook her head, "I can't, you won't be able to channel energy from the water into it. You could drain your well, maybe even kill yourself."

"I don't need to channel it." Ally opened just enough of a link between them for Pasha to feel the power coursing through her body. "I can use what I took from the siren."

"But, what if I'm not back by the time you use it all?"

"We can *help*," Vesi said again. "Once we're free, we can help."

"We've no time to argue," Ally slid her hands below Pasha's on the spear shaft. The green stone sparked to her touch. "Your skeletons won't last forever. I can do this. Trust me."

Nodding once, Pasha released the spear. The full weight settled into Ally's hands, and with it a sharp tug beneath her breastbone. Like a fishhook. Like the irresistible pull that'd once drawn her to the sea. The spear syphoned the energy Ally'd taken from the siren, and the shield held.

"Go on," she told Pasha. "I'll be right here."

PASHA

CHAPTER ONE HUNDRED-NINETEEN

Leaving Ally with the spear filled Pasha with anxiety. But in the end, she knew Ally was right. Pasha wasted no time. She tore through the shield and into the fight, charges already gathering in her hands. She'd have to constantly release them, without the spear as a channel. Even if there was no target nearby.

The skeletons had done well, the sirens' numbers were already cut down by half. Still not enough to break the cage entirely, but it was more than Pasha could've done on her own. Their ranks were dwindling, just as Ally'd said. The skeletons might've been able to rejoin, but only if enough of their bones remained intact.

Throwing charges left and right, Pasha hunted for the blonde siren who seemed to be in command. She had many stolen scales embedded into her arms, and Pasha had an idea.

Pasha found the leader fending off a hoard of skeletons. Her tail whipped through the water, knocking the skull from a human's neck. When she spotted Pasha through the clamoring bones, her lips pulled back into a snarl.

"You! You may have revived this stupid trick," she slammed her tail clean through an alligator skeleton trying to bite her, "but you will *never* be as strong as the mermaids who stole our freedom. These pitiful kin are all you have left, all your warriors are gone."

Something about the siren's words tickled the back of Pasha's mind. What exactly made a mermaid a warrior, that she was so sure there were none left?

Pale blue eyes blazed with contempt as the siren slammed a mermaid's bones into the cave wall. Her lips opened wide and a set of fangs slid from the roof of her mouth. "I will savor every drop of fear I wring from you."

A shot of pain lanced through Pasha's right arm. The scar on her forearm burned, the healed-over tissue attempting to split open.

If wielding a weapon didn't make Pasha a warrior, then maybe something else would. Pasha released the tenuous hold over the thing that'd brought her such shame for so long. What she'd always assumed to be a punishment bestowed by the elders before they left her alone beneath their island.

Her scar split open, dark droplets of blood mixing into the already tainted water. The tentacle she'd tried to ignore for most of her life slid out, mottled purple skin writhing with the excess energy still coursing through from the water. The siren's fury faded, tail coiling erratically beneath her. Pasha and the siren moved at the same time. One attempting to flee, the other in pursuit. Taking aim, Pasha struck, catching the siren by the throat. Jagged nails sunk into her flesh, but Pasha gritted her teeth and pushed the charges from her arm into the tentacle. Shocking the siren hard enough to make her arms go limp and eyes roll back.

Dragging her closer, Pasha hissed, "Not all warriors are gone, it seems?"

Using her other arm for support, Pasha hurled the siren into the shield held in place by Ally. When the siren struck the wall of raw energy, the entire cavern quaked and the last of the cage disappeared.

CHAPTER ONE HUNDRED TWENTY

Ally felt the massive release of energy when the cage came down. The force propelled her forward until she flattened her tail fins to absorb the impact.

Hands landed on her shoulders, Vesi and the elder mermaid. They opened new currents, even more energy drawn from the water, routed through them into Ally, and then through the spear. The glow that permeated throughout the caves dimmed considerably, leaving the shield and spear as their main sources of light.

As Vesi and the elder supported Ally, the handful of mermaids strong enough to fight darted past them to join Pasha. Not even bothering to use charges on the remaining sirens. Instead they attacked with tooth, nail, and centuries of bottled rage.

Within moments it was over. No more sirens appeared through the tunnel. The sirens who hadn't been shattered against the shield lay sprawled across the cave floor. Blood clouded the water, Ally could taste metal on her tongue. Pasha's energy was spent. The threads dancing over her skin fizzled out as the tentacle retracted into her arm, leaving a shiny, pink scar behind. And with that, the remaining skeletons collapsed, bones clacking together as they landed on the ground.

Watching from behind the shield, Ally'd been in awe of Pasha. In a way it was like the first time she saw Pasha's tail emerge beneath the sea. The mermaids flanking Ally released her, their energy faded as their hands slipped from her shoulders. Ally tried to lower the spear, to break the connection holding the shield in place.

Ally's heart raced and a sliver of dread crept into her heart. She couldn't put the spear down.

This can't be good. Ally tried again to throw the spear away, but it stayed firmly in her grip.

More... The hunger buried deep in her chest seemed to be saying. *More.*

No, that's enough! Ally searched for Pasha.

She was across the cave, caught up in an embrace by Vesi and looking unsure if she should reciprocate.

"Pasha!" Ally shouted, or at least thought she shouted. She couldn't hear her own voice over the roar of the energy funneling through the spear.

Her mind flashed back to the day Pasha changed her into a mermaid. The sensation of energy filling Ally up until it threatened to spill out of her eyes. Only this time, Ally felt as if she might split apart.

Ally had no idea how long she floated there, wrestling with the hunger and the spear. Only that one moment she was alone, and the next she was surrounded by mermaids.

Pasha's face came into focus and Ally nearly wept. She was speaking, shark-like teeth flashed as her lips moved, but Ally couldn't hear her either. Multiple pairs of hands attempted to pry the spear from Ally's grasp but her fingers remained locked in place. More mermaids came to their aid. Palms pressed against Ally's shoulders, her arms, her back, even on top of her hands. Pasha cupped her face, coaxing Ally to look at her. Pasha said something else, and the current flowing through Ally ground to an excruciatingly slow halt.

It was as if the cave itself was holding its breath, then each mermaid claimed a portion of the energy and *pulled it out.*

A blanket of hollowness settled over Ally and she finally released the spear. The rush as the last of the energy left her body left Ally reeling Pasha caught her, and they sank to the floor of the cave together. Lights popped and flashed in Ally's eyes. The roaring was finally gone, but when Pasha spoke, the words were still muffled.

Unable to understand, Ally could only turn her face into Pasha's palm as she touched Ally's cheek. Everything else faded away.

FORAOISE

CHAPTER ONE HUNDRED TWENTY-ONE

"Tell me more about this bell concealed beneath Kingfisher Island." Foraoise had taken the helm herself for a spell. A cool night breeze whispered into her ear.

Swain leaned against the navigation table installed nearby, a flickering lantern held close to the map. Not that they needed it, with the sirens steering the ship towards the Isles like homing pigeons returning to roost. But Swain was nothing, if not prepared.

"What about it?" He glanced up, the orange glow of the flame flickered across his face.

"I know why I'm the one to ring it. The sirens gave that up early on," she mused, hands propped atop the wheel. "They need a human willing to do it, and I expect no other human can hold their breath as long as I can now."

The Captain Who Could Not Drown. The words came to mind before she could stop them, Foraoise shook the memory aside before it could consume her. The avarice of that day on the *Maiden's Revenge* still haunted her, how superior she'd been. So obsessed with her legacy that she didn't see the trap laid out before her until it was too late.

"Aye, that's true," Swain agreed, unaware of the turn in Foraoise's countenance.

"But they neglected to specify what the bell will do once it's rung."

"Did they?"

"What will it do, Swain?"

"Well," he hedged, "I heard tell it must be rung thrice, for the magic to take hold."

"And then?" Foraoise pressed.

"It'll release the curse put on the sirens all those years ago. The bell's what cursed 'em to begin with, so the bell has to undo it."

Regarding the quartermaster for a moment, she adjusted the ship's wheel. "Swain, is there something else you're not saying?"

"Nay, Captain. Nothing of importance."

Chapter One Hundred Twenty

Swain remained on the quarterdeck after the captain returned to her cabin. He'd been eased when Foraoise didn't press him further about the bell, but now that he thought on it, that wasn't like her. The Captain Dare that Swain knew would've demanded, or possibly threatened, the answer out of him. Since she'd returned, Foraoise only seemed to show her old self when the opportunity for revenge was presented.

Come to that, Swain wasn't sure anymore if he needed to keep the bell's other purpose to himself. The redheaded siren had been very loose with her tongue early on, and yet the thought of damning the Known World hadn't factored much into Swain's decision. Not when weighed against the prospect of rescuing Foraoise from an eternity trapped on the ocean floor.

They'd reach the waters around the Birde Isles in a matter of days, judging by their approximate position on the map. And the closer they got, the more agitated the wretches became. Morning and night, Swain's captor urged him to get Foraoise to the bell's resting place as soon as possible. And something must've happened the day before. Swain couldn't say what, but it ignited a new fervor in the other sirens accompanying them.

They already knew the cursed hunk of metal had awakened the year before. Based on what he'd learned, it had to be when the mermaid who tried to kill the captain followed Alphonsine Kingfisher out to sea.

And now, they had proof the mermaid had left again. Which meant the bell was unguarded, ripe for the taking.

ALLY

Chapter One Hundred Twenty-three

Ally woke to the sun warming her face. The bed beneath her rocked with the steady to and fro of the tides. Stretching as best she could beneath the heavy blanket, Ally sighed when something cool and impossibly soft touched her brow.

"Ally?" A voice like waves rolling onto shore murmured. "Can you hear me?"

She wanted to answer, but the bed was so comfortable and Ally couldn't remember the last time when she'd slept so well.

"Al," a deeper, but no less welcome, voice spoke next. "It's time to wake up, Al."

With the greatest reluctance, Ally cracked one eye open, then the other, blinking hard against the light streaming through the windows.

"Good morning, sweetheart." Pasha sat next the bed, her back to the windows. Sunlight shimmered against her silvery gray skin.

"You are so beautiful." Ally smiled, utterly besotted and feeling a little silly.

"How about me, Al?" Maher chuckled from her other side.

Head turning on the pillow, Ally grinned dopily up at him. "Of course, you're beautiful too, Maher. But different from Pasha."

"Thank the gods for that." He shook his head, while Pasha blushed and snorted into her hand. Maher looked at the mermaid sitting across the bed. "You weren't having me on after all about the effects of all that energy. She's three sheets in the wind."

"What?" Ally frowned. "I don't understand."

Pasha held her hand. "Do you remember finding the mermaids?"

"I..." Ally stared off into space for a few seconds. Her sluggish memory began unearthing images of deep, underwater caves and a crackling cage built from stolen energy. "The mermaids!" Ally shot up in bed, only to fall back with a wave of dizziness. "What happened? Are they alright? What about the sirens?" She glanced around. "Where in the goddess' name am I?"

"One question at a time, Al." Maher squeezed her other hand.

"The mermaids are fine," Pasha soothed. "There were a few injuries, but we lost no one else fighting the sirens. They're free." Voice catching, Pasha looked down for a moment to collect herself.

"You're back aboard the *Foxglove*," Maher took over. "Marielle's family will look after the mermaids too weak to leave The Riddles, but there are some who felt well enough to travel home with us. They're beneath the ship right now, correct?"

Pasha nodded, "They'll stay with us until we reach the bay. They were most surprised to find Euphonia down there as well, but they're glad to have her help once again."

"Euphonia's back? Where's she been?"

"We think she tried to hunt down the other snapjaw that was with Dare's ship. But I can't gather if she had any luck."

"I'm glad she's back." Ally resolved to go down and visit the sea monster when she was able. "Do you think the siren who attacked you before knows the rest are dead?"

Pasha shared a look with Maher that did not inspire Ally's confidence. "According to Vesi, there are more sirens than those we faced in the caves."

Ally's stomach twisted. "But where are the rest of them?"

"They must be with Dare's ship," said Maher. "On their way to the Birde Isles."

"They're most certainly going after the bell," Pasha added.

"What? No!" Ally struggled to sit up again. Which set the room to spinning.

"Don't fret. We have a plan."

"Precisely," Maher said as he and Pasha helped Ally lay back down. "We have far more information than before. They may've gotten a day's head start, but we know exactly where they're going and what they're after."

Later that afternoon, Ally stood on the bow, watching the ship slice through the waves. A flotilla of boats from The Riddles flanked them on either side. They looked like toys compared to the *Foxglove*, but easily kept pace with the larger ship. Even with the extra push being channeled by the merfolk with them.

Ally hadn't yet gone below to greet the other mermaids or Euphonia. After much cajoling from Maher, she agreed to recover and wait until the following morning. She'd been astonished to learn that she'd been asleep for nigh on two days. Much had been discussed while Ally slept, with Pasha relaying everything they'd learned while down in the sirens' nest. And all that Maher and Marielle had discovered on land.

Now she finally understood the rest of the murals Ally and Pasha had found hidden in their home. The humans depicted in those carvings were the early Riddle Islanders.

What a bargain to have made, knowing they'd be largely cut if from the rest of the world.

Wind plucked at her clothing, a lovely, loose-fitting Riddles gown in a pale shade of blue. Their majesties had been astounded, overawed, really, when they learned of the defeat of sirens who'd remained in the islands. They'd apparently offered a number of rewards. Which Pasha'd declined, rightly so. All she'd asked was for the injured mermaids to be cared for in their absence.

Pasha was in the sea now, discussing their plans with the mermaids. Much depended on if they reached the Birde Isles before the sirens found the bell. Or if they'd picked up any other allies along the way.

"Al?" Maher approached and laid a hand on her shoulder. "You alright?"

"Yes, I am."

"Marielle is about to come aboard, would you like to come with me to meet her?"

"From her brother's boat? Won't it be difficult at the speed we're sailing?"

He pulled her hand through the crook of his arm. "You'd think so. She just said to have a ladder ready and wait for her signal."

They walked down to midship, where Pimm waited with Kamharida. Marielle's gun belt was draped over the first mate's shoulder. Out on the water, Costan maneuvered his boat closer to the *Foxglove*, but it was still some distance to go without a longboat.

"She can't mean to swim!" Ally said.

"Aye, that's exactly what she means to do," said Kamharida.

When the boat was apparently as close as it was going to get, Marielle waved and Kamharida gave the order for the ladder to be unrolled down the side of the ship. Marielle clapped her brother on the back, then dove into the sea.

Ten tense minutes later, Marielle was pulling herself up the ladder.

I knew she was a strong swimmer, Ally said to herself. *But she stayed under for so long between breaths.*

"Impressive," Pimm noted as Marielle's shorn head appeared at the base of the railing.

"Indeed," Maher chuckled, moving to offer her a hand up.

Beads of water trickled down Marielle's face and she breathed heavily, but she looked exhilarated when she finally stepped onto the deck.

"I haven't done that in ages." she panted.

Maher smirked. "Your previous job skills came in handy."

"Great goddess!" Ally blurted. "You were a selkie."

"That's right." said Marielle.

"How did you know?" Maher asked, brows raised.

"It makes sense, I saw the scars on her hands and arms when we first reached the sandbar. But just now it came to me, I've seen you before, Marielle, when you were still a selkie. So did you, Maher." A slow smile spread over Ally's face. "Marielle was part of my coming-of-age celebration, and I didn't even see it."

"What do you mean?" Pimm asked.

"There's a painting hanging in my room at the manor," Ally explained, "of the selkies preparing to dive early in the morning. Maher painted it for my seventeenth birthday. And Marielle is with them."

"What?" Maher squawked, rounding on Marielle. "Did you know this whole time?"

"Not about the painting," the gunfighter admitted, "but I vaguely remember a young artist sketching us for days on end."

"I... you... but..."

Ignoring Maher's rare moment of speechlessness, Ally turned back to Marielle. "I hope you don't mind the painting. As a child I'd watch the selkies whenever I could."

"I don't mind." Marielle smiled, a dimple appearing on her cheek. "I remember that too."

BEAR'S DEN

PIMM

CHAPTER ONE HUNDRED TWENTY-FOUR

Pimm tried not to look too amused at Maher's shock. Though they supposed it was good for the person who held both titles of Magpie and Intelligencer to be flummoxed once in a while.

The Riddles boat had returned to its formation with the others. Marielle's brother led one half of the flotilla, while her cousin commanded the other.

It was indeed a good turn that Marielle's parents were so prepared to face the sirens. And willing to come to the Bird Isles' aid. They knew best how to deal with the sirens, knew their weaknesses and strengths. Every weapon supplied by the queens was tipped and trimmed in gold. Even their lightweight, leather armor fastened with gold buckles and studs.

Pimm was fascinated, to say the least. Not only with the tale of the ancient bargain made between the islanders and the mermaids, but with how the people of those islands had adapted to their situation.

Movement on the quarterdeck caught their attention. Ten more birds were released. As soon as they'd returned to the *Foxglove*, Pimm took it upon themself to recommend the ship send as many messengers ahead as possible. To their allies, as well as the Isles. But which allies, was the question posed by Maher. From what he'd learned from Costan's records, some might not be as friendly as they thought. With any luck, at least one pigeon would reach Kingsport ahead of the pirates. And if the worst were to come, at least their friends would be forewarned. Whether or not they believed it at first

If the unthinkable does happen, they'll soon be made to believe.

FORAOISE

CHAPTER ONE HUNDRED TWENTY-FIVE

As the sirens escorted Foraoise through the murky depths, she reassured herself there was no need to hold her breath anymore. Now the saltwater flowed into her lungs and back out as easily as air. There'd been an initial spike of panic, the memory of drowning readily returning. But Foraoise was glad, in a way, to see the familiar emotion present so strongly. Thinking back to earlier that evening, she'd almost been envious of Swain's apprehension. He'd been in quite a state as the turbine was fired up and the sirens absorbed as much of the resulting electricity as their bodies could take. Pacing across the deck, worrying if anyone would notice the strange signature of the machine just outside of Trader's Bay.

For her part, Foraoise'd wanted to confront Cal first thing. But Swain begged her to fulfill their end of the bargain first.

Behind them swam one of the monstrous, crocodile-like things that'd allied with the sirens. Even in the darkness of the night sea, its bulk cast a long, ominous shadow.

The sirens seemed to know exactly where they were going. It must've been some instinct Foraoise couldn't perceive, for certainly the ever-changing ocean floor had shifted in the centuries since they were last here.

Soon they came to an opening in the base of Kingfisher Island. At least Foraoise had retained some sense of irony, as it dawned on her that this was her first time back in the Birde Isles since her own family sent away like some foundling. And instead of stepping onto the shore, she was sneaking in like a thief.

Once inside the tunnel, a cluster of corals set into the walls began to light up. But once the lead siren got close, they blinked erratically before snuffing out.

Seems we're not welcome here, even with the mermaids gone.

Growling, the siren slapped a hand against the wall and pushed a jolt of electricity into the corals, forcing them to light the entire tunnel. "Keep moving. We're getting close."

Standing in the middle of a massive cavern, Foraoise turned in a slow circle, taking in the carved murals that took up every available inch of wall space. The mermaids had certainly made this island their own once the sirens were driven out. Leaving no sign that this had once been another fantastical creature's domain. The sirens spread out the moment they exited the tunnel into the cave system. Leaving Foraoise to wait while they sought out their precious bell's location. Judging by the size of this place, it could really be hidden anywhere. Occasionally a siren would emerge from a connecting cave or tunnel to cross the cavern into another.

Foraoise began to notice that they particularly avoided the enormous depiction of a mermaid with a bony crest running down the center of her skull. Foraoise walked closer, feeling somewhat disconnected from herself as her boots stayed firmly on the sand floor. She felt none of the buoyancy she associated with being in the water, nor did she feel the natural pressure her body should be experiencing at this depth.

There was a small pile of shark teeth, in many shapes and sizes, sitting on a stone ledge beneath the carving. Some appeared to be quite old. Just as Foraoise reached for one to examine it more closely, the redheaded siren approached.

"Come." She glanced up at the image of the crested mermaid and sneered. "We've found the bell."

Following the siren across the cavern and through a doorway with debris scattered around the opening, Foraoise realized they were descending into a crypt. The rows of sealed, or in some cases unsealed, graves shook loose vague memories of the catacombs of Old Pravil.

About halfway down, they met a few more sirens, the rest must've still been exploring the caves.

"There, down at the end," pointed a siren with inky black hair. "You must break through the door and ring the bell once, to bring it from its resting place."

Foraoise could just make out the dead end ahead. "How am I to do that?"

"The skill will come to you once you're there." The redhead gestured around them. "We cannot go beyond this point, but we will lend the energy to you if needed."

Still unsure how she was expected to fucking figure this out on the spur of the moment, Foraoise continued the rest of the way alone. Reaching the dead end, she scanned the wall for some sort of clue. The water here was inexplicably colder, nearly freezing, though it didn't cause her any discomfort. An intricate pattern was woven into the rock, filled with bones from different sea creatures. Set into the middle like some kind of guardian, was a mermaid skeleton.

Placing a hand against the stone sent a shock up Foraoise's arm. Even with her limited knowledge of how this magic worked, she could tell a tremendous amount of power was used to hide this bell away. One of the scales embedded onto her face began to itch, perhaps recognizing the magic of this place.

Foraoise stayed like that for a long time, trying to tap into whichever of her new abilities would have some effect. She was ready to tell the sirens to give her some godsdamned directions, when there was a light tickle against her ear. As if someone were humming from quite far away. A strange, yet oddly recognizable tune. Her other hand touched the stone and Foraoise concentrated on that sound. If only she could get closer, she might be able to figure out what it meant.

Pushing with all her might against the wall, she nearly faltered when the distinct smell of electricity hit her nose. The sirens sent sizzling bolts of lightning down the tunnel. They bounced along the walls before absorbing into the stone beneath Foraoise's palms. Now all the scales set into her skin began to respond. Some going cold as ice while others burned like lit coals. The one on her face itched so badly now, Foraoise wanted to rip it off.

The electricity kept feeding into the rock wall, until the harsh brightness was too much to bear. Squeezing her eyes shut, Foraoise leaned into the craggy surface until something deep within began to give. The rock beneath her hands took on the texture of wet sand. Bowing beneath her weight, the wall shuddered once, then Foraoise was pulled right through.

When she opened her eyes, Foraoise was in a small, enclosed cave. It was barely large enough to house the massive bell that sat in the center of the room. The tune that'd filled her mind as she fought her way through had stopped.

Slowly approaching the bell twice her height, Foraoise eyed the strike bar set into its crown. She'd have to climb the side to reach it. Bracing one boot against the flared edge, Foraoise hoisted herself up. The metal was surprisingly warm, given the frigid temperature of the water.

A few more steps, and she'd be high enough to ring it. But when Foraoise tried to scoot farther up, her hands stuck to the bell.

"What the…" She tried to pry one hand off, but it held firm. "What is this?"

The metal grew hot enough even for Foraoise to feel. She flinched away when a voice belonging to no one filled her head.

"*You must trade.*"

"Trade? Trade what?"

"*You must trade.*"

The water touching the bell began to bubble and evaporate. "Tell me what to trade!"

"*A memory.*"

"A what?" Foraoise couldn't breathe, she was going to drown after all.

No. Not here. Not again.

"Fine! Take it!" she gasped. Beneath her, the bell instantly cooled.

"*It is a good trade,*" The voice answered and the cave plunged into darkness.

The Meredian physician prodded the angry wound in Jon's back as he lay curled on one side on the examination table.

Injured during their last attempt at a prize, the place where the sword had caught him between his shoulder blades wasn't healing. Now Jon was sick with fever, unable to do much else but sleep and swallow the broth his wife ladled down his throat. As a privateer under Meredia's authority, the provost had sent them to a doctor in a wealthy section of New Pravil. Foraoise'd half-expected to run into one of her parents' acquaintances as she and Swain had helped Jon walk down the street. But everyone on the street had given them a wide berth. None got close enough to recognize Foraoise as someone who'd been raised as one of their own, once upon a time.

Now Swain was keeping watch out front, while Foraoise and Jon saw the doctor.

"Just as I thought," the older man nodded to himself. "The corruption of the flesh is quite severe. Calomel is the thing to treat an infection of this severity."

Foraoise shook her head. "Isn't calomel dangerous?"

"When taken orally and in incorrect doses, it can be. Just like many medicines. But I myself have been developing a new topical method of administration, which is much safer."

"You're sure?" Her heart constricted as Jon groaned, burying his face into his arm.

"Madam, the provost sent you to me for a reason. If you wish to ignore my medical advice, that is your choice."

Jon twitched and shuddered, his face slick with sweat. The doctor had retrieved an unlabeled, brown bottle of coarse white powder from a cabinet and measured a portion into a flat dish. Now he looked at her, waiting for her answer. The provost wouldn't have sent them to a physician with no knowledge of his work. And Foraoise would give a limb to have Jon healthy and whole again.

"Alright," she relented. "Please, do what you can to help him."

Months later, Foraoise ventured into Pravil on her own. At first it appeared the doctor was right, the calomel treatment done in his office and then continued back on the ship scoured the infection and filled Jon with renewed vigor. But, gradually, things began to change. He disciplined the crew for no reason, the violence escalating until he was sewing sailors up in their hammocks alive and tossing them overboard. Jon had always been a tough captain, but also a fair one who'd been well-liked by the crew. Now, it became more apparent each day that he was slipping into madness. When Foraoise discovered he was still secretly using the calomel, despite his wound having healed, she knew something must be done

Foraoise and Swain were already planning to have her step up as captain, to get help for him somewhere else on land, when Jon found them out. By then, he couldn't see Foraoise as the woman he loved anymore, only as a faceless enemy. He challenged her to a duel and they fought up and down the deck of the *Tide's Last Revenge*. The crew only stayed back when she told them not to interfere. Jon was taller and stronger than her, but in his madness he was sloppy.

After Jon's burial at sea and the cut on Foraoise's head had mostly healed, she tracked down the physician who gave Jon the medicine. He was sleeping soundly in the expensive rooms above his office, and didn't even notice Foraoise's presence until she dragged him from bed.

Not long after, the doctor knelt on the floor of his examining room, hands clasped tightly to his gut to stem the tide of blood and entrails threatening to escape.

Foraoise leaned against the counter, wiping the blood from her dagger. "Where is it? The poison that robbed my husband of his sanity?"

"Please! It's not my fault! He must've used the powder wrong, he –" The doctor's mouth snapped shut when Foraoise held the blade to his throat.

"Where is it, doctor? I won't ask a third time."

"T-top shelf, the large bottle."

Opening the cabinet, Foraoise grabbed the square, brown bottle and shut the door. "Is this all you have? There's no more stored elsewhere?"

"That's all of it! I swear," he gulped, hands slipping in his own blood.

Holding the bottle up in the light from the single candle she'd lit, Foraoise tsked. "You really should label your supplies, every ship's purser knows that."

"I – I will, I promise..."

She knelt in front of him, holding the bottle in his face. "You will never force this bilge, or anything like it, on another soul under the guise of medicine. Do you understand?"

"Yes, of course, as long as I live, I'll never use calomel again."

Foraoise stood and her boot landed square in the center of his chest, sending the doctor sprawling onto the floor. "I'm glad to hear it." She stood atop him, wrenching the cork from the bottle and tossing it across the room. "Because you don't have long to live at all."

She tipped the bottle, dumping his store of the white powder into his open stomach cavity as he screamed for help that would never come.

The cave slowly came back into focus. Light emanated once again from the bell and Foraoise's hands were finally released. Before anything else could trap her in place, she scrambled the rest of the way up.

It took all her strength to lift the strike bar. Wedging her shoulder beneath the lever, Foraoise pushed with her legs until she was standing atop the bell. All she had to do was let the bar drop and the clapper inside would strike the curved metal. Taking a moment to get her bearings, Foraoise froze when she felt a soft touch brush against the back of her neck. But there was no one else with her in the sealed cave.

Shaking off the sensation of no longer being alone, Foraoise shifted the bar off her shoulder and let it fall. The clapper struck hard, the resulting sound thunderous in the enclosed space. When the tone faded, Foraoise waited for something, anything to happen.

"What are you doing, my green-eyed girl?"

Foraoise slipped, catching herself against the sloped side. When she looked up, Foraoise thought the clang of the bell might have scrambled her mind. Jon was standing before her. Not his body, but a hazy outline that blurred and moved with the water.

"Jon?" She reached for him, stopping just short of touching his face.

"Are you willing to give me up so easily?"

"How can you say that?"

He smiled forlornly and faded away.

Then, the walls around her began to crumble.

PASHA

Chapter One Hundred Twenty-six

Pasha's eyes flew open. She'd been sound asleep, arms wrapped around Ally as they rested in the cabin given to them on the ship. "Tides protect us."

"Pasha?" Ally rolled to face her, voice thick with sleep. "What's wrong?"

"The bell, they've found it. The call has begun."

LUTHAIS

CHAPTER ONE HUNDRED TWENTY-SEVEN

There'd been little time to rest since they set sail for the Birde Isles. If Luthais wasn't performing his usual duties as captain, he was attending strategy meetings with the officers or their new allies from The Riddles.

Every other spare moment was spent writing as many missives and warnings as they had birds to carry them. Though, for some reason Pimm had requested one particular bird be left in peace. No replies had come, but any number of obstacles could prolong the deliveries. They would reach the Isles tomorrow, goddess willing, and Luthais could only hope his father had received at least one of the letters.

Maher had been just as busy. They'd had a brief reunion at the villa belonging to Marielle's family. But since then Luthais had only seen him during meetings, then he would disappear. It was beginning to feel like they were already home. Passing ships in the night. There were so many things he wanted to say to Maher, if they could manage to be alone for any sufficient amount of time. Gods only knew when that would be.

Back in his cabin but still unable to sleep, Luthais sat alone at his table and stared at a map of the Birde Isles. There were a few places where Dare's ship could make port while avoiding Trader's Bay, but none were anywhere close to Kingsport. Much depended on whether any of their warnings reached Lord Kingfisher, with enough time to prepare for the pirates' arrival.

Pressing his palms against his eyes, Luthais breathed deeply. It would do no good to tangle his mind with what ifs. There was a soft knock on his door. Lifting his head, Luthais asked who was there.

Please, let it be anything but another problem.

The door clicked open, and Maher walked through, a tray balanced on one arm.

"Evening, Captain," he grinned.

"Maher?" Luthais' weary brain took a moment to catch up. "What are you doing?"

"You've hardly been eating, and you won't be of use to anyone if you're faint from hunger." With a small flourish, he set the tray down. There was indeed food, but also water and a mug of tea. "There's also a treat for later," Maher took the seat across from him, as relaxed as he would be in the drawing room at the manor, "but only if you finish your dinner."

Chuckling despite himself, Luthais shook his head. "You sound like Mrs. Thorley." He helped himself to the tea and drained half the mug. "Thank you, really."

"Of course." Maher's eyes softened. "You have to look after yourself. If anyone's learned that it's me."

Luthais started on a small pie filled with meat and potatoes. "I'd say you've had your share of bodily injury up to now, you could use a change of situation."

"True enough," he snorted. "I've survived going overboard on two of your ships now. Don't know if that's good luck or bad."

Luthais dropped the fork in his hand. "That isn't funny."

"You brought up my lack of luck first."

"I meant you should stop putting yourself in such dangerous positions!"

Maher crossed his arms. "Says the sea captain."

"Leaving ships out of it, during the last year I've watched you run yourself half-dead. How about you take your own advice and look after yourself."

His head tilted, not rising to the provocation. "When did this become an argument? I thought you'd be glad to see me."

Luthais stood and paced away from the table. When he turned around, Maher had also left his seat. "Do you have any idea how worried I was? Watching Marielle pull you overboard and being powerless to stop it? You may have been lucky up to now, but you're not immortal," He snapped. "Do you understand that?"

"Of course, I do." Maher crossed the cabin, stopping just within reach. "I'm not mad, no matter what the rumors might say. That's why I'm trying to help you see past it. It's over, and I'm still here."

CHAPTER ONE HUNDRED TWENTY-EIGHT

Taking Luthais' hand, Maher held it to his chest. Letting him feel the heart beating steadily within.

"I'm still here."

Swallowing hard, Luthais' fingers flexed against the fabric of his shirt. "But you might not've been."

"We can't think that way, else we'll make ourselves afraid to do anything."

"I don't want to lose you when I've only just found you." Luthais' voice cracked. "I'm sorry it took so long." He began to pull away, and Maher closed the remaining distance between them.

"It'll take a lot more than all that's happened to get rid of me." Bending until their mouths nearly touched, Maher enjoyed the hitch in Luthais' breath. "You may not've finished your dinner, but would you like to have your treat?"

Maher wasn't certain which of them kissed the other first, but that didn't matter when Luthais was opening up to him so readily. He held Luthais' face, one hand sliding back to test just how securely that blonde hair was tied. Nothing would please him more in that moment than to run the sun-bleached strands between his fingers.

Gripping Maher's shirt, Luthais reached back with his free hand and removed the tie for him. It fell down his back and over his shoulders in waves.

"No fair," Maher huffed against his lips. "I was going to see if I could untie it without looking."

Pulling back far enough to fix him with those moss green eyes, Luthais sighed. "Maher Villaon, what am I going to do with you?"

"I bet I could think of a few things."

There was a moment in which Luthais seemed to pop a cog in his brain. Then, a look that could only be described as brazen appeared on his face. "I'm sure you could."

"I'm just saying, there's no need to be formal all the time. Although I certainly don't mind a bit of wooing."

"You've been talking to Pimm, haven't you?"

Declining to answer, Maher recaptured Luthais' lips. His mind was already turning over a few ideas, wondering what exactly would work best on a moving ship. Then Luthais caught Maher's lower lip between his teeth and all thoughts took flight.

A fist pounding on the door nearly made Maher knock their heads together.

"Not again," he groaned. "I even made sure Kamharida'd retired for the evening."

"Luthais!" More banging on the door. "Are you there?"

"Ally?" Luthais answered.

"Al?" Maher said at the same time.

Ally burst into the room as the two men untangled themselves. "They found it, they found the bell!"

"What?" Maher straightened his clothes. "How do you know?"

"Pasha felt it. If she's right, then they've already rung it once!"

"Fuck," They both muttered.

"She's gone down to ask if the other mermaids felt the same thing." Ally herded them out of the cabin. "Come on, you can tumble each other later."

ALLY

CHAPTER ONE HUNDRED TWENTY-NINE

Ally and Pasha waited on the deck of the *Foxglove*, watching the pink light of dawn steadily approach on the horizon. They would be home in a matter of hours. There was no way to know what awaited them, but Pasha and the other mermaids were certain the bell had only been rung once so far. It appeared, time was needed between each ring of the bell's call.

With the bell already found, the mermaids formed a new plan. A few would still go straight to the underwater caves, but the rest would stay with the *Foxglove* and the Riddles boats. They would see any sirens, or other predators, coming long before the sailors and would sound the alarm. Ally'd finally gone below to properly greet the other mermaids and to check on Euphonia. The sea monster was excited to see her, crooning loud enough to shake the hull of the ship. It certainly didn't lessen the deference the merfolk showed Ally from the moment they saw her. At first, she assumed it was because she was a made mermaid, which most of them hadn't seen before. But later, when they'd returned to the ship to relay the new plan, Pasha explained it had more to do with what she'd done to the siren.

Not that either of them could explain how that happened. But the sensation in Ally's chest had been so similar to when she was Sea Kissed, that she was sure there had to be some connection. The hunger was quiet now, and Ally hoped to keep it that way. She'd been glad to have the weapon at the time, but the idea of using such power often was unsettling. She understood far better now why Pasha'd kept her own hidden weapon a secret for so long.

At least they'd learned how Pasha was able to create such a powerful shield against the sirens. Vesi was proving to be a font of knowledge, able to impart all the lessons Pasha missed as a child. Though Pasha'd been able to wield the spear from the moment she found it, the ancient weapon didn't belong to her until that moment. When there was enough energy, and enough will, being pushed into it by Pasha. The crested mermaid warrior's spirit was still a part of the spear, but now it identified Pasha as its owner.

Though she was hesitant to think of the future at this moment, Ally hoped to learn much more about the history of her new shoal. Once this was all over.

Ally and Pasha weren't alone on the deck for long. As the sky brightened, the space around them filled until it seemed every soul not actively engaged in sailing the ship had gathered to watch their approach to the Birde Isles.

There was no sign of Dare's ship, but some of the messenger birds must have reached the city in time. Hastily erected barricades were barely visible above the docks and an answering message was sent to Luthais the moment those on land became aware they were close to the Isles. It wasn't until they were halfway across Trader's Bay that they could see the damage already done by the bell. Half of the docks were underwater, the tide risen far above what was normal. Workers scrambled to secure vessels set loose from their moorings. Ally glanced at Luthais, knowing how the sight must upset him. He was speaking to the ship's officers, but the firm set of his jaw told her all she needed to know.

Maher was off to the side with Pimm, scanning the city with a spyglass. "Some of the buildings closest to the harbor look as if someone's taken a hammer to them."

"Like an earthquake?" asked Pimm.

"The bell was concealed beneath the island," Pasha said softly. "Raising it could have shaken the earth around it."

Pimm looked through the glass for themself. "How far could that tremor have spread?"

"I'm not sure."

They nodded and looked to Maher. "We must warn everyone in the Lantern. If they're not already evacuating, they must go. There's no telling if there will be another quake if the bell is rung a second time, or how far it will reach."

Ally frowned at the approaching land. "If the bell was raised, then where would it be now?"

"How large is it?" asked Maher.

"Taller than you." Passing Ally the spear, Pasha asked for the spyglass and moved farther down the deck to view the shoreline beyond the city.

"I thought she'd never seen it before?" Maher stepped into the spot Pasha vacated.

"She had a dream about it once," said Ally. "We didn't know that's what it was, at the time."

"Well that couldn't have been a coincidence."

"I think you're right."

"Ally!" Pasha called. Hurrying towards the foremast where Pasha stood, Ally heard Maher and Pimm not far behind her. "What is it?"

Pasha traded the spyglass for her spear and pointed south. Towards the farthest end of the coastline visible from the bay. It took Ally a minute to focus, but she soon saw a massive hunk of rock missing from the cliffside, leaving a gaping hole in its craggy face.

"It must've emerged there," Pasha said. "The stone was moved from the inside."

Sweeping the glass upwards, Ally stopped when she reached the end of the old seawall closest to town. There was something large set atop it, but it was too far to know if it was the bell or another chunk of displaced rock.

"What do you see, Al?" asked Maher.

"We'll have to get closer to be sure, but we might've found the bell."

LUTHAIS

CHAPTER ONE HUNDRED THIRTY

The *Foxglove* made port at one of the only intact docks left in Kingsport Harbor. Leaving Kamharida to handle things on board, Luthais disembarked with Maher, Pimm, and several sailors handpicked from the crew. One of the Riddles boats would dock as well, so Captain Vas could meet and confer with Lord Kingfisher. The rest were already spreading into formation throughout the bay.

Luthais' boots hit the dock before the gangway came to a complete stop. Striding through the workers, sailors, and Kingsport Guards, he found his father and Gai outside the harbormaster's office. They were speaking with Agnes Heper; the set of the older woman's face was grim, for good reason. She departed just as Luthais arrived, shouting rapid-fire orders at her staff.

Gaius swept his middle son into a crushing hug. "Luthais, thank the goddess you're home safe."

"Father," Luthais squeezed him tight before Gai stepped into his place.

"We received your missives, brother. All twenty of them."

"Glad to hear it." Luthais nodded at the barricades just behind them. He turned, expecting to find Maher and Pimm, as well as Vas. But only the guard captain stood there. Head swiveling, he glimpsed Maher and Pimm headed for the street above the wharf. When they reached the cobblestones, Maher turned back and their eyes met. Mather pointed at Pimm and then into the city. Heart in his throat, Luthais nodded. With a wave and a wink, Maher was gone.

"Luthais?" Lord Kingfisher brought his attention back to the matter at hand.

"Right, yes, Captain Vas of The Riddles Royal Guard has come ashore with us. Has there been any sign of Dare?"

"We've had reports of a Fraollish warship off the southern coast," said Gai.

"Makes sense. Ally and Pasha believe the bell was raised near the cliffs beyond the seawall."

"Ally? Where is she?" Their father scanned the dock.

"They've gone to confirm the bell's location,"

"By themselves?" Gaius demanded.

"One of our boats will ferry them closer to the cliff, Lord Kingfisher," Vas interjected. "They will be guarded the entire time."

"Much appreciated, Captain." Gaius collected himself.

"It's our honor," the Riddles Islander bowed slightly. "What else has been done to prepare?"

"The city is being evacuated by district. Our entire fleet is mobilizing, with reinforcements expected from Swan and Gull Island," said Gai. "But I don't know how we're expected to fight against undead sailors, if your letters are to be believed."

"I doubt they'll come ashore," Luthais said, waving over the crewmates who'd accompanied them onto land. "Dare will need as many as possible to hold a ship that size steady, which I'm sure she knows."

"Our first priority is stopping the bell from being rung again," said Vas. "The Riddles soldiers will do everything possible to keep the sirens away from the shore, but we must prepare everyone to face them."

"We've sent instructions to each ship." Lord Kingfisher offered.

"Those on land must be warned as well. If you are close enough to hear their song, then it matters not if you're on land or at sea."

"Olebile! Weams!" Luthais called.

"Aye, Captain?" Weams answered as he and Olebile approached.

"You know what to do," said Luthais. "Pass the word along to everyone you can. No names are to be spoken near the water from this moment. Everyone is to pair up and look out for one another."

"They should partner with someone they love, if possible," Vas added. "Or at the very least care about."

"Why is that?" asked Gai.

"It's more difficult for the sirens to enthrall those whose affections belong to another. A song that might have once been captivating becomes irritating, at best."

"Well noted," said Olebile, their hand hovered at the small of Weams' back.

"Go to it," said Luthais. "Then return to the *Foxglove*."

Weams and Olebile saluted their captain and left with the others to deliver Luthais' instructions.

Gai looked out at the bay, counting the number of boats Vas brought. "What now?"

"For now, we wait," said Vas. "With any luck, they will be stopped before the bell rings again."

MAHER

CHAPTER ONE HUNDRED THIRTY-ONE

Maher and Pimm raced into the city, dodging the crowds as people fled inland for safety. The Kingsport Guard were sweeping the buildings closest to the wharf, ensuring all citizens were able to evacuate.

He hated to leave without saying goodbye to Luthais, but they didn't know how much time was left until, or if, the bell rang again. The superstitious part of him also didn't want to tempt fate. If there were no farewells, then Maher and Luthais would have to see each other again. For good measure, Maher made the Saprean sign against ill fortune over his heart.

Take no chances. It's gotten me this far.

The streets that bordered the Lantern were somewhat calmer. But once they crossed into the district, the sounds of a skirmish drifted out from the square.

Maher halted so abruptly that Pimm crashed into his back.

"What the fuck is going on?" they demanded.

"Everyone seems to have lost their minds."

The Lantern square was currently the site of one massive brawl. One group that'd taken up position by the fountain was distributing a cache of clubs and other blunt weapons to its allies.

Lantern employees guarded their buildings as the intruders tried to push in, some hurled whatever they could get their hands on from the windows. A woman on the second floor of Nitya's blue lantern establishment hurled a ceramic chamber pot that smashed over the head of a man trying to knock their gate down.

"Maher! Pimm!" Archie ran over, his establishment was only two doors down. "Don't just stand there!"

"What's going on?" Maher asked as they followed him into the nearest door alcove.

"The street crews, they've joined together to ransack the Lantern." A shallow cut over his eye bled sluggishly. "They assembled just before dawn, started attacking soon as the last establishment closed for the night."

"Thought they'd catch everyone unaware," Pimm scoffed.

"Aye, we've sent for help. The guards that've been patrolling for months weren't fucking here!"

"It had to be the earthquake that took them away." Maher frowned. It seemed too much of a coincidence.

"What earthquake?" Archie stared at him.

Maher opted for the simplest answer, "There was an earthquake that hit the harbor districts last night. The Kingsport Guard were all called in to help people evacuate."

"Gods save us, I'd no idea."

"We passed them on the way here," Pimm ducked when a wayward projectile flew into the alcove and shattered against the wall. This one appeared to be a little dog figurine.

"Let's get inside, you can shelter at my place," Archie offered.

"Thank you," Maher clasped his shoulder, "but we need to get to the black lantern and we can't wait."

"Get your people out of here soon as you can," said Pimm. "We've no way of knowing if there'll be another tremor."

"Best go the back way," said Archie. "Take care, both of you."

"You as well," said Maher.

They parted ways, Archie back to his brownstone and the other two down the nearest alleyway.

"I hate leaving them," Pimm looked back.

"I know, so do I, but they're holding their own for now and the guards weren't far behind us."

"One thing's for certain," Pimm said as they cut down an even narrower side street, "there's no way the street crews picked today to attack at random. It's as if they knew the guards would be pulled out of the district."

"I was thinking the same thing."

MARIELLE

CHAPTER ONE HUNDRED THIRTY-TWO

Holding the rudder steady while her brother secured the sail line, Marielle watched their soldiers check their weapons and tried to control her pounding heart. Everyone else on the boats sent by their parents had already known what Marielle only learned a few days ago. The sirens were *real* and every bit as dangerous as the stories said. While their people were the most equipped to deal with them, Costan admitted he'd never faced one. In fact, they'd become so good at avoiding the creatures, most of the younger soldiers hadn't seen one in the flesh either.

Marielle was more grateful than ever that the mermaids were patrolling the waters beneath them. And Maher'd said something about a sea monster loyal to Ally staying nearby. She'd thought he was having her on at first, but then Kamharida confirmed it. The first mate witnessed the creature knocking a ship around as if it weighed nothing and catching the pirates who fell overboard in her open jaws. Marielle couldn't imagine how a sight such as that would stay with you.

Kamharida. She was docked with the *Foxglove* for now. But they'd lead the charge if Dare's ship sailed anywhere near Kingsport Harbor.

Marielle hoped very much that Kamharida would stay safe on land. The thought of a siren getting her claws into the Utollmir woman made her stomach turn.

BEAR'S DEN

PIMM

CHAPTER ONE HUNDRED THIRTY-THREE

By the time they reached the black lantern, Pimm could hardly hear the noise from the square. They hoped that meant the Kingsport Guard had arrived to break up the street crews, and not something worse.

The surly door guard let them in immediately and without complaint. Even when Maher gave him a quick, "Many thanks, Eustace!" he only grunted and showed them to where everyone waited in the Madam's sitting room. Mama Bear was there with her mother, along with Kit and, of course, Sweetpea.

"Oh, thank the gods, you're back!" Mama Bear rushed to embrace them both.

"Hello, dear," Maher kissed her cheek.

Kit was right behind her. "Pimm, you're a sight for sore eyes."

Pimm wrapped an arm around the lad's shoulders in a quick hug. "I'm glad to see you too, Kit."

"Have you seen the row in the square?" he asked.

"We came right through it. A ceramic dog nearly brained me."

Sweetpea's blocky head lifted from the floor, tilting to one side.

"Is there anything that can be done?" asked Maher. "The Kingsport Guard are headed this direction, but they're evacuating each district along the way."

"Everyone we could spare was sent just before you arrived," the Madam said, gesturing for them to sit. "We are aware of the evacuation order."

"It seems so unlikely," said Mama Bear. "An earthquake in the Birde Isles."

"It wasn't a natural earthquake," Pimm hedged, looking at Maher.

"You can elaborate on that later." The Madam rested a hand on Sweetpea's head. "First, tell us what you learned on your journey. I expect you are back so soon for reason."

Maher sighed, "Indeed, we are."

Kit prepared and served tea for everyone while Maher recounted all they'd learned about the origins of the false Saprean coins.

As he spoke, Kit began to give Pimm pointed looks, as if he had something important to impart. Finally, Maher finished with the explanation behind the so-called earthquake. Silence hung heavily in the room. The crackle of the fire and Sweetpea's soft snores were the only sounds.

"I can't wrap my head around it all," Mama Bear said, at length.

"I can't believe Marielle is a princess," Kit muttered.

"Speaking of Marielle," said the Madam, completely bypassing the revelation about mermaids, sirens, and other deep sea myths, "We've learned quite a bit in your absence as well."

"Thanks largely to Kit," Mama Bear added proudly.

"Do tell," Maher invited the lad to speak.

Flushing a light shade of pink, Kit said, "We found where Ezmira's been hiding."

Pimm and Maher gave Kit their full attention as he told all that'd happened since they set sail for The Riddles. Apparently, they'd found the location of Ezmira's hideout soon after they left.

She escaped the raid on her rooms in the city, but they caught a few of those that worked for her and found evidence she'd been one of the key suppliers of the silver coins to the street crews.

"But *how* did you find her?" Pimm asked. "We've been searching for months."

"Ezmira made a mistake," Kit shook his head, golden curls flopped across his forehead. "When she learned you'd left Kingsport, she tried to go after your building."

Pimm's stomach dropped. They were half-out of their seat when Kit grabbed their arm.

"Everyone's alright! I promise!"

"Next time, maybe lead with that," Maher suggested while Pimm sank back into their chair. They'd been ready to run to the northern district if that's what it took.

"What happened?"

Now Kit grinned, "Your tenants outsmarted Ezmira's gonys. There was a little damage from where they forced their way in, but not a scratch on anyone or anything else."

When Pimm was too gobsmacked to speak, Maher chimed in, "I'd dearly love to know how that came about."

"I was due to pop by that day to check in like we'd agreed," Kit explained. "But first thing that morning, I got a note from Ms. Orel asking that I come right away. When I arrived there, they were, six of Ezmira's men tied up in Ms. Orel's washing line."

"I'll be damned," said Maher. "They should've known better than to mess with anyone in the northern district.

"By the way, Pimm, you never said Mister Bernhard was an imperial guard in Tjordun."

"I didn't know," Pimm murmured.

Kit blinked in surprise. "Well, he was, and he was already awake when the gonys broke in. Laid them out flat, he did, while the couple on the second floor pelted them with all the garbage they'd collected from everyone to dispose of that day. Then Ms. Orel tied them up so tight we had to cut the ropes to get them loose."

"We replaced her laundry lines," Mama Bear added.

"Thank you," Pimm felt as if they were dreaming. "And they revealed where Emira's been hiding all this time?"

"Yes, and that's not all they said." Kit glanced at Mama Bear. Her mirth at the story of Pimm's tenants faded, but she nodded for him to continue. Concerned blue eyes darted to Maher.

"What is it?" he asked, and Pimm had a sudden feeling they knew what was coming.

"The reason we had so much trouble locating Ezmira, is because she'd been put up in rooms in the financial district, right near the Treasury."

"And we didn't think she could've been anywhere close to an official building," Pimm noted.

"Who put her up?" Maher asked, though his tone suggested he already knew the answer.

"Ambassador Villaon," Kit said. "Ezmira's been working for him longer than we thought. And when Jerd got pinched at the Treasury, he gave Marielle up to Khafra almost immediately."

"Of course he did," Maher muttered.

"We'll take care of that as well," said the Madam, setting her teacup down with a soft clink.

Gods, I wouldn't trade places with Jerd for all the treasure on the ocean floor. Pimm thought.

"Right," Kit cleared his throat. "So it was the ambassador who told Ezmira to take care of Marielle. The fact that she was spotted at the Den was just more incentive to attack the way they did."

Maher's face was stricken as he turned to Mama Bear. "I'm..."

"Don't say it," she held up a hand to stop him. "It's not your fault, Maher."

"But I'm the one who asked you to hide her in the first place. And Khafra..."

"Listen to me, my Magpie, you've no business apologizing for the deeds of someone you happen to be related to, understand?"

Maher kissed the top of her hand, arguing no further, but Pimm could hazard a guess at his thoughts. He'd already known his father was a political schemer, but to also learn Khafra was the source of so much destruction and so many lives lost? Turning someone like Ezmira loose on the city was an exceedingly stupid thing to do.

"I'm sorry, Maher," said Pimm.

"Don't be, I should've known…" Maher's reply was drowned out by the peal of a bell, so loud that Pimm felt the vibration in their teeth.

As the tone faded, Sweetpea stood from her place by the Madam's feet. Jowls curling back, the dog stared at the door and growled.

Fuck. Pimm started to rise from their seat, only to be thrown to the floor as the building around them began to shake.

CHAPTER ONE HUNDRED THIRTY-FOUR

Everything was eerily still as the unmistakable note of the bell echoed through the harbor. From his position outside the harbormaster's office, Luthais could see Kamharida standing on the quarterdeck of the *Foxglove*, looking out towards the distant cliffs. The first mate knew to sound the alarm if anything seemed amiss, apart from most of the docks already being underwater.

The long sound finally faded, leaving Luthais even more on edge as the seconds passed and nothing happened.

"What's the second ring supposed to bring, again?" Gai whispered to him.

"Legends of the deep," Luthais recited what Ally and Pasha had told them.

"That bell sat underwater for centuries, maybe all those creatures are long gone."

"Wait," their father squinted at the water. "Do you see that?"

After a moment of searching, Luthais saw a massive ripple spreading from the open ocean towards the Isles. Any boats it met rocked gently with the impact, but it never rolled or crested into a wave. The ripple quickly reached the harbor and the moment it touched land, the ground beneath their feet buckled.

The sea roiled, tossing unmoored ships about and sending some crashing into one another. Waves surged, hammering against the shore. Before their eyes, the water level began to rise again.

"Get to higher ground!" Luthais shouted, running after his father and brother.

Further down the harbor, a ship careened out of control and smashed through the barricade. Climbing atop a wagon sitting on the main wharf street, Luthais called out directions to the fleeing dockworkers streaming into the city. Out on the bay, only the Riddles boats appeared to be weathering the rocky sea and staying in formation. The sails of his own ship were slacked in some places and tightened in others as Kamharida wrestled with the wheel. Luthais had no time to wonder what kind of nightmares were just unleashed. He'd hoped Gai could be right, that it had been long enough that the worst of them had perished. But now he had a feeling they just needed a little more time to wake up.

MARIELLE

Chapter One Hundred Thirty-five

Marielle and the other Riddles sailors felt the shift in the sea just before it struck. The thrashing waves were enough to capsize most smaller vessels, but their boats held fast. They were rocked violently, even as the swells grew farther apart. Near Costan's boat, a mermaid with silver hair surfaced and waved to get their attention.

"What is it?" Marielle called. "Are the sirens close?"

"Not the sirens!" she shouted back. "Bigger!"

A long, dark shadow moved beneath the waves. As it drew near, the mermaid ducked under again. Clutching the side of the boat, Marielle watched as the shadow came to an abrupt stop, then twisted. A dozen lights sparked to life beneath the water, all aimed for whatever creature had arrived in the bay. The lights hit their target and the sea monster's snapping jaws came surging out of the water. Its narrow head was attached to a neck as long as a mainmast. Marielle wasn't sure if it was some kind of serpent, or if that neck was attached to something's body. But it was big, and it was angry.

"Archers!" Vas bellowed from his own boat. Every soldier who could wield a bow grabbed their weapons, trading the gold-tipped arrows meant for the sirens for those made of iron.

"Ready! Aim!" Vas waited until the sea monster was distracted by another barrage of charges at the parts of it that remained underwater. "Loose!"

BEAR'S DEN

PIMM

CHAPTER ONE HUNDRED THIRTY-SIX

The brawl in the Lantern square broke up once the tremors began shaking the district. One of the Madam's men reported the Kingsport Guard had also arrived moments before. Luckily, she'd had the foresight to get all their guests out earlier that morning.

Maher agreed to stay with them, to ensure both Mama Bear and her mother made it to safety. With that arranged, Pimm and Kit set out into the district. While the black lantern had withstood the initial quake, aftershocks continued to roll through the city at odd intervals. Not every building was as sturdy, and Pimm wanted to satisfy themself that no one else needed help.

A more orderly form of chaos had taken over by the time they reached the square. The Kingsport Guard were evacuating everyone they could, but a few of the surrounding buildings had indeed come down. Oddly enough, the brownstones on either side of where the Den once sat were still standing.

Starting at one end of the square, Pimm and Kit worked together to aid the people fleeing the Lantern. Whether that meant helping them climb over rubble' discouraging them from trying to bring more than they could carry; sending them in the direction indicated by the guards; or assuring them that yes, the guards did know what they were talking about, and evacuation was in fact necessary.

Sweat dripped down Pimm's temples and their throat was hoarse from shouting over the din, but they'd nearly covered the entire square. Twice more, the earth trembled, but everyone kept moving.

More crowds began to stream through, directed into the Lantern from neighboring districts. Pimm nearly lost sight of Kit in the throng, but the lad stayed close.

They didn't know what became of the street crews, but from the general chatter Pimm gathered those who didn't retreat when the guards arrived all scattered as soon as the quake hit. But the guards had secured most of their weapons left behind, so at least that was something.

Pimm and Kit climbed atop the fountain base to check the square once more. Nearly everyone from the Lantern was already gone, the people still crossing the district were from other parts of the city. They spotted Archie, one of his employees leaned on him for support as they followed the flow of people.

"I think we can leave soon ourselves," Pimm started, then cut themself off when a commotion erupted across the square.

"What's happening?" asked Kit, raising onto his toes for a better look.

"There's a basement club in that building," Pimm couldn't see much beyond the guards gathered around the door. "Perhaps someone is refusing to evacuate?"

Finally the line of guards parted and another group of people emerged into the daylight.

"Pimm!" Kit grabbed their sleeve, but Pimm didn't need him to point out what he'd seen.

A tall woman with gray streaked hair stumbled up the stairs from the club and onto the street, trying to blend in with the crowd. Ezmira.

"Come on," Pimm jumped down from the fountain, weaving their way through the river of folks moving inland. Kit was right behind them. As they angled across the square, Pimm took a spare, sheathed knife from their waistband and passed it to him. "Take this, keep it hidden unless you need it."

Ezmira stayed close to the line of buildings. Twice, she tried to duck down a side street, but was turned around by the guards stationed throughout the district. And she couldn't risk arguing with the Kingsport Guard during a city-wide emergency.

Kit and Pimm made it to the same path, about a block behind her. Gears turned in Pimm's mind as they worked out a plan. They wouldn't let her escape again. When she tried a third time to veer off and was rebuffed, Ezmira spun around in the street. No doubt looking for another way out.

Wild, bloodshot eyes locked onto Pimm and Kit. They all halted as the crowd continued to move around them.

"She's gonna bolt," Kit hissed.

Face twisting with rage, Ezmira grabbed a fallen brick from the nearest building and charged right at them.

"Apparently not," Pimm flicked their wrists, releasing a blade into each hand.

Kit spun around and began directing people around them. "Back away! Go around!"

A bubble of space formed around them as people noticed the knives in Pimm's hands and the enraged woman pushing against the current to reach them.

"You! Stop there!" the nearest guard shouted at Ezmira. A whistle pierced the air as she called for assistance. If Pimm could just keep Ezmira distracted until the guards came, then at least she'd be in custody.

As she barreled down on them, Ezmira screamed and threw the brick. It sailed over their heads and shattered a window. She scrabbled for more on the ground. Pimm suspected she'd soon escalate from throwing bricks to trying to bash their skull in. More whistles sounded, the guards weren't far off.

"Give it up, Ezmira!" Pimm backed up a few steps, knives held steady by their sides. "You won't win, not now."

"No, I won't," she rasped. "But at least I can kill you before I'm done."

Pimm shifted their stance, adjusted their grip on the blades as she closed in. Then they felt it, a new tremor rumbling up from deep underground. Ezmira stumbled, dropping the bricks to catch herself against the nearest building.

Cracks ripped through the cobblestones and the people broke into a run. The guards stopped on their way over to try and regain order. Pimm fought to keep their balance, eyeing the remaining distance between themself and Ezmira. A loud crack ripped through the air and more bricks rained down.

"Pimm! Watch out!" Kit grabbed Pimm by the shoulders and hauled them back. The last Pimm saw of Ezmira was the hand she reached out as the building collapsed.

FORAOISE

Chapter One Hundred Thirty-Seven

The sound of the bell echoed around Foraoise, bringing her to her knees. Every ring seemed to cost her something.

Knocked bow over stern by the first, she'd awakened to find herself on land. Lying next to the bell, it took hours to summon the will to stand. Swain found her just as the sun rose. He fussed over Foraoise until she could sit up on her own. They were on a hill, at the edge of an antiquated stone wall. There was nothing else as far as she could see, but Swain said they were just outside of Kingsport.

Below the wall was a stretch of beach. While he described the damage already done to the harbor, Foraoise watched the tide lap at the pebbly beach. Out beyond the breaking waves, a shock of red hair appeared above the surface. The siren called Swain's name, the sound of her voice plucked at Foraoise's nerves.

"Ah, right," Swain clambered to his feet. "I'll only be a moment, Captain."

Descending a set of steps built into the wall, Swain went out to meet the siren in the shallows. Their conversation was short, and then he was making his way back up the hill.

"What do they want now?"

He sighed, tugging on his mustache. "They wanted to know when to expect the next ring of the bell. It appears the Kingfisher ship we left near The Riddles arrived back this morning."

"Did it?" That piqued Foraoise's interest.

"Aye, along with some of the mermaids they were holdin' captive and an escort of Riddles boats. They've come ready to fight."

"And what of the sirens that stayed behind?"

"All dead, I suspect," Swain glanced out where the siren still waited. "That's why they need the spell finished, now that its begun. I told her that you needed time to recover, but they're getting a mite anxious."

Foraoise took stock of herself, using the pause to mull over what he'd just told her.

"I'll be able to ring it again soon."

The tension in Swain's shoulders eased. "Aye, we'll finish the task and be rid of them. While you attend to that, I'm to meet Smith down the shore. She's bringing a special delivery."

Foraoise didn't lose consciousness after the second chime of the bell. Instead, the vibrations sent her entire body into agony, from her hair down her bones.

Curling into herself while the ground shook and the sea rose halfway up the wall, Foraoise rode out the waves of pain until everything settled into a dull, thumping ache.

Why am I doing this? Foraoise screamed at herself. *I didn't make this bargain. I'm not some puppet or tool for the sirens to use!*

The words she'd heard in the sea caves, spoken in Jon's voice, came rushing back to her. "What are you doing, my green-eyed girl?"

No. It wasn't real. A hallucination from the memory taken by the magic of this thing. Foraoise glared at the engraved hunk of metal. *Whoever forged this bloated wind chime ought to be keelhauled.*

"Captain."

Foraoise looked up to find a row of sirens holding onto the edge of the seawall. The ends of their long tails dipped into the water below.

Swain's siren gave what Foraoise supposed was meant to be an endearing smile. It did not have its intended effect.

"Are you well, Captain?" she asked sweetly.

"Aye, well as I can be, under the circumstances."

"We're nearly there, Captain. You need only ring the bell a third time."

"When I'm ready, I will," Foraoise sniffed.

The siren's face contorted into something ugly.

"What is the delay?" a deep, gravelly voice rumbled.

Rising stiffly, Foraoise moved close enough to see three of the crocodile monsters lift their snouts above the water. Red eyes fixed on Foraoise. In another life, those eyes would've curdled her insides. Now, she only stared back with mild interest. "I'm not quite ready to raise that fucking heavy strike bar again."

"You will do it when you are told!" another siren ordered.

"Shouldn't you be returning to the water soon?" Foraoise goaded. "After all, you can't breathe for long on land."

The crocodiles' tails thrashed as the sirens snarled at her.

Jaws gnashing, one of the sea monsters threw its weight at the wall, scattering the sirens. "Don't forget, we broke a contract to rejoin your side."

"Yesss," another other hissed. "You promised us blood."

CHAPTER ONE HUNDRED THIRTY-EIGHT

"What's going on here?" Swain arrived back at the bell and found Foraoise baiting the sirens. Smith was just behind him, leading a bound Calder Kingfisher to his fate.

A grimace of pain crossed Foraoise's face as she turned, but she quickly schooled herself when she saw Swain was not alone.

"Well," she took in Cal's bedraggled appearance, "it appears we have a visitor."

"Aye, that we do, Captain," he signaled for Smith to stop. "But what was all that commotion as we arrived?"

"I simply don't appreciate being ordered about like a deckhand."

The redheaded siren clawed over the edge of the seawall and spat out his name. It was like a knife jammed into his ear.

"Swain! Captain Dare refused to ring the bell the final time!"

"So it is true," Cal's hoarse cackle drew their attention. "I thought the idiots who held me captive on that damned boat were having me on. Or mad. I didn't care which."

"Quiet," Swain snapped, then turned back to Foraoise. "I know ye need time to rest between each time, Captain, but the bargain is nearly done."

"A bargain *you* made, not me." Stalking closer to their guest, she clasped her hands behind her back. "Not what you expected is it, nephew?" Cal cringed at the familial term and Foraoise grinned. "My quartermaster was determined to have us meet at last, even if it meant making a deal with those creatures back there. What do you think of that?"

"I think they must've made an improvement." Cal shook his shaggy hair from his eyes. "The less you resemble the Kingfishers, the better. Don't mistake me, I don't want to be associated with them either."

The captain's gaze roved over him, the pleased look on her face making Smith retreat a few steps. "If I'm being honest, I'm surprised to find you alive. After the lengths you went to betray the Kingfishers, it's a wonder you weren't put to death for treason."

"Gaius is soft. You should have no trouble besting him. Besides, I had to do something. I gave you Rochelle on a fucking silver platter, and you still let both her and my half-sister slip from your grasp!" Cal sucked in a breath when Dare's knife pressed against his throat.

"Thank you for admitting you were the one writing those letters. I thought you'd try to deny it, plead your innocence."

"Plead?" Cal sneered, his dry, cracked lips peeled back over his teeth. "Plead for what? The opportunity has passed us by, *Aunt* Foraoise. The Kingfishers never would've known it was me if you hadn't kept that godsbedamned journal. So you might as well just kill me now and get it over with. Come on, one slip of the blade is all it takes. Do it!"

"Enough!" Swain jerked Cal away by the rope around his wrists. His chin caught the edge of the knife, blood trickled into the uneven stubble on his face. Pushing the boy back into Smith's charge, Swain rounded on the captain. "That's enough, you can toy with him to your heart's content after we've settled this bargain."

"No, I don't think I will."

"What?" Swain's heart stuttered as the waiting sirens all shrieked. "Why are you doing this now?"

"It's fairly simple," the captain said, any spark that'd returned to her eyes upon seeing Cal already fading. Foraoise looked at the blade in her hands. Turning it over, she dug the tip of the knife beneath a nail until blood welled around it.

"Stop her!" one of the sirens hissed.

Ignoring the creatures clinging to the wall, Foraoise held her bleeding hand up for Swain to see. "I barely felt that. In fact, the most I've felt since I awoke was the bone-twisting pain caused by ringing that bell a second time. I'm not particularly inclined to find out what will happen to me if I do so again."

"I can't believe I'm hearing this," Swain raked his hands through his hair. "Do you realize everything I've done to bring you back?"

"And I was grateful, at first. But what kind of life will this be if all I can experience is pain," her black-rimmed eyes cut over to Cal, "or a brief moment of excitement at taking revenge. Eventually, it all fades." A look of pity flashed his way and bile rose in Swain's throat. "It's been, what, a month spent in this new life, and already I grow weary of it."

"*No*. I did *not* go through all that, Jon, only for you to give up!"

"Foraoise."

"What?" Swain stopped cold.

"You called me Jon. I'm not Jon and I never will be. He's *gone*, Swain, and keeping me in this half-life won't bring him back"

Chapter One Hundred Thirty-nine

Ally and Pasha were aboard one of the Riddles boats when the second chime came. As the sea tossed the small vessel about, they disposed of their clothes and dove into the frothing waves.

The water rose so high in only a matter of moments, they decided to swim past the place where the bell had come to rest. If they could climb onto land near the manor, and as long as no pirates awaited on shore, it would be easy to circle back around unseen.

"We're nearly there." Pasha flexed her fins as a high swell swept over them.

"Do you think I'll be able to go far inland?"

"It's been more than a year since you changed, you should at least be able to make it past the seawall."

"Good, because I..." Ally trailed off. A sense of unease started at the base of her tail and traveled up her spine.

"What's wrong?" They both slowed and Pasha lifted the spear.

"Did you feel that?" Ally turned in a small circle. There was nothing but open water as far as she could see. "Something's coming."

Pasha's head tilted as if she were listening to the currents. Eye ridges lifting, she grabbed Ally's wrist. "We have to go. Go, go now!"

Swimming as fast as their fins could take them, Ally and Pasha shot for land. It didn't matter what part of the coast was ahead, if they reached it before whatever was stalking them caught up. Ally didn't dare look back, even when that same feeling touched her spine again.

Something behind them let out a low, rumbling growl and Pasha's nails dug into her skin.

"We can't outswim it." Pasha's words seized Ally's brain. "You keep going, Ally, I'll hold it off."

"No!" Ally's heart leapt into her throat. "I won't leave you."

"Then we'll make it harder to catch us. When I say the word, you go left and I'll go right. Ready?" The creature hunting them growled again, much closer this time. "Now!"

Ally hooked a sharp turn to the left. She felt the wake of something very large passing between her and Pasha. Angling towards the surface, she looked down and gasped. It was one of the statues in the manor come to life. Some of Ally's earliest memories involved sneaking off to the statuary hall built just off the library. She would run her hands over every carving until she knew them by heart. Ironically enough, this creature had been one of her favorites.

Swinging its wedge-shaped head back and forth on a short neck, the sea monster used four long flippers to propel through the water. A thin, spined crest ran from the back of its head to the tip of its long, flat tail. Even from this angle, Ally could see the sharp, overlapped teeth curving out of its snout. The beady eyes on either side of its head wouldn't see them if they stayed above and slightly behind it, but how long before it caught their scent again?

Ally and Pasha looked at each other across the creature's back. They had to get to land, but they wouldn't reach it if they had to keep circling back into the creature's blind spots. Pasha motioned with the spear. "If I can shock it with enough energy, maybe that will give us time."

"Your well is still recovering," Ally shook her head. Searching within herself, Ally sought out the hunger that came to her in the siren's nest. But nothing responded. Was it still sated from before? Couldn't be, it was ready to devour everything in sight before the mermaids severed the connection.

"We have to do something," said Pasha. "It's going to turn around soon!"

Ally knew Pasha was right, but as she spoke there was a faint tickle at the back of Ally's mind. *Wait.*

Pasha shifted the spear, prepared to draw a charge powerful enough to shock the sea monster's tough hide.

"Wait," Ally insisted. The creature began to swing around and one of its eyes locked onto Ally. Its jaws cracked open.

"Ally!" Charges gathered at Pasha's hands, drawing the sea monster's attention.

"Wait for it!"

"Wait for what?" Pasha swept the spear into an arc.

Just as the creature angled to strike, a halo of light bloomed beneath it as Euphonia surged up from the depths. Her teeth closed onto the other sea monster's underbelly and dragged it back down. Darting over to a stunned Pasha, Ally linked their arms and pulled her towards the island.

"For her. Let's go!"

Ally pushed open the door to her mother's parlor and they crept inside the house.

The higher water line enabled them to walk onto land very close to the manor grounds. Everything had been abandoned in haste. Gardening tools dropped on the lawn, a mop and full bucket of water left in the entryway, even the chickens cooped near the kitchens were all set free.

That was good, it meant everyone had gone inland for safety. It also meant they wouldn't have to explain their presence to anyone and could move about freely.

Racing through the house, they grabbed clothes from Ally's room and threw them on.

"This is the first time I've seen your family home," Pasha noted as they let themselves out.

Ally wished it were under different circumstances. She wanted to show Pasha each room, share the memories built into every brick and beam

"With any luck, it won't be your last visit either."

Sneaking down to where the bell sat by the seawall was a pleasant summer's walk compared to their swim to the island.

Well before the huge iron piece came into view, they jumped down into the ditch on the opposite side of the Kingsport road. They couldn't see much as they approached, but the sounds of an argument were hard to miss.

"I can't believe I'm hearing this!"

"That's Swain, Dare's quartermaster," Pasha whispered.

"And I was grateful," When Dare's voice responded, Ally clutched handfuls of the tall grass growing by the road. It was like she was sitting in her spot high above the cliffs, as she used to, holding tight to the earth to stem her fear of the sea.

None of this sounds right, Ally breathed deeply, in through her nose and out through her mouth. *Will she not ring the bell the final time?*

Dare's voice rose and Ally winced. "He's *gone*, Swain, and keeping me in this half-life won't bring him back."

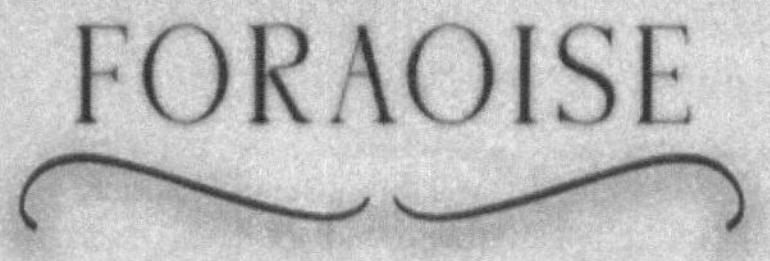

FORAOISE

CHAPTER ONE HUNDRED FORTY

Swain stared at her, eyes glazed over as each word landed like the strike of a sword.

She'd been so intent on understanding her new existence, on harnessing the powers of her new body, Foraoise missed Swain's true intentions for striking the deal to bring her back. It was never about Foraoise and who she was to him. It was about Jon. So many years had passed, and she wasn't the only one still in mourning.

"Don't do this," he begged. "Don't you want control over the Birde Isles? To take revenge on the family that abandoned you?"

"Excellent question," Cal snorted.

"Shut it!" Smith cuffed him on the shoulder.

"What good is any of that if I can't enjoy it?" Foraoise snapped, her limited patience fading. If Swain thought he could goad her into ringing that fucking bell, he'd be sorely disappointed. "What good is keeping this body alive if I'm not really living?"

"Spare me," Cal muttered and Smith hit him harder.

"SWAIN!" The siren shrieked, fingers digging into the stone wall. Her breath came in ragged gasps. "Enough time has been wasted. Make her ring the bell!"

"*Make* her?" Swain rounded on the creature. "You think Foraoise Dare can be made to do anything? My only leverage was that bilge-drinking idiot over there, and even *he* can't hold her interest for long!"

"The bell must be rung!" Blue veins pulsed beneath the pale skin of her face. A set of hooked fangs dropped free. Foraoise couldn't recall seeing those before. The other sirens on either side of her hissed, their own fangs appearing.

"Fine!" Swain roared. "You want the damn bell rung so badly?" Stomping past Foraoise, he raised his arms to climb up to the strike bar.

"*The trade is not complete,*" a disembodied voice whispered into Foraoise's ear.

"Swain! Don't!"

Swain never made it to the top. The moment his hands touched the metal, he began to scream.

Lunging to pull him free, Foraoise was pushed back by invisible hands. There was a flash of green, so bright it was like looking into the sun. She covered her face against the glare.

When Foraoise's vision cleared, she found Smith and Cal cowering on the ground. The sirens had all fled back into the sea.

Ally Kingfisher and her mermaid stood in the road just behind the bell.

And Swain was dead.

ALLY

CHAPTER ONE HUNDRED FORTY-ONE

Ally couldn't say what she'd planned to do, exactly, when she stumbled out of the ditch with Pasha chasing after. But once she heard Dare's quartermaster move to ring the bell himself, something had to be done.

Pasha caught her halfway across the road, just as Swain touched the bell's side. Terrible recognition seized Ally when she felt an answering twinge deep in her chest. It was the same as when the hunger first appeared. Pasha threw an arm over her head as light flashed around them. Though Ally couldn't see what was happening, she could *feel* the bell draining the life from Swain. As she'd done to the siren, but wasn't able to call upon to use against the sea monster.

I don't understand this. Ally clung to Pasha until the bell finished its work and the light faded. When Ally looked up, she met Captain Dare's eye.

Movement from the other side of the bell drew their attention. There'd been two others with Dare and Swain, but Ally wasn't sure who they were.

Slowly, Ally and Pasha edged around until Dare was between them and the people still laying stunned on the ground. Though Pasha kept the spear angled towards Dare, the captain made no move towards them or the bell. Ally refused to let herself hope, despite Dare's earlier words.

The woman climbing to her feet, a sailor by the look of her clothing, grabbed the bound arms of a young man and pulled him up. Shaking his long, filthy hair from his face, the man finally noticed the two mermaids.

"My, look at you, squirt," he ground out.

"Oh dear goddess," Ally gasped. "Cal!"

"Captain?" The woman's eyes darted between the mermaids and Swain. "What... what happened?"

Dare took the rope tethered to his wrists. "You should leave now, I think," she said to the slack jawed sailor staring at Swain's dead body. "Go."

Not needing to be told twice, the sailor took off down the road towards Kingsport.

"I must say, this is quite a transformation," Cal sneered.

"I could say the same," Ally murmured.

Had Cal not spoken, calling her by the childhood nickname that now turned her stomach, she'd never have known him. Gone was the boyish roundness of his face, replaced by sharp angles and harsh lines that aged him ten years. His freckled skin was sallow, his clothes worn and tattered, hanging off his frame. Had he been held captive by Dare's crew since escaping from prison?

"That's your mermaid, is it?" Cal stared greedily at the spear in Pasha's grip. "Kind of puny to be holding such a large weapon."

"Come closer and I'll show you how it works," Pasha growled.

Unfazed by the threat, Cal laughed. The wild, unhinged sound raised the hair on the back of Ally's neck. "You think I'm scared of dying? As I was telling our long-lost auntie here, you might as well kill me and get it over with."

Dare's brows snapped together. "Call me 'auntie' again and you'll get your wish."

They all stared warily at each other, until Ally asked, "So, you really won't ring the bell again?"

"I will not."

A low growl floated up from the other side of the wall. Followed by another, and another.

"Snapjaws," Pasha's lip curled back.

"Is that what they're called?" Dare's head tilted. "I suspect they're unhappy they broke their other agreement for nothing."

What does that mean? Ally looked at Pasha and the mermaid's brow ridges raised. She wanted to know what Pasha was thinking, but wouldn't ask in front of Dare or Cal.

Unsure of what to do next, Ally turned back to Dare. "What will you do now?"

"Do you mean, what will I do with him?" The captain jerked her chin at Cal. "Does it really matter? He did try to have you murdered."

"I had every right!" Cal spat. "My mother was *perfect*. She deserved better than to be replaced by some Balahn whore the moment her body was in the ground."

Ally's gaze hardened. "I don't know who told you Lady Glenna was so easily replaced but –"

"Don't you dare say her name!" Cal lunged at them, only to be jerked back by the rope in Foraoise's hands.

"That's enough of that." Dare hooked an arm around his neck. Backing up a few steps, she nodded at the bell. "I suggest you find a way to destroy that thing."

"What are you doing?" Pasha frowned.

"I have an appointment to keep," Foraoise dragged Cal to the edge of the seawall, "and this time, I believe I'll be able to make it."

"What are you..." Craning his head, Cal saw the snapjaws circling just below. "No! Let me go!"

"I thought you didn't fear death? Trust me, it's not so bad once you're used to it." Tightening her hold, Foraoise looked at Ally. "Goodbye, Alphonsine."

Cal struggled harder as the heels of Dare's boots slid off the edge.

"You want blood? Come and take it."

FORAOISE

CHAPTER ONE HUNDRED FORTY-TWO

Foraoise heard the snapjaws circling below. Waves splashed against the stone, mist filling the air. She thought of that first year on the *Tide's Last Revenge* with Jon. Standing together on the bow, side-by-side, the wind in their hair and the spray of the sea coating their skin. Before she ever learned the true meaning behind the trinket she'd carried since birth.

In fact, it was Swain who recognized the old Kingfisher crest stamped into the golden ring that'd always been in her possession. Told her the nearly forgotten fishwife's tale about the early Birde Islanders trading born daughters for their sea goddess' favor.

"Perhaps you're one of them?" he'd joked.

That story stayed with Foraoise, but even as she grew convinced of its truth, there was nothing she wanted from the Kingfishers or the Birde Isles. She would create her *own* story. Foraoise Dare, a pirate that all on the sea knew to fear.

Then, the letters began arriving. And it wasn't enough anymore to merely rule the seas.

The source of all those letters was squirming in her grasp, too weak to break away. Ally and her mermaid watched, their uncertainty evident.

Pebbles slid beneath the soles of her boots as Foraoise reached the edge.

Well, the captain thought as she bid her niece goodbye. *If I didn't make it into the history books before, I'll certainly be included now. Captain Foraoise Dare, Savior of the Known World.*

She called down to the waiting snapjaws, "You want blood? Come and take it."

Stepping back off the wall, Foraoise threw herself into the frothing waves, dragging Cal along for the fall.

As the sea enveloped her and the first snapjaw closed in, the face she'd been longing to see appeared in the surface above.

"I've missed you, my green-eyed girl."

PASHA

CHAPTER ONE HUNDRED FORTY-THREE

Pasha and Ally ran for the edge of the seawall. The waves were too rough to make out what was happening beneath the surface.

"Why did she do that?" Ally whispered.

"Perhaps she was telling the truth. She didn't want to exist in some half-life, no matter what power she obtained."

A flurry of bubbles burst up from the depths. Pasha stepped in front of Ally, spear raised.

Perhaps she isn't so easy to kill.

Cal resurfaced alone, sputtering and splashing wildly. Within seconds, two of the snapjaws surfaced as well. They circled Cal, red eyes trained on their prey. Ally gripped Pasha's arm. Spotting them above, Cal screamed, "Help me! Ally, help me please!"

Before either of them could react, the snapjaws struck. Pasha spun around, pulling Ally's face into the side of her neck and turning them both away.

Soon, it was over. Pasha held Ally as her tears soaked into their borrowed clothes.

When she felt it safe to look, Pasha helped Ally to sit down on the grass. Moving back to the seawall, Pasha found all three snapjaws still there. Were they waiting to see what would happen with the bell? The sirens hadn't returned, but they must still be nearby.

Something Dare said shortly before her death had stayed with Pasha. How the red-eyed predators had broken an agreement to align with the sirens.

"What are you waiting for?"

One of the snapjaws raised its long snout from the water, teeth stained with blood. "For you, little mermaid. What will you do now?"

Planting the spear's end cap into the stone beneath her feet, Pasha showed her own teeth. "I haven't decided yet. But hear this, if you want even a chance of remaining free, I'd remember who you bargained with to leave that trench in the first place."

The snapjaws grumbled and rattled amongst themselves for a moment. Then the same one addressed Pasha again. "Why don't we find the last of the sirens for you? We heard what you did to those that remained in the nest." Ruby eyes glinted at her. "There won't be that many left now."

"Deal."

PASHA

CHAPTER ONE HUNDRED FORTY-FOUR

Summer faded and autumn settled in, cooling the sea along with the changing foliage on land. In the great cavern, Pasha gazed up at the carving of the crested warrior. A large crack ran right down the middle. There was no way to bring the two halves back together, but thankfully one of the mermaids rescued from The Riddles knew how to repair the damage so it wouldn't worsen. She was the only stone carver left among the shoals, and had a great deal of work ahead. At least there were others willing to assist, perhaps even learn the skills.

When the bell rose from its hiding place, it left half the caves that made up the shoal's home in shambles. As the remaining mermaids were brought to the Isles to heal, they were all made as comfortable as possible in the less damaged caves. Their numbers might have dwindled, but they would rebuild their communities. Some were already talking of hatching eggs, but Pasha suspected they were still too weakened for that.

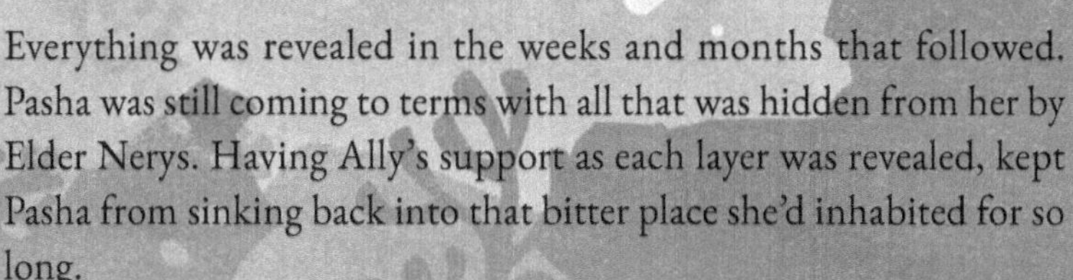

Everything was revealed in the weeks and months that followed. Pasha was still coming to terms with all that was hidden from her by Elder Nerys. Having Ally's support as each layer was revealed, kept Pasha from sinking back into that bitter place she'd inhabited for so long.

The choice to leave Pasha behind had nothing to do with Pallagia or her love for Ealasaid. There was already a plan to leave in search of the other shoals, but Nerys needed a plausible excuse for leaving one so young alone. And Pasha *had* to be the one to stay behind. She could speak to bones, have them do her bidding, a talent that hadn't been seen in centuries. So rare that most of their shoal had never heard of such a thing. A talent that marked her as a future warrior, that would enable her to receive the mark on her arm and the weapon that came with it.

Despite that explanation, Ally'd still questioned the need to leave Pasha on her own. The indignation from when she first heard Pasha's story flickering back to life once the returned mermaids began talking. Vesi claimed the elders felt they needed every spare mermaid to search for the other shoals. Especially if the sirens were involved, as Nerys suspected. And they didn't want Pasha diving too deeply into her power before she came of age. If another mermaid was left behind with her, they'd have to know why and might've been tempted to teach her. They never expected the trap waiting for them. Never imagined they'd be gone for so long.

All of that, Pasha found she could forgive. What she had a hard time accepting was how Ally'd been changed by the decisions of mermaids. Not only from the bargain Pasha struck with Gaius I, but hundreds of years earlier, when the bell was concealed beneath the island.

There were no humans there at the time, and no way to know how the bell would react to their presence. But after they first arrived, strange things began to happen. Not often, but enough to begin recognizing a pattern. Young humans who refused to leave the sea, to the point of being dragged away by their families, only to sneak back at odd hours while the rest of the growing settlements slept.

It took years for the elders to connect the odd behavior they were seeing with the presence of the bell, their own use of energy, and the cycles of the moon. Many merfolk rituals required a full moon, therefore any human born on that island could be caught in the cross between the bell's magic and their own. Those humans would, as they grew, become more and more drawn to the sea. It called them home, to a place where they couldn't hope to survive. Not without the aid of the mermaids.

The condition became known among humans as being Sea Kissed.

When all but one of the mermaids had gone, with both Pasha and the bell fallen into a deep sleep, the Sea Kissed stopped appearing. Then Pasha woke and made her bargain with Gaius I, beginning the cycle anew. Ally'd told the story of her mother praying to the moon the night she was born and all the pieces fell into place.

Pasha and Ally's lives were tied together before either of them was born.

"Pasha?" A gentle touch roused Pasha from her thoughts. Ally was there, with the tapestry map in its case across her shoulder.

"Ready to meet Maher and Luthais?" she asked softly, the care in her eyes making Pasha's breath catch.

Pasha leaned in to kiss her cheek. "Let's go."

CHAPTER ONE HUNDRED FORTY-FIVE

There was still much to rebuild in Kingsport. Being so close to the bell when it rang, the city took the brunt of the damage. From the sudden rush of water as the tides rose higher than they'd ever been, to the tremors that toppled buildings and split foundations. Though the destruction of property meant nothing next to the lives lost. A day of remembrance was declared, to be observed every year on the anniversary of the Battle of Kingsport. As it was already called.

Only the northern district appeared untouched. Whether because of the distance from the bell or the structure of the buildings, they weren't sure. If it turned out to be the latter, Lord Kingfisher was determined to use the same architecture style to fortify the city. Luthais sat in such a meeting now, listening to a progress report on debris removal. He'd already said his piece. The water line had steadily gone down, but most of the docks had to be rebuilt to a new height.

There was also the ongoing discussion about the sea monsters that'd been released back into the seas. Not as many as The Riddles anticipated – thank all the gods for that – but these creatures were now hunting in waters that hadn't seen predators like that in centuries. It was a new nautical world out there, and they had to learn to navigate it.

Which was why Luthais and Maher were working with the mermaids to draw up new maps. Comparing the old maps that used to warn sailors of sea monsters, back when people still believed in them, with the mermaids' knowledge of these creatures and their habits. A squadron of mermaids were guarding the *Foxglove* at this moment. Accompanying it and the remaining Riddles boats back to their islands. Queen Maeva and Queen Sefina had traveled to the Birde Isles to meet with Lord and Lady Kingfisher. They agreed to take the bell back with them and keep it secure. The barrier around their islands would play a large part in ensuring it stayed hidden.

They would also scour their own records, in the hopes of finding a way to destroy it. Though Ally'd assured everyone the bell would cause no trouble with no mermaid magic around to provoke with its own, it was still agreed they would still err on the side of caution.

Across the table, Maher sat in his green tufted chair and scribbled notes onto a slip of paper. He looked more rested than he had for months prior. Not that either of them had slept much since Luthais moved into Maher's rooms in the guest wing.

He caught Luthais staring and winked. Heat tinged Luthais' cheeks as he tried to refocus on the fascinating topic of debris removal.

Maher was finally accepting help with some of his responsibilities. There were still plenty of challenges ahead, unpleasant tasks that needed to be done. Still, they were building a new life together and, to their own surprise more than anyone else's, they were allowing themselves to enjoy it.

ALLY

CHAPTER ONE HUNDRED FORTY-SIX

Ally and Pasha swam towards their meeting place with Luthais and Maher. They took their time, enjoying the calm ebb and flow of the current. The sea had come down considerably since the bell was removed, but the stretch of beach that ran along the seawall was still quite narrow. And it may never fully go down, they would simply have to wait and see. Sunlight streamed down through the water, making the blues and greens of Pasha's tail shimmer. Ally smiled, feeling surer than ever that this was the life she was meant to have.

Even with all the rebuilding still to be done and the snapjaws hunting the last of the sirens, Ally was content. She still didn't have the same abilities as a born mermaid, but that didn't bother her any longer. There were skills she possessed that were hers alone.

After much practice and talking with mermaids from other shoals, Ally was fairly sure she was a conduit. Energy pulled from the sea could flow through her, a great deal as it turned out, but she couldn't call on it herself. Her innate well of energy was also different, in a constant state of refilling itself. In her mind, she saw it as a strand of thread being spun from a never-ending supply of wool.

Then there was that place in Ally's chest that she still thought of as the *hunger*. That piece of herself that resulted from the most unlikely set of circumstances. The thing that made her one of the Sea Kissed. Pasha was angry that the mermaid elders knew this was happening to humans on the island and did nothing to stop it. But Ally questioned if there was really anything they could've done, even if they wished.

Besides, there were other, more pressing matters awaiting their attention. The sea monsters for one, at least five different species had been spotted over the last few months. Some showed little interest in humans and were just eager to roam the ocean once again. But others, like the sea serpent faced by Marielle and her people, were another story. So the mermaids were helping Maher and Luthais devise the best ways to share the seas with them once again.

There was one sea monster whom Ally would give anything to see again.

When she heard the news about Euphonia, Ally didn't want to believe it. She was severely injured while fighting the spined creature that'd gone after Ally and Pasha. Vesi came to them and said she didn't have much time. The other mermaids led them to the place where Euphonia'd come to rest. When she crooned at their arrival, it nearly broke Ally's heart in two.

"Could we heal her?" Ally asked, clinging to a last shred of hope.

"We've already tried," Vesi said softly. "Our tears don't work on her kind. Every form of magic has its limit."

Ally stayed with Euphonia, rubbing her smooth head and thanking her for all she'd done. The rest of the mermaids stayed at a respectful distance, all waiting with Ally until Euphonia's eyes slid closed.

Luthais and Maher were already on the beach that ran alongside the manor grounds. They'd set up a small table and were looking at a newly made copy of one of the ancient Known World maps. The two men seemed so comfortable in each other's presence, Ally almost didn't want to interrupt. But then Maher noticed the mermaids walking out of the surf. The way his face lit up made Ally that much happier to know she could come onto land now to visit with him and her family whenever she liked.

"I have news," said Ally. "I've been offered a leadership position within the shoal." She sat with Maher on the seawall steps, taking a short break while Luthais recorded all Pasha had to say about sea monsters they'd identified so far. Maher'd also brought one of the sewing projects she worked on now when on land. Having the hoop in her hands, moving the needle in and out as the pattern came to life, brought Ally such joy.

"That's quite an honor, isn't it?"

Nodding, Ally paused as Pasha laughed at something Luthais said. *Never thought I'd see the day.*

"Did you ever think you'd see something like that?" Maher guessed her thoughts. "Now, tell me about this new position."

"To be honest, they wanted Pasha at first. But becoming a shoal leader wouldn't be right for her."

"I can see that. Whereas you've grown up absorbing your family's lessons in governance, whether you wanted to or not."

"Exactly." Ally returned her attention to her needlework.

"Will you accept?"

"I think I will. They need someone to represent merfolk interests on land. My family may've taken on the task of educating the other human nations about mermaids, but we're going to need help if there's any hope of reestablishing any of the former shoals."

"And you're the only one who's lived as both a human and a mermaid," Maher noted.

Ally sighed, "The renewed knowledge of the existence of mermaids is already spreading. We'll have to balance fighting the old superstitions with reclaiming their homes and coexisting alongside humans again. It won't be easy."

"I know," he snorted. "Remember that hawker who tried to pass off oyster scraps as mermaid scales?"

"Don't remind me," she muttered. "We've a lot of work to do."

Slinging an arm around her shoulders, Maher pulled Ally close and tucked his chin into her hair. "You are an exceptional person, Al."

"I may need you to remind me of that after I accept this position," she wrapped an arm around his waist.

"Not a problem, Al. I'll be here."

MAHER

CHAPTER ONE HUNDRED FORTY-SEVEN

Maher waited in the alcove across from Lord Kingfisher's study. He'd grown so accustomed to being on the other side of those doors during meetings, it was almost nostalgic to find himself lurking in the hallway again.

At this very moment, Gaius was delivering the good news to those gathered: The source of the illegal Saprean coins that had spread throughout the Birde Isles was finally unearthed and the entire operation shut down. However, the person responsible for distributing the coins, a known criminal named Ezmira, was killed during the Battle of Kingsport. Whether she was working with anyone else was still unknown.

The stolen coin press was being recovered and would be returned to Saprea as a gesture of goodwill, once the investigation was completed. It would take time to collect the silver circulating through the Isles and beyond, they'd likely never find it all, but there was a plan in place for that as well.

He's probably in there congratulating himself on his escape. Maher adjusted his position, leaning his good shoulder against the wall. *Better not be sitting in my chair.*

At long last, the study doors opened. Luthais was the first to leave, crossing the hall to where Maher waited.

"Well?" Maher glanced past his lover as various officials began exiting the room. The Utollmir ambassador gave him a strange look as she passed, no doubt wondering why Maher hadn't attended the meeting.

"Everything went according to plan. He even asked a few questions," Luthais snorted.

"Where is he now?"

"Gai is regaling him with yet another travel story from his time in Saprea."

"Gai must be enjoying himself immensely," said Maher.

"He'll ensure they're the last to leave the room, that's for certain." Luthais paused. "You're sure you don't want me to stay while you confront him?"

Maher hooked a finger into Luthais' belt. "No, but I appreciate you asking. His true colors will only appear in the absence of others."

Lord Kingfisher walked into the hall and nodded at Maher. Giving a short bow in return, he released Luthais so they could leave together.

"I'll only be downstairs if you need anything." Luthais rumbled.

"Thank you," Maher murmured, the weight of the impending conversation heavy on his chest.

Ten minutes later, by Maher's watch, Gai finally left the study. The jovial expression on his face dropped the moment he turned to follow his father and brother.

Maher emerged from the alcove and crossed into the study. Khafra was alone, gathering his papers and muttering under his breath. No doubt he felt inconvenienced by Gai and his travel tales. Walking silently into the room, Maher closed the door with a snap.

Khafra's head jerked up, carefully schooled features dropping into a scowl at the sight of his son. "If you're here to attend the meeting called by his lordship, you've missed it."

"I'm here to speak to you, actually."

"As usual, your timing couldn't be worse," he sneered. "I have no room in my schedule to entertain whatever grievance you've concocted this time."

"You do have time, as a matter of fact." Maher blocked his father from leaving. "I've cleared your schedule for the rest of the day."

"Don't be absurd,"

"Sit down, Khafra."

"You dare to give me orders? Get out of my way!"

"I said," Maher squared his shoulders and stepped into Khafra's space, forcing him to retreat, "Sit. Down."

Maher didn't raise his voice, there was no need. His tone brooked no argument.

Slowly, Khafra backed into one of the vacant chairs. His gaze was wary as Maher circled the table and sat in his green chair. Reaching into his jacket, Maher withdrew a few Saprean coins minted in The Riddles and one of the documents given to Costan by the so-called delegation from Saprea's queen. Placing the items on the table between them, Maher sat back and laced his hands together.

"We have a few things to discuss."

As Maher spoke, Khafra's expression slowly evolved from shock, to indignation, to fury, and finally to something akin to wry acceptance. When his son finished, Khafra sat quietly for several minutes.

"It was a risk," he said, almost to himself, "to use my own seal. But then, I thought, if the Riddles prince tried to confirm its validity, he'd find it to be the true seal of the Villaons."

"You're not going to deny any of it, then?" Maher raised a brow.

"I thought about it. I could always claim the seal was stolen." Khafra's eyes glittered. "But it appears you are very good at your job, Intelligencer."

Fighting back the urge to be sick, Maher took a sheaf of blank paper and set it down in front of Khafra. "Lord Kingfisher has requested you document the entire affair, in detail." He placed a pen on top of the paper.

Khafra's long fingers drummed on the table. "And what do I receive in exchange for this full confession to my crimes."

"You get to abide by the deal I've made for you."

"Am I not able to set my own conditions?" Khafra sniffed.

Hands braced on the table, Maher rose from his seat. "You have no idea the strings I've pulled to make this happen. You're lucky to be given the opportunity to tell your side, the Kingfishers wanted you locked up weeks ago."

"Well, we all know how you convinced at least one of them to let you have your way."

Not so long ago, a barb like that would've lodged beneath Maher's skin and festered. Slipping into his Magpie mask, Maher leaned closer and grinned wide. "Exactly and, I can assure you, Luthais took the most convincing by far. I can show you the bite marks if you'd like, Father."

Khafra reeled back as if he'd been struck, staring wide-eyed up at his son.

"Call me sentimental, but even I don't want to see you imprisoned or executed." Backing off slightly, Maher sighed. "This is what's going to happen. In exchange for a full confession, including the names of anyone else involved with this scheme, you will be allowed to leave the Isles on your own power. You will be stripped of all Saprean titles and honors. If you set one toe on Saprean soil, you will be arrested and tried by her majesty's government for treason. I've arranged passage to the one country willing to have you, the ship sets sail in three days."

"That's how it's to be, is it?" Khafra shook his head. "My instincts were correct then. After your behavior during Lady Kingfisher's capture, I knew I couldn't trust you to understand the importance of this, Maher."

"I don't care anymore why you did it. Just write it down."

Picking up the pen, Khafra toyed with it for a moment. "Perhaps I did all of this for you, for your future."

"Perhaps I'm really prince of the jellyfish people. Don't insult either of us by claiming you were acting for anyone but yourself."

Three days later, Maher stood with Luthais on one of the newly built docks, watching Khafra Villaon board the *Agate*, bound for Meredia.

When Luthais offered again to accompany him, Maher accepted without hesitation. Khafra's signet ring burned a hole in his pocket. It was confiscated during the raid on the former ambassador's rooms in the city. Lord Kingfisher gave it to Maher, but he wasn't sure about keeping it.

Khafra'd confessed to everything they suspected. The scheme to weaken Saprea's economic power with the influx of currency. Taking advantage of Kingsport as a trade hub to make the Birde Isles the distribution point. Sourcing the silver from Meredia, all to tip the scales of commerce. There was no solid evidence the silver was supplied by the Meredians, they were more careful than Khafra, but the Birde Isles would watch them closely from now on.

Cal's escape from prison was also orchestrated by Khafra. Although no one could've predicted his subsequent capture by Captain Dare's crew. The story of Cal's death had been a difficult one for the Kingfishers to hear.

And Khafra'd told the truth when he boasted to Maher about his relationship with the youngest Kingfisher son. When Gaius learned it was Khafra encouraging a young Cal's hatred of his family after the loss of his mother, he nearly ripped up the agreement Maher brokered for Khafra's exile to Meredia. Not that Maher blamed him. The disgust he felt over everything his father had done would stay with him for a long time.

"Are you alright?" Luthais' hand rested on his back.

"Not particularly," he admitted, trying to clear the growing lump in his throat. "But I will be, eventually."

"You did right by him, even if he never acknowledges it. Maybe starting over with nothing will make him more appreciative of what he has."

Maher nodded as Khafra disappeared onto the ship without rooking back. "Maybe, but somehow I rather doubt it."

MARIELLE

CHAPTER ONE HUNDRED FORTY-EIGHT

"You're sure I can't convince you to stay?" Costan asked.

Marielle stood with her brother on the shore. The crew of the *Foxglove* was loading the reclaimed Saprean coin press and everything that went with it.

"I'm sorry Costan, but I can't." She wrapped an arm around his waist. "I have too much waiting for me in the Isles. And the work we do in the Lantern is important."

"I know," he sighed, resting a hand atop her head. "You'd better write more often from now on."

Marielle chuckled, pushing him off. "I promise. It'll be much easier now with the new trade route opened between us. And I expect you to keep me informed on what you learn about that bell."

"Of course, I will. Father has every historian on every island digging through their records." Costan paused, thinking. "To forge something that large would've taken tremendous resources, even with help from the mermaids."

Marielle hummed in agreement. It was a question that had to be answered if they had any hope of destroying the bell.

For their last night in The Riddles, Sefina and Maeva threw a feast. The royal villa was opened to allow in as many guests as possible.

Music floated through the air, long tables groaned with dishes of every kind piled high. Marielle even wore the circlet of her station, as Mam requested, and a gown borrowed from Mother. She felt naked without her gunbelt, but at least it was safely stowed aboard the ship. Standing by a garden screen dripping with flowers, Marielle enjoyed a break from the sea of well-wishers and old friends.

Vas approached and handed her a drink. "Trying to blend in with the foliage?"

"You could say that." She sipped the sweet, fruit-laced wine. Across the courtyard, Costan was deep in conversation with Kamharida. Rather, he peppered her with questions while she answered patiently between bites of her dinner.

"I heard Costan's been trying to convince you to stay," Vas observed.

"He has."

"There's nothing that would change your mind?"

Marielle smiled when Kamharida practically shoved a piece of fruit into Costan's mouth to make him take a breath. "Nope. You're all welcome to visit, but I have several reasons for returning to the Birde Isles."

BEAR'S DEN

PIMM

CHAPTER ONE HUNDRED FORTY-NINE

Pimm studied the maps and city diagrams laid out in their temporary workroom at the black lantern. They removed the pins that'd marked the areas at sea where the ghost ships were found. There hadn't been another since before the Battle of Kingsport, thank the gods, but most crews were still being trained to watch for signs of the few remaining sirens. The pins clinked together as Pimm dropped them into a small bowl.

Next to come down were the markers for the districts where most of the Saprean coins were found, and the hubs of activity for the Kingsport street crews.

The new crews financed by Khafra, through Ezmira, wouldn't go away overnight. But between the destruction in the city and the cutting off of their funds, some had already disbanded on their own. And with the two original crews in new arrangements with the Lantern and the harbor, they'd not be ceding any territory. More pins down, more pins into the bowl.

A soft coo from the corner of their room drew Pimm's attention.

"What is it?" They crossed to the open cage where a contented pigeon perched inside. The bird fluffed its feathers and cooed again. Gently stroking a finger over the pigeon's head, Pimm smiled when he began to preen the nonexistent feathers on their hand.

Pimm tried to release the pigeon a few times, even thought it might enjoy living in the Kingfisher aviary. But the silly thing kept coming back. And if the bird now had a spacious cage and free run of Pimm's rooms in both the Lantern and the northern district, who could begrudge them the companionship?

Maher arrived just as Pimm finished with the maps. They'd not been expecting him, but the visit was still welcome.

"Ahoy Pirate, old boy," he greeted the pigeon. "Sacked any ships today?"

"I should never have told you about that name," Pimm chuckled, giving Pirate a treat. They were still getting him used to other people being in Pimm's room. Kit was the only one the bird hadn't chased out at least once. "Staying long enough for tea?"

"Please," Maher took a seat at the table, noting the cleared maps. "Quite an adventure we've had these last few years, wasn't it?"

"An adventure is one way to describe it, I suppose." Pimm tugged the bell pull twice to signal the kitchen for tea. They missed having their own stove in the room, but that would soon be remedied. "Did you hear the new Bear's Den will be ready to open in a few weeks?"

"I did." He crossed one leg over the other. "In fact, that's why I'm here. Is Kit ready to take over as door guard?"

"That all depends on if I accept your offer." Patting their vest pocket for a tobacco pouch, Pimm sighed when they found nothing. "I forgot, it's not there."

Maher arched a brow. "You've not given up smoking."

"Only indoors." Clearing their throat, Pimm glanced over at Pirate. "He doesn't like it."

They fully expected Maher to laugh. Maybe tease them for not letting a broken rib break the habit, only to willingly quit for a bird.

Instead, Maher's expression turned thoughtful. "I expect he's seen his share of cannon fire. The smoke might remind him of that."

"That was my guess as well."

After tea was brought up by Olga, who'd also found temporary work at the Madam's establishment while the Den was rebuilt, Maher broached the subject again. "What do you think, Pimm? Will you accept my proposal?"

Pimm already knew their answer, but they had to ask, "You won't regret giving it up?"

"I won't, I'm sure of that. It's time for a change, and my work with the Kingfishers will keep me plenty busy. Besides, you'll be able to boast that the Intelligencer of the Birde Isles is in your pocket."

"It's a good trade, I accept," Pimm smirked. "Do I have to keep the nickname?"

Maher chuckled, "Well, you could always call yourself the Pigeon instead."

CHAPTER ONE HUNDRED FIFTY

Maher stood by the fountain in the Lantern square, watching as the final touches were made to the new Bear's Den.

When Pimm took over as the Magpie of Kingsport, it would lift a tremendous weight off his shoulders. Granted, the Lantern would still be part of his life, but now he'd have one job alone to focus on. Maher wouldn't have proposed the change if Pimm couldn't handle it, or if they weren't interested in the position. But Pimm was looking for a new challenge themself, and Maher had a feeling they'd be a better Magpie than he ever was. Of course, Pimm would keep their workroom at the Den. Mama Bear wouldn't hear any argument about that.

There was quite a lot of activity in the square for the middle of the afternoon. Much had to be rebuilt throughout the city, enough that it was necessary to order materials from the continent. There'd been some valid concern over the cost, until Maher told the Kingfishers exactly how much silver had been confiscated from the street crews over the last few years. A small fortune, enough to finance most of the second rebuilding of Kingsport.

After some heavy negotiations with Saprea, they agreed to exchange the materials needed in return for the falsely minted coins. The silver itself was good, they could put it to other uses. Even better, Meredia couldn't claim the silver without admitting they supplied it to Khafra.

That thought alone cheered Maher to no end.

"If it isn't Maher Villaon."

"Marielle!" He grinned as the gunfighter crossed the square and they clasped hands. "Welcome back. When did you arrive?"

"Just this morning, we docked at the northern wharf." She took in the progress on the Bear's Den. "My, that looks fine. The Madam and Mama Bear must be pleased."

"Indeed," said Maher. "Will you be returning to work at the black lantern, now that things are settled?"

"Yes, and I'm looking forward to it. I'm finally back in the Madam's good graces."

"That reminds me, I still owe you another favor. Any thought on how you'll use it?"

"I think I'll hang onto it for now," Marielle winked.

"Just as well," he laughed, straitening his waistcoat. "I must run, I've another appointment."

"Something fun, I hope?"

"Very much so." Maher bid Marielle goodbye and strolled out of the Lantern. Checking his watch, Maher confirmed he was on time. He wanted to reach the manor before Luthais returned home from the wharf.

It amazed him how comfortable he was sharing quarters with Luthais Kingfisher. There was still much they had to learn about each other, but even the occasional stumbles seemed to bring them closer in the end.

That Ally was happy for them made it that much sweeter.

After making a few stops in the market, Su's Perfumery, Mrs. Ekmekci's bakery, and the shop that carried Luthais' favorite brandy, Maher hired a carriage to take him the rest of the way to the house. Luthais would be leaving soon on Lord of Trade business, for at least two weeks. It would be the longest they'd been apart in months. For his part, Maher intended to make the coming days especially memorable.

ALLY

CHAPTER ONE HUNDRED FIFTY-ONE

Ally and Pasha sat together on the cliff edge behind the manor. The late afternoon sun cast a warm glow, even as the chill of autumn plucked at their hair and thrown-together clothing. Someday soon, Ally planned to make garments for them both that would be easier to take on and off. These were good enough for quick trips to the shore, but Mama expected something a bit more put-together for family dinners.

So much had changed about the world. Fantastical creatures that'd faded into myths and legends, released after a centuries-long sleep. Humans learning how to share the world with them again. The return of the mermaids and the rebuilding of the Birde Isles shoal. It wasn't easy, and sometimes scary. But it was also delightful.

Ally looked at Pasha, taking in the way the sun made her silvery skin shine, the way it transformed her scales into glistening jewels.

"I really do love you, Pasha," Ally murmured. "Do you know that?"

Pasha's head turned slowly, as if she couldn't quite believe what she'd heard. "I love you too, Ally. You have no idea how long I've wanted to say that. I thought... I thought it wasn't safe."

"I expect we'll find many more superstitions that can be tied back to the war with the sirens, for both humans and merfolk." Ally caressed the side of Pasha's face, fingertips tracing along her jaw. "But that's one thing you can always say to me. As many times as you want. As often as you want."

Pasha's hand slipped beneath her drying curls, sharp nails scraping against her scalp in a way that made Ally's toes curl. Drawing her close, Pasha kissed Ally's brow, then the crooked bridge of her nose, then her cheeks. Between each kiss, Pasha whispered "I love you" until she reached Ally's lips and couldn't say any more.

They kissed there in the place where Ally'd spent so many sunrises gazing out at the sea. Wondering if she'd ever conquer the fear and longing that warred within her whenever she beheld the endless expanse of blue. They kissed until the sun began to set and the grass beneath them cooled with the evening air.

Reluctantly, Pasha broke the kiss. Pecking Ally once more on the nose, the mermaid helped her to her feet.

"Shall we?"

Ally nodded, "Yes, let's go home."

But when Pasha tried to lead the way back down the slope, Ally stopped her. Confusion creased her brow as Ally slipped out of her dress, the thin material fluttered to the ground. Smiling, Ally held out her hand.

"Care to take the shorter route?"

CHAPTER ONE HUNDRED FIFTY-TWO

Pasha looked at the hand Ally offered, the scales capping her knuckles catching the fading light. Remembering how she'd once offered her arm to Ally, the first time they walked side by side into the sea.

Ally knew what she was asking. This was the place where Pallagia made her great mistake with Ealasaid. Losing her love and, eventually, her life in the process. But this was different, they were different. They were ready to leap together.

After a last moment of hesitation, Pasha tugged the knot of her own makeshift dress free and let it drop. Sliding her hand into Ally's, Pasha couldn't help but compare this moment to how empty her world was not that long ago. Now, she didn't think her life could be any more complete.

"Ready?" Ally smiled.

"Always, as long as I'm with you."

With one last look back at the manor and the faint outline of Kingsport beyond, Ally and Pasha broke into a run. They raced through the tall grass, onto the cliff's stony edge, and dove off together.

Acknowledgements

Writing this series has been an incredible labor of love, a tremendous learning opportunity, and one of the most amazing experiences of my life.

Thank you to my parents, family, and friends for your support and encouragement. For all of the random questions asked and answered, the nerves soothed, and sharing my joy as each book in this series was published.

To Christina, for holding my hand through the most stressful pre-publication process of my career and for being so proud of me when I had trouble celebrating the smaller milestones. You are amazing!

To my fabulous beta and sensitivity readers, this series would not have turned out the same without you! Thank you so much for your time and thoughtful feedback.

To my editor Rowe, you are the absolute best! I'm so proud of the books we've created together and can't wait for the next one!

To my cover and interior design artist Sandra at Maldo Designs, you've made this series into one readers are excited to have on their shelves! I look forward to designing many more covers together, and thank you for putting up with all of my "how about this?" requests.

To my map artist Rachael at Cartographybird, you took one of the worst sketches in history and made it into the gorgeous maps that represent this world.

To Jessie at Book Blurb Magic, I've learned so much from you! I freely admit the blurbs for this series wouldn't have turned out nearly as well without your coaching.

To Foraoise, Captain Dare's namesake, and my amazing character artist, Celipher, I'm so glad we finally got to meet in person and I can't wait to see you both again!

As always, I have to thank my wonderful online community of writers and readers. I'm always so excited to see you reaching your own writing goals!

Last, but not least, thank you so much to everyone who read, loved and shared *To Kiss the Sea* and *To Brave the Deep*. Knowing that my characters and their stories resonated with so many of you gave me the confidence to keep going. I truly hope you enjoy *To Free the Waves*!

Index: Places

Index of all places in the *Kingsport Chronicles*

<u>The Known World</u>

The Birde Isles (bird): Capital: Kingsport (kings-port); Symbol: Kingfisher bird holding one fish in its beak; Worship: Henotheism (The Goddess of the Sea and her messengers); A collection of islands off the east coast of the continent, the three main territories are Kingfisher Island, Swan Island, and Gull Island; They are the only stopping point on the Unending Sea crossing, built into a bustling trade hub by Gaius Kingfisher I.

    Balah (bah-la): Capital: Ehlafi (Eh-lah-fee); Symbol: Stag; Worship: Polytheistic Trio of Deities (Sun, Moon, & In-Between); Prosperous country on the southeastern end of the Split Sea; Known for cultivating beautiful gardens and home to many world-renowned jewelers; Strong Birde Isles ally.

    Saprea (say-pree-ah): Capital: Laleseir (lah-lei-seer); Symbol: Double flower tulip; Worship: Polytheistic pantheon of deities, varied by region; Large, mid-continent nation that relies heavily on trade; Their major export is textiles and they hold a strong influence over fashion trends; Political intrigue runs rampant through much of the country.

    Fraolland (fray-oh-lund): Capital: Laivastho (Lah-ee-vahs-thoh); Symbol: Crossed cannons; Worship: Nature based; Located at the northeastern end of the Split Sea; They hold a large territory on the Zavatleo and Saprean borders, a holdover from the old Continental

Wars; Powerful naval presence, they hold the highest number of warships on the Eastern Sea.

Meredia (mare-eh-dee-ah): Capital: Pravil (prah-vill); Symbol: Crossed gavel and quill; Worship: Henotheism; Western neighbor to Balah; High level of control at the mouth of the Split Sea; They have a strong, but strictly regimented, arts culture; Generally more concerned with their own affairs over mutual needs; Those raised in the capital tend to call it New Pravil.

Tjordun (sch-ohr-doon): Capital: Midthe (mid-teh); Symbol: A horse with an empty saddle; Worship: Polytheistic pantheon of deities; Shares the inner Split Sea border with Fraolland and Meredia; Strong ally with Balah, they control most land travel from the Eastern Sea coast to the Split Sea coast; Tjordun horses are said to be the finest in the Known World.

Utollmir (oo-toll-meer): Capital: Darajha (dah-rah-ha); Symbol: Circle of waves around the sun; Worship: Ancestral; The largest southern nation on the west side of the Split Sea, they are a major stopping point on the Southern Strait; Utollmir sailors learn to sail through the powerful Strait currents and are often sought after by foreign crews; There is a prominent farming culture throughout the inland portions of the country.

Kharabo (kh-air-ah-boe): Capital: Botsa (boat-sah); Symbol: Crossed scrolls in front of a flowering tree branch; Worship: Ancestral; Landlocked northern neighbor of Utollmir, also their strongest ally; Known for the Great University at Botsa and multiple advancements in modern science; First nation on the continent to implement education for all citizens.

Char-range (ch-ah-r-raynj): Capital: Illsik-yun (ill-si-ck-yoon); Symbol: Mortar & pestle filled with various herbs; Worship: Deism; The largest country on the continent, Char-range takes up the entire west coast and has the strongest naval presence on the Unending Sea; Known historically for alchemy, later channeled those skills into mass herb farming and production of concentrated oils.

Teratsu (teh-rah-tsoo): Capital: Ine (ee-neh); Symbol: Three trees of staggered age framed by a mountain; Worship: Mix of Deism and Non-theism (ethics based); Landlocked country between Char-range and Zavatleo, the country is mountainous and heavily forested; Teratsu controls the largest mining interest on the continent and are known for a specialized type of woodworking that integrates metal throughout each piece.

Nuvwaan (noov-wa-ahn): Capital(s): NuvLunsoh (noov-loo-n-soe) (Left Star) & NuvDamseh (noov-dahm-say) (Right Star); Symbol: A constellation with stars representing each island; Worship: Celestial; A collection of islands, the two largest are connected by a string of smaller land masses called the Bridge of Islands; Their closest neighbors are Utollmir and Char-range; Known for beautiful coastlines, secluded coves, and export of rare fruits.

Agriya (ahg-ree-yah): Capital: Muevat (Moo-eh-vah); Symbol: An ornate metal brazier with high flames; Worship: Nature based; A smaller nation that sits in the middle of Saprea's southern border, they have had tensions in the past over access to the Southern Strait; Primary exports include carmine powder and other paint pigments; Known for elaborate funeral processions that include the use of massive decorative pyres to burn the dead. People will travel to Agriya just to say they've witnessed one of their funerals.

Myrre (meer-ay): Capital: San Aveth (sahn-ah-vett); Symbol: Multiple hands joined together in a circle; Worship: Mixed, largely taken from their surrounding neighbors; Smallest and newest nation on the continent, they broke off from Agriya more than a century ago. They border Saprea and Agriya, and control the western shore of the mouth of the Split Sea; There is a strong culinary culture, many professional cooks will travel to Myrre to study their methods.

Zavatleo (za-vaht-lay-oh): Capital: Straihorn (stray-horn); Symbol: Two bulls locking horns; Worship: Henotheism; Closest ally to Teratsu, they boast the northernmost settlement ranging into the expanse of largely uninhabited northern tundra; Lost their entire territory along the Split Sea to the Fraollish during the Continental Wars; Known for hardy livestock breeding, also their biggest export.

The Riddles: Capital: Unknown; Symbol: Unknown; Worship: Unknown; Volcanic archipelago known for pink sands and clear seas; The Riddles are surrounded by an abnormal water formation, known to most sailors as the "current" or the "barrier", that makes sailing to the islands nearly impossible unless the crew includes someone who has made the passage before; Mostly isolated for centuries, only in the past decade have their uniquely designed ships been making the passage across the Unending Sea to trade at major ports like those in the Birde Isles. But, those who make the crossing remain secretive about their homeland; From a young age, Riddle Islanders will cap a portion of their teeth with gold.

Major Bodies of Water

Eastern Sea, Western Sea, Split Sea, Southern Strait, Unending Sea, the Fraollkin Inlet.

Index: Cast of Characters

Index of all named characters in the *Kingsport Chronicles*

The Sea

Birde Isles Shoal:

Pasha (pah-shah): Mermaid; Last member left in the Birde Isles shoal; Location of Pasha's remaining kin: Unknown. (she/her)

Pallagia (pah-la-gee-ah): Mermaid; Member of the Birde Isles shoal; Pasha's older sister; Deceased. (she/her)

Nerys (neh-riss): Mermaid; Elder of the Birde Isles shoal; Location unknown. (she/her)

Hama (ha-mah): Mermaid; Member of the Birde Isles shoal; Cousin to Pallagia and Pasha; Location unknown. (she/her)

The Manor

The Kingfishers:

Gaius Kingfisher I (guy-uhs): Former Lord of the Birde Isles; Ally's great-grandfather; Deceased. (he/him)

Gaius Kingfisher II: Former Lord of the Birde Isles; Ally's grandfather; Deceased. (he/him)

Gaius Kingfisher III: Current Lord of the Birde Isles; Father to Gaius IV, Luthais, Calder, and Alphonsine. (he/him)

Glenna Kingfisher (glen-nah) Former Lady of the Birde Isles; Mother to Gaius IV, Luthais, and Calder; Deceased. (she/her)

Rochelle Kingfisher (roh-shel): Current Lady of the Birde Isles; Mother to Alphonsine; Step-mother to Gaius IV, Luthais, and Calder. (she/her)

Gaius "Gai" Kingfisher IV: Eldest Kingfisher child; Heir to the Birde Isles title by birth order; Ship: None. (he/him)

Luthais Kingfisher (loo-tye-iss): Second-eldest Kingfisher child; Lord of Trade by appointment; Ship: the *Pike.* (he/him)

Calder "Cal" Kingfisher (kal-dur): Third-eldest Kingfisher child; Former sea captain and Birde Isles trade representative; Ship: the *Wave Skipper*; Currently imprisoned for treason. (he/him)

Alphonsine "Ally" Kingfisher: (ahl-fahn-seen/ahl-lee): Youngest Kingfisher child; Only child to Rochelle and Gaius III; Ship: None; Maher's best friend. (she/her)

The Villaons:

Khafra Villaon (kah-frah : vill-ay-on) : Saprean ambassador to the Birde Isles; Maher's father. (he/him)

Maher Villaon (Ma-hehr): Khafra's only child; Also known as the Magpie of Kingsport; Ally's best friend. (he/him)

Staff:

Mrs. Thorley (thorr-lee): The Kingfishers' housekeeper. (she/her)

Kingsport

The Lantern:
Mama Bear: Owner of the Bear's Den, a private, green lantern afterhours club; Given name unknown; Friend of Maher. (she/her)

Pimm: Door guard at the Bear's Den; Friend of Maher; Origins unknown. (they/them)

"Barkeep": Bartender and general strong-arm at the Bear's Den; Originally from Swan Island. (he/him)

Olga (ol-guh): Kitchen maid at the Bear's Den. (she/her)

Gertie (ol-guh): Kitchen maid at the Bear's Den. (she/her)

Dr. Tambara (tahm-ba-rah): Physician kept on payroll by the Bear's Den. (she/her)

The Madam: Owner of the black lantern establishment; Mama Bear's mother; Given name unknown. (she/her),

Marielle (mar-ee-ell): Gunfighter; Employee at the black lantern; Originally from The Riddles. (she/her)

Eustace (yoo-stuhs): Door guard of the black lantern; Dislikes Maher on principle. (he/him)

Kit Naumenko: Former employee at the Whistle & Bells orange lantern club; Assistant to Barkeep at the Bear's Den; Originally from Zavatleo. (he/him)

Archie (aa-chee): Owner of the Whistle & Bells orange lantern club. (he/him)

Nitya (niht-yah): Owner of a blue lantern club. (she/her)

Temple of the Sea:
Eschina (eh-schh-ee-nah): Former Head Priestess in the time of Gaius Kingfisher I and II; Deceased. (she/her)

Aithne (eye-ehth-ne): Former Head Priestess; Studied under Eschina; Deceased. (she/her)

Esa (ee-sah): Current Head Priestess; Ally's former tutor; Studied under Aithne. (she/her)

Citizens:

Ms. Orel (oh-rell): Elderly tenant in Pimm's Northern district building; Originally from Zavatleo. (she/her)

Bernhard (burn-hard): Tenant in Pimm's Northern district building; Indeterminate age; Originally from Tjordun. (he/him)

Parvan Dayal (pah-r-van : duh-yahl): Head of the Birde Isles trade guild. (he/him)

Edgar Dayal: Parvan's husband; They love to wear matching outfits. (he/him)

Su-Yonn (soo-yo-nn): Owner of Su's Perfumery. (she/her)

Su-Minn (soo-min): Su-Yonn's daughter; Helps her mother at the perfumery. (she/her)

Agnes Heper (heh-per): Kingsport harbormaster. (she/her)

Kamharida Anyanwu (kahm-ha-ree-dah : ahn-yahn-woo): First Mate of the *Pike*. (she/her)

Ga-Seung (gah-seh-yung): Bosun of the *Pike*. (he/him)

Anya (ah-n-ya): Barrelman of the *Pike*. (she/her)

Grant (gr-ant): Helmsman of the *Pike;* Deceased. (he/him)

Olebile (oh-leh-bee-leh): Crewmember of the *Wave Skipper*. (they/them)

Weams (weems): Crewmember of the *Wave Skipper*. (he/him)

August Tapper (aw-guhst): Birde Isles Trade Guild member; Has trade connections to Agriya through family. (he/him)

Beitris Tapper (bee-triss): Daughter of August Tapper. (she/her)

Thara (ta-rah): Former Agriyan ambassador to the Birde Isles, now retired; Related by marriage to the Tapper family. (she/her)

Etty (eh-tee): Thara's wife; Younger sister of August Tapper; Originally from Gull Island. (she/her)

Safiye (sah-fee-yeh) & **Latife** (lah-tee-feh): Twin sisters from Saprea who often follow Beitris' lead. (she/her)

Ealasaid (eal-ah-saych): Pallagia's lover; Deceased. (she/her)

The *Maiden's Revenge*

Foraoise Dare (fora-shuh): Captain of the *Maiden's Revenge*; Privateer; Origins unknown. (she/her)

Jon Dare: Former captain of the *Tide's Last Revenge*; Privateer; Foraoise's husband; Deceased. (he/him)

Swain: Quartermaster (first mate) of the *Maiden's Revenge*. (he/him)

Smith: Crewmember of the Maiden's Revenge; Loyal to Swain. (she/her)

Frossard (froh-sah): Crewmember of the *Maiden's Revenge*. (he/him)

About the Author

C.H. Carter is a fantasy author with a lifelong love of the genre in all its forms. In middle school, she wrote a fan letter to Tamora Pierce and received the most encouraging reply! That experience cemented her desire to become an author. (She also still holds out the hope they can meet in person one day!)

When not writing, you can find her working on a number of rotating projects (Crochet, anyone?) and obsessing over her two rescue dogs.

The *Kingsport Chronicles* is Carter's debut series.